MW01488100

RIFT

Book Three of

RISE OF THE REALMS

D. FISCHER

Rift (Rise of the Realms: Book Three)

Copyright © 2019 by D. Fischer

All rights reserved.

No part of this book may be reproduced in any printed or electronical form without written consent from the author. This book is fictional. All names, characters, and incidents within are pure fiction, produced by the author's vivid imagination.

This book contains adult content. Mature readers only. The author will not be held responsible if a minor reads this book.

ISBN: 9781794360204

BISAC: Fiction / Fantasy / Epic

D. FISCHER

|THE CLOVEN PACK|

A Gifted Curse   Out of the Darkness

Above This Grave   Caught in the Crossfire

|RISE OF THE REALMS|

Reborn   Disobedient   Rift

The Vault   Decimate   Ruin

|NIGHT OF TERROR|

Book One   Book Two   Book Three

|GRIM FAIRYTALES|

When Hope Was Forgotten   Cure the Enemy

A Cold Soul

FIND MORE at D. Fischer's Amazon

Everything in this book is fictional. It is not based on true events, persons, or creatures that go bump in the night, no matter how much we wish it were…

To K. Bond –

You have given me the power to be courageous.

CONTENTS

Chapter One   9

Chapter Two   26

Chapter Three   45

Chapter Four   58

Chapter Five   81

Chapter Six   103

Chapter Seven   115

Chapter Eight   132

Chapter Nine   149

Chapter Ten   163

Chapter Eleven   181

Chapter Twelve   199

Chapter Thirteen   216

Chapter Fourteen   241

Chapter Fifteen   252

Chapter Sixteen   264

Chapter Seventeen   279

Chapter Eighteen   289

Chapter Nineteen   301

Chapter Twenty   309

Chapter Twenty-One   320

Chapter Twenty-Two   333

Chapter Twenty-Three   345

Chapter Twenty-Four   354

Chapter Twenty-Five   363

Chapter Twenty-Six   379

Chapter Twenty-Seven   390

I never thought this would be my life. I never imagined I'd be the center of destruction. The choices I've made, and will make, will be the end of the beginning. And now, in the middle of our rift between fear and fate, we're out for blood to save those we love. Can you blame us? - *Katriane DuPont*

CHAPTER ONE

TEMBER

DEATH REALM

"Was that necessary?" Jaemes asks. Disgust flattens his lips as though his tongue is glazed with a bitter bite, and his throat bobs, suppressing a gag.

The immediate threat gone, I dim my halo's glow and observe him with narrowed eyes. Halo gone, we're cast back into ill-lit darkness which weakens the evidence of his disgust inside the Colosseum's tunnel.

Jaemes' underlying contemptuous expression reminds me of Erma's angelic features twisted in a snarl, the one she'd been sneaking my direction when she believed me to be unaware. But I felt it like nails raking the back of my neck. Under her scrutiny, it chisels at my heart, but with Jaemes, it raises invisible hackles along the knobs of my spine. If I still had them, my feathers would ruffle, and I can almost hear the sound of them rubbing against one another in telling agitation.

I miss Erma's affections more than my discarded wings, though. My heart needs her more than an angel needs flight.

Squatting to the floor, Jaemes smears black vampire blood from the tip of his arrow to the stone floor. It's different than normal creature blood, more thick and sticky with the lingering stench of rotting flesh. He grunts with further disgust when his efforts have no effect. The goop smudges along the arrow, already partially dried.

My right eyelid twitches in annoyance to Jaemes' question, and I take in our surroundings to quiet my clicking tongue. Since we've ventured away from his village together under the orders of Mitus, his father, he's continued to taunt me with words meant to break my spirit. My reactions provide him with entertainment.

To our left, rows of cells are filled with people while our shoulders hug the wall on our right. The tunnels are skinny yet well-constructed with low, smooth archways instead of corners or squares. It's what I had envisioned this structure to look like while we stood on the outside of this maze, but nothing compares to seeing it with my own eyes. Even I, a creature who's lived many a year, wasn't prepared for this.

Precisely every ten feet is a candle on top of a plain metal candelabra, the flames too small to provide sufficient light. The details of the metal wax holders are absent and plain, providing no beauty for the prisoners to gaze upon before they're marched to their deaths.

I wasn't yet created when the first Colosseum was built, but I know a few who were. Jax, an angel disgusted with my adoration for Erma, was one of them. The angels who were present in that era often recounted the devastation with sorrow etched on their handsome features. To this day, they're still traumatized by the loss of their charges.

During that precarious time, they had been forbidden to interfere by Erline and Erma, for fear of possible discovery, though angels have stepped in before and after, continually, throughout history. And each time we had raced to the rescue, devastation would soon follow. It's a lesson we can't learn, doomed to repeat our mistakes over and over again in hopes to save one, or many, lives.

Erma believes it best to pull the strings from behind the curtain, and I fully agree with her. But it's times like this, observing the helpless in the Death Realm, I want nothing more than to call the evidence a liar.

My fixed stare lingers too long on the humans, concern wrinkling my forehead and stiffening my shoulder blades. They're no longer shades. Instead, they're owners of a brand-new beating heart inside a solid body. My brain screams at the impossibility, and my shock is clear, leaving me speechless for several moments. Now that they are once again human, are they subjected to never have a guardian - an angel - forever?

How has this slipped through my species' regard?

Charges are divided among angels by Erma's decree. She wouldn't have left these resurrected humans to fend for themselves in a realm where they cannot. Perhaps she has no jurisdiction here, no way of knowing what's happening under Kheelan's watchful eyes and ham-fisted agenda.

Death isn't supposed to be like this. Guardians shouldn't have the need to protect the dead, and I know with certainty Erma would have done something about it if she knew.

Angling my head, I look as far down as I can see, Jaemes' question momentarily forgotten. They're all human. Every. Last. One.

A few sit, slouched against the wall with a blank expression. They're most likely contemplating their very grim futures while coming to terms with enduring another death. Others try to reach through the electrified bars, the bright cackling lights mixing with shadows and casting flickering reflections along the walls behind them. As soon as they touch lights, however, they're physically shocked back into their cells with their legs knocked out from beneath them.

Fearful hope crosses the closest cell members' faces when they notice we aren't the typical creatures roaming this realm, and their spines straighten to attention. Aside from the echoes of battle rumbling through the tunnel, silence stretches as they study us, the two who had massacred a handful of vampires with swift ease.

A gangly man slowly stands and shuffles his bare feet across the gritty floor until he's inches from the bars which hiss their warning. His dusty blonde hair is unkempt as though he's been pulling at the roots repeatedly. The clothes he wore, when his first death transpired, hang from him in tattered strips, and his old life's blood stains them with splotches of burgundy.

His guardian must have been absent the day he first died. It happens from time to time. We all have

12

multiple charges, except for me, who had given mine to another when I sawed off my wings.

"Please," he whimpers and then swallows with difficulty as though he's perpetually parched. The blue bolts cast dancing hues along the empty valley of his thick, pinched together eyebrows. "Help us."

I take a scramble back and bump into the wall, recoiling internally at the plea. The edges of the stone dig into my skin and jar the length of my spine.

Neither Jaemes nor I have the power to help him, or them, and the last thing I desire is to make it seem as though we're here to free everyone. Even if we could lower the bars, where would they run? Where would they hide? Nowhere is safe. Our mission is Katriane. Retrieve her and bring her home. There's nothing we can do for this hostile realm and those who must endure it.

I reluctantly turn away without responding. The soles of my shoes rub against vampire dust, echoing the shame twisting my gut. Jaemes' face is carefully blank when our eyes meet. He, too, struggles to control the urge to aide.

Wiping my mouth with the back of my hand, I straighten my shoulders, ignore the sobs of denial whimpering from the humans about to be slaughtered, and take a deep breath before answering Jaemes' first inquiry. He had questioned my motives about kissing a vampire, and it seems like a far less emotional question to answer while surrounded by victims.

"I dropped Ire," I begin. "The kiss was instinctual. What more did you want me to do?"

He raises one eyebrow and then plods backward through the tunnel. "Instinct?" he mocks, a hint of relief in his voice to the return of topic. "To kiss a fanged, dead fool?"

I roll my eyes and allow the gesture to swipe away the rest of my guilt. "It's the Angel's Kiss. Not a lover's affection. The fool would be you for not knowing the difference."

The bright glow of the kiss had blinded the entire tunnel, including Jaemes who was forced to kill his vampire on instinct instead of sight. The pompous elf relies much on sight instead of the rest of his senses, I've noticed.

Opening his mouth, intent on a quick-witted retort, he quickly snaps it shut, raises his bow and dirty arrow, and aims. The string whips the still air when he releases his curled fingers, vibrating my eardrums. Splitting through my brown curls at the curve of my neck, the arrow flies by my head and snuffs a candle's small flickering flame. A thick, wet thud resonates behind me, the arrow embedding in its target.

In a slow turn, I witness the silent attacker flake to ash and the tiny black particles drift to the floor.

Watching the last floating flake while the breath is trapped in my lungs, I wonder what the vampire felt as his body molted to nothing but a pile, all the while knowing he's headed to a dark place for eternity. He will become something else entirely, a smudge in a dark void. Did he feel fear? Or did he feel nothing at all?

One would think vampires would be more careful with their non-living life. There's literally no second chance for them, not like the shades who are human once again.

But, with an abundance of ego and ignorance, they blindly follow the trail of food and a chance to curb their desires without a second thought to where it may lead them.

"I should be keeping track of how many times I've saved your life," Jaemes proclaims, chipper with pride. "One day, I may collect."

He retrieves his arrow and flicks the fresh goop from the tip. The droplets splat against my cheek, and I growl, lifting my shoulder to swipe the affected skin against my sleeve.

"I'm sure I'll find some way to repay you, Elf," I grumble.

He turns on the balls of his animal-skin-covered feet and swaggers his way down the tunnel. "A wingless guardian will never have anything I desire," he calls over his shoulder.

"Then keeping tally would be a waste of your time," I retort.

He chuffs, a rude passing of breath. "Everything about you is a waste of my time." Though the words were quiet and meant only for himself, I heard them perfectly clear.

My carefully controlled patience snaps. "If you're going to have a tantrum with every kill, then perhaps we should call Erma to take you home."

Peeping at me over his shoulder, his face void of emotion such as a true warrior, he lifts his foot higher in stride. "Not a chance."

The wails filtering down the tunnel from the Colosseum's arena grow louder as we travel, and the inhuman cries of pain carry, bouncing off the stone and raising the hair on my arms. As I follow Jaemes to what appears to be doom itself, my mouth salivates. Every part of my being wants in on the action - to guard and protect. To taste a sliver of adventure. To kill the enemy.

I clear my throat and squash the urge to pick up my pace. "Are you prepared?"

"Prepared?" Jaemes chuckles. "Have you learned nothing? Are you so obtuse? Do you not use your eyeballs for anything more than ogling your forbidden love?"

My heart sinks at the implication of her name, and I flex my jaw to banish the emotion. "Right," I say, dripping with sarcasm. I'm not taking the bait. Not this time. "Are you prepared to work with me? To fight alongside me? Or are you going to continue this hero complex you're so adamant to display?"

The questions replaced the sounds of battle and my desire to leap into it even if it results in a bickering response. I already know the answer, no matter what he says. Jaemes can't help himself when it comes to my emotional faults, and I fully believe he never will.

Our footfalls pad a dreaded echo as we near an entrance, passing several empty cells, and I look to him when he doesn't immediately respond.

"Perhaps," he begins, drawing out the word. "I will hang my cape. Just this once. If only but for our new friendship." He changes his tone, petulant, his accent thicker. "I wouldn't want to anger you. There's no telling the vengeful capabilities of a side kick gone rogue. Even a wingless one."

We enter the ascending tunnel, which leads to the center of the Colosseum, and pick up our pace to a light jog. Each step echoes in the tight space, and the sound spikes my adrenaline. Once at the opening, we halt, and Jaemes curses in his native tongue at the sight before our eyes.

KATRIANE DUPONT

DEATH REALM

The Colosseum's crowd cheers in one wave of roars. It's like a single, brilliant stroke of a cello. Instead of being beautiful and giving me delightful shivers, it does the opposite. The scales on the back of my legs stand on end, enough so that my long teeth ache.

A memory flashes in my thoughts, reminding me of the time I strode into my first rock concert as a teen. I had almost walked right back out. There was an alarming number of swaying bodies and a chorus of ear-splitting music blaring from each speaker. It had raised my anxiety to the point of smothering claustrophobia.

The roar leaves the mouths of thousands of superior predators - the fortunate among the less. And definitely the ugliest. The creatures of the dead and harborers of terror are enjoying the massacre they came to see. It's disgusting, but I'm the twist they didn't anticipate. They came here to watch and bask in blood and fear.

This is their rock concert, I realize, and we're the band.

When they had first seen me - the beast I am, the fire swelling my chest, the ultimate slayer - their wails of excitement had slowly hushed. For that moment, it was blissfully quiet. Peaceful, almost. The fog swirled in the sky, dipping and folding unnaturally inside itself like a fog machine on a black stage. There was no wind to blow, no gentle caressing breeze to potentially antagonize the flames I plan to unleash. The clinking of swords, battle cries, and my heavy breathing were almost too loud.

Their new roar is absurdly louder than the previous, thinking I'll take flight in my display of stretching dragon wings. It offends my hearing, and my head automatically ducks lower to the ground just to get away from it. I flatten the spikes on my neck and shake my head, desperate to rid the offending vibrations. To my dismay, the orcs in the sandpit mirror it, spittle flying from their large mouths and decaying teeth.

I desperately work to block it out and, instead, focus my senses on my stretch and the ripple of muscles. My spine shivers in delight when my talons dig deep into the sand and find a pocket of cold to chill my heated veins.

My dark side sings with this new freedom, and I eternally balk in fear of the powerful emotion.

What I do next is for me, I tell myself, desperate to convince the evil rooting in my soul. A victorious result is for me, the unjust across the realms, and the innocent. For my misfortune and all those who've fallen as my consequence. This will be my penance.

I have two choices: to spend the last of my strength squashing the dark beginnings of no return and possibly die, or to internally retreat and let it save my friends while forfeiting my mental state of health. The choice sounds explicable, simple, when I put it that way. It echoes, bouncing in the limitations of my skull, willing me to take action. One life isn't worth hundreds, possibly thousands.

My red-hued gaze swivels to Gan's broken body smushed against the sand, then to the Sandman and Dyson's wolf, all fighting an enemy just to survive. Tanya and Jane run and duck under my substantial frame, deeming me the lesser evil. They look to me for protection against a battle completely out of their motherly depths.

No. The realms. One life isn't worth all the souls, dead or alive, in all the realms. A self-sacrifice, even if it's just mental sacrifice, is all I have left to give. I have to keep them safe. If I don't, who will?

I lower my mental block with certain, cringing dread, and the invading evil intentions squander the available space. Like a starving, rabid pup in chase of a plump rabbit, my darker half shoves reason, and my seemingly frivolous convictions, aside. And I allow it.

Shifting my weight, I face the thundering orc stomping in my direction. His thick body rocks on his boney, single-horned steed - the creature which resembles a unicorn of the dead. The vibrations travel through the sand, and I can feel each hoofbeat rumble up my thick legs.

Tanya and Jane squeal.

My darkness snickers with anticipation.

I shiver.

He was built for this. Death and destruction are what the orc craves, and just as its rider, the skeletal unicorn holds no hesitation or fear. A typical horse may shy from all the noise - from the obvious death thick in the air. Instead, its strides are determined. It makes me wonder if it knows what it's headed toward, if it's aware of the bigger threat, or if it's designed only for killing.

As it nears, my talons quickly lift and lower in heavy stomps. Sucking in a deep breath, I feel heat blossom in my chest, an opening rosebud in the morning's ray of sun. It curls tight then enlarges, swirling and forcing my ribs to expand. The pressure becomes painful, begging immediate release.

Fire sizzles along my esophagus as it travels up. The heat licks my tongue and exits my mouth, a thick stream of flames targeting the orc and his steed of bones.

The unicorn skids to a halt. Sand flies in every direction, and the billow of fire engulfs the creature. It screams its bereavement, rearing and flailing its front hooves before falling over, dislodging the orc. The shriek is loud, high-pitched, and otherworldly.

Rolling as best it can, it tries to escape to no avail as my flames continue to consume. Victory sings through my veins and into the depths of my soul.

The orc scoots his rump backward across the sand, attempting to get away from the scorching heat and impending death. But he's a moment too late. The minimal cloth covering his lower half catches on the tip of a flame.

Hungry orange fire rapidly spreads, and he wails, deep and rumbling, when his body is devoured. It licks up from leathery legs to torso. Puffs of black smoke rise and mingle with dust the two creatures create in their desperation.

The orc's massive arms swing like trees in a strong wind, slow and weighted, and I suck in another breath, unleashing the fire once more. It's a straight shot. Streams of scorching flames reach the burning creatures, and the orc's shrieks expire in unison with the unicorn's. Their blackened limbs fall limp to the sands, and pieces of bone break away from the charred bodies, tumbling a few feet.

The crowd erupts once more, a fuel to my new dark desires of revenge. The smell of burning leather reaches my nostrils, filling me with a sense of overwhelming cravings for more death and taking chunks of my humanity with it.

I need more.

My gaze sweeps the battle, searching for the next target. The red haze deepens to a darker hue, and my rigid muscles relax into the mental transition.

The loose sand makes it easy to quickly turn, and I swiftly do so. I select the next target – the next challenge to my immediate revenge. This is all too easy, the battle on fast forward, and I haven't had enough bloodshed.

There will never be enough.

I whip my tail as I face the fee in their low stone gallery, careful to avoid the two women under my belly. A rumble vibrates in my chest when our eyes don't lock, prepared to roar to gain their attention. I want to see the fear on their faces, watch them tremble on their thrones of superiority while they question all they've done to receive my wrath.

But instead, their backs are to me, their attention on a red-headed woman alight with blue lightning. She hovers a few feet from the stone platform, radiating a graceful and elegant power. I can taste it. It's thick, bright, and charged like crisp air during a snowstorm, the kind that steals the air from lungs.

Concern and confusion envelope me in a blanket of curiosity, worried she's a bigger threat than my original targets. But as I take a closer glimpse, adjusting my vision to a more detailed perception, it quickly flees. The fee are cautiously backing away, and even Corbin's posture hunches with uncertainty. Her threats are for them alone.

This is her unleashing of revenge, I realize. This is the woman Mrs. Tiller, my shade escort into the Death Realm, spoke of.

Her arms are held out to her sides, and her red hair waves in a wind which does not blow. Lightning plays across her pale skin and the open space surrounding her. And though the fee back away cautiously, one man does not. A demon, I quickly note. What kind of creature doesn't fear what she threatens?

Unless he's the bigger threat.

Stretching my neck, I roar, menacing, in their direction, but he's too consumed in her display of impossible power to notice my challenge.

Distracted by another object, my eyes dart to an arrow sailing through the air. It shoots a direct path to the

22

galley and embeds in Corbin's upper arm. His head tilts back, and his balance sways as he screams to the foggy sky.

A smirk pulls at my dragon lips. He deserves hundreds more of those arrows until he's mistaken for a porcupine. If I get my way, he'll have more than that small misfortune for leaving his wife in the hands of vengeful humans and a dangling noose. Myla didn't deserve that fate, and he has much to pay for because of it.

Rustling my wings against my sides, I arch my neck and turn my head in search of where the arrow came from.

Down by the tunnel we had entered, Tember stands like a Greek god. Ire is in her grips, and an electric arrow is positioned on her index finger of the hand curled around the bow's middle. Like me, she's immediately distracted by the magical woman. She aims, but it drops slightly when she becomes transfixed with the disturbing anomaly, eyes wide.

Someone else stands beside her – a creature I've never seen. Not even in lessons at the Demi-Lune coven and pictures in the ancestral books passed down through the generations of women witches. He's striking, powerful, formidable. A trained warrior from another realm.

Horns protrude from his skull, and his entire body is tattooed in stripes of black. Silky dark hair shines despite the lack of light. The glistening strands cascade to the small of his back, and he grips a bow and arrow as well though his is much grander than Tember's Ire to meet the needs of his frame.

Swiveling his upper torso causes impressive muscles to ripple along his bare abdomen, and his eyes sharpen when he spots something. A female demon, with equally flowing white hair, jumps over the edge of the climbing seats and drops sure footed to the sands. She snarls at the warrior, intent on protecting her master.

Tember's friend takes first aim, eyes sharp and focused, much like the tip of his waiting weapon. The speed in which he releases is evidence to the skill his body speaks. But, just the same, the shock is still there even as I watch him kill the demon and three more after in a matter of seconds.

And then he aims at me.

I hear the whistle of his sailing arrow, and it thuds into a demon just below my chest. The blow knocks the demon into my leg. This strange new ally meets my gaze, and he curtly nods. I snort my gratitude, and puffs of smoke snake from my nostrils. Not that I needed his help. My scales are armor. I doubt the demon would have been able to penetrate them, whatever his choice of attack. But he could have harmed Jane and Tanya.

On my right, a flicker of pale white pulls my focus once more. A vampire. At full speed, he barrels toward Tanya and Jane, leaving a trail of rising dust and knocking even his companions out of the way for his chance of twisted glory.

He's a brave soul, I think to myself as Tanya and Jane scream my name. The voice inside my head is deep and raspy like the brush of fierce winds against old pane windows. And when he's close enough, I strike. My neck stretches, snapping forward, a whip. My razor teeth slice into his rotting flesh, and I pick him from the ground, a plucked weed.

I bite, hard, blood gushing, and throw his body to the stone wall before he turns to ash in my mouth.

CHAPTER TWO

AIDEN VANDER

DEATH REALM

Chaos unfolds on the field of sick and twisted games. Blood sprays, mixing with the disturbance of sand. The sound of the dragon and the victims she consumes are deafening.

Kheelan's face is scrunched, a shadow of scarlet, and his black eyes are wide and wild. He shouts at Eliza though I can't hear what he says past the battle's thunder.

Eliza's eyes are glowing a blinding shade of blue. The scent of freshly-charged air with a hint of iron wafts from her body. Lively currents strike along her skin as though her pale flesh is a brewing storm.

I pull at my thumb. I don't know what to do, and I don't know how to help her, not when I have no idea what's going on with this new power she possesses. Instead, I stand like an idiot.

Looking to Corbin, I search for answers across the shocked face of the fee. Was it him who had screamed a moment ago?

He growls, his eyes as black as the souls of the demons he creates. My gaze drifts to the stick protruding from his arm and his fingers which are firmly curled around the middle of it. Biting his top lip, he rips the arrow out in one swift yank and tosses it.

Turning swiftly, he views the battle happening below before the arrow can clank against the stone platform. I'm sure he's searching for the culprit of the deliberate attack. It's what I would do. The arrow rolls across on the uneven platform.

Demons and vampires jump from their stadium seats, swarming the arena to join the fight. The black dragon roars, sharp teeth dripping with saliva and dark liquid. Bodies burn around the beast, resembling the tiki torches that had lined my foster home's back patio. My mother and Eliza's shuffle under the belly of the dragon, desperate for protection.

Arrows arch above the battle before descending into the chests of demons and vampires. Two new creatures had joined the slaves, I note, watching as they work as a team. They pick off the enemy, one by one, formidably so.

Corbin doesn't turn back to me, doesn't check to see if I'm still here or bother to seek my counsel. Instead, his back stiffens with telling concerns, his shoulders bunched. This didn't go the way he'd planned. He knows he's outnumbered, outwitted, and caught mid-manipulation. Without action or retaliation, he shimmers away, leaving his demons, and me, to fend for ourselves.

"Coward," I whisper, hoping he hears me from wherever he fled to. He's a waste of breath, and these demons follow him blindly into whatever trap he lays.

I flick my gaze to Sureen, wondering what she'll do next. Her long fingers grip the top rim of her throne's backrest. Eyes darting from Eliza to the dragon, she snarls viciously, a cornered rabid animal.

Dark eyebrows smooth as her face falls, void of any emotion except shifty eyes observing the scaled beast and the fire sprouting from her mouth. I don't need to follow her line of sight to know what she sees. The flames are scorching - I can feel it from here. Through all of the mayhem, the spraying blood splatting along my forearm, and the heat boiling my blood, my subconscious strives to gain the upper hand. The chaos of the situation scatters all my thoughts and what action I should take next.

Shaking my head, I feel a hiss of breath squeeze through my nostrils. I blink, and when my eyes reopen, Sureen is no longer there. She disappeared as quickly as Corbin had. The fee, all of those who were so desperate for death and power, have a fear. This fear happens to be wrapped in scales. The legend I was told had mentioned that only a dragon can take down Corbin, and I briefly wonder if this is the dragon.

More fire devours bodies - a wall of moving flames - while they scream their last breath of dusty air. A demon closest to the platform turns, eyes visible through the orange-hued sand dust, and he sweeps the platform, searching for Corbin. I can see the hope leave those soulless black orbs before he drops to the ground, dead, with an arrow poking between his knobby shoulder blades.

I stare at it, unable to move my eyes from the demon's still form.

A sliver of sympathy works its way through me, an unusual pang to my chest. I lift my hand and clutch my sternum with surprise. These are my people, my kindred, though I despise them and their weaknesses. The fee's creations die while they run to hide. They didn't even stick around for the outcome. Where is the devotion? Where is the compassion?

Blue hues to my side brighten the immediate atmosphere, and I turn.

Kheelan's arms light with the same bolts of electricity Eliza has, snapping me from my query and the scene below. Eliza's body floats, magnificent and powerful, and my pinched and confused face falls in a rush of something I thought I'd never feel again.

A flood gate. That's what this feels like. A dam bursting with frigid waters, overcoming everything in its path. Beginning in my heart, it rushes through my veins to each limb, each organ. I stagger against the intensity and the accompanying pain and lower my hands to grip my stomach where it settles.

I gasp and am driven to one knee. I shake with the intensity, each muscle rippling in a separate wave. Sweat beads above my brow. My vision blurs and refocuses. All the oxygen rushes from my lungs as a roar bellows from my mouth, a cry to the extreme assault of returning emotions. I drop the other knee, kneeling before the woman with palpable power. I suck in another breath,

29

tasting the air in a different way as it crosses my tongue, and then I fall to all fours.

Huffing and puffing, I angle my head and stare at Eliza from under my dark lashes. The flood settles, a gentle stream of flowing, colorful emotions.

Love. Hope. Water to a dying man.

Eliza's eyes snap impossibly wider, and her mouth opens in a scream with no sound. Bolts of electricity hit the stone like a second voice to her rage, a threat. Her gaze jerks to Kheelan's immobile frame, a whip of fury pinned to the cruel man.

I've never seen Eliza like this. I never knew Eliza was capable of these violent thoughts and actions. I can practically see them behind her eyes, speaking to me on a level I understand. Ferocity has replaced her compassion, and it makes me wonder all that she's endured in the hands of Kheelan to make her feel this way.

"You have no choice," she begins, her voice like a recording of Kheelan's. "You have no say. This is no longer your life."

Kheelan visibly pales and takes a step back, his words are thrown back at him.

She continues, her voice returning to her own. "Be still, King of the Dead. You'll pay for what you've done."

Goosebumps riddle my skin, her threat tangible and thrilling. I can taste it. I bask in it. I feed from it.

Red hair flows like ribbons down her back as she tilts her head toward the sky. Her spine bows, puffing her chest. A stream of blue electricity departs from the center

30

of her sternum and strikes Kheelan's abdomen. The force sends him into the air and over the edge of the platform, his greasy hair whipping in the wind of gravity.

My lips part, a wheezing breath hushed between my loose lips.

Gathering myself to my feet, prepared to finish him off, I rush to the edge and watch Kheelan disappear, his body vanishing before he hits the sand.

I swivel back to Eliza, noting her feet already planted on the stone. The crackling lightning fizzles along her skin until it's absorbed back into her body. Blue veins are left behind, shining under her flesh. Her legs wobble, and for a brief moment, her eyes catch mine.

My breath hitches.

So many emotions are held within those swirling blues, so many questions on the tip of her tongue. I open my mouth, ready to declare these new-found feelings, to tell her what she's done for me if she doesn't know already.

She saved me from myself. It was she who returned the emotions. Who else would be responsible if not the woman I love?

As I inhale to speak, cold air tickles my tongue, but I'm halted mid-word. Her eyes roll, and her knees buckle beneath her. I swiftly jump forward, and my arms catch her limp body just before she almost flattens against the platform.

Hoisting her up higher in my arms, I nestle her head against my chest and stare into her eyes. Sluggishly, she searches mine while her hair tickles my arm.

"Aiden," she hums, eyelashes fluttering with exhaustion. And then she faints, her head rolling to the side.

"I'm right here," I mumble, deep-toned. I marvel at the smoothness of her skin, shimmering veins, and flawless complexion. So fragile in a body warped with too much power.

A surge of protective instincts replaces my need to declare what I am and what I feel. She's mine, and now that I'm back, I'll never let her go.

Gathering her higher in my arms, I glance once more at the chaotic scene below as her head falls against my chest. A pang of sympathy, the need to help even the odds, to save my mother and Eliza's, overcomes me.

I could. I could help those who fight for justice. Or, I could hide Eliza and keep her safe.

The image of her vulnerable state bargains a plan into my thoughts, but the voice isn't my own. It drowns the cries of battle below in its few words of wisdom to my jumbled mind.

Seek the one you trust most, a male voice says.

I grit my teeth, weighing the hard path of the greater good against my own selfish desires. I know what I have to do - what I should do – but neither my gut feeling, nor the voice, is easy to ignore.

Eliza is my responsibility, and I'll be damned if I ignore my instincts again.

I shimmer for the first time in my third life, my body fading from this realm to the next. Selfishly taking an unconscious Eliza with me, I seek the first creature I feel I can trust.

KATRIANE DUPONT

DEATH REALM

My energy is depleting, and I'm struggling to think straight. Each muscle under my black scales screams, begging for relief, for a millisecond to pause and unbunch them. The darkness ignores the discomfort because relief would be my end – all of our ends. It's this thought I take some comfort in - knowing it will prevail where I cannot.

Our enemies remain merciless, allies turning on allies just for a taste of victory. My eyes flick to the left. Dyson rips apart vampires and demons as they come, his growls menacing. He's coated in an odd black substance, and for a moment, I worry it's his own blood. But the concern is fleeting when goop sprays from a gash in a vampire's neck and lathers his fur with another layer. The wolf's teeth grip the black-veined throat, and he snarls, shaking his head and shredding the thin skin.

Tember and her odd companion were forced into hand-to-hand combat with the oncoming assault. They wade through those who are attacking their friends as one team, delivering deadly blows, ducking and weaving. Tember's halo shines bright, a beacon to the enemy. She swings her leg, wraps it around a demon's neck, and twists him to the ground. The force snaps his spine before his face is shoved into the sand.

It's taking everything they have to raise the death toll on our enemies. They just keep coming like the stadium is breeding them by the dozens. My mom used to use the phrase *popped from the ground like daisies.* It applies here.

Tanya and Jane call my name once more, drawing my attention from Tember and her friend. A few vampires leap from the last bench and dive toward my back. I lurch forward without lifting my feet and pluck the first from the air with my teeth. Using my tail, it snaps at the second and third, connecting to their torsos with a thud. I chomp once, severing the body in two.

I take extra care to avoid my two charges when I swivel back to the main battle. They're not mentally built for this, and they lack in combat skills. It's not their fault – they're mothers at heart. Brutality and a barbaric nature aren't something they've ever thought they'd have to endure, just like all those who have fallen today. Just like Gan. I shouldn't have to endure it either, but I've made my bed. This, all of this, is my doing. My ripple of consequence.

The sandman is in battle with the last wounded orc, his skills far greater than I thought a passive creature could be capable of. The orc's skeletal unicorn is in a heap by the wall, discarded in a cringe-worthy mass. He holds the sword I left behind, hacking a path back to us while swinging the spiked ball with the other.

34

A whack drowns the yells and roars when the sandman swings the ball like a bat, striking the orc square in the jaw with the spikes. The orc crumbles to the ground, and blood oozes from his now half-missing face.

The sandman turns fluidly and slashes his sword through the air, dancing around Gan's bloody mess. The sword connects with a demon's arm, severing it clean off. He's proficient, but even I can see he's exhausted. His attack is becoming less forceful, his energy depleting.

We can't keep doing this, my conscience whispers in the small pocket of my mind to the darkness.

Even though many of the enemy have begun attacking each other for sport, there are too many of them and not enough of us. We'll die if we don't retreat, but how can we when there isn't a place to hide in this realm? Any which way we could turn, we'd have demons on our tail, trailing our fear, and vampires on us like leeches inside a murky pond.

We have to leave the realm and live to fight another day. We need a plan – a better plan. One which gets us all out of here alive.

I was ignorant to think I could do this on my own - to come here and save Dyson while destroying the fee. Dead fee wasn't part of the original plan, but I couldn't pass up the opportunity, not after I saw all the captives and their treatment. Not after Gan, whose dead body is being protected by a sandman, a griever for the loss.

Revenge comes with its own set of consequences. *Seek revenge and dig two graves.*

It's now or never.

I roar above the noise, catching Tember's attention. Holding an unconscious demon's head in her grips, she snaps its neck with minimal effort. The head of the demon droops to an odd angle. We hold each other's eyes for a moment, and then she grimly surveys the mob, picking up on my train of thoughts. Her chest rises and falls, her eyes picking through every detail and weighted options. I'm sure she's engaged in many battles throughout her life, but I've never seen anything like this. Has she?

Two more demons head her direction, approaching from her back. I swivel and lash out my tail, knocking them back and crushing them against the wall. A boom vibrates the air, and the wall cracks and crumbles from the force. It crashes to the ground seconds later. Smoke and dust rise, clouding our vision. But as the wall falls, it distracts our enemies, leaving their heads swiveling that direction instead of ours.

Tember looks back to me and uses her hand to shield her eyes. She nods once. "Let's go!"

Plunging from the racing cloud of smoke, Dyson's wolf skids to a halt under me, almost knocking Tanya over. I blow another stream of fire, engulfing two vampires who thought to chase him. They don't have time to scream before they're piles of ash.

A dark, heavy thought crosses my mind, a sliver of desperate hope trying to convince me that the fallen wall is our chance to even the odds. The thought basks in the thrilling possibilities, flicking new scenarios through my mind. I push against it, attempting to swipe it away, to wash my hands of it and regain some mental composure past the visions of crumpled bodies beneath my victorious talons. But I can't. Instead, I feel it darken me further with

36

cold tendrils of invisible fingers wrapping around my heart. A stain to my pure soul. It's a branding, one I'll never be able to ignore. A branding of what I'm truly capable of.

Once you dwell in the dark, it always drowns the light.

Dyson's bones crack and reshape as he returns to human form, albeit naked, and grips the scales around my leg like a rock-climbing wall. I swing my body, shooting flames at a group of vampires attacking each other. The movement almost throws him off, and I can hear his grunt when his ribs slam into one of mine.

I still my movements, my muscles rippling with effort to contain myself. He climbs up with ease and nestles himself between the dip of my wings.

More rush our direction, aware of our plan, but it does nothing to pull me from the thought of his bare body touching my scales. Warmth settles there, right where he places himself in a haste. His skin touching mine feels… right, like a flower blossoming inside my stomach, twisting in a ray of sun, and a flock of butterflies swirls around it.

The sun . . . My mind's eye feels it, thirsts for it. I reach for the light, wanting more, needing more. I reach a little more, desperate for his bright soul to touch my dark one. To ease the smothering discomfort that threatens to swallow me whole.

The screams and roars pull me from a full mental grasp, forcing me to regain focus to the matter at hand and the incoming enemy. I shake my head to clear my thoughts, and the blossoming flower and butterflies disappear as quickly as they came, replaced by a cold sensation – a bucket of ice dumped on an already chilled body. I almost sob.

The sandman takes a running leap and grips the curve of my back leg. He's quick to climb, a practiced skill. Tember's odd companion follows directly afterward, his approach closer to a swinging monkey in a cluster of close trees.

My dragon head swivels, looking for Tember with wild eyes.

Jumping into the air, fist pulled back, Tember punches a demon upon descending. Her fist cracks the bones of his wide protruding cheek, the sound unmistakable, and he falls to the ground. Taking another running leap, she catches my scales with one hand. With a grunt, she swings her legs, grips another scale, and climbs.

My back is heavy with passengers, straining my spine and leaving me to wonder how I'll fly from here with each on my back. Jane and Tanya have yet to be seated, but we must try. I must try. I won't leave them behind.

"Tanya, Jane, let's go!" Dyson screams from the top before I have a chance to roar at them in frustration. I'm agitated and anxious, and my scales prick my muscles, an uncomfortable sensation similar to goosebumps.

Expanding my wings, I stretch and test them. I've never flown before. I've never seen their full expanse or felt the wind between each crevice.

I flap once, and the creeping sand cloud is pushed back from the breeze of it. The feeling is like no other, like a lover's fingers trailing through thick hair, massaging my scalp. It sends a thrill of adrenaline coursing through my hot veins.

Resist the dark, a voice warns. I remember them, my mother's words, but the tone is all wrong. It's male, deep, but just as loving as the woman who brought me into this world.

I whip my head to look beneath my stomach, using the voice to anchor my thoughts. Tanya and Jane look to one another, tears streaming down their aged faces. It's their blissful moment in chaos - a silent communication - and I nudge Jane's back, letting her know we don't have time for it.

Tanya squints up at my underbelly bowing with the weight on my back, and she shakes her head. "You can't -" she begins, screaming over the noise and shaking her head. "Run! Fly! Leave us!"

She pushes one of my legs, and my instincts force me to chomp at the air. Jane startles with fright but quickly recovers.

The dust starts to settle from the falling wall, and the demons and vampires roar, aware of our impending attempt to escape. They run with pumping arms, some with speed, some lumbering due to massive size. It's intimidating, looking at it from this perspective when I harbor every person I could lose.

The pounding of their feet nears and my adrenaline spikes, desperate for a few more moments to convince the women that here isn't the place to die a second time. I whip my head from underneath my belly. In quick succession, I release a wave of fire, engulfing the first line and creating a barrier of flames to buy us time.

My heart drops. The flames reach to an impossible level - not because it's not working. It is. My hope sinks because of Tanya's words and the truth behind them. My spine is already pained, an ache which reaches to my skull. I'm inexperienced in flight, and if I add another person to my back, I may not even make it off the ground.

I roar in fury, directing it at the demons and blaming them while they disintegrate into charred bones.

Jane and Tanya are sacrificing themselves because someone has to. The enemy is close, too close. Even if I could get both women on my back and manage to lift my talons off the ground, the enemy would bring us down. If someone were to stay behind, if someone were to distract, it would allow us the time we need to escape. It makes me sick thinking about it.

I chomp my teeth, a snarl, and stomp my talon. I don't want to lose someone else.

"Go!" Jane shoves one of my legs this time, soft flesh against my armored scales. "Go!"

I stare at her, searching one pleading, wet eye. It glistens with my flames, and tears continuously flow to the edge of her jaw. I search the other, finding the same emotion. She's scared. Worried. Broken... I can see her heart shattering to pieces with this one look.

"No!" Dyson yells. "Kat, no!"

Jane nods to me, slow but certain, and brings her trembling fingers to her lips. She knows this is her end, and she's aware of the costs. She'll be taken to the void, forever a trapped soul.

"Kat! There's no place for the twice dead. Don't do it!" Dyson attempts to sway me once more, but there's resolve on the women's stances even as they begin to back away from the safety of my underbelly.

Nothing I say, nothing I do, will save them from their own choice to save us from the inevitable if I were to try. And I won't take choice away from them. Not like it has been for me.

"We have to go!" Tember's friend yells. The vibration of released bow strings whips the immediate atmosphere while Tember and the man fend off those who have leaped over the wall of burning bodies.

Our time is up.

Jane reaches forward and strokes the scales along my jaw. "Tell Eliza to be strong. Tell her I love her. Tell her . . ." her voice cracks. "Tell her I choose this fate because a realm without her in it is too dim for the darkest of souls."

I briefly close my eyes against her gentle touch, feeling the depths of her last request through the contact - an unruly beast to a compassionate human. A mother saving her daughter. The selfless rescuing strangers. It sobers me, yet mentally brings me to my knees. My legs wobble, echoing my thoughts and jostling those on my back.

Grinding my teeth, I nod my head against her palm, vowing to honor her wishes. A tear streams down my scales, hitting the sand below. It sizzles when it meets blood and goop. My tears cure, but they can't cure this.

"Kat!" Tember yells in desperation.

It's now or never. I turn from Jane's compassionate touch, and, against my conflicting judgement, I beat my wings through the cold, dusty air. Dyson screams and protests on my back. His fists pummel my scales, but he soon reduces to sobs that quake his body against my aching spine. My heart shatters with his.

I'll live with this for the rest of my life, knowing I allowed their deaths and stole their freedom, even if it was their choice in the end. And I'll accept this burden as my own.

The darkness, once gripping my thoughts, dampens in my sorrow. The cold fingers wrap more tightly around the chambers of my heart. This time, however, I accept it for what it is - an emotional disconnect I willingly accept.

Gently, I lift into the air, my wings pushing against the pressure of the wind gathering underneath. Dyson wails, and my eyes well with tears. I shift my flight slightly for fear he'll fall with his grief, and the sandman grabs Dyson's arms to hold him in place. My heart pounds in my ears, sorrow gripping.

Higher and higher I fly, my feet tucked against my belly. We're almost to the top of the Colosseum, and a rush of unexpected wind pushes me slightly off kilter. My riders' grips tighten with their legs, squeezing my sides.

"Steady, Kat!" Tember warns.

Once balanced, I look down and watch as the wall of fire dissipates to a low wave. The vampires and demons take advantage, cheers of pure delight when they leap over the embers. As one, ants swarming from their hill, they take over our vacated spot without pause.

Dyson screams when they circle Tanya and Jane, and in a blink, they pile on top of them.

I close my eyes, wetness chilling my cheek. There will be nothing left of the women when they're done. Nothing but the haunting memory etched behind my eyelids for the rest of my life.

Angling my wings, I tilt us in a new direction, flying along the fog blanketing the sky and leaving my humanity behind.

"Hurry, Kat," Tember urges. "We need a portal!"'

A growl rumbles in my chest, a warning to the demanding angel.

"Now!" she screams again.

More tears stream down my scaled face, dripping from my muzzle and falling the hundreds of feet below. I chomp my teeth in fury, my grief quickly changing to rage because of Tember's demand, but knowing she's right. Soaring through the Death Realm's sky while coming to terms with what I've done will leave Tanya and Jane's sacrifice in vain.

Erline, I whisper in my head, an unpreventable mourning tone. I know she'll hear me. She's heard me before, back in the forest so long ago. *Erline*, I call again. *Portal*.

High winds from our gathering speed whip my tail behind me. When I don't think she'll answer my plea, the portal finally forms, mixing with the misty fog ahead. It swirls, large and circular, a broken promise for a place far safer than here.

Tucking my wings, I detect my riding companions hugging my spine, and we dip, soaring toward the swirls and leaving a part of ourselves behind.

I'll never forget this day. I vow to avenge them even if I'm the only one marching in an army.

CHAPTER THREE

AIDEN VANDER

DEMON REALM

I shimmer in, choosing the only place I know she'll be. The battle cries still vibrate inside my skull, and sand pebbles cling to my clothes, but everything here remains the same. Except me.

My trust in the creature I search for is almost humorous. I've only met her once, and even then, she tried to lure me to my death. When I recall that memory, her searching eyes had said everything she couldn't, and I feel as though I can trust it. She had made a point to tell me about Corbin's weakness, as had my reluctant escort. Who would do such a thing if there wasn't an underlying reason?

She's the one creature I can ask for help. I feel it in my bones.

Sulfur stings my nose, my first deep inhale of the Demon Realm. I haven't been gone too long, but the stench is overbearing.

The lavafalls tumble slowly down the cliffs, the backdrop to this realm. It's the only sound to be heard, and I get goosebumps at the eerie atmosphere. This truly is a place of harbored terror.

I search the surface of the gentle flowing black lava sea, looking for Ferox. There's a rift between her kind and our creator; it was evident in the way she spoke about him. But I need to find her and quick. Time isn't on my side.

At this moment, Corbin is wounded and vulnerable, and his remaining demons seem to be absent. I didn't expect them to be. I had anticipated them to be roaring with battle rage, bustling from one place to the next, and scrambling to find their baring.

However, their absence works in my favor. What I plan on doing next is reckless, even for myself.

Eliza can't stay in this realm - she'll be fed from until she dies a terrifying death. It's prudent I get her to safety, somewhere Kheelan can't find her. And then, I'll return to deliver the death to the fee who doesn't deserve his position. He is weak, pathetic, a disgrace better suited as the grit clinging to my shirt.

Still unconscious in my arms, Eliza's long red hair tickles my bicep, waving with each shift of my weight. I wait beside the lava sea, the same area I met Ferox in. I glance left, look right, paranoid of discovery before I can go through with my impulsive plan.

In the distance, the flow of lava travels upward, forming the castle walls of Domus Timore. Perhaps the remaining are tending to their wounded creator inside the home of demons. I smirk at the imagery, but it quickly fades while my wait stretches on.

No one knows of my betrayal yet, I remind myself. No one is aware I don't plan to remain under the pressed thumb of Corbin. The attention was on the bloodbath and not on my shimmering exit, and that works in my favor.

Jaw flexing, I inhale an impatient breath. Where is she? How do I call upon her? Do I speak her name? I mentally shrug. It's worth a shot.

"Ferox," I rumble to the open, quiet space.

Eliza stirs in my arms, her face pinching toward her nose. I study her features once more in hopes of diving into her unconscious mind. Though my demon nature is consuming and still fueling my purpose, everything I used to feel for her has come back with a powerful intensity. My heart swells, my blood pumping for her, but my pulse hammers to the tune of my nature, begging to be fed. And because of that, I know I'm too unstable to keep her safe myself. I have to get her to safety. She can't stay here, and she can't stay with me.

"You beckoned?" a familiar voice sings.

Tearing my eyes away from Eliza, I look to the voice. Ferox's hypnotizing face stares back at mine, an annoyed expression narrowing her eyes. Her tentacle hair twitches, submerging the ends into the surface. Above the surface, the thick hot goop drips down her deep green, slender shoulders.

47

"I do not enjoy being summoned, Thrice Born," she growls, exposing sharp teeth.

I flick my tongue and lick my bottom lip, uncharacteristically nervous. I hold no weight with the pyrens. They don't owe me any favors, and yet, I'm about to ask for one. This may not go over well.

"I need your help."

Her gaze drifts to the woman in my arms. "I, or we?" she drawls sluggishly.

I straighten my spine, irritation swirling in my stomach. Slitting my eyes to match hers, I lower my voice. "We," I demand with more conviction. What I'm asking isn't up for negotiation. She'll do it, or I'll kill her and ask the next pyren I come across.

Slowly, her gaze lifts back to mine, voiceless threats twitching her plump fish lips. She angles her head, considering me and my demand, and as she does so, her gills flutter. The corner of her eye twitches, and we hold each other's stare in a silent challenge. I'm ignorant to the pyren's true capabilities, but I'm sure it's deadly. Her abundance of confidence displays as much.

"What have you done, Thrice Born?" she nags sharply, accusing.

"Nothing yet, but I will if I need to," I threaten, smirking and tucking my chin. "I wonder what happens to a pyren when a demon feeds from them. Are you all connected?" Her lips twitch, and I know I've hit truth. "If I feed from one, does it drain the rest? That sounds like quite the meal, don't you think? The ultimate power boost."

"It's forbidden," she growls, and her tentacles quiver.

It takes a moment for her to compose her anger. She shakes her head and chuckles, bravely brushing it off. Holding up a hand with long and pointed fingers, she returns her gaze to mine and runs a nail over the small curve of her chin. The pads of her palms and tips of her fingers have tiny suctions on them, and as the black lava drips, it reveals six fingers, yet every two fingers are webbed with a transparent layer of skin.

Unspoken questions surface in her eyes, the possibility of manipulation at the root. It's expected. It's our nature. But I still prepare myself for her demands.

"Have you caused a rift, Thrice Born?" She toys with the lava, swirling her finger in the goop. "Is there something I should know?"

"Not yet." Shifting my bottom jaw, I grind my teeth. "There was a battle in the Death Realm. The dragon you spoke of was there. Corbin was injured, but it wasn't because of me or her. The dragon had friends. Powerful ones."

She waves her hand in the air. "Corbin will heal if he hasn't already. What of the dragon?"

"The dragon?" I frown and shift my weight, impatient with her interests. She's no longer intrigued with what she can demand from me but rather what the dragon means for her. It's obvious and has me curious about her alternative motives, yet annoyed for the impending conversational direction.

Ferox says nothing.

"Yes." I sigh and look to the Domus Timore. "She came. She's alive. I have no doubt she had plans for Corbin, possibly Kheelan and Sureen as well, but I don't think it went in her favor." I return my attention to her. "Look, I don't have a lot of time here."

She waits, patient, and a dramatic scrunch of her forehead wrinkles her smooth skin. "You have devious plans of your own, don't you, Demon?"

Speculating, she tilts her head to the side, her eyes flicking to the black lava castle. She bites her bottom lip, and her pointed teeth easily slice her skin, yet blood does not pour from the wounds. Instead, it leaves puncture holes that visibly close before my eyes, the flesh sucking back together like poked cake batter.

"What is it you want my help with?" she asks.

"I need to find a place where neither Kheelan, nor Corbin, will travel to," I begin, talking rapidly. "They cannot find her, Pyren. Do you understand?"

One tentacle points at me. "Why?"

I snarl. "You don't need to know."

"I do." She smirks, eyeing my bared teeth. "I've heard the angels are rebelling. The shades tried but failed. Are you planning a rebellion of your own, Demon?" She jabs her finger at Eliza. "You're harboring the wife of Kheelan. I'm sure she has many new gifts to aide you in doing so." She swims closer and lowers her voice. "Why not use her? Why stow her away?"

I think about that for a moment. My eyes traveling to the lavafall behind her, and my mind wanders with each slow dribble. The first and only solid plan is to keep Eliza safe, to find a place she can remain undiscovered. But it won't be enough, will it? They'll come for her. They'll find her. If I hide with her, they'll come for me as well, and anyone who's around me will die. Besides, I can't be trusted. I don't even trust myself. And I won't use her.

Something Ferox said echoes in my head though, nagging at my thoughts. The wife of Kheelan. New gifts. Did their union bestow his powers to her? I saw it with my own eyes and know it to be true. She holds the same kind of power as a fee; this much is obvious.

It would make sense. We are their ultimate creations – their weapons of mass destruction. We're their strengths in whatever they have planned, but a strength is also a weakness. Without Eliza, Kheelan will be the bottom of the food chain compared to those he's allied with. Without me, Corbin will be lesser of a fee, and his plans for what is surely to be a power-struggle will be lost. He can't compete against the dragon, against me. Not if we joined forces.

She giggles at my silence. "You plan to find the dragon."

The dragon is Corbin's weakness, his power source. If I find the dragon, I can develop a more solid plan.

I return my eyes to her and wonder how she feels about that. "Yes. I'm planning a rebellion," I say, ignoring her intuitive behavior. That knowledge in the wrong hands could be dangerous.

Ferox's giggle deepens to a darker tone. It's musical, like a harp's song, flowing and smooth. I said the exact words she wanted to hear.

"Very well. Come." She turns, the veins of fire crackling with disturbance. Floating forward, she wades through black lava, slow enough for me to keep even pace. Puffs of smoke rise in her wake, filling my nostrils with a more potent sulfur stench.

I find it mildly interesting the smell never bothered me before now - now that I have someone in my arms who can't breathe this air for long. She needs oxygen - pure, clean air.

"Wait." I jut my chin, frowning. The only reason Ferox would agree to a plan involving Corbin's death is if she gains something from it. "What's in it for you?"

Slowly, Ferox looks over her shoulder and touches the edge of her teeth with the tip of her tongue. "You're not the only one who desires freedom, Thrice Born," she spits.

Nostrils flaring, I grunt my response to her hostility. What I desire at this moment is to rip the truth from her instead of small chatting filled with nonsense and riddles. I know it wouldn't be easy though. These beasts, the fire-swimming mermaids, are strong. They swim through thick lava as quickly as water, despite their slight musculature. The most formidable opponents hide their strength.

From what I've been told, pyrens are Corbin's favorite. They're the ones he confides in at any given chance. As cherished creatures, he favors them like a loved pet, and yet, the pyren before me claims hatred for him and his affections. Why?

I look at my feet, gathering my senses, and hesitate with the question on my tongue. Then, I take the first tentative step onto the black moving lava. It takes several seconds for me to fully place my foot down, rolling my heel and arch until the toes inside my shoes are firm and sure. I keep my exhale of relief quiet and briefly examine the lava, watching it move under my foot. It holds my weight as though I'm not even standing here.

A sliver of doubt creeps into my abdomen, clenching my stomach, but I mask my uncertainty of its hold by clearing my throat. If I were to fall through, I'd survive. But would Eliza?

"What do you mean?" I ask, distracting myself more than wanting her answer.

Ferox turns back forward, wading through the lava once again. She continues her path, swimming toward the nearest lavafall. The thick substance parts around her body. "Ignorant child." She speaks in the same captivating sing-song voice which once held me under its spell. I'm surprised it holds no effect on me this time. Perhaps it's due to the woman unconscious in my arms.

Does Ferox know the woman in my arms is my anchor - my only weakness? I could be making a mistake. The pyren could be fooling me into false security. I grind my jaw, hoping I didn't make the wrong choice by seeking Ferox's help. I'm a desperate demon. She could easily make a fool out of me.

"We Pyrens may be able to travel to all realms," she answers gently. "But we are still on a leash. Corbin demands us to do his bidding. When we are not finding humans at sea, we are to spy on his enemies. It's not an easy feat, and we keep much knowledge to ourselves. But you would be surprised how much you learn in the blue and clear waters."

I tilt my head and take another careful step, untrusting of the lava and the creature who lives in it. "What do you mean? What do you do with humans?"

"We climb their ships and drag them to the depths of their ocean and sea," she mumbles, her words clipped. "Afterward, we destroy their ships and bring the humans here, half dead." Her voice changes. The tone, the personality of each vowel, it shifts as though another part of her soul is speaking. The evil slowly drips from her lips and causes me pause. "They fight and plead, eyes swimming with the salty sting of their waters. By the time we reach this realm, their lungs are filled but their heart still holds on, still beats with the last remaining hope."

"And then?" I growl when her silence stretches on, frustrated with her fascination in death. I'm tired of probing for answers and sick of death itself. Death and I have had too many encounters. One more, and I might as well move in with Kheelan, kiss his feet, and call him master. The thought raises invisible hackles along my spine.

The ends of Ferox's tentacles curl as though they brushed against something hot and quickly recoiled from the burn. A sign of disgust, maybe? "Corbin turns them. Adults, women, children. How did you think he made demons?"

I raise my eyebrows. I wasn't expecting this answer. "I don't know. I've never asked myself that question."

"Well," she whispers. "Now you have the answer." Her tail flicks under the lava, and droplets splat against my forearm, sizzling. It tingles. "To be a creature of terror, you must be changed during the moment of highest fear. It's only a sliver of a moment in which Corbin can change them. When their heartbeats falter, but their brain function continues."

"Do you like what he asks of you?" I speculate when she finishes.

Ferox sighs. "None of us do."

She reaches the black lavafall first and turns to face me with a look I've worn many times in this third life: Pinched. Starved. Thirsty. "Death is beautiful. It is fascinating. It is the only sure bet in the realms. But no, Thrice Born. We have no choice but to do as he wishes. It is this reason alone we hunger for freedom."

"Freedom," I mumble, nodding to her.

"Freedom," she echoes and tips her head to the black lavafall behind her. "This is your portal to the Guardian Realm. You could shimmer there, but unfortunately, I'd wager you've never been. A demon cannot shimmer to a realm he's never been. This," she waves to it, "is your way in. I will travel with you, Thrice Born, but only this once. Do not ask favors from me again unless it benefits me and my kind."

My eyebrows pinch above the bridge of my nose, and I narrow my eyes in disbelief. "And this doesn't benefit you?"

She purses her lips, resembling a tight rosebud. "I have no idea your intentions. You want to be free, and we want to be free. At this very moment, you're the only one escaping, yet your judgement is clouded by a heart created to never feel love. You say you plan to rebel, and this could be good for my kind. But how can I trust you'll come back for us? Will you leave the woman in your arms with a stranger to keep her safe? You have not given me your word, and even if you do, how do I trust it?"

I inhale deeply, seeing her point. "Demon's aren't trustworthy, but as you've said, I'm not a normal demon, am I?"

She smirks, and her face smooths once more. "No, you are not." Reaching up, she softly trails her fingers over the skin of my forearm. "Come. There isn't much time. The pyrens are to convene by Domus Timore. I can hear the call."

I frown and tilt my head, listening for a sound that isn't there.

Her smirk widens to a cocky grin. "The frequency is too low for anything but our ears."

"What are you gathering for?" I ask.

"Corbin," she spits, looking to the castle. "I surmise he's lost many demons today. He'll be needing more."

I stretch my neck, popping my spine. In other words, many will be dying today on the Earth Realm. A part of me cares, but the other part of me is resigned to a nature I have no power to stop. The humans' safety isn't my chief concern.

She swallows, and her gills close as she does. "I will travel there with you, but I will not stay. If there was a battle as you say, each realm will be on the defense. This is an up-hill climb for you, Thrice Born. The tribes will not be welcoming."

Gripping my forearm, she quickly leads me forward. The lavafall parts on its own, revealing blue, sparkling water behind it.

"Tribes?"

CHAPTER FOUR

TEMBER

GUARDIAN REALM

We emerge through a separate portal than the one all angels take when we travel to and from the Guardian Realm. It's the main portal inside the Angel's Ground and would surely have shredded Dyson and the sandman to pieces. Only fee born creatures may pass through it, walk among the angels, and live to tell the tale. Even Jaemes wouldn't survive it as he was born the traditional way.

No, this portal is nature made. It feels as though the air is forced from my lungs, the winds too high, too strong for anything but asphyxiation. I remember it well from when our makeshift fee group traveled to the Dream Realm to save Katriane from Sureen's smite.

Erline created this portal for our escape. Kat must have called for her. Or perhaps, Erline knew we were in need. Both could be true.

Since Myla is no longer in Kat's body, it tips to the conclusion Katriane and Erline's bond is on a solidified and unique level, one which I'm beginning to understand. Erline loves Kat, but I know better than to suspect the adoration is mutual. It's hard to love the fee who are all corrupted by their own desires. Somehow, I've managed that emotional feat despite Erma's shortcomings.

Death clings to me, a heavy weight settled between my shoulders, slicing through my spine and exiting my chest pressed against Kat's scales. It clings like a sickly internal dread.

I release some of the tension I've been holding between my shoulder blades by shifting my arms. I breathe deep, the first inhale of fresh, normal air since we had departed to rescue Kat from her heroic efforts.

Dyson, who is tucked under the sandman's tall frame, gasps as the oxygen returns to his lungs. His intake is loud and desperate, his body too mortal for such a transition from one realm to the next.

Our torsos are flat with our cheeks pressed against the rough scales lining the back of Kat's dragon. Her wings beat once, an automatic instinct to right her off balanced body. The correction is a mistake, her wingspan too large for this area, and the edge of her wing clips a thick, black marble pillar.

The pillar crumbles like the wall had in the Death Realm, raining chunks of rock into the common area. I grind my teeth and lean as a piece narrowly misses my shoulder. It hits Kat's ribs instead.

Screams of surprise erupt from the angels who, until our unexpected arrival, had been leisurely roaming.

Their shouts carry and bounce in echo until they reach the top, exiting through the structureless ceiling to join the starry sky.

I imagine this wasn't what they were expecting - a dragon and her riders disrupting their peace and calm as an unannounced arrival, but we had no choice. This is the only safe place, the only realm where our enemies have no eyes. Erline was clever to send us here.

Kat dips her long head in an attempt to regain balance, but it shifts us instead, further teetering her flight. I grip her scales tighter, the edges of my knuckles white, and my thighs tighten to keep my rump firmly seated. Jaemes curses in his native tongue, and I feel his body tense in front of mine.

Dyson lifts his head for a peek and shouts as the belly of Kat's dragon thumps into the black marble floor. The Grounds, which float in the sky of the Guardian Realm, shake from the force of her weight while she slides across it.

The sandman grabs Dyson's hips to steady his slipping frame, and the bounce's second impact almost knocks me from her back. Spinning, we skid several feet, her scales scraping marble. I squeeze my eyes shut, hoping we miss the pillar we're fast approaching. The air whooshes from my lungs as we come to a full stop.

A groan - partial relief, partial pain - rumbles up Kat's ribs, her head thumping to the cold floor which perfectly reflects the sparkling stars above.

Hushed, violent mutters enclose before any of us can uncurl our fists from scales. We wait for several moments, catching our breath and calming our hearts.

We're safe.

Slowly, I stretch my cramped limbs and slide backward down her back. My pants catch on a spike of her tail, ripping a hole near my calf. The sandman, Jaemes, and Dyson are sluggish to peel themselves off, dismounting and snapping their legs.

I push my disgruntled curls from my face. A few locks are stuck to the enemy's dried blood streamed across the hill of my cheek. Carefully dislodging them, I rake the same hand along my scalp and turn on my heel to face the approaching group of curious and furious warriors.

I assess the situation quickly - their tones versus their body language - and see they present no immediate threat to me or mine. Their eyes are flickering and darkly brooding, but their palms remain open and their wings twitch with the need for information.

Pulling my shoulders back, I head to Kat's passengers. One of my eyebrows raises while I watch Dyson try to cover his manhood with both hands and failing, his face brightly red. Although unharmed by Kat's scales, he's naked as the day he came screaming from his mother's womb.

Kat groans, and the sound vibrates the entire floor. Hot breath wafts soon after, curling around my ankles and chasing the chill from the room. The three men take several wide steps back from the sprawling beast, and then Jaemes pins Dyson with a disgusted frown.

His elf-tinted accent speaks in clipped, barking syllables. It's his version of chastising, I've learned. "Why are you naked?"

Ignoring Dyson's stuttering, unintelligible answer, I glide around to the front of Kat's head. It's as long as I am tall, and I marvel at the sleek, smaller scales pinched between the tight dips of her face's skeletal structure.

Bending my knees, I block out the men's bickering and allow it to fade into the background. Her fire orange eyes gaze back into mine, a sigh rushing through her nostrils.

She's much bigger when I stand this close, more magnificently dangerous and mighty, even as she lays, vulnerable, in an undignified heap. Each muscle ripples with every breath, and her scales are sharply defined like carved steel.

I reach forward with a careful hand and touch her muzzle with the tips of my fingers. The scales are softer here, smooth and leathery. I flatten my palm, tilt my head, and run my hand up her face. I stop between her grieving eyes.

"Are you okay?" I murmur, concerned. I don't know if I'm staring at the beast or at Kat. I'm certain Kat almost lost herself in the bloodbath back there.

I also know her heart is filled with sorrow and deep regret for leaving behind Jane and Tanya. If it were my charge, I'd need a moment to myself as well. But here isn't the place to shed emotions. Here is not safe for the powerful or the least bit different.

A soft wind exits her lungs, and this time, it's tinged with the smell of burning wood and white smoke. With much effort, she tucks her massive legs under her and stands on all four shaky legs, looming over me and all those who gather. Chomping her jaw once, she curves her long neck and surveys the audience.

I follow her lead and study my home. The angel's portal glistens and shimmers behind me, almost invisible to an untrained eye. The black pillars rise to a star-speckled sky. White flecks move inside the marble, and laughter quietly rings down the hall from another part of the Grounds.

Throughout this colossal area, angels are shocked still, gaping with their mouths wide open at the dragon who invaded their peace. Some of their wings flutter, agitated when she meets their gaze, while a few halos banish dark corners of the room.

The shock quickly fades, however, and the air becomes smothered with hostility. I tense, ready for what may come.

Turning stiffly, my back to my dragon charge, I glance at Jaemes as more angels rush into the common area, Ires ready. Unaffected by the possible danger he faces, his feet pad against the floor as he comes to stand beside me. He narrows his eyes to the angels while flicking his thumb at Dyson behind him.

"He's naked," he proclaims with a tone of disgust.

"I'm aware," I mumble distractedly.

As if it just occurred to him he's on enemy grounds, Jaemes leans in to whisper in my ear. The gesture makes it clear to the circling angels that we're together as a team, and I cringe. The angels hate the elves, and vice versa. And… they hate me.

"Is this when I should cower in fear?" he asks.

I scrape my bottom teeth over my top lip and ignore his crass question. "We need Erma before this gets out of control."

The Angel's Ground is no place for a breathing enemy. However, here we stand, a wingless angel, an arrogant elf, an unsteady dragon, a silent sandman, and naked shifter, breaking the rules set about for the safety of our home.

I tilt my head up and peer at Kat's dragon. "Can you shift back?"

A rumble's soundwaves tickle the soles of my feet while she returns the hard stare to the angels, a battle of wits. She must feel it as well – the hatred, the uncertainty. Perhaps she's telling me she doesn't want to shift back in case we have another fight on our hands.

Her orange eyes flick back to mine, and her pointed spikes flatten along her spine. She tucks her wings tight against her back, and we endure a moment of silent communication. I watch as her irises darken, and the slitted pupils enlarge, taking the glow with it.

What I would give to understand what's going on in her head - to know the secrets she keeps tucked away to spare those around her. She doesn't trust me enough to share the burden, and perhaps, it's not my place to demand it.

I nod to her, gently encouraging while keeping my face soft and free of increasing concern. I turn back to the angels and give her the privacy she deserves, forming a tiny wall with Jaemes. Together, our stances are wide and portray our desire to protect her.

Cracking and popping quickly follow, and Jaemes' body practically hums with his own desire to witness the transformation, shifting from foot to foot. But he resists, gripping the curved handle of his bow instead.

She groans, confirming her discomfort and soreness. When the sandman and Dyson suck in a sharp breath. Jaemes peeks over his shoulder and scoffs. "Why is nudity the theme of the day?"

"When they shift, they lose their clothes," I mumble, preparing to further explain. I'm cut off from the details of the transformation when screams erupt. With the echo it generates, it takes me longer than it should have to discover where it originated. I blink hard and Jaemes curses, swiftly leaving my side.

I sharply turn, the movement uncoordinated. For a moment, I'm frightened the angels might be attacking my charge. But they remain as still as before.

My heart thumps hard against the veins in my wrist. On the ground, the sandman and Dyson clutch their middles while curled into a fetal position on their sides. Their hands clench their chests, agony creasing lines on their youthful foreheads. Through a pained expression, Dyson looks to me, his eyes wild and his face visibly paling.

"What is it?" I demand, striding to the men and looming over Dyson while Jaemes hovers over the sandman.

Kat quickly rushes to our sides, her bare feet slapping the marble, seemingly unconcerned about her nudity. It feels like yesterday we were standing in the alley after she defeated a nest of vampires. Then, she had cared much about her exposed flesh to peering eyes. But now, she doesn't seem to notice. This isn't the same Katriane DuPont, though. I'd be a fool to believe otherwise.

Together, we quickly bend and sit on our knees. Jaemes' gaze sweeps the sandman's shaking body, looking for obvious injuries where there are none. Slowly, he lifts his eyes back to mine. It's the first time I've ever seen him display true emotional concern.

"My – chest –" Dyson spits between clenched teeth. Curling tighter, he screams again. The crowding angels jump in surprise.

"His heart!" Kat yells over their synchronized agony. She places her hands on his calves, tendrils of bright lights swirling below her palms. She raises them past Dyson's hips to the area where Dyson claws at his ribs.

"What about it?" Jaemes demands.

Dyson rolls to his back, completely still, and after displaying the same power over the sandman, Kat's magic disappears. The two men look to be sleeping though their body's still twitch.

"They've fainted," I announce, distracted by Kat's power. I've never seen her do that before. Magic usually requires spells, but she didn't utter one word.

A dark expression crosses her face. I can almost see the flames behind the irises. "Their hearts belong to Kheelan," she growls.

"Move!" Erma shouts from the other end of the common area.

She parts the sea of angel's silently gathered around us and emerges through the crowd, Erline right behind her. Erma bends to the sandman, kneeling beside Jaemes, and examines him. She's clothed in her black dress, the one which exposes the pale skin along her shoulder blades and the feminine dips of her spine. It pools around her knees, a dark puddle.

Erline positions behind Kat with her arms crossed. A hostile and vicious expression contorts her gentle features, crunching her small pixie nose. I know what she's doing - she's placing herself between the Angels' smothering tension and her sole responsibility: Katriane DuPont.

Hovering her hand above him, a yellow glow emits from Erma's palms just as Kat had done. She nods grimly, coming to the same conclusion as Kat.

"They're tied to Kheelan," Erline confirms, speaking for Erma. "Kheelan is calling back his hearts."

I ball my hands into fist, my nails biting the skin, and slam it on the ground next to my thighs with a crack. "I've had enough of this!"

All the death, all the games and open hostility. What has become of the realms to stoop to such a low level?

After taking a calming breath, per Erma's pointed glare, I direct my next question to Erline. If anyone knows Kheelan best, she does. "How do we stop it?"

Erline doesn't look at me, and her lips press together. "You must tie them to you, Katriane."

Kat visibly stiffens, and slowly, she turns her dark eyes to the fee hovering above her. "Excuse me?"

"You must tie their lives," Erline states, pointing to the writhing, unconscious men as though the action would explain everything. "To yours."

I laugh cynically. "That's impossible. Kat doesn't have that much power." No one answers me. "Does she?"

Kat hesitates, staring at her realm's creator. She doesn't want to, this much is evident. This will be not one but two other lives on her hands. If she dies, they die.

"Why don't you do it?" Jaemes asks Erma while tugging at his pointed ears.

Erma shakes her head and tucks a hand under the sandman's shoulder. "I won't tie myself to another." She focuses on Erline like a child urging its mother.

What does she mean?

My face relaxes as the conclusion hits me. Erma is tied to every creature she creates. It's why she holds them so dear - gave them hearts to care and appease the reckless behavior we barely hold at bay. She's not only preserving our longevity; she's ensuring hers.

"Why not?" I ask, flabbergasted.

Erma gracefully stands and holds out her hands in the open air. The atmosphere cracks for a split second, and a plush white blanket finds its way into her waiting fingers. She snaps the fabric and drapes it comfortingly over Kat's naked shoulders.

"Need you ask, angel?" Erline barks, eyeing the white fluff.

I growl, protective over Kat who has yet to respond to Erline. She shouldn't have to do this. She just lost two lives. Adding more may break her completely.

I can feel Kat's emotions waver, witness them cross her face as she watches Dyson with a telling sparkle in her eye. Her gaze lingers far longer than it should for a normal person.

"I – I can't," Kat begins, her eyes watering.

Erline flicks her wrists, clothing Kat in tight jeans and a black v-neck t-shirt, the blanket remaining where it was placed.

"You must," Erline mumbles. "Our futures - your future - will be grim without them." She lowers herself to Kat's level, her blue dress billowing like the skirt of a bell. "This, I promise you, daughter of my daughter. If you lose him," she eyes Dyson, "all will be lost. They are important for what's to come."

A tear reluctantly spills over the rims of Kat's tired eyes and trickles down the slopes of her cheek. She angrily swipes the heel of her hand across the chapped skin and hardens her face. "How do I do it?"

Erline smiles weakly, a reassurance, and I cringe internally. I don't trust her - not after what she pulled with Myla's spirit. She continuously endangers my charge.

"The tears of a dragon and a little magic," she coaxes.

The angels behind us murmur in one hushed wave.

"And what will –" Kat begins, but Erma cuts her off.

"We don't have the time for questions, Dragon. If you want your friends to live, we must act now." Erma pauses and sucks in a calming breath. "We will aide you in this. You needn't worry."

Without explanation, without further verbal consent, Erline lifts her slender yet powerful hand to Kat's increasingly reddening cheek. She gathers a stray tear on the pad of her thumb. Sluggishly, the droplet dribbles down her knuckle and cups in the scoop of her hand, glistening.

With a lick to her bottom lip, Erline scurries around Kat, and leans to Dyson. She rubs the tear on his forehead then makes her way to the sandman, repeating the same action.

I gather to my feet when the black floor and pillars quake. The Angel's Ground groans with power, and a drafty breeze dips into the common room, whispers in the wind.

At first, nothing happens to the two men. But then, a strike like a crack of thunder booms in the space around us. The men's backs arch as though a string is attached to their sternums and pulls at their abdomens.

Kat gradually gathers to her feet, the blanket tumbling from her shoulders to the floor, and is pushed across the expanse by the wind. "What's happening?" she asks.

Erline holds out her hand to Erma, and they each hook the other's fingers.

Jaemes and I exchange glances as they close their eyes, dip their chin, and chant words I can't make out above the noise. The space around us glows a vivid white, blinding light. The winds gather further, a treacherous gale that whips my hair.

I duck my head and wrap my arms around my face. The surrounding angels' wings lose feathers in the gusts, and they swirl in the open space, pummeling my exposed skin.

Gritting my teeth, I fight the elements to stay upright, to not allow it to carry me away like a plastic sack in a storm. With a thundering crack, a few marble pillars crash to the floor.

Just when I think the sea of winds will beat me to my knees, they quickly die to a gentle trickle, leaving my skin chafed and raw.

Jaemes coughs beside me, and I lift my head, glancing at him first. He's closer than he was before. When did he reach my side? His long, black hair is in disarray, and his jaw is set to a sharp angle of courage. "Remind me" he begins with a mumble, "to never underestimate the might of a fee."

I turn to what he stares at. Such pride is set in his eyes, a rare show plastered on this warrior's appearance.

Kat's arms are held out to her sides, palms up, her face slanted to the stars. Whatever the two fee did seeped an abundance of extra magic inside Kat's form. She looks every bit the force she'll surely become. An expression of peace keeps her features relaxed, and slowly, she lowers her arms back to her sides, the transaction complete.

Dyson and the sandman are still sprawled on the floor, seemingly untouched by the gale, but their bodies no longer shake with pain. Feathers are sprinkled along the marble as they float around the room and find a final resting point along its surface.

"Is it done?" I ask, my voice cracking.

"Yes," Kat answers.

Erline holds out her hand and waves it in the air, clothing Dyson with black jeans and a crisp white buttoned-down shirt. "They're safe." She looks pointedly at Erma, one brow raised. "But they can't remain here."

Frowning, I survey the area and the possible danger it poses. And then I scoff, crossing my arms to contain my disgust. Every angel who was gathered around us has fled the room, and silence has taken over the Grounds, which surely can't be good. None of them stuck around to help my injured party, not even to converse about what had transpired. I shouldn't have expected them to. Every being in this room is their enemy. They've already drawn their own conclusions. Coupled with the gossip spreading about my relationship with Erma, Erline is right. We can't stay here. We don't know what to expect in due retaliation, and safety won't be welcoming in my home.

Jaemes curses when he too notices the absence of his enemies. "Trouble follows you creatures everywhere," he says as though he isn't a part of the problem.

Kat's cheeks are burned a bright shade of pink and slick with tears. The peaceful look has fled, and her face droops before she rubs her fists against her tired eyes. She's exhausted, today's emotions finally taking their toll.

"We should find Katriane a place to rest," I mumble and reach forward to place my hand on her shoulder. She sticks me with a hard stare before I can, and I pull away and cross it back over my chest, grimacing. She's still upset with me for my manipulation which resulted in her being shoved into Myla's past. I believe, on some level, she blames me for Myla's death.

Erline speculates and studies the exchange with a scrutinizing eye. She slowly turns to Kat. "I know you despise me, and I know you're angry with Tember. At this very moment, the realms are in your debt. But..." She pauses, waiting for Kat to meet her gaze. "It would be wise if you attempt to give your guardian a set of wings."

Kat's head whips back like she's been slapped. I open my mouth to protest that it isn't necessary, that I can do without them, but quickly snap it shut. Again, Erline is right. I can't continue to protect properly without them, and according to Jaemes, their absence makes me half a warrior.

My shoulders droop. This is a favor I don't deserve.

"There's a battle coming," Erline continues before Kat can abruptly decline. "We will need every advantage we can muster."

Lifting a hand, Kat roughly rubs the wrinkles lining her stressed forehead with the tips of her fingers. She nods behind her palm, lowers her trembling hand to her cheek, and gathers the necessary moisture.

"Kat," I defend, shaking my head. "You don't have to do this."

"Of course, she does," Jaemes barks. "You are useless without them, and I'm tired of intervening in their absence."

Looking only to me, she holds her hand out in front of her. Her eyes harden like she's tucked away her true feelings, and the muscles twitch around her eyelids with the effort to keep them hidden. "I will," she says, her voice thick with the beginnings of anger. "They're right, Tember. We barely made it out of there alive. If you would have had your wings, you could have saved Tanya and Jane. I won't make that mistake again. I won't be unprepared, and I'll be damned if I lose another."

I gulp at the memory of Jane and Tanya, overtaken by hungry beasts.

She lowers her voice to a deep and dark husky tone, one I've never heard her use. "I refuse to be half of the team we could be. This is only the beginning. We can't have you half the warrior. Now, lift your damn shirt." She eyes my shirt, knowing full well it's one I've borrowed from her but says nothing to that front.

Jaemes chuckles beside me, an unpleasant sound in the heat of the moment. "Does this mean I can no longer call you my mascot?" he asks.

I call him a colorful name in response, but it only widens his grin.

"Do it," I tell Kat drily, if for no other reason than to smear the grin from his face.

Gathering the hems at the back of my borrowed shirt, I turn and fully face Jaemes. The cloth is stiff from dried blood, and a few specks of the Death Realm's sand dislodge from the stitching and ping against the floor.

I shimmy the cloth up to my shoulders but leave the front lowered to cover my breasts. Jaemes had made his feelings known. He doesn't find nudity charming. It's a conundrum since he and his people barely wear any clothes themselves.

Jaemes' arms are folded, a smug smile slanting his lips. He baited me with his goad, but I already knew that before I turned to face him. His pointed ears jerk, tangled in his nest of black hair discolored by clinging dust.

I smirk as I gingerly lift the rest of the cloth over what's left of my wings. "Nice hair," I tease.

His shoulders bob in a shrug. "Trying something new."

Kat gasps and curses in French when she sees what's left of my wings. "Christ, Tember," she mumbles. Her bare feet make a sticky sound as she closes the short distance to me. It takes a moment for her to do anything, and this reluctance causes me doubt.

A finger trails down my spine and over the space on my shoulders where my wings once sprouted. I hiss between clenched teeth. It doesn't hurt, but I can feel the chill as the tears from a dragon trace the unhealed wounds. Though guardians heal quickly, the severance of wings do not. It's a visual reminder of what was sacrificed.

My shoulders hunch forward on their own accord, and my skin rips along my back, splitting to make room.

Feathers tickle the flesh at the small of my back as they grow.

I look to Jaemes between the curls obscuring my vision. He tilts his head. "Black?" he ponders, scowling.

A warmth leaks through my veins, and goosebumps rise over my thighs. My balance wavers as the additional weight is added to my backside, and my arms sway to center my gravity, dropping my hold on the shirt.

"It's done," Kat whispers.

"What's black?" I question Jaemes.

He nods to my wings as I test their strength, fluttering the extra limbs. They're heavier than I remember my first set of wings being.

Standing fully upright, I peer over my shoulder and watch the feathers grow their last inch. I twirl and examine with speculation. Their feathers are black instead of the traditional white, and each constructed one perfectly matches the other and shines in reflection from the stars above. I reach back, touch one, and my face drops in awe.

"They're hard," I comment. "Like metal." But it's not metal. It's different, flexible yet sharp like knives.

Erma gapes in disbelief, reaches forward, and strokes the tip of her fingers along my wings. Kat's fingers rhythmically tap her lips, her elbow propped and supported by her arm tucked around her waist, and Jaemes rocks on the back of his heels.

"My stars," Erma breathes.

"What does this mean? What went wrong?" I ask, spinning in full circle.

"I don't know," Erma mutters.

I stop rotating, close my eyes, and take a deep breath to temper the anxiety. Will I be able to take flight with these?

"They are weapons," Erline says with pride. A ghostly beam tugs at the corners of her lips when I snap my eyes to hers.

"Weapons," I repeat, the word rolling across my tongue as though it's the first time I've spoken it.

Indeed, they could be weapons. The white wings may be more flexible, but this metal substance would surely protect against any object from an assault behind. I flex them, displaying their width, and curve them to fold around me. Immediately, I bask in their glory with a gasp of surprise. There's enough space in here to keep another safe as well.

It's a shield.

Ideas and scenarios pop into my head, ways I can use them to my advantage. Tucking my wings to my back, I'm promptly reminded of the innocent victims on the floor as their bodies come back into full view. My gaze lingers on their slumbering forms.

I point. "What do we do with them?"

Erma blows out a breath, fanning her red ringlets, and turns with her hands on her hips. "Erline is right. They can't stay here." She looks to me, swiveling her head over her shoulder. I make my way to my creator as though she beckoned me forth, and Jaemes tags along with me.

She continues. "Since the two of you left, there's been talk about an uprising. I have no idea how they plan to do it, but this is hostile ground, Tember. You - none of you - can stay here until it's sorted. The rift between us all cannot be our center focus."

I nod, fully agreeing with her. We have larger issues across the realms than a few who disagree with the rumors slithering through my home. The gossips may be warranted and held in truth, but this won't stop a retaliation, I fear. Favoritism is their chief hypothesis, and there will be no swaying those opinions until the dust settles.

This also explains why Erline is here - to add extra protection for her sister fee. The angels wouldn't dare uproot their creator with two powerful beings roaming the halls. If she's here, matters are far worse than Erma is portraying.

Turning to Erline, Erma taps her chin and then flicks her eyes to Jaemes. "The tribes?"

He sucks in his lips and tightens his crossed arms, releasing his lips with a wet pop. "I'm not sure -"

"It's worth a shot," I blurt before Jaemes can completely decline. "There isn't anywhere else in this realm more safe than your tribe. We need the protection of warriors. Surely Mitus will allow it."

He is, after all, hoping Jaemes and I will continue to work together, to show the elves and the angels that history doesn't have to repeat itself. We can work together to protect this realm, and the elf leader knows it. He's a good man, a kind elf below an intimidating exterior. He may not have used as many words to portray his complete approval of this arrangement, but I did witness the twinkle of hope when we last met under the tent which gathered all four tribe leaders. None of them were welcoming aside from Mitus' reserved judgment. I was made to parade my severed wings then, too.

"Tribes?" Kat asks. She frowns, following Erma's speculative gaze to Mitus' youngest son. "What are you?"

I click my tongue. Do I introduce her to this tyrant? "Katriane, this is Jaemes, an elf of the Igna tribe. He is one of the many sons of their leader, Mitus, head of the tribe's Council."

"Elves are real?"

Jaemes inclines his head, a bow of respect. "Dragon," he greets.

Kat exhales. "Don't bow," she grunts quietly. As a distraction, she angles herself to look upon Dyson. A mix of emotions crosses her face, a blossoming spark in the air, peaking my interest.

"Are you okay?" I ask.

She nods. I don't believe her. The gesture was automatic with no truth or thought behind it. What is she keeping to herself now?

"Are we ready?" I ask the group instead of further pressing Kat. If she wants, and when she's ready, she'll forgive me for my wrong-doings enough to trust me with her troubles.

Kat holds up a finger smudged with dirt and dust and jabs it in Erline's direction. "Since you owe me a debt you'll never be able to repay, I'd like to call in a favor."

I bite the inside of my cheek. You don't ask for favors from the fee, even those who manipulated you to do their own bidding.

"Oh?" Erline quirks an eyebrow. "And what is this favor?"

"I want answers," Kat growls. "Real ones. Not the wooly crap you keep pulling over my head."

CHAPTER FIVE

KATRIANE DUPONT

GUARDIAN REALM

Firewood sizzles, and embers pop inside the hole in the ground of the Igna tribe's village. The hole is surrounded by a layer of quickly melting snow, the heat too great for the fragile crystals to withstand. Taunting memories of orc roars and demon screams echo within each glowing log, the battle on continuous repeat like a song I can't get out of my head.

In my mind, the hole itself represents the Colosseum, a barrier to keep the rage: fire; and the wood: victim within. I can't seem to keep the fresh memories at bay. The Guardian Realm is far from the dark creatures of that tragic event, but they're still with me nonetheless. The fire plucks the recollection of it and those I willingly chose to burn alive.

It's some time after we arrived in the tribes. I had already attempted sleep in one of the teepees quickly erected by the elves who weren't eager to do so. They weren't happy to see us here, and many had raised their voices even after Erma put her foot down with her almighty magic. However, my dreams were realistic, death after death, making a restful sleep impossible. I gave up soon after, venturing to this hole, and erected a fire on my own with a simple flick of my wrist. The display had shaken some of the neighboring elves, but for the most part, they had to work hard to pretend I didn't exist.

Tethered to posts outside my neighboring tee pee, their dog-like creatures have their eyes glued to my every twitch or subtle shift. They don't trust me, and if I cared enough to guess, it's because whenever I stare at them, they sense the dark tendrils gripping my heart and fiercely growl their warning in return.

They don't look like ordinary canines, but they do sound like them. The absence of eyes doesn't stop them from assessing their surroundings, either. Their forms waver, ghost like, as if time exists differently for them. A lime-green-tinged aura surrounds their blurry outline, a constant distraction.

A small part of me desires to run my fingers through it just to see what it feels like. Is it airy? Or does it defy logic and have a more solid texture despite its looks?

No lips hide their sharp, imposing teeth, and a glow from inside their throats brightens the snow beneath their paws when they open their mouths. Each muscle is impressively defined with the absence of fur, and they jolt in surprise when I scratch my chin, testing their tentativeness. Their nostrils and ears are large like pigs and twitch when I do so. I suppose they have to make up for their lack of sight somehow with other heightened senses.

The creepy canines shift their heads from me to something behind me gimping in the snow, a slight limp in the gait.

"Kat?" A voice booms though it's meant to be a whisper.

The tone is deep. I know exactly who it is, but my shoulders tense anyway. I'm also not sure if I want any company.

Sandy shimmies between the narrow space of the log I'm sitting on and the teepee's animal skin wall flapping in the brisk wind behind me. His new shoes - also animal skin - break the snow's thin caps, crunching the barrier. He sits beside me, gracefully bending despite his obvious leg injury. The bandage around his arm gleams in the fire's light.

The sandman had fought hard. I'm not surprised to see him alive and well. He's proven his worth in more ways than one. This sandman is probably one of the few who can take care of himself.

I don't answer my new companion with any sort of greeting though he has yet to look at me expecting one. Instead, my eyes remain on the dog-like creatures and my focus on the echoing memory of battle inside the fire.

"Prenumbras," he conveys, pointing at the canines. "Nasty hunters, they are. They are blind, similar to bats, but sense by auras instead."

Interesting, I think to myself. And useful. It is said aura's can be felt from an astounding distance, and their color depicts the being's nature and intentions.

Instead of peppering him with questions about the beasts, I remain quiet and still.

Around us, the tribe bustles from teepee to teepee, working to accomplish their daily tasks. They have extra mouths to feed, and their displeasure is evident when they slam pots on solid boulders acting as tables and flick glares our direction when they believe us unaware. I can feel their eyes like daggers flying in our direction, but at this moment, I couldn't care less.

The sandman and I both lost Gan. Even though we didn't like him, the cruel death he had endured shouldn't be subjected to anyone. The way he died, the tragic occurrences we had to go through to get here - it's something neither of us wants to voice.

And the others - the humanized shades still on the Death Realm, stuck in their cells - what will become of them?

I know we aren't the only ones plagued with the memories, but it's different for them than it is for us.

Dyson will be fine - he's seen battle, he's seen death. With shifters, it comes with the territory. The sandman and I have not. At least not to this magnitude.

And myself? I was never meant to be the bloodthirsty beast that had come over me. I'm ashamed to have allowed it. Even now, I can feel the evil rooted at my core, orchestrating the hums of battle cries. It's what this feels like, its frigid fingers like a vice around each chamber, pulsating my heart to the same tune. It's ensuring I don't forget it's there, what I'm capable of, and a constant reminder of how far I've gone.

I can feel the sandman's heart as well, and Dyson's too, their lives now ultimately tied to mine. If I die, they die. I wonder . . . if my slithering madness continues to consume, will it take them next, a plague to the mind? Goosebumps riddle my skin with pricks and tingles at the thought. This is yet another thing I'm responsible for.

Blood. Screams. Death. Bones poking through skin. Flashes of things I want nothing more than to forget surface, and no matter how much I try not to, a smile spreads across my face, victory in an evil's eye.

Uncomfortable with my increasing dark vibes and wicked grin, the sandman shifts in his seat. "Your thoughts will drive you mad, Katriane DuPont. You must cap them."

"Too late," I hiss, hushed, my concentration moving from the canine creatures to the fire.

An ember pops from the orange glowing wood, floats above its prison, and travels with a new gust of wind into the forest of snow-capped trees. It's a breathtaking contrast - the bright orange and the stark white.

With envy, my gaze follows the dips and sways, its break for freedom. The smile drops from my face as the ember twinkles its last and disappears, snuffed by the cold.

Freedom is but a hope, I realize. Is hope truly so far out of grasp that the guilty can't reach it?

A snowflake glides to a rest on the tip of my nose, pulling me from my thoughts. I grip the blanket tighter around my shoulders and tilt my head to the sky overtaken by tree branches canopying the village.

We're deep in a forest, surrounded by an elf tribe I didn't know existed. The constant revelations are exhausting, and my rattled brain can barely keep up. There is not one but four tribes, each having their own purpose, I'm told. Four tribes I knew nothing of until now.

I raise my voice a notch above a hushed whisper. "On Erline's realm, nobody knows this place exists."

The sandman scrutinizes me from the corner of his eyes. "Humans are unaware of all beings outside of their own reality, though they speculate and consider the possibilities." He pauses, letting me digest this. "Myla was created by a seed of life and a seed of death. It is why she was a dragon with tears to heal and fire to kill. These are the tales which cross to each generation in our realm. Tales are often lost over time just as the witches' power has depleted over time."

Sighing deeply, I slouch forward. "How did everything go this unnoticed for so long?"

Swiveling his head and squaring his jaw, he considers me fully.

I continue. "There are legends and folklore in books and movies, but they're nothing like the creatures around us. This is reality, and the lives the blissfully innocent are living are built on ignorance. The humans I can understand, but how could everything I've discovered on my own be lost to an entire generation of witches?"

"The elf tribe did not want to be involved with guardian duties aside from their own realm," Sandy answers my unasked question. "Choosing to not interfere will have this result."

I mull that over. Is it racism keeping them away? Or is it egotism? I suspect a bit of both by simple observation.

The snow falls heavier from the sky and sprinkles my exposed skin. I close my eyes, the chill cooling the heat in my veins. "With all the creatures across the realms, it's unbelievable how lonely it is, no matter which ground you stand on." To the elves, all the other realms are beneath them. I shouldn't care, but I do. It hurts to be unwanted even by creatures and beings who were folklore to me until recently.

The sandman grunts and then grants me a moment of silence to revel in the snow's soft fall, but not for long. His voice lowers from the peeping listeners around us. "The only person who can fix this is you. Remember that, Katriane DuPont." He proclaims my last name with a crisp "t" and stops, forcing me to hang on his last syllable.

I look at him and immediately get lost in his eyes. They're completely white and swirl like fog, churning slowly. All the answers seem to be in those orbs, intellect and wisdom, a crystal ball.

"You are not alone," he adds.

But I am. The darkness, the evil I'm capable of, is proof I'll never be normal. It grips my heart with one good squeeze, a reminder of who's in charge. I attempt a reassuring smile anyway, but my lips spread more like a wicked grin, tightening the chilled, chapped skin of my cheeks. Sandy narrows his eyes, searches my face, and grimaces at what he finds: A broken soul, gripped in the clutches of evil desires.

"I am alone," I say, but it doesn't sound like my voice. It rumbles, coming from a deep place within. I'm ashamed to admit, even to myself, that I enjoyed the deaths. I want to return to the arena, addicted to death.

A howl rips from within the forest as he swallows. The sound is ear piercing and raises goosebumps across my skin. The prenumbras lift their gaze to the forest, their pig-like ears perking. Inside those trees, predators roam just like inside me.

He grips my chin with a large dark hand, painfully pinching. It's enough to push the loneliness away, and I draw in a sharp breath. Leaning closer, he forces me to meet his gaze. "You are only if you wish it. Don't allow it to swallow you."

Briefly closing my eyes, I count to three before I open them and switch the subject. "I still need to find a way to tell Jane's daughter that she's dead. Do you think the red-headed woman is still alive? The one who was a human plasma ball? Eliza?"

The sandman gracefully drops his hand back to his lap and turns to the fire. His clothes snag against the rough bark below his rump. I watch as the snow swirls around us, illuminating his dark and mysterious features.

"Kheelan's queen was a hostage, Katriane," he begins. "I believe she is still alive. I saw the demon take her. It is a small victory. She is no longer in the hands of Kheelan, and this brings me joy."

"The demon?" I chuckle without humor, shaking my head. "She's definitely dead then."

A demon would take her back to Corbin. There's no telling what Corbin would do with Kheelan's wife. She's a power source - a wealth of information. Even if Corbin is seemingly siding with Sureen and Kheelan, I'd bet my last dollar he has another angle. He's conniving enough to do so.

I should have killed that demon when I had the chance.

"The demon was once her love," the sandman murmurs, snapping me back to attention.

My mind reels. How is that even possible? "Do I want to know the details?"

With a hushed, gruff voice, the sandman replays the events which ultimately led me to be in the Death Realm in the first place. The demon, once named Aiden and now dubbed Thrice Born, was pulled from the void after his resurrection and second death. The shades had been recruiting the dead instead of the reapers, and in doing so, Aiden had fallen in love with a woman before they crossed to the Tween together. By the end of his story, he retells the demon's detailed second death, and the tangled web of disasters hurts my brain.

Some of the information I already knew, however. But I'm surprised to hear that every creature in every realm is rebelling against their creator, including myself.

The short black hair along my scalp feels gritty as I push a hand through it in exasperation, tugging on the ends dangling above my eyebrows. "So, they were trying to uproot Kheelan?"

His head dips in confirmation.

"But Aiden - Thrice Born - is a weapon," I growl, my attention to the number of topics flitting from one to the other. "If Corbin made him from his own little brew, wouldn't he have no emotions like the rest of the demons? Wouldn't he be a servant? If he took her, his intentions aren't angelic, Sandy. Surely you can see this."

This statement raises another question and many other possible angles. What's to stop Corbin from making more Aidens? And if he does, or already has, what would be the result? Aiden has to have unimaginable capabilities. It's catastrophic any way you look at it, and the void is chock full of fresh and old lost souls. And with the hundreds who died in the Colosseum, the total number has risen significantly.

My lips pinch. He wouldn't . . . would he? Would Corbin raise all those who died a second death? My heart aches thinking about it. What if he pulled Jane or Tanya from it? Would they be the same? Or would they be pure demon - physically and mentally?

The sandman rubs his hands together and squeezes the fingers. "He loves her, and she loves him. Love is power, Katriane. Not a weakness. Fear is the true rift of possibilities. It can do many a great thing, or many a terrible."

A strong demon roaming the realms with the wife of Kheelan, who clearly shares his powers . . . I'm going with 'many a terrible thing.'

His words are wistful like he wishes he had the chance to find out for himself what love would have in store for him and what it would feel like to fear for them, to have the opportunity to do so.

Sandmen aren't supposed to feel emotions, yet this one does. It's most likely a result of me and the deal I made with Erline. He was my sandman after all - the one who sprinkled dust over my nose to aid me with dreams. Everyone I come in contact with either dies or is altered from their original purpose, all because of that one night in the forest.

I almost tell him that having feelings can either be a blessing or a curse. Twitching my nose, I sniff and squash the desire to rip the hope from him and save myself from enduring further philosophy.

"He's right," a musical voice announces beside me.

I narrow my eyes and whip my head to Erline. The assault of the growing blizzard burns my eyes with its frigid wind and stinging flakes, but I force myself to not blink. Blinking would defeat my expression's purpose: to show that her presence isn't wanted.

With a serene countenance as though everything around her is of little consequence, she sits on the log directly beside mine. Her posture is straight and proper, unlike my slouched and huddled torso.

"You," I growl, jabbing a finger in her direction.

"Me." She nods, turning her eyes to the fire. "I can see your memories in the flames," she whispers, frowning. "Are you doing that?"

"She's attempting to transfer the memories from one entity to another in hopes of destroying them," the sandman tattles.

This must have been how he knew what was troubling me. I had assumed it was a perceptive ability, and the howls inside the fire were only happening in my mind. Knowing they can hear my inner struggles sends a swirl of anxiety through my lower, cramping gut.

I growl, and my thinned lips vibrate from the sound. I don't like being talked about as if I'm not even here.

In truth, I have no idea what I'm doing - transferring the weight of my burden to be consumed by the fire before me. It scares me, and I swallow thickly. The power I have is too great for even me to understand.

"You mustn't," Erline chides, bending closer to the fire and listening to the sounds. "You must take this burden and use it."

"Use it?" I bellow. The prenumbras bark at my outburst. "For what? To do more of your bidding? To be the one who brings justice to the realms you and the other fee have destroyed?"

She closes her eyes, hiding the guilt in her black orbs.

I'm not fooled, nor do I have an ounce of sympathy for it. I continue with a quieter, more fierce tone. "This was planned. All of this. You knew about The Red Death. You knew a witch would break the rules and ask for help. You had every intention of rebirthing your daughter into another and calling it a 'deal.' Instead, it was manipulation. You knew I'd help those I love." She flinches, and I press on, unloading my burdens back onto the shoulders which they belong. "You played on my emotions, on my need to help others, and it turned into a bloodbath. When I travelled to the Death Realm, did you hope I'd destroy your enemies for you? Is that why I'm here?"

Her body is rigid and statue-like except for her jaw where a muscle works profusely as she takes the full brunt of my words' blows.

Pulling the blanket tighter around me, I allow my tone to lose its ferocity. "I bet you didn't count on your daughter being lost to the void forever, did you?"

"No," she says after a moment of silence. "She was a casualty I didn't anticipate."

My heart thumps hard, flooding my face with pressure and heat. How dare she act like Myla, her own flesh and blood, was a casualty of war!

I lunge at her, the blanket falling from my shoulders to the gathering snow. The sandman strikes forward, impossibly swift, and grips me around the waist before I can reach her with outstretched, flaming hands. I have every intention of taking the life from her soulless body, no matter the consequences. She's more to blame for everything than I am.

The sandman's grip tightens as I squirm in his arms. I could easily wiggle from his grasp, use a little magic and make him soar across the realm, but his next words reach me through my crazed haze.

"Her death won't fix anything, Katriane."

Closing my outstretched hands, the fire dissipates when his advice sinks in. He's right. Killing her would only bring more problems though I wouldn't feel anything as I did it aside from utter relief. This, I'm sure of. I have little love for the fee, especially the one who has manipulated me the most.

I relax, if but a little, in the sandman's arms, and the heat drains from my face. Tears prick my eyes in its absence, and I fight the lump in my throat as my emotions level once more.

"You manipulated everything, Erline." I angrily swipe at my face. "I wouldn't be here - none of us would - if you hadn't intervened."

Tucking a strand of white hair behind her head, the color matching the blizzarding flakes around us, she sighs through her nostrils, impatient. "You're right. Dyson would still be in the Death Realm. The sandman would have remained Sureen's unwilling lover."

I gulp at the revelation. Unwilling lover?

She continues, ignoring my stiffness. "Eliza would be hostage to her fee husband. Aiden would be a powerful weapon in the hands of a sociopath with a vengeful agenda. The witches would be extinct." She flicks her black eyes to mine, jutting her chin. "And with all that, to what fate, I ask you, do you think the madness would end?"

"All would be destroyed," Sandy mumbles over my head, his deep voice vibrating my spine pressed against his chest.

"So, I was your weapon to even the odds," I state.

Crossing her arms, she glares. "Yes. I am not proud of it, but I must do what I need to preserve life. Their fate remains in my hands, Kat. Mine. If I need to use you to ensure a peaceful outcome, I will."

94

Sandy slowly releases me, uncurling his arms from my waist as Erline glowers back to the flames. Instead of scooting away and returning to my own seat, I continue to rest against him, untrusting of my own actions.

"And the red-headed queen, Eliza?" I ask. "What will be her fate?" After all, she's the one we currently need to worry about. She and her demon lover. She's a life - surely Erline has interest in preserving it even if she is wed to Kheelan.

Erline doesn't speak for a long while, and the hushed chatter wraps around us while the snow blankets the remaining, unoccupied logs.

Lifting her hand, her magic licks the streams of a crisp breeze and the snow dances in it. The small flakes deter from their path and swirl in a circle of the space before us, building a moving picture. Two figures appear, and I watch, fascinated at the extraordinary detail the specs create. It's abundantly clear that it's a man and woman.

"When a fee takes a mate, it isn't for love," she begins. A few passing elves stop to watch the moving picture of snow. "Not usually, and not in Kheelan's case. The evil can't love."

The snow sculpture of the man leans toward the woman, passionately kissing her. But the image quickly changes. The man and the white flakes take on a different hue, one of blood in color. The woman grips the man's shoulders, attempting to push him away before she too is consumed by the red.

Erline's fingers flick, and the image changes once more, swirling in obedience. "When the fee mate with one human, our power is shared, linked. It is our greatest strength but also our greatest weakness."

When he breaks the kiss, the man's hands raise, outstretched to his side. Soon after, the woman's form floats above the man, her chest bowed, and her arms dangled behind her. Snowflakes shoot from her chest like a bomb, only to circle around her, a tornado, until all that's left is a red woman matching the man.

"If the fee dies, the mate dies," Erline murmurs.

She lets the image fall by the drop of her hands. The man and woman's image dissipate with the next gust of wind, carrying the snowflakes across the village.

Erline huffs. "If one wishes to call upon the other, they can. If one wants to draw on the magic of the other, they can. But there is one twist. The mate can kill the fee, and live."

I release the breath I've been holding, a curse passing my lips.

"She doesn't deserve this," the sandman fumes.

I turn to him, his face strained with unease. "Are you okay?"

He nods though his expression says otherwise. "She is Dyson's friend. She helped save him at a great cost to herself. She is honorable."

Across the path dividing the teepees, past the canines who've lost interest in my presence, I spot the teepee where Dyson is sleeping off the rest of his exhaustion. What had Dyson gone through in Kheelan's dungeon? Perhaps . . . perhaps I misjudged the situation in believing Dyson would be fine and his sorrow couldn't possibly match mine.

The sandman continues, "Kheelan took her for a bride as a final act to hurt Dyson."

I glower. "How would that hurt Dyson?"

The sandman's throat constricts as he swallows his troubles. Busying his hands, he squeezes his nail beds, one by one. "Dyson was the one Kheelan forced to kill Eliza's love."

"I see," I respond.

We're quiet, and it takes several minutes for me to sense Erline's wavering nervousness.

I turn to her, knowing she has something else to say.

Ticking her jaw, the intensity of my lingering expectation too much, she meets me square in the eyes. Fear flicks along her features before she masks it.

"There's more," I spit, accusing, and wave my hand in the air.

"Yes," she says evenly. She reaches forward, her pale fingers brushing the tips of the flames. The fire responds and plays with her skin, a cat arching its back against the palm of its owner.

During her stretching pause, an elderly male elf storms by, slinging his native language in our direction. By the tone, I imagine the words aren't kind. The sandman hisses in return.

"Myla and Corbin's mating contract-" she starts.

"Is now void," I cut her off. "She's dead."

"I know she's dead, Katriane," Erline snarls, the fire roaring once and engulfing her hand. "There isn't a need to keep reminding me of my failures."

I snort, begging to differ.

"The contract still holds. Corbin was able to continue living because I did not allow his mate to die completely. And once I inserted her back into the living, he grew in strength."

"Myla's death does not affect him because the contract was swapped for another," the sandman summarizes.

A shockwave scores under my skin, burning my bones and aching my joints. Like a slap across the face, my head whips back in disbelief. "Now, how is that possible? Contracts are void once the other is dead. You can't hold a contract with the dead, and you sure as hell can't keep one when the other is in the void."

Removing her hand from the flames, she leans back to her straight posture and clasps her hands in her lap, resembling an impatient teacher. She stares at me, her eyes searching mine, waiting for me to draw my own conclusion.

I gasp, my mouth widening. "No."

"Yes." She nods, hissing the "s".

"What?" the sandman asks, his head swiveling back and forth. "What is it?

98

"The contract exchanged to me, because I was merged with Myla," I whisper in horror. "Her DNA runs in my veins, her magic now mine."

Erline blinks affirmation.

"What does this mean for your future?" he asks, foreboding in his tone as if this signs my death sentence.

A new voice calls behind me, and I almost jump from my skin at the abrupt intrusion.

"It means Corbin can draw from her power whenever he wishes."

I turn and watch Erma and a bulky elf approach our circle of misfits. The large elf's expression is dark and settles on me. His trudges are lumbering, and he's a striking resemblance to that of Tember's friend, Jaemes. The bridge of his nose is wrinkled with fury, his eyelids tightened in contempt.

He blames me for all of this.

Join the club buddy, my answering scoff speaks. I'm done cowering, even to an elf who could squash me with his pinky finger.

My eyes bulge when I look past him. Clomping through the village's path is a horse, but not the normal kind. Everything here resembles so much of the Earth Realm's animals but much darker in creation. This horse has two heads, six hooves the size of skulls, and a mane and tail which blend with the snow, smoky and wistful. Its spine's vertebrae stick out like knobbed spikes.

A female elf is on its back, guiding the creature with mere thought instead of reigns. She swivels her head, searching for something, and impossibly black hair falls over her shoulder.

Adjusting her bow slung over her chest, she considers the small gathering of creatures of importance while her horse trots by. The weight of the animal quivers the ground and disturbs the snow rested there.

Erma continues as I blink at the creature and the elf who rides it, watching as they disappear behind a teepee. "It means he's more formidable with the bond of the contract. With you, he is stronger and also weaker. You are the power source he needs to rule all the realms, but you are also the only one who can bring him to his knees."

The words are sluggish to soak in, but when they do, I tut several times in obvious denial. I turn to Erline as Erma and the giant, angry elf brush the snow from the logs and take a seat.

"This is why you brought her back, isn't it?" I say it as a statement, knowing the truth as it filters into my mind. She doesn't answer, but I continue anyway. This explains everything. "You hid Myla's spirit from Corbin, from Kheelan, and when they started invading your realm to search for her, killing all those in their path, you let her loose once more in hopes she'd be able to destroy them. I wasn't your weapon. She was."

Erma inclines her head, pulling my attention. "But now you are."

The sandman shifts uncomfortably. "The fate of the realms now rests on Katriane DuPont's shoulders."

A darkness roars inside me, rising to the challenge while I struggle to rein in my anger. A gust of wind speeds through, ruffling my hair, and the fire roars to a bellowing flame, ready to do my bidding. Smoke curls from my nostrils, and as it does, the two women stand to their feet.

I rise to my own, my movements sluggish and coiled. The tips of my fingers warm as my inner fire settles there.

A nearby village child steps out from the inside of his teepee, a playful grin sparkling his miniature features. Once he spots me, he stops, wide eyes trained on the flames at my side. The canines bark and growl, their front claws raking the snow.

Stretching one arm above his head, the large elf reaches inside his quiver and grips an arrow.

"Mitus," Erma warns and places a small hand on his bulging bicep, stopping him.

My breaths huff and puff as I keep close watch on his movements.

"She's unstable," Mitus says gruffly.

A glow blossoms at the center of Erma's chest, a warning to me. She's prepared to use her magic to protect her people, and she meets my gaze head on, granting me choice. Calm myself, or tangle with her.

Erline, however, slowly observes all that's around her: the wind, the flames. Me.

A cold hand is placed firmly on my shoulder, and the flames licking my forearms dissipate like water is doused over my body. I suck in a deep breath, feeling as though I'm coming up for air, and goosebumps pepper my skin once more.

"Kat," the sandman whispers, squeezing my shoulder once. "You cannot change what they have done. This is your fate now. Make the right choice."

I already know the answer to my choice. I made it back in the forest that overwhelming day. I won't let these people die any more than I'd let my coven, but I sure as hell won't let these two women dictate my future.

I tightly close my eyes, resisting the urge of a violent revenge.

"Don't let it consume you," he says when he feels my bones shake under his large palm.

"If you want a weapon," I begin, snapping my eyes open. "You have it. I won't leave the realms in the hands of the fee."

Ripping my shoulder from his grasp, I turn and stalk from the fire, heading to the trees where the ember had winked from the realm.

CHAPTER SIX

AIDEN VANDER

GUARDIAN REALM

Fresh water replaces the open curtain of lava. The frigid flow cascades down my body and clouds my vision. I blink and roll my eyes behind the lids, dispersing the uncomfortable pressure.

Eliza is still asleep, tucked in my arms and completely unaware. I thought the water might wake her, but she has yet to stir. Her once bright blue veins have returned to a normal hue, leaving behind glistening pale flesh.

I stand at the ledge of a cave, the waterfall tumbling from the cliff behind us. In front, a hefty river expands, tucked between two forests. It's clear, void of all colors, and I can see the red sands deep below.

A school of … something swims inside the river. They're unlike any other fish I've ever seen with six thick short legs, webbed between each limb. Their bodies are a matte dark blue, and no eyes rest inside their pointed heads.

One unhinges its jaw, wide and unlawful to typical nature. With impossible speed, it swims toward another and bites the head clean off. Black blood obscures the water before it dissipates, and the headless swimmer sinks to the bottom in the red sands.

I look down and to my right. Ferox lays along the jagged rock by my feet, and I study her as she watches the water with longing.

Out in the open, her full body is revealed. Her blue tail is thick, void of scales, and the fin is quite large. Its tips come to sharp points, razor-like almost. I imagine the tail is as deadly as it looks – a weapon on its own. She has no breasts, an oddity, and I tilt my head as my eyes sweep her length. If I had to guess, pyrens have no gender.

"I must get back," she mumbles. Her tail flicks and slaps the damp rock. "This is where I leave you. Others of my kind are here, I can feel them, but they won't be for long." She tears her eyes from the water and squints up to me. "Do not step foot in this river, Thrice Born. The creatures here will eat you alive."

"What do I do?" I ask as she turns, creepily crawling back to the waterfall in a jerky army crawl, preparing to leave me.

"You travel along the cliff," she proclaims, pointing to a narrow path. She speaks as though my journey will be simple.

"The tribes will come?" I ask warily.

She nods and flicks a glimpse to Eliza. "You must wake her, or it'll give the wrong impression."

Following her pointed gaze to Eliza, I ask what I should expect from the people here. I receive no answer and glance up with a frown. She's gone.

After minutes of staring at the trail of dried lava she left behind, I raise an eyebrow with a sigh and scan the horizon. An array of somber gray clouds claims the sky, and the river bends around the cliff, disappearing from sight.

Hoisting Eliza higher in my arms, I take the first step on the narrow path, shimmying when necessary. Several rocks crumble under my weight and plop to the water.

Briefly, I think about shimmering from the cliff's path onto the bank but think better of it. Ferox made it clear I'm to travel exactly to her instructions.

The path eventually leads to a dirt one, nestled along a grassy hill, the blades hip-height and backdropped by rows of barren trees covered in crisp white snow. The blue swimmers had followed me the entire way, hoping I'd lose my footing and drop into the river, providing them a snack. But as the trail leads a short distance from the bank, they disappear.

Snow peacefully falls inside the forest but stops as soon as we reach the last tree. It leaves the grass untouched by the flakes and chill. A shaky breath swells my chest concerning the anomaly. Weather shouldn't work that way. Temperatures and elemental nature should be gradual, not sudden.

I adjust Eliza's weight and use my free hand to cross the tree border. I yank it back when the bite of wind circles my hot fingers.

Turning my hand, I stare at my palm, mystified. How is this possible? I scan the realm with a different take than when I had entered. Instead of a gradual climate change across the lands, it's instant. It is a complete contradiction to the Earth Realm climates, terrains, and weather. The creatures and beings who roam this realm must be quite formidable to survive in such an atmosphere.

I stand there watching the serene scene for too long, listening to the silence only falling snow provides. It distracts me, and when Eliza speaks, I startle.

"Aiden?" she calls, a cracked whisper.

I look down into her blue eyes sparkling with so many questions, and her brows bunch. How long has she been watching me?

A corner of my mouth raises in a half-reassuring smile. This confuses her further, and she gently pushes against my chest, hands trembling. It's a wordless gesture requesting I set her on her feet. I oblige, lowering her to the soft grass swallowing my legs.

"Where are we?" she asks. Her voice is quiet, too quiet, and as she pushes a hand through her damp tangled locks, she takes in the realm with wild concern. "Did I faint?"

"Yes, you did," I mumble, matching her tone in hopes to ease her edge. "This is the Guardian Realm."

The wait for her to meet my gaze is agonizing, a torture to a starved love, but when she does, I suck in a shattered breath. Her expression is soft toward me, and fear doesn't surface in them like I had anticipated. I don't want her to fear me, and my greatest worry is that I'll accidentally feed from her. I don't know if I'd be able to control myself if she did feel frightened.

"Why are we here?" she asks then bites the inside of her cheek.

I lick my bottom lip, wondering how much she remembers. "To keep you safe. To hide you."

"From Kheelan," she proclaims. She releases the assault to her cheek and closes her eyes.

"Yes." I take a step toward her, hand outstretched.

The desire is too great to touch her, to feel her soft skin with my own fingertips instead of taunting memories. She's so alive, so innocent, a reminder of what I am not. I don't deserve her, yet here I am, asking anyway.

"Eliza," I call, my voice a gentle plea of desperation. My heart can't take much more.

She opens them back up, tears welling along her bottom lids. They glisten and refuse to shed. Her lower lip twitches with a slight shiver.

I take another step, blowing out a quiet breath.

"What are you?" she asks.

I blink, slow, and plant my feet. It's a question I don't want to answer but know she deserves. What I truly am isn't ordinary. I evade the truth with a statement. "You know what I am."

She gulps. "A demon. But demons don't feel. They destroy."

I incline my head, drop my hand, and stuff both sets of fingers in my pockets. My fingers find a piece of lint and toy with it, rolling and pinching. *Please don't deny me*, I silently beg.

"You're correct. Demons are built to prey on the innocent." I look back to her, peeking under my lashes. "But I am not one of those demons. Not really. Not with you."

"Then what are you?" she tilts her head, eyes sweeping my body. It's practically visible - her line of thought - as she reconstructs her preconceived notions.

I consider how to answer her question. Most of the realms know me as Thrice Born, but it's underestimated. I am more, and when I'm with Eliza, I am blissfully invincible. "I am a demon standing before a woman who makes him feel as though I'm nothing but an ordinary man. I see only you, all of you, and nothing more."

She says nothing, my declaration yet to convince. I step toward her this time, and she adjusts her head to search my face.

"I am a man who can't breathe when I'm not touching you. You are my sun, and I am but a feeble planet caught in your orbit."

Abandoning the lint, I lift a hand from my pocket and brush my thumb against her cheek. Her dusty red lashes fan the space between us. This easy acceptance stitches the gaping hole in my soul.

"What does this make you?" I ask, wanting her to declare her feelings.

"Ignorantly in love," she vows, the beginning of a bright grin tugging at her ruby lips. "I'll always love you, Aiden."

I moan and close the distance, selfishly taking her as my own. My lips brush hers, once, twice, like a butterfly's wings opening and closing. The movement sizzles my skin with a delightful tickle under the surface. The touch empties my heart and fills it with something else - sorrowful relief, warmth, and something no language can describe.

In response, she exhales a whimper. Her breath fans the bridge of my nose and coats my tongue with her deliciously charged scent.

Flattening my hand against the side of her face, I push it along the expanse of her cheek and then to the nape of her neck. My fingers knot in her soft hair, and I gently pull her head back, deepening the kiss. Our tongues touch, desperation behind the wet, soothing strokes.

I never thought I'd kiss her again, our last a broken memory tainted by the void. I never thought I'd hold her, smell her, feel my heart sing only for her. She restores me.

Another gentle stroke of tongue, another sigh.

Could it be she's my salvation from what I've become?

My fingers tighten and she moans.

Is this what true love feels like? Is this what it does to the spiritually and emotionally lost?

She whispers my name, soft against my lips. So much longing behind one gentle word, and I wonder . . . I wonder if she has the same questions I have fleeting through my own mind. I wonder if she can feel her soul knit back together, too.

Snaking her arms around my waist, she presses her body to mine, and my stiff posture relaxes against hers, another acceptance. Of its own accord, a tear squeezes out of my eye and trickles down my cheek, containing the evidence of my relief with it.

Eliza is my everything. This woman is the end of my agony. She is the keeper of my soul, my life forever tied to hers. I will always find her, and she will always find me.

A sob shakes her body. I use my other hand to hold her steady, curling it around her waist. The kiss deepens, the tears mixing.

"I love you," I declare, wishing I would have said it before I died my second death.

I feel her smile in the kiss, a tug at our intertwined lips, and it's then I know for sure: I'm hers. She's mine. My very essence, the one I'll worship until my last breath. I'll destroy for her, become anything she needs me to be. I'd die all over again with a grin on my face just to keep her safe.

Ahhh--oooo.

My muscles tense at the strange howl resounding in the distance. The sound travels through the forest and barrages my hearing with violent vibrations.

The hair raises on my arms, on the back of my scalp, and Eliza tenses against me. I break the kiss, the breeze cooling the saliva against my swollen lips.

Another howl. And then another, each one closer than the last. I zone my hearing and focus my senses. Before I can pinpoint the direction it's coming from, three green-glowing dog-like beasts skid out of the forest tree line. Two flank our front, and one at Eliza's back, their heads slightly taller than the blades of grass.

Their forms are unwavering like green glowing soundwaves, and their ears and noses are oversized and pointed. No eyes meet mine, but their teeth drip with a silky thread of lime-colored drool. It plops to the grass and instantly soaks in the blade, leaving no traces behind.

I keep my gaze matched to the dogs, their faces contorted in a fierce growl. I can feel the venomous rumble through my shoes and push Eliza behind me.

"Eliza," I mumble in warning, barely moving my lips.

"Aiden?" she asks, tinged with worry. "What are they?"

I don't respond. I don't have the answers.

I hear her sharp intake of breath, and she grips below my shoulder blades, gathering my shirt in her clutch, trembling. The movement is slow, but the dogs' growls deepen, and their faces whip to the side, threatening and eerie. Their heads are a shaky blur as they conceive us as a threat.

Eliza's fear coats my back and seeps into my pores before I can stop it. It's strong and delicious, begging me to suck in more. I grind my teeth, forcing my demonic nature to halt its feeding.

"When I tell you to, I want you to run," I murmur to Eliza. "Do you understand?"

She doesn't have time to answer. The three dig their back claws into the soil and barrel toward us.

"Go!" I yell.

I take off at a run, and we meet, dog to demon. I grab the closest approaching creature around the neck, and it chomps at the space between us. The creature's spittle slaps my cheek, burning my skin, and I match his snarl with my own deadly growl. Its legs kick and squirm. The neck slips through my fingers, it's wavering aura impossible to fully grasp.

Deepening my audible threat, I inch my face closer. I don't want to kill it if I don't have to. Our purpose here isn't death. But the creature persists in ours. It's either us or them.

Heat floods my hands and my lava-flowing eyes mix with the hues of the creature's green. Sharply, my fingernails dig into the wavering flesh, soaking in the aura like my pores drink fear. The creature's glow reduces as I feed from it. It's a piercing taste, sour and potent, and leaves the scald of heartburn in my chest as an aftertaste.

The next dog lunges. I snap my free hand forward, intent on it meeting the same fate as its packmate. An electric bolt beats me to it, and I pull my hand back just in time. It strikes the dog in the chest. The animal flips in the air and lands without a thud on its side. It gathers itself quickly, gleaming, to all fours. This grants me a split second to peek over my shoulder.

Eliza's hands are crackling with blue bolts just like before. Dark circles rim her bright, electric eyes, the toll of magic almost too much for her. I tense, emotions crippling me. I can destroy these creatures, but if she's intent on using magic to help, it could force her into another deep slumber. She isn't ready to produce more magic. Not yet.

I drop the dead animal in my hand and prepare myself for the next who returns with a vengeance.

A perfectly tuned whistle irritates the air behind me. The high-pitched sound, and the possibilities of where it came from, bristles my spine as though I, too, have hackles to raise. The dog stops and skids to a halt feet from me, the grass seemingly untouched in its path. The fierceness of bared teeth leaves its snout just as quickly as the whistle blew. And then it sits.

"Aiden," Eliza screeches. Her scream makes me half-crazed. Are there more of these creatures? Is the owner of the whistle a threat? I whip around, believing her to be in more danger than what currently presents us.

When I turn, my face contorts and warps before it smooths with recognition. A substantial boat with no sails float in the river. A smaller boat - a raft with railings - and its passengers - horned, tattooed men and women - row our direction.

Elves, I realize, recognizing the pointed ears from my youth's fascination with fantasy legends and books. They are quite different than what I imagined could be real, and in a moment of awe, my shoulders relax.

Their tattoos are red, striped to the same pattern as zebras, and the exact shade of the sand at the bottom of the river. A maroon patch surrounds each eye socket, like a racoon's mask. They're all the warrior Ferox told me they'd be, roped with the kind of muscle only the test of nature could develop.

The front elf lifts his foot and perches it on the ledge of the boat. He peers at me, his face carefully blank as he tightly grasps his long wooden spear tipped with an arrow the size of my hand.

Internally, my emotions dance with glee. This wasn't the way I'd hope to gain the attention of the guardians, but it'll do.

"Don't worry," I say to Eliza, palming the cotton of my shirt to straighten the wrinkles. "This is our ride."

CHAPTER SEVEN

DYSON COLEMAN

GUARDIAN REALM

A shiver stirs me from a deep, comforting sleep. The air is bone-chilling cold, but despite the temperature, I feel different. Restful, and trouble-free.

My heart beats rhythmically and layers me in a sense of internal warmth, something I haven't felt in a very long time. Keeping my eyes closed, refusing to fully wake with every intention of falling back asleep, I scrunch my eyebrows as I wonder what changed to cause me to feel this different, knowing it can't possibly last. Anything that feels like this doesn't last. Not with me - a magnet for trouble.

I pull the blanket I'm tangled in tighter around me. If I go back to sleep, this new sense of protection won't flee the moment I fully wake. But my clutched fingers tighten when I realize what they're touching. The blanket is soft, the strands long and thick. *Fur.*

Slowly, I open my eyes.

At first, my vision is blurry and fixes on the leather walls sprawling to a triangular point. There's no square, cornered ceiling like a normal roof would have, and the walls come to a point, a circular opening at the top. The weathered and cracked leather-like walls flap in a breeze and a few flakes of snow drift down from the opening, lingering with a rising smoke.

A teepee.

A crackling fills my ears, the sound of fire being fed, and the unmistakable smell lingers in my nose. Some of the smoke loiters in the large space between slanted walls, creating a hazy glow with the minimal light filtering in before it exits the hole.

I blink and lick my chapped bottom lip.

Memories surface. Memories of the battle, my mate, and the place she took us. Where did she take us? I remember the feathered people. Is this where I am? Their realm?

This structure looks vastly different than the massive room of black marble floors and pillars fit only for a god. I remember the angels had surrounded us, but it wasn't them nor their infuriated glances who I had paid attention to. It was seeing Kat, her dragon form, calm and peaceful instead of the beast she had become. In the arena, she was frightening and deadly. But, as she stood in the big room, she was a creature worth marveling.

Each scale had reflected the stars, and her intense eyes had met the gaze of each warrior without an ounce of fear. She had prepared herself to defend her friends in the face of their hostility. Her beauty and bravery is truly one of a kind.

My heart thuds faster, my wolf stirring inside me, interested in my train of thoughts. His ears perk, and he internally nudges, urging me to seek our mate. It's different, this reversal of roles. Normally, a male shifter fiercely protects his mate, not the other way around. He's stronger than she is, more capable of defending. But this is not the case with my Katriane DuPont. Nothing is ordinary when it comes to her.

Ignoring him for now, I begin to stretch but then freeze. Kat has no idea she's my mate. With everything that's happened since I discovered it myself, I haven't had time to tell her. What will she do when she finds out?

It's different for pack members. We actively seek our mates and easily accept it. For an outsider, the idea, the very notion, will be difficult to even consider.

I mumble curses, my voice harsh.

"Are you going to wake, sunshine? Or do you need another hour of beauty sleep."

My eyes widen, and I nearly jump from my skin. The voice, that wit-laced personality, is one I could never forget.

Slowly, I turn my head, coming face to face with my best friend, the one I had thought I lost forever. Shades hold no hope of ever seeing loved ones again, and we accept our limitations for what they are in hopes they'll find us after their death.

Sandy brown, close cropped hair, a half-cocked grin, Flint sits on a fur-carpeted floor, one knee propped to support his elbow. His other hand holds up his top half, sustaining his posture behind him while his coat billows around his torso. The smirk pulls at the skin on his chin, the famous look that has most women falling head over heels for him. I used to envy that.

"You should learn to muffle your ear-splitting snore," he jokes. "There's no telling what the freak-show outside will do if they hear it." He raises a hand, shaking it, closed fist in the air, and mocks. "Gather your torch and pitchforks!"

"Flint," I croak.

"Dyson." His grin widens, and he nods toward me. "You're looking pretty good for a dead person."

My lips twitch, and tears well in my eyes. "You're here." I frown, blink, and a tear tumbles down my cheek. Pushing back the fur blanket, I sit upright. "Where is here?"

Flint looks around. "I was told this is the Guardian Realm." He shifts, finding a more comfortable position, and flicks his thumb behind him. "Dude, you wouldn't believe what kind of Ozzie shit is going on out there."

He reaches forward and slaps my shoulder. I grab his arm, gather myself to my knees, and wrap him in a hug. It's a warm embrace, disrupted by the crinkling of his coat.

"I've missed you, man," Flint mumbles over my shoulder.

I sniff and match his tone. "I was never really gone."

We part, and he helps me to my feet. My knees shake, and I mentally question how long I've been out. His calloused hands hover at my sides to make sure I don't collapse.

I roll my shoulders to work out the kinks, and my mind returns to his earlier statement. "What do you mean? What's going on out there?"

Flint flings an arm in the air, sweeping the expanse of the teepee dramatically. Everything he does is dramatic, and the familiarity is comforting. "Elves, man. Elves everywhere. It's a mythical wonderland, without the wonder. There's even an angel with these weird wings." He shakes his head in exaggerated disbelief. "It's a horror show."

"Wait." I scowl and cross my arms. "How did you get here?"

Flint's chest puffs, and he sighs through loose lips. His sweeping arm reaches up and over his shoulder, and he scratches the back of his neck. "The night you . . ."

"Died?" I supply, my eyebrows flicking once.

"Yeah." He shifts uncomfortably. "Kat had told us about the fee the night you died. It was almost unbelievable, but well . . . you know how the witches are. Half mad but deliciously wise."

I curtly nod. Flint has never been a fan of witches, but Kat was his mate Irene's friend. She had performed the mating ceremony between Brenna and Ben, and Kenna and Evo, the Beta and Alpha couple of the Cloven Pack. It was the first time I had met her, and even then, I didn't stick around to introduce myself. If I had, I would have known she was my mate, and the entire course of my following history would have been changed.

He drops his arm with a slap to his thigh. "Mother Nature herself swooped in like a damn tornado, right in the living room, and demanded we gallop into the night by swirling vortex."

"Is that so?" I grin.

Life-like scenarios of Kenna verbally assaulting Erline to high-heaven over a broken vase would be a laughable experience. You don't tangle with my old Alpha female, tornado or not. She could make a titan cower.

He frowns and smooths stress wrinkles above his eyebrows with his fingers. "I wonder if now would be an appropriate time to bring up the weird virus spreading among the humans to Queen Earth."

I pucker my lips. "She'd probably send you flying through another portal. The fee don't take orders well."

He locks on to the fur below his feet, the strands in disarray due to pacing and foot traffic, and his face turns a shade of green. "Portals are like being flushed down a toilet. I feel sorry for the fish I returned to the sea when I was twelve."

I know the feeling, the wave of nausea which accompanies traveling through a portal. I felt it when Kat's dragon took us through one, a swirling vortex of wind. It's not an experience I wish to repeat if I don't have to.

"What's wrong with the humans?" I ask while reaching over and stroking the leather walls. They're as

120

rough as I thought they'd be, ruined by the chilling elements outside.

"Flu-like symptoms. Unexplainable blood loss," he divulges, ticking off his fingers.

"Vampires," I grumble and slowly drop my fingers from the wall.

He scratches his chin, and the sandpaper sound accompanies the soft smoldering crackle of fire as his nails rub against short and thick brown stubbles. "Can you believe humans fantasize about these creatures that are currently killing them? And they don't even know." When I don't answer, his voice sobers. "We can't really go to the humans and say they have blood loss because two-legged leeches are strolling through the night and sucking from their veins."

"No." I sigh. "You can't. The vampires are looking for Kat. Probably all of us now."

"What would they want with a witch?" Flint asks, his top lip curling.

I avoid his gaze by pretending deep interest in the structure of this shelter. "She's not an ordinary witch."

I'm not sure how much I should tell him, nor how much Erline did. A part of me wants to keep the information to myself in hopes of sparing him the details of my problems. The game we are playing - the rebellious streak - it may very well get us killed in the end. The last thing I want to do is bring Flint down with me.

Kheelan has us marked. It's better to leave my old pack out of it than to drag them in just to lose them all over again.

I suck in my cheeks as their imaginary death scenarios plague my thoughts.

Part of the beginning of our conversation floats back into my head without being called upon. My eyes widen, and I snap my head back to Flint. "Who else came with you?"

Flint smirks again as if to tease me about the late revelation. "Us."

The one worded answer is almost drowned by a song, the villagers chanting a catchy tribal tune not far from my teepee. It's a hauntingly beautiful melody, their voices bouncing precariously like the dance of fire itself. A few bouts of child laughter accompanies it and the beat of a steady, tight drum.

I tuck my chin and blink hard. "As in . . . *us*?"

"Yep." He pops the 'p' just like Brenna always does, and my heart pings with excitement in an uncanny resemblance to the music outside.

Brenna is another packmate, Beta Female to the Cloven Pack. Out of them all, she's the most loving and motherly. I've missed her kind words and gentle smile.

"I practically had to tackle Brenna to be the one waiting by your bedside." He shakes his head slowly. "That girl is stronger than she looks, and Ben has taught her too well in the art of Krav Maga."

Rubbing his arm, he frowns at a memory of Brenna besting him.

A dull light enters as the flap of the teepee is pushed aside, casting deeper shadows inside. One by one, Evo, Kenna, and Brenna duck through, allowing snowflakes and a gust of wind into the barely warm space. Goosebumps riddle my skin, and the fire crackles its displeasure, outraged by the disturbance to its gentle roar. All three have arctic winter gear strapped to their bodies, the cloth swishing as they close the distance.

I smile. "This is the last thing I'd ever expect," I mumble, my voice choked.

With determined long strides for such short legs, Brenna shoves Flint aside with her shoulder and wraps her arms around my middle. Her sharp chin digs into my chest when she laughs with melodious joy. Evo slaps my shoulder, jostling my sturdy stance. My lips catch a few stray yellow hairs, and I wiggle my cheeks to free the strands. Her hair is much longer than the last time I saw her, and my stomach churns with grief for all I've missed. Life continued on while I was dead. It unsettles me how much it hurts.

Brenna pats my back and carefully peels herself from me as though I have brittle bones and may break by a single gale of wind.

"You've lost weight, Dyson," she declares, accusing. "How do the dead lose weight?"

I clear my throat and stretch the sting from Evo's slap by arching my spine. "I wasn't dead for long."

I'd rather not tell them the specifics. They don't need my past's situation distorting this happy moment. My past is my burden to bear, and if I told them, they'd feel the urge to help shoulder it. It's what packs do, and they've been through enough.

Kenna folds are arms across her chest with much difficulty, due to her puffy coat, and cocks a foot out in front of her. This is a legendary Kenna gesture, which states she isn't buying anything I'm saying, and she's prepared to beat me to a pulp for it.

Not only is Kenna Alpha female, but she's a Queen Alpha. Every Queen Alpha has a gift, a supernatural ability above all other shifters. Kenna's gift is empathy. She can feel what others are feeling and spot a lie faster than the whack of a fly swatter.

"Sweet baby Jesus, Dyson," she swears, incredulous. I mentally prepare myself for the tongue lashing. "What kind of crap have you gotten yourself into? The wench wizard said you've been in the Dream Realm, starting trouble. The entire circus village wants us dead. An angel is pining for her creator, as if that's not disgusting enough - I mean, that's basically her mother, right? And now, you're telling me you weren't actually dead this entire time?"

Flint hums happily. "I was wondering when you'd burst," he says to Kenna. "Angels aren't born, they're made. I think what you're thinking is wrong thinking."

Internally, I sigh with happiness despite Kenna's meltdown. I've missed them.

With a deep sigh, knowing she's hurting under her charging exterior, I grasp a handful of her coat and wrap

124

her in a hug. Her coat is chilled, and I shiver despite my best efforts.

By not returning my embrace, Kenna deflects my affection, but I can feel her lean into me. Her crossed arms fidget between us. I rock us side to side, knowing it'll make the interaction less comfortable for her but unable to resist coaxing her present irritation.

After a bit, she mumbles against my sternum. "Where the hell have you landed us? Have you seen it out there?" Her voice cracks at the end.

"I was just telling him about it," Flint states. He takes two long steps and stands next to Evo. As Brenna's brother, Evo shares the same hair color, and just like his sister, it's cut differently than when I last saw him.

Sharp Alpha eyes roam my body, looking for obvious injuries.

Ever the protector, I think to myself. My wolf perks and yips inside me. I deny his request to be let loose by a quick swipe in my mind, and he growls in response. Now isn't the time for a frolicking wolf pack.

With a nod to Evo, I silently tell him I'm unharmed.

It's an Alpha's job to ensure his wolves are cared for, but I'm not his wolf anymore. I don't feel the mental connection I once had, though I'm a little surprise it hasn't clicked back into place. Maybe it's because I'm also not the same man I once was, but even thinking that's the case rings false in my own assumptions. This is something more. I can feel it. Like a second beat of a heart, my life is tethered to another in the similar way it was with my old pack. It's as though invisible strings are tied around me, guiding me to the one who holds the ends.

I release Kenna, her long brown hair catching on the stubble of my chin. Stepping back, I place my hands on my hips wearing a boyish smile, and glance back at the door.

"Where's everyone else?" I ask, my grin faltering. This group gathering is missing several of my old pack, and for a moment, I worry something terrible has happened to them.

Evo shifts his large frame from one foot to the other, and a joint pops. "At our territory. We couldn't leave it unattended. You know that."

Closing my eyes, I feel a sudden ache throb behind them. I raise my hand and rub in hopes of relieving some of the pressure. My joy flees as quickly as it came, and the weight of my responsibilities heavily returns.

It'd be unwise to leave an entire pack territory unattended, especially with an increasing number of vampires roaming the Earth Realm. He's right, I should have known that. With everything going on, with my mind in a million places, it had slipped through the cracks.

"Right. Of course." I drop my hand and look at my old packmates. "Where's Kat?"

Kenna frowns and wrinkles her nose. "The witch? The gothic-looking one?"

"She's not a witch," I correct, quickly coming to Kat's defense with a series of ramblings. "Well, she is, but it's more complicated than you think. She's pretty cool

126

once you get to know her. Amazing, actually. You'd like her."

At Kenna's scoff of disbelief, Flint tucks his chin, crosses his arms, and widens his stance. "Spill."

"Didn't anyone tell you?" I question with a quirked brow.

They shake their heads as one, and at the same time, wind pummels the side of my little home. The teepee's thin wooden beams groan in complaint, and for a moment, we remain silent, watching the structure, unsure if it'll stay upright.

I sigh. This might be a longer conversation than I want to endure. I might as well get straight to the point. "Right. Well, she's a dragon."

Kenna gapes. "You've got to be kidding me."

"This explains everything," Brenna murmurs, glancing at Kenna. "There's no way a normal witch could have done what she did the night we were attacked by vampires."

Flint's face softens, and then he rolls his eyes when his mind visibly draws on a conclusion. "It's the secret Irene's been obsessing about."

"Your mate can hold onto a secret like a squirrel with a nut," Brenna mumbles in a grudging growl.

"It's complicated," I mumble, glancing at the feeble doorway. There are many ears around if the chatter, song, and children's laughter is anything to go by. I don't need anyone overhearing this conversation, and I'm reluctant to tell a tale that's not mine.

They're silent with icy gazes, expectantly waiting for a more in-depth depiction of all things Katriane DuPont.

"Dyson, who is she to you?" Evo asks in a gruff tone.

I look Flint straight in the eye, avoiding Evo, and search his dilated pupils. He's my best friend. I used to tell him anything and everything. Naturally, he's the comfort I seek first because he'll understand my situation better than anyone else.

The skin pulls around my throat as I swallow with apparent difficulty, willing my thoughts to register in his mind. He's been through something similar with his own mate, though she's a Shifter and not a hybrid witch.

Flint tilts his head to the side and grins dazzling white teeth. "No. No that's impossible." The expression on his face completely contradicts his words.

"What?" Evo asks, his tone full of authority.

"They're – He's – She's –" he splutters, pointing at me and then gesturing with a twitching hand as though the shock of the situation settled in his joints.

A small, brave breeze trickles in from the hole above our heads, and Kenna rubs her gloved hands up and down her arms. "Mates," she mumbles, her teeth chattering. She stiffly rotates to Evo. "Oh my god, they're mates."

I suck in a deep breath, the cold air burning my teeth while I wait for the inevitable outburst.

"No, they're not," Brenna blurts in denial, fixing me with a hard stare. "That's impossible."

The flaps of the makeshift door open again as someone enters, and a blizzard made of big flakes quickly follows. The crystals melt on the fur, shrinking before they thaw to beads of dew.

"Our kidnapper is back," Flint mumbles.

"Erline," I correct him in a quieter tone and turn to face the woman in question.

"Of course, she has a name," Flint responds sarcastically. "But kidnapper fits better. Or maybe Majesty of Destruction."

A blonde, almost white haired and slender woman with curves in all the right places, and wearing nothing but a flowing pale blue dress, glides in. Her hands are clasped in front of her, fingers neatly puzzled together. She's strikingly beautiful, and her hair flows in one wave down to her waist. An authoritarian air moves about her, impossible to dismiss. This is the famous Mother Nature, Erline.

The door sways to a close but the remaining snow she brought with her continues to swirl in the increasingly small shelter. Add any more bodies in here, and we'll need a bigger teepee.

She blows in the offending flake's direction, irritated at the pesky blizzard who had dared to follow. We watch, hypnotized and rigid. A small trickle of wind whistles between her red lips and the flakes obey her wordless command, gathering as one and quickly darting out the hole at the top. Her eyes are just like Kheelan's, black pitiless orbs, and they slowly sweep my group of shifters.

"Snow is not my favorite thing," she admits when the reticence to her display of magic becomes uncomfortable. "Even if it is needed to restore balance in my realm's atmosphere."

The group snaps back to reality when she finishes, her tone a demand despite her choice of conversation.

"How?" Brenna asks Erline. "How is a dragon his mate?"

The woman ignores Brenna's question, her face sweeping across the space with her gaze until she looks upon me. Moments tick by, and our hot breaths gather in the space around us while we wait for her truth.

"Little wolf, nothing is the same as it once was." She glances at the pack to my back. "It is best if each of you grow accustomed to this anomaly. Since Katriane DuPont shifted each realm, impossibilities have occurred. I am to blame for part of that." She closes her eyes, consumed by obvious guilt, then opens them. They're etched with sorrow, soft and jagged at the same time. "I am Erline, fee of the Earth Realm."

"We know," I mumble, and then I clear my throat, embarrassed for my rude interruption.

Honestly, there's no need for formalities. The situation we're finding ourselves in is far past good-natured manners. If she can explain it better than I can, then I'm hopeful she'll persuade them how Kat is what's best for me. At a time like this, needless introductions grate at my nerves, and immediate action and explanations would best ease my anxiety.

She takes a step closer, her mood switching like an unruly toddler in need of a nap. I gulp at her stiff demeanor. It's not that I fear for my own safety in the presence of basically a god, but I worry all the fee have an unchecked temper. I had witnessed Kheelan's, and it was far from admirable or desirable. I worry, too, what their unpredictability truly means for the future safety of the realms and those they've created.

"She is your mate," Erline continues, clipping her words to discipline. "And the one who saved your heart."

"My heart?"

"Oh yes," she says gravely, taking the last step and gently lifting a hand.

She presses her cold fingers to my chest, my heart jumping at the chill of her skin through my thin button-down shirt. "The beats of your heart were owned by Kheelan. He called it back to him when you arrived at the Guardian Realm. I suspect something tipped him off to your whereabouts, Dyson, but I know not what." She pauses, hesitant. "The beats are now tied to Katriane's. She saved you."

Kenna curses behind me, and the shuffle of feet indicates she's begun to pace. I stand, still and statue-like, hanging on Erline's every last word. This must be the feeling I felt when I woke. This is why I feel no ties to my old Alpha and pack.

"As your creator, I sense the tie she constructed to keep you and the sandman alive. You are tethered to her, wolf. In more ways than one." She pauses when my head snaps to attention. My wolf's green glowing eyes shine against her pale skin. "Yes, I feel your wolf's need for her. What matters now is what you do with it. How far will you go to keep her safe?"

CHAPTER EIGHT

TEMBER

GUARDIAN REALM

"Where's Kat?" I ponder aloud, approaching the fire I saw roaring to a high flame just minutes ago from inside the forest. Jaemes walks to the gathered group with me, his stride silent and predatorial despite the crunching noise my steps make in the snow.

A freshly killed zipra is slung over his shoulders. The blob of creature had been lumbering through the forest as we wandered in search of fresh meat to feed the hungry elven children.

In secret, I believe we both had desired to get away from the smothering hostility of the village and had quickly volunteered to do so. None of the elves want us here despite the fact that James and I have moved past our differences. I just wish everyone else would as well. It would make this stay more pleasant.

We had bantered during the entire hunt, hushed words slung under our breaths, but I know without a doubt I can trust him with my life. He's proven that time and time again even if he uses mockery to justify his intent.

We each had hoped to get the first kill, and the friendly competition was welcome as we prowled from tree to tree and tracked prints before the falling snow could bury them. We had one condition: I wasn't allowed to fly, in order to keep the odds even, and I had grudgingly obeyed this rule. Now, I wish I hadn't.

I had hoped the victory would have been mine to gain favor. I need every piece of leverage to show these creatures I mean them no harm, and the best way to do that would be to feed the village. But Jaemes had carried out the striking blow and smirked openly about it.

According to Jaemes, my kind has been stealing their food source for sport. He felt it justice, in a way, that the zipra wasn't slung over my own shoulder in seeming victory. The words had stung, but Jaemes was completely oblivious to my plight, or he chose to dismiss it, needing someone to hold accountable and blame over their stolen goods.

The animal's hooved front legs sway at the small of his back, its leathery skin loose and covering his entire shoulder. Tribal songs are being sung in beautiful harmony throughout the village. It's as though they're using the tune to calm the edge of their nerves.

When we saw the flames reach higher than the teepees, we looked at one another and rushed back on the path we travelled. I was worried the entire village would be consumed by the time we returned, and several twigs had caught and torn my clothes in my haste. It would make sense the village used their music to calm their people. We had slowed our trek to watch a few of the elves dance once we saw it wasn't burned to the ground.

Their arms had swayed, and their horned-heads hung with their eyes closed as they breathed in tune to the music and allowed it to flow through their limbs. It was a beautiful dance, one which resembled the graceful swing of the tree's top branches pushed by the wind. Together, the blizzard, the moving trees, and the dancing elves were a breathtaking sight.

Now, as we approach, Dyson, his pack, Erline, the sandman, Mitus, and Erma, all hovered around the fire, chat in fervent voices.

Erma whips her head toward our approach at the same time Mitus' dangerous expression lands on Jaemes. The rest take their time to look us over with little interest as we add our bodies to the collective circle.

"Where's Kat?" I repeat again.

"She marched into the woods," Erma exclaims, puffing her cheeks and running a hand through her short red curls. She's beautiful when she does that, an action so innocent despite her powerful position and carefully diverted truthful emotions.

The heart in my wrist pumps, driving me to her as though she's the antidote to the ache in my chest. I keep my feet firmly planted, however, and grit my teeth against my internal struggle. Now isn't the time.

"It's dangerous in the woods," Jaemes explains, passing the slayed zipra to another elf's awaiting arms.

134

The elf is flocked by children bouncing from foot to foot with pure glee sparking in their eyes and punctuated with giddy giggles.

"I know," Dyson growls, tugging on his earlobe. His eyes shine a brilliant green, illuminating the falling flakes.

His wolf is dangerously close to the surface, and I frown at his defensively stressed posture. Why is he so protective over the mention of Katriane? Is this part of the repercussions of their tied lives? Overprotectiveness, perhaps?

A pang of jealousy rocks me where my chest aches for Erma. Kat should be my responsibility to fret over. Not an emotional wolf shifter's.

Jaemes and I step over the circle of logs surrounding the embers and trespass into the circling group, shoulder to shoulder.

"Why?" I ask, my eyes on Dyson.

Mitus and Jaemes begin a heated argument spoken in their native tongue while Erma watches them closely. Their attempts at a hushed tone are laughable, their voices and deep baritones carrying anyway.

An array of expressions flick across Erma's face, understanding every word uttered from Mitus' shrewd lips. Whatever they're saying, she's not agreeing with but is choosing to allow Jaemes to endure the argument alone.

Jaemes has proven he can hold his own. The fact that he is openly challenging his father and leader of the Igna Tribe's prejudices in verbal brawl is proof. He will make a great leader of his own someday. With his authoritarian straight back and piercing eyes which dare a challenge when he isn't mocking those beneath him, he'll surpass his brothers for the head seat.

I know he doesn't desire it, though. Jaemes would rather be a protector - a warrior - than a leader. But those who don't want the head seat tend to be the best at it, for they aren't corrupt with greed and gluttony. Their rule will be fair and just. Jaemes is capable of such, and I believe, down to my bones, Mitus is aware of this. When his life comes to an end by battle, he will leave his place as leader in the capable hands of his youngest son, even upon his son's refusal.

The sandman gingerly sits back down on the log, picks up a stick, and pokes at the flames with provoking jabs. His mind travels elsewhere, and he blinks rapidly like he's afraid to leave the fire unattended for the mere second a proper blink would take.

I turn my gaze to Erline and glare, placing immediate blame. "Why is Kat in the woods, unprotected?"

Mitus scuffs. "She is anything but unprotected. She's unstable. I've never seen such power in all my existence. Not even our legends mention something its equal."

"Oh?" I say, quirking a brow at him. I do not enjoy the hostility behind his accented tone, and I sense Dyson bristle with me.

Katriane DuPont has power even the fee can't comprehend. Though they've never said it aloud, I can see it in the fear in their eyes whenever her name is mentioned. She's an unpredictable creature, now more so than ever. But still, I feel as there are many to blame.

136

"Who pushed her?" I growl. "Who made her feel the need for solace?"

Dyson whips his head to Erline, eyes narrowed.

"It was I," Erline says simply. "She didn't like the answers she bargained for."

"And that is?" I fist my hands on my hips to hide my fingers. They're twitching with the need to call Ire. Dyson snarls at Erline. Behind him, a large blond man grips his shoulders and mumbles softly in his ear. I catch a few of the words, and tense further when one of them graces my ears: 'mates.'

"What the hell is going on?" I ask.

The sandman, ominous in tone and tending the fire, recaps all he has heard. I listen, quietly seething. It feels like the wind is blown from my chest by the time he's done, and I take a heavy seat on a log behind me, wings drooped in defeat. The madness never ends.

One particular statement ricochets inside my head: the fee can't take a mate without sharing their power - without vulnerability on both parties' behalf.

Is this why Erma has denied me? It would explain why she's held back from what we shared when times were simpler, when sneaking was easier. Our relationship is on display for the entire realm, and more.

Corbin knows of it, too, along with all the angels. All the elves must be aware as well if the stare Mitus has directed at the side of my head is anything to go by. His gaze feels like daggers, twisting and turning against my cheek in hopes it will become uncomfortable enough that definitive answers will be revealed. I don't plan to give him any. My business is mine alone.

It would also explain why Erma finds it all too easy to despise me. By keeping me at a distance, she's effectively saved me and herself. Mates can kill their fee mates, but I can't believe she'd ever think I'd do such a thing. It hurts more than I care to admit, like all the hope is sucked from my world.

Aside from that, if we were to mate and share what power she has, if the angels were to retaliate, it would destroy the entire realm. A mated couple taking on hundreds of powerful warriors would end in sure demise.

Fee mating isn't common knowledge, nor are the repercussions of it, and to share it with this group must be hard for the fee. This is their weakness, a chink in a carefully guarded chain. Though it cripples me with despair, it can be used against our enemy.

I look to Erma, her hard eyes directly on mine. The black orbs speak volumes - fear, anger, aggression, wariness - but I see behind her exterior. She can't hide from me. I'm tautly aware of everything about her.

Those eyes lack the one thing I search for, however. There may be an abundance of longing for what we once shared, but there's no relief that I now know why we can't be together.

"You all are tim-tato," Jaemes mumbles at my side.

I shoot out a hand and punch the back of his knee, grateful for his distraction and outlet for my emotions.

Falling to the ground with an *oof*, his landing causes puffs of white fluffy snow to rise like dust. He surely called us an unkind name, but I'm used to it by now. I don't need to understand his language to know he is calling us all crazy. His honesty and truth are irritating, but he's quite right. All of this does feel that way - a hopeless impossibility. A tangled web.

I never thought the day would come when I'd find myself agreeing with him. Perhaps I'm spending too much time with this creature.

Erma stiffens without cause, and I glance up at her at the same time Erline calls her name.

"What is it?" Erline asks quietly.

Erma surveys the group, meeting each of our curious gazes. "Someone new is in my realm."

"Who?" I ask, running a hand over my face. This is what true exhaustion feels like, and for a moment, I envy those who can sleep.

Neither Jaemes nor I have rested yet. Black blood and goop from our enemies are dried on our skin, and my clothes are close to tatters. I don't sleep, but a soft bed would be welcome nonetheless.

"Friend or foe?" Erline asks, gripping Erma's shoulders.

She smacks her lips. "Salty. It tastes salty."

"Demon," Jaemes grumbles, knowing that the creature's realm is filled with sulfur. "Do you have any demon friends?" The question is rhetorical. A guardian never makes allies with a demon, let alone their creator.

They're too unpredictable, and just as vampires, their only goal is their next feed.

Erma's eyes widen, and she gapes down to me. "Tember?"

I know this look. I'm the one she's entrusted most with missions, discretion and honor neatly tied together. I close my eyes and nod, accepting her unvoiced request. It is my duty to obey my creator, and I'll do it to the end of my long life even if my loyalty means I'll never get to hold her again. I'll remain hers, forever, no matter my title or purpose.

"Get up, you fool," I grunt to Jaemes, thumping his thigh with the back of my hand. "It's time to go."

KATRIANE DUPONT

GUARDIAN REALM

In front of me, a crystal lake gleams unnaturally, surrounded by frost-capped trees and fallen logs. To be honest, I can't tell if it's a lake or a large pond. What makes a pond a lake? Who decides this, and what measurements do they use?

Snow falls against its surface, gentle and calming, very much unlike what I feel inside along with the village noises echoing in the distance. Every part of me urges to erect a fire across the surface of ice, just to see if it simmers and melts, and watch the beauty be destroyed by

140

my hand. Just to spread the pain. Just to ease the need for destruction.

The flames sizzle under the surface of my skin, ready for immediate use if I decide to melt the fantasy around me. I mentally grasp it, refusing to let it go, and give one internal yank to settle this feeling back in the pit of my stomach, accompanying the evil fingers around my heart.

There's no white flag here, I tell myself. *And I can't give up the hope that someday, I'll be free of all this.* But how am I supposed to come to terms with everything I've learned?

I close my eyes and breathe deep, willing this *feeling* away. When I exhale, I open my eyes, marginally calmer than before, and lift a hand vibrating with awaiting magic.

There are no birds here chirping from tree to tree, no distractions from my own inner struggles. Mitus was right. I am unstable – my power, my emotion, my certainty - and I don't know how to correct nor balance it.

Slivers of ice crack under my weight, but I ignore it. I'm only on the edge of the frozen body of water, and if it were to break, I wouldn't fall in too deep.

Snowflakes run along the snow-covered forest floor, tumbling over each other with a small surge of wind as though a giant invisible hand is sweeping a finger through the landscape. The flakes reach the frozen lake and swirl in a vortex, hovering inches from the surface and waiting for an elemental demand. I watch it for a moment, marveling as each crystal catches a reflection and twinkles, a sparkle.

Lifting my other hand, I clap my palms, weave the fingers between their counterparts, and rip my hands apart. The snowflakes combust from their miniature tornado, falling to the lake smaller-sized than they were before.

Power, my thoughts darkly marvel, and I blush, ashamed for my weakness.

What I've become is almost too much for me to understand. Myla may have left me all of her power, but I have the blood of three fee and the first born witch running through my veins. I have my darkness as a leader. I have other lives pocketed in my very being. I'm more, much more, than they believe me to be, even more than I believe me to contain.

And there wasn't enough time for Myla to teach me how to wield what she was born with. My heart aches for what could have been.

It's amazing how one vessel can hold so much without self-destruction. Perhaps I will be destroyed in the end, but I have every intention of taking the fee down with me, even if that means Erline falls by my hand. Balance will be restored, and vengeance will be sought. Myla would have wanted that for me.

"Is that what you wish?" a male voice chimes in the wind. "Vengeance? I demand more of you, Child born of Compassion."

Startled, I whip around, my breath hitching. Heat floods my cheeks once more but for an entirely different reason this time.

"Who's there?" I ask the open woods.

Nothing is there. Not a body, not an entity. Nothing but the trees blanketed in white.

There's no answer for several moments, and I narrow my eyes, preparing to lay the responsibility of my palpable fear on the branches.

"Do you truly need to know who I am?" the voice finally responds when some of the hostility drains from my stiff shoulders. "Or are you looking for an alternative target to place blame for the things you cannot control?"

I whip back around to the frozen body of water, my eyes wide, and I take a step back.

Small dotted lights, consisting of black and gold, shimmer in front of me, resembling the shape of a tall human, male body. I can't make out features, just a silhouette, but the body is still and undisturbed by the small gusts of wind whistling through the trees.

I flick both arms at my sides, calling upon the flames. "Who are you?"

"You shouldn't do that," the voice says calmly. A light reflects from some of his specks, and they sparkle just as the snow had.

I tilt my head. "Do what?"

"Call upon what you don't understand," he responds. "You're fueled by the evil intentions growing inside you." The body lifts a hand and points to my chest where the black darkness has its grip around my heart.

"And what would you know about it," I snip, taking a challenging step forward.

Unaffected, the body matches my advance in kind, and it's then I realize he isn't walking on ground but hovering in the air. "I know you don't understand it. I know it's dangerous. I know this addicting darkness is an asset of what's to come, but I also know it will consume you like the flames licking up your arms, heeding your every secret desire as you tap into it. You ignore the offerings of relief around you."

I gulp, and the flames extinguish, doused by his blunt honesty. "Who are you?" I ask, oddly calmed and a little mystified.

"I am everything," the voice whispers, tickling my inner ears. "I am part of four."

When he says four, the word is carried by four different voices as though he's speaking for others as well.

"Part of four?"

"Where there is one," the breeze buzzes his voice, "there is another."

I roll my eyes. "A yin and a yang?"

The head bobs, slow, as though to assure I see the gesture. "In a way."

"Friend or foe?" I ask, looking back to the landscape. I don't feel any anger nor challenge coming from him, whatever he is. Instead, I feel an obsession, a craving, blossoming in my chest. He's the brightest, most calming sensation I've come across, and I struggle not to drink him in.

"That Choice is yours."

From the corner of my eyes, I scrutinize him. He says it like choice is a person, a being such as himself. An inkling nags in the back of my thoughts, but I can't fully grasp it as though the memory is a picture warped by time.

"What are you?" I demand again, this time more cheeky.

"Fate," he breezes.

I close my eyes, my heart pattering against my ribs, and the memory fully forms. I recall lessons about him, on his counterpart Choice, and their opponents, Hope and Despair. Some say they closely resemble the four horsemen, but the Covens always spoke of them as legends and pure myths.

"The Divine Realm," I divulge.

The Divine Realm is told to have many wondrous creatures and entities: people who move with the shadows, misty wisps in the absence of wind, and strange voices who manipulate. The land is made of bizarre vibrant colors and deadly objects. It's a coveted place, and yet I've never met anyone who has seen it. I've often wondered where the tales come from.

Fate chuckles, the sound so father-like it raises goosebumps along my skin. "Very good. I see the witches have continued an excellent education."

"Sure. You mean before they cast me out?" I grunt maliciously, deepening my voice.

"Don't," Fate says, reaching forward with a sparkling arm. "Don't let it rule you. Hate can turn even the brightest star into something so dark there is no return."

I look away, my eyes landing on fallen tree limbs. "It isn't a choice."

It doesn't feel like I have a choice, I add to myself. No matter how hard I try, I can't banish this cold pressure nor resist the taunting thoughts of revenge fueled by this crippling hatred he speaks of. It's a rift between a coveted pure conscious and feared dark greed.

"Oh, but it is." His voice holds much wonder, so much conviction. I'm drawn back to him, a slow turn of my head as his next words captivate me. "Everything is a choice."

I chuckle, shake my head, and scratch my jaw. "Coming from a Divine whose mate and enemy is Choice itself."

Though there are no eyeballs, I can feel its gaze and irritation. "You know a great deal about us, Katriane DuPont."

"I do," I meet his gaze. "Perhaps I'll come to your realm someday, Creator of All Fee."

The Divine - Fate, Choice, Hope, and Despair - all created the fee together, as well as the realms the fee modified to fit their needs. The fee built upon these realms to resemble themselves and their desires, but The Divine built the platform and set them loose. They're not evil. They are, in fact, the glue. Without them, all life, all creatures, all realms, would never have existed, and at the same time, if they were destroyed, the realms would immediately follow.

They resemble the four horsemen because of that fact alone.

Cheeks puff from the black and gold orbs, and I imagine the action to be caused by a smile. "I have no doubt you will."

In the comfort of Fate, I lean into a tree and rest my head against rough bark. "I'm gone. If you're purpose is to help me discover a brilliant future, I fear it impossible."

"No," the voice says right in my ear. "Your future is not brilliant. It is shrouded by death. And though you are lost now, you will become the map for all those who are."

"How, when I can't even find my way back?" I mumble, my throat thick.

"The darkness is a line, Katriane DuPont. You choose to step over it. No one pushes you."

I open my eyes. He no longer resembles a man but a swirling circle of dots, hovering right in front of my face. This close, the dots smell like sage.

"It is okay to dip your toe across that line, and it is also okay to take the hands of those you love and ask for help. The lightness is in love, young one. Love is the light. Hate is the dark. You cannot find your way in the dark. Forgive yourself or be swallowed by it." He pauses dramatically. "Choose."

He begins to dissipate, and I panic. He'll take the warmth with him, the only thing presently holding my emotions at bay.

"Wait!" I scream to the air.

Fate chuckles, the last of his dots disappearing, but his voice remains. "Do not fear, dragon. I'm always with you. Find your future in your heart. Seek Hope with your eyes. Discover the greatness of Choice. And whatever you do, don't cling to Despair."

CHAPTER NINE

AIDEN VANDER

GUARDIAN REALM

It takes everything I have, everything I represent, to allow this unnecessary manhandling. Firm and boney hands grip my shoulders, and snarls of surrounding hostile elves vibrate my ears. Their growls are animalistic, deep and rumbling yet subtly threatening. At least to me.

The row on the raft is short. Not once do we struggle against their force even when they push us onto the main boat. It is, however, difficult to remain a willing hostage with this level of disrespect. I can feel my power swirling within, my demonic side prepared to unleash a wrath even I'm not prepared for. I haven't tested them and have no idea the strength though I have an inkling it's grand.

The only thing holding me back from gaining the respect I deserve is Eliza. The last thing I want to do is frighten her. A show of strength to that magnitude would make me seem unpredictable.

The water gently laps at the wood, and the extra breeze ruffles my short hair, caressing my scalp. It's like affectionate fingers weaving between the short strands and massaging the muscles under the skin.

The wind is warm and tangy on my tongue, and I wonder; if I were to touch the water, would it be as warm as the breeze which carries it?

Our elf entourage leads Eliza first, straight to the middle with an egotistical strut. The surrounding elves beat the bottom of their spears against the boat, a sound of drums which grate at every nerve.

They think they've caught us tramping through their lands and haven't yet drawn the conclusion that perhaps we were looking to be caught. But this was the plan all along. This is what Ferox advised me to do.

Every being on this realm is a guardian. A worthy warrior. A survivor. They're meant to protect, and it's due to that fact alone they're still breathing.

On the main boat, the absence of sails is oddly unnerving, and it's too small for a quarter deck, rocking precariously with each subtle shuffle of feet.

To guide the boat, instead of sails and a quarter deck adorning a helm, two creatures wade in the crystal clear water, tethered with thick, handmade, and fraying ropes. The swimming creatures are long, like snakes, and spikes line their spines. Their bottom jaw is massive, and the teeth poking from them are just as impressive. How did the elves tame them to do their bidding? I wouldn't get near them if I could help it.

They remind me of a documentary I watched as a teen. I was in the living room of the Tiller's foster home. The program covered dangerous areas of the ocean and parts rarely explored due to the extreme depths and danger of the water pressure. What fascinated me most was a species of a deep-sea fish, the kind that never see the light of day and preyed on those who wander their way. They were frightening. The hair along my arms had stood on end when they displayed this fish across the small boxed screen, and their predatory features are quite like the slaved creatures who pull this boat.

Stealing my pondering thoughts back to the present, the two who lead me dig their thumbs into my shoulder blades, a warning to watch my actions. I discretely study them and their scent of confidence, unafraid of the threat I present. I suppose a warrior should never show fear.

Their skin is white but striped with red like the color of the sand below the water. Sharp, long horns halo their heads, meshing with pointed ears. Long black hair cascades down one side, reaching their waists when the wind doesn't whisk it away. If it wasn't for the delicate difference in facial features, they'd all look identical.

As I pass each watching member, only half a dozen and both male and female, they peer into my eyes. They surely see an oddity. I'm not a humanoid even though I look like one on the outside, and they openly inspect me as though I'm a wild beast. Eliza isn't the only one I need not frighten today. If I raise too many alarms, they won't provide the protection I seek for her.

My escorts and I come to a complete halt, and I glance over at Eliza, catching her pinched and concerned face. She's confused, and I don't blame her. Having woke in another realm and been captured by creatures she's never heard of should cause such confusion. She was a doctor. Doctors believe in what they can see, touch, and then explain. This is beyond easy explanation, and the realm is outside the scientific laws of nature. We all are, I suppose.

Unexpectedly, fear doesn't waft from her body and feed me. Her concern mingles in the humid air instead, salty like the water. It's concern for me, I realize, when her eyes flick to mine with hundreds of unasked questions.

In front of me, at the point of their haphazard circle surrounding their willing hostages, is a burly elf. His eyes are fierce, heated, and if I weren't what I am, I'd surely quake in my shoes by the intensity of it. Eliza, however, trembles when he pins her with his gaze.

I tick my jaw, waiting to see what happens next, and force myself not to feed from Eliza's new-found fear. I'll kill them all if I must. No one will touch or harm her, including myself.

"Shi-shu isu?" the male creature says, his last word's tone rising in that of a question.

I smile as his words filter into my mind. Not only do I understand Latin, I understand his language: *Who are you.*

"Monto Aiden," I rumble, matching his challenging stance.

He double blinks over dark eyes, the only sign that I've taken him off guard. Is he expecting to make a fool of me?

Recollection crosses his features. "You speak our language," he quips, his English heavily lilted in an accent I've never heard.

I don't move except to center my stance in an attempt to counteract the sway of the boat. The knowledge that I know their words shakes the other elves, and their delicious answering emotion coats the air when their spear's drumming stops altogether. Instinctively, I pull their fear into my body, careful not to touch Eliza's, and use it to fuel me. I need all the energy I can muster in case this doesn't turn out in our favor. If they won't help us, I'll find another who will.

"What's going on?" Eliza asks, her voice tinged with fright.

I tilt my chin toward her but keep my eyes on the elf in charge. "It's all right," I coo.

"Spokeo isu-ate livate?" he asks, taking a step forward and curling his fingers tighter around his spear forever stained with black blood. The red stripes on his knuckles turn a shade of vibrant pink with the effort, and the boat's boards creak under his massive weight.

"I want nothing," I respond. "It is her I want for."

Eliza's eyebrows dip, and she moves to reach my side. The elves holding her shoulders dig their fingers into her exposed skin, and she winces, halting her mid-stride.

He considers Eliza, hanging his head while stroking his chin. "Shi-tu isu tire?"

"I'm here for her protection, and her protection only." I drop my voice to a dangerous whisper. "I would appreciate it if you speak English and take your eyes off her."

The way he's looking at her - the expression of a steaming meal in front of a starving man - escalates my protective instincts to the woman I love.

"You come to my realm, creature of dark, and ask for the protection of another?" Dark eyes shift back to mine, threatening, slow, the look of a predator. Two can play that game.

I smirk, wicked. "This isn't your realm."

Along the square of his sharp jaw, muscles ripple in agitation. Internally, my demon soul raises a fist in triumph though my conscience screams to be cautious in my choice of words.

"These are my waters, demon," he counters, lifting his top lip in sneer. He angles the tip of his arrow at my chest with brilliant, formidable speed. It doesn't come in contact with my body, but it does hover a few inches from it, a promised threat. It's not his fault he doesn't know who he is dealing with. Maybe I should show him.

Fear spikes around Eliza's form, knocking me back to the present and restoring my main goal with the delicious taste. I whip the idea of a challenge from my mind and focus with much effort.

Quieting my voice, my tone asks for forgiveness without a cowering lilt. "And this is the one I love. She needs protection from me, my kind, and those who wish to see her dead."

If nothing else, this shocks the elf. He takes a step back as though he's been physically shoved, and astonishment glitters in his eyes. Demons can't love - they're not supposed to.

"And here I thought she was your hostage," he whispers, watching Eliza with a renewed look of adoration.

"Hardly," I snort at the same moment the creatures pulling the boat slap against the surface of the water. Their long tails flick, agitated at the standstill. I don't believe I could control Eliza even if I wanted to.

The elf holding Eliza grips his fingers tighter around her shoulder. I growl at him, visibly baring my teeth and allowing a flicker of lava to swell in my eyes. "If you don't get your hands off her, I'll consume your every emotion and leave an empty husk for your tribe to bury."

Wide-eyed to the blatant threat, the elf shifts his full attention back to me, and I give him a small taste of what I can do. My lips firm and my stare hardens, shoulders pulled back despite the strength of my own captors' grips. By the twist of expression, my eyes are brilliantly molting. I leech some of his fear, sucking it into myself with only a thought and a sliver of will. The elf gasps and drops his hands as though Eliza were too hot for his touch.

The boat, the atmosphere, hushes. The water lapping once more and spilling over the edges is the only sound.

"Peplato," the giant elf muses.

I immediately stop drinking the emotion from his minion. *Love,* he had said, reminding me of my purpose.

I turn to him and shirk the elves holding my arms. They drop their grips willingly after the elf in charge nods to them in approval.

"Yes," I say simply. "I love her."

"Impossible," he spits. "A demon cannot love."

I laugh, the sound from deep within my chest, and then straighten my shirt as if the action is evidence to my point. "Not for this demon."

He stares at me, and his lips become shrewd once again. "What is your true name?"

Licking my bottom lip, I consider if I should answer his question. A demon should never give his true name. It is power, I was told, but my goal here isn't to gain power. It's to gain protection for Eliza while I go back to my realm and deliver my revenge. She must be safe, and if that means putting myself in danger, then so be it.

"Thrice Born." Gasps emit from the other elves surrounding us. I chuckle darkly. "So, you've heard of me?"

The elf sucks in his top lip and considers his next answer. "They gossip - the pyrens - and carry tales quite often to our realm."

"You know what I am then," I mumble, dipping my chin. No soul has been taken from the void except me.

"We do." He nods once and smacks his lips as though the very thought of how I was made sours his taste. "But rumors are just rumors, and a demon, no matter the miraculous form, cannot be trusted." He flicks his spear to his elf minions in an obvious command, and they swarm once more like bees after their nest has been promptly poked. "Feed them to the calimates."

They pick up Eliza around the waist, and she screams and flails, rocking the boat. Their strides are long and determined, and they hoist her in the air at the ledge. Even with all the power she has inside her, she won't be able to control it enough to protect herself from the creatures pulling this boat. Despite their repurpose, they're predators, the jaws of this river.

"No!" I yell, hand outstretched.

With my next inhale, I cripple the boat's residents by pulling their souls to me, tethered to their emotions, just as I did with the scraggly demon escort of my realm. It's all too easy, my power closer to the surface than I had originally thought.

It's a glorious feeling to have so many lives I could snuff with a single thought. I hadn't planned on playing my trump card, but I'll be damned if Eliza dies.

Grunts and groans are my reward, and the weakest elves among the boat's residents fall to their knees, swiftly overcome. I'm quickly rewarded for my efforts as I press on. Those who hold Eliza above the water stagger back and drop her to her feet, clutching their chests. A smoky trail exits through the dip of their joined collarbones, arching before descending into my pores.

I spread my arms, prepared to take more, but the boat sways. More bodies appear as they step through a glowing circle of light. I fix to inhale again, this time to take on the new reinforcements without a second thought as to who they are.

"Enough!" A small woman, a fee, I realize, blasts a yellow light to all those on the boat.

I stagger at the force of her power, close my fingers into fists, and pin my eyes to the fee. She's accompanied by an angel with black wings and another elf tattooed in brown, almost black stripes.

It's mere seconds later, when I sweep my gaze across my captors, that I realize their bodies are stiff, unable to move as though each of their muscles has been cemented under their flesh.

Eliza darts to me, curls her arms around my bicep, and presses her cheek to my skin.

DYSON COLEMAN

GUARDIAN REALM

Erma and the two creatures, named Jaemes and Tember, disappear into the fee's bright lights. Their scowls speak volumes. No one should be allowed on the realm without permission. There is possible danger here, and I mentally prepare for it. If Jaemes' grip on his arrow, pulled from a quiver slung on his back, and Tember's calling of her magical bow called Ire are anything to go by, they're expecting trouble.

For several moments I stare, transfixed, at where they had once stood. I've barely been awake, and already, I feel the weight of exhaustion. It's still so new to me, this exhaustion. On the Death Realm as a shade, we never slept. Time is broken there. Or perhaps time is always broken, and we only try to control it.

The whack to wood breaks me from my fixation. I exhale slowly and turn. Not far from where I stand, logs are being chopped into quarters by a female elf. Her children run, crazed and giggling, along the nearby path. Next to her, the dead, blubbery animal Jaemes had brought back is being peeled of its leathery skin like a ripe banana. It hangs upside down by a rope stained with past kills. Blood pours from its body with each rip of flesh and muscle, and hot iron taints the wind, rolling my stomach.

As a wolf shifter, I've heard the sound many times, mostly by the shredding of my own teeth, but somehow, this feels different. I've never been a fan of hunting, though the elves do it without sport. They hunt to survive and feed the many because it's the only way to eat in a frozen land. But with such a public display to a slaying, I start to sympathize with their food source even if it feels normal for them.

Every part of me hums as I turn, yet again, and look to the barren forest where my heart begs to explore as that creature once did. My wolf, eager for the same, urges me to seek out Kat as well. She has yet to return, and I'm beginning to worry. What is she doing out there?

Evo's hand squeezes my shoulder, and I jump. I had forgotten I am flanked by my pack, completely lost in my own thoughts. "She'll come back, Dyson."

"Are you sure about that?" Kenna mumbles, and an *oof* quickly follows. "What was that for?" she growls in a whisper.

"Do you want his wolf to rip through this village?" Flint says, angry, much unlike his normal demeanor.

Kenna's quiet for a moment while I watch the branches sway in a breeze and the snowflakes that play across the landscape. This realm is beautiful, a white wonderland. The trees and smells are unlike any I've ever encountered and I drink it in, collecting the aroma and stuffing it in a pocket of my sensory's memory.

"Probably wouldn't be a bad thing," Kenna mumbles. "These elves' horns could poke someone's eye out. He'd be doing everyone a favor." Another *oof* follows. "I am your Alpha Queen, Flint. Slap my stomach again, and you'll pull back a bloody stump."

"Would you knock it off?" Flint snarls, rising to the challenge and feeling the need to protect me. He's just gotten me back and knows what my wolf is going through. After all, he went through something similar with his own mate. He knows my wolf is riding me hard. Even now, I can feel his temperament rising, the claws of his paws raking my insides. It's taking everything I have not to hunt her down and sling her over my shoulders like a barbaric caveman.

Evo squeezes again. "Ignore her, Flint. Kenna will make her own bed."

I hear her gasp, her fists thump against her hips, and the abrupt swish of her coat. "Are you telling me you'd let these elves spin me over a fire?"

Brenna chuckles in front of me, seated on a log and heating her hands over the orange embers. She pulls her hands away from the warmth and brushes snow off a neighboring log. "Kenna, why don't you come sit by me."

Grumbling under her breath, she does as the Beta Female asks, grabbing the sandman's stick along the way and stoking the fire. The sandman had departed minutes before, abandoning his acquired stick in favor of leaving the present hostility behind.

"What do I do, Evo?" I ask in a mumble while stuffing my hands in the pockets of my heavy coat. The pack had brought it for me, had even kept my things. It stung as much as it touched me to be reminded of everything I've lost. That kind of simple life is no longer for me. Instead, I'm tangled in a web even I can't grasp.

Flint rakes a hand through his hair and stands at my other side, peering into the forest with me.

"There's nothing you can do," Erline says, quietly observing by the teepee. She'd been so quiet in her approach that Kenna startles and openly growls at the fee.

"What do you mean?" Evo roughly inquires, sliding his hand from my shoulder in favor of crossing his arms. Like his mate, he's not a fan of Mother Nature either.

"That's his mate," he adds.

She looks only to me, her dark eyes peering into my borrowed soul. Perhaps she, too, isn't a fan of the

Alpha pair. "A darkness consumes her. The choice is hers if she decides to stay there."

My eyes flutter shut. I had felt that at the Colosseum, but at the time, I had thought it only bloodlust.

"A mate should be able to cure that," Flint chimes in.

She nods, and takes a step toward me, closing the distance. Lifting a delicate hand, she grabs my chin and forces me to meet her eyes. "Remember? You are tied to her in more ways than one."

Mine, my wolf growls.

"You all seem to be linked to the witch," Flint observes.

"We are," Erline mumbles, peering into the forest. "In a way."

"So what do I do?" I ask, tired of the petty chit-chat. I want my mate, and I want her to see me and what she is to me. But how do I reach her in a place she's buried herself?

"Be patient," she cautions. "Do not force it."

"Woo her, man." Flint slaps my shoulder, jarring the joint. His jokester attitude is once again at the forefront. I've missed it, and my heart sings if but for a moment. I turn a half grin toward him, and he shakes my top frame, returning the smile.

"Don't worry. I'll help," he adds, bending his head closer to mine for a quick lesson on romantic topics I've never cared of learning.

CHAPTER TEN

ELIZA PLAATS

GUARDIAN REALM

I remember the day I first saw Aiden. It was the dream before my first death, and the fog had swirled around his breathtaking transparent form. Those steel eyes pierced my soul and reached me on a level I'd never been touched. This was back when things were simpler, with a scalpel in hand and dreams of a man I couldn't have, for he was a ghost.

In that clearing, he had been standoffish yet innocent. He was caring and full of love waiting to be freely given. He was Aiden. And most importantly, he was mine.

The scorching kisses he had fluttered against my lips said everything he didn't know how to say. It was an ease no stranger possessed, as though he'd been waiting for me his entire life and then some. And me? I had been waiting for him, too.

This is not what I see now. He is not the same man. That Aiden had died twice and will never return. It makes me second guess if I can love the man I see now.

Beneath the contact of our skin, I feel a demon, pure evil, evident with molten eyes. But deep within, tucked in a dark corner, is the man my heart twisted and twined with until we became one. I don't think I could ever love him differently, no matter what he becomes.

He brought me here to save me, he had said. From what, I don't fully understand. Kheelan isn't here to take me away. I'm safe when I'm with Aiden. Surely, he knows that. So why is he asking these creatures to watch over me? Why can't he do it himself?

And then it hits me. He doesn't plan to stay. He's going to abandon me. Again.

Aiden glares at the small red-head holding her glowing hands in the air, possessing a power just as great as Kheelan's. I can taste it, a creamy sensation across my tongue. It begs me to call my own, to match its challenge, but I won't. Aiden brought us here for a reason, and I'd bet it wasn't to challenge the fee of this odd realm.

Though my grip around Aiden's bicep says otherwise, I fear his power more than I do the fee's. I can see it; a smoky hue pulling from their chest and being absorbed into his own. He's feeding from these frozen creatures, and there is nothing they can do about it from their current state.

"Who are you?" the woman asks Aiden, her voice musically venomous. "Why are you here?"

When Aiden doesn't answer, she drops her hands, and the glow goes with it, freeing the elves. His mind is occupied by a plan carefully forming if the tick of his jaw is anything to go by. This new turn of events isn't something Aiden banked on; that much is clear. Perhaps he's choosing his next words wisely.

The creature with brown stripes steps forward, away from the fee, and steals the spotlight. The elves, huffing and puffing from Aiden's assault, bow to one knee, using their spears to anchor their balance and the teetering of the boat.

"He was in the Death Realm's battle," the darkly-striped elf says. "They both were."

Aiden straightens from his defensive hunch, recognition crossing his features, and fully faces the three, ignoring our captors. He doesn't fear her, and a niggling feeling inside tells me what I need to know. She's an asset to our plans.

"Erma," he says as though he's recognizing her for what she is.

Erma looks to the elf speaking, ignoring Aiden. "Jaemes? Are you sure?" She swivels back to Aiden and me. "Is this true?"

Aiden inclines his head in confirmation. Though these elves are completely intent on our demise, Erma is the one who can halt such an assault if she sees fit. But first she must see us as innocent, and right now, we don't exactly scream helpless. At least, Aiden doesn't.

Erma strides briskly to us, and I grip Aiden's arm tighter. His muscles ripple against my palm as he attempts to hide his bristle to her closeness. She narrows her eyes when she's directly in front of us, scrutinizing, and sniffs a whiff.

The tiny fee's eyes widen. "You've been pulled from the void."

"I have," Aiden rumbles.

Erma shakes her head. "That's impossible," she quietly declares in palpable anger.

Aiden crosses his arms, and his next words are a hiss of disgust. "Not for the ruler of demons."

His anger toward Corbin causes me to shiver. Until now, I haven't been entirely sure where his allegiances lay. I know he'll never harm me, but I haven't been sure if he is leaving me here to return and do the bidding of his creator. It is what he was made for, after all.

She huffs. "You detest Corbin."

"With every fiber of my being."

The angel's eyes prick my forehead. I've felt her gaze on me the entire time but have chosen to ignore it and let her study me instead. If she can see I mean no harm, then perhaps her protective instincts will rise in my need of it.

"You," the angel says, pointing. "What are you?"

Erma turns her eyes to me, a whip-like movement. "I know who she is."

Taken aback, I hide my shock by clearing my throat. Under the attention of this fee, my mouth is as dry as if I had swallowed a handful of sand.

Aiden lifts a hand and closes my fingers tighter around his skin. It's a calming gesture, wordlessly telling me he has every intention of protecting me, no matter how this turns out.

"Well?" Jaemes scowls, impatient. "Spit it out then."

I double blink. I've never heard a creature talk to a fee in such a way. Doing so in the Death Realm would be a sentence to the void. Perhaps things are much different here, and Erma trusts the beings she creates. I can't tell if that's a smart move or an ignorant one.

I decide to speak for myself. "My name is Eliza-," I begin, carefully keeping my emotions from my voice.

"Kheelan's new mate," Erma finishes. "Tell me why I shouldn't kill you now."

Aiden uncrosses his arms and releases a gusting sigh. The weight of the world is on his shoulders, and the word mate had stiffened his spine. He doesn't like that I'm married, and neither do I. I'd give anything to ease that burden from Aiden's shoulders, to be free and with him until the end of times. But my fate has been stolen from me just as it has been for him. I'll never truly have Aiden. I should have known this in the forest of my dreams - a ghost pressing his body against warm human flesh, entwined in a forbidden love. We're two contradictions meant to forever love each other apart.

"Because she needs protection," Aiden says, his voice clear and calm.

167

Erma tilts her head, and her tight curls bounce across her shoulder. "Protection?"

"Don't we all," Jaemes starts, and a snort quickly follows.

"Quiet, Jaemes," Erma spits. "Protection from you, perhaps?"

Aiden nods reluctantly. "And from Kheelan."

Erma contemplates that for a moment and raises her hand up, palm out, to silence the elves' leader who had opened his mouth to speak. "Your input is not needed, Ica."

I swallow at the demand, not daring to look at Ica at our backs.

"And what side of the line do you fall under, Thrice Born?" Erma asks after a moment of contemplation.

Aiden double blinks before smoothing his features. I, however, hiss as I suck in a breath, the sound masked by a new lap of waves against the rocking boat. How does she know his name?

"The side that ends with Corbin's death."

Satisfied with his answer, Erma nods her head and sweeps his body with gentler eyes, reevaluating her first impression. "Even if that means your own death?"

"Yes," Aiden answers, his voice firm.

And I know it to be true, plucking the emotion from his mind. He'll die before he loses me again. I don't know if that's a comfort or a great weight to an impending loss. Will

Aiden be taken from me again? I don't think I could bear it another time. I know I couldn't. This time, if he dies again, I'll go with him.

Erma turns to me, and I almost miss her words as my thoughts churn with oily dread. "And you?"

I think for a moment, but my thoughts are stolen when Aiden's gaze locks with mine, the lava depths returning to the colors I remember so well - the colors I fell for. The swirls are pure. They're Aiden. Vivid. Captivating. A safe place to the depths of his true soul. They take my breath away.

I hold his gaze as I answer. "I fall on the side of Aiden. I choose him."

Aiden's lips quirk in a smile, and those eyes seem to shine just a little brighter. Until now, I believe he thought I feared him. I do but only a part of him - the part that could so easily kill without guilt. I want him to know I fall on the side of us being together. I'll do anything to kiss those lips without having to look over my shoulder.

"A lover's conviction. Adorable," Jaemes mocks. He wipes a fake tear from under his eye along the black skin which raccoons them.

Erma sighs, forcing me to break my gaze, my silent promise that Aiden is my forever. "Keep your feelings for another in check. Don't let it consume the mission."

"Creator," Ica begs. She silences him with a deadly look.

"Mission?" Aiden questions, his eyes still on me, caressing my cheek as he searches my face.

Suppressing a laugh, Erma's small shoulders bob, and she touches the tips of her hair, patting the curls. "Did you think you'd escape from the grips of the fee by hiding here?"

The angel's black wings rustle, and she presses her lips into a thin line. Her hand lifts, and it is then that I see the large black bow gripped tightly in her other. Who does she protect? The protestor or the General? I can't tell which. Not from where I stand. She's too guarded for such inquiries.

Aiden's eyebrows flick, a sign that he did, indeed, think so.

Erma peers at the angel. "Tember, explain while I talk with Ica."

Tember smiles, almost wickedly, like she's excited for the future and what we mean for it. "The only way you'll be free of them is if they're dead."

Jaemes claps his hands once. "I never thought I'd endure a war in my lifetime," he proclaims, far too cheerful for someone who may not survive it.

TEMBER

GUARDIAN REALM

As soon as we step through the portal, safe from the Uji's hostage proclamation, Eliza bends and retches all over the snow. A few Igna elves grunt their protest and clear disgust, but Jaemes quiets them with one stern look.

It must have been some wordless expression for the elves to wipe the disgust from their features so quickly. They back away immediately and return to their tasks.

Interesting. Obedient, even.

I lick my top lip and smirk. "Has a great elf taken a charge? Perhaps we shall make a true guardian of you yet. Maybe even the leader of your tribe, one day."

His lips twitch, hiding a sneer, and he flicks his head to Aiden and Eliza. "If two extra creatures mean a victory in war, then I'll make sure they live to fight in it."

Aiden bends his long, bulky frame and tends to Eliza, murmuring sweet tones in her ear. Strong hands gather her hair behind her shoulders while continuously flicking his eyes to the elves, keeping a close watch as they roam by. I imagine his preconceived notions of them and their prickly attitude has everything to do with the temporary hostage situation they'd endured. He's untrusting of them, just as most angels are.

I can't blame him. If I were under the clutches of a threatening tribe, I'd be wary of the entire species as well, even the ones providing reluctant solace.

Approaching Erma, we immediately search each other's face. Jaemes had first proclaimed war on the boat, and though we've never spoken it aloud, I've known this day would come for quite some time. It is inevitable, and many will fall, including those we love. I am not blindly believing I won't lose someone I care for. The battle on the

Death Realm was the first move, but an alliance seems to be forming on its own.

What deaths will come before this is over? Who around us will survive it? Am I to be counted among the odds? These questions have never halted my thoughts and pondered my future. Before, it was a battle of my own realm. This time, it's the all realms, and I have much more to lose.

Erma must be thinking the same as I. Her eyes soften, and she lifts a tender hand. Her frigid palm cups my cheek, and I place mine over the delicate back of her hand. I close my eyes, basking in this rare affection, the warmth in such a cold hand. The heart in my wrist flutters, the same beat as the butterflies flapping in my stomach.

Jaemes turns his back to the display, pretending he's unaware of this private moment between two forbidden lovers.

Erma leans in closer to me and drinks in my scent. "Do you understand now, Tember?" she whispers, pleading. "Do you understand my anger when you cut your wings? Do you understand it is your life I'm trying to save?"

At the mention of my wings, I flutter my black steeled feathers to prove how wrong she is. I may have severed my original set, but I have a formidable pair now. I have Kat to thank for this unimaginable gift which Erma herself wouldn't have been able to give.

She continues. "Can you comprehend the disaster of what would come if we mated?"

I tick my jaw against her palm and nod once into it. My skin slides easily along hers, and the touch sends a thrill of pleasure to every nerve. Gripping my fingers tighter around hers, I swallow the knowledge with difficulty. I refuse to let her go.

"I do understand." I swallow. "But what if this is how it's meant to be?"

A slow grin puffs her angelic cheeks, and impossibly, her eyes water. "The fee are meant to take mates, you know. The Divine created us this way to ensure we don't lose our way. They wanted us to have compassion, Tember. This is what I'm showing you. Every part of me has so much compassion for you that I can't bear to put you in harm's way. That thought alone hurts me more than knowing I'll never be able to touch you in the way that I want. To call you mine. To kiss you under the stars of my chamber's bed. To tell you I love you, every day, for the rest of time."

She pauses to let this sink in, and her throat works to her emotions. "But those of us who care more for what we have created know how reckless and irresponsible that would be. It would be favoritism. It would be jealousy and destruction. It would cause a rift in all those we've created, my sweet Tember."

She steps back and slides her hand from under mine, despite my grip. Wetness clouds my vision, blurring the falling flakes. These are unshed tears for what she has yet to say aloud and rings in my head before her lips have a chance to form her next admission.

"I will always love you, Tember," she discloses with such passion. "But I cannot subject you to your own death. I am done sitting on the sidelines while others do my work for me. We are a distraction to each other. It can be no more."

And with that, she briskly turns and walks away.

It takes some time for me to gather myself, to banish the pain carving deep gashes in the pit of my stomach, and for the surrounding noises to penetrate my hearing. But when she disappears from my sight, bending around the corner of a teepee, I'm pulled back to the matter at hand. Her words continue to echo in my thoughts, and I vow I'll discuss this with her again after she's had some time to collect herself. To see reason. To take me for what I am: the rest of her life. After the war, perhaps, when it's safe for her to love me as equally as I do her.

Jaemes, who heard the entire exchange, meets my eyes squarely. His head is tilted, and his body is positioned to have shielded the entire exchange between Erma and me from curious glances. He reaches forward, slow, as if to not scare me or be the wrath of anger, and gives my shoulders a firm squeeze.

"I see now," he says, a mild murmur. "When this is over, my friend…" He leaves his promise open-ended, and I curtly nod for his blessing. Perhaps Jaemes and I are more than we appear – friends who will forever be enemies - and for his own version of compassion, I'm grateful.

He's right. When this is over, I will pursue the matter at hand and cut down all those who object. I have an inkling Jaemes will be there right beside me, a looming tower of power to all those who protest a union between creator and creature.

Aiden gathers Eliza to her feet, and Jaemes drops his hand back to his side.

"That's impossible," Dyson's clear, shocked voice rings from behind me. Where he came from, I do not know. It's hard to hear an approaching body when this village is crawling with them.

I look over my shoulder and spot Dyson's awe-filled expression. A pang of sympathy overcomes me. Dyson's day has been full of revelations and life-altering situations. Perhaps I shall reserve my reservations about him until I have the full picture of the man himself. It is clear he's had a harder life than most, and I share this with him. My life has not been easy either.

"Aiden?" he questions, shuffling to his friend. His pack hangs behind, gathered around the fire and watching with intense curiosity.

"How?" Dyson wheezes as he passes me.

"It doesn't matter how," Aiden responds, his voice rumbling as he steadies Eliza to her feet with a firm grip to her elbow.

The three begin to speak in low murmurs and bowed heads, discussing the time they've spent apart. Three friends reuniting under one realm, each altered from the last time they were together. It is clear they care for one another by the soft eyes and gentle touches of reassurance. Dyson's head hangs with pure guilt bowing his spine, and Aiden bends to meet his gaze. It's touching, almost, to see a demon care for another. To see him feel for another, to console and accept. I don't know what the three of them have been through, but whatever it is warrants apologies and forgiveness.

175

Goosebumps riddle my skin with obvious envy. If only forgiveness would be delivered to me in such a way, I wouldn't have to fight so hard to receive it. I've never had what they have – an easy acceptance - except. . .

I look to Jaemes from the corner of my eye and wonder if I may be deceiving myself. He may not care for me the way Aiden, Eliza, and Dyson do, but he has his own way of showing he cares – continually saving my skin and banishing my self-doubt with mockery that uncovers my confidence.

"How is it everyone seems to know everyone?" Jaemes asks, a murmur in my ear when he catches me peering at him.

"These three survived a great wrath by Kheelan's hand," Erline proclaims.

Jaemes' muscles tense in obvious fright, and he growls his annoyance. "Must you fee sneak up on everyone?"

Erline smiles, small but tinged with humor, while she observes the three. "We're quite good at it."

I chuckle my agreement and angle my body to Erline. "Did Erma -"

Cutting me off mid-sentence, her smile fades quickly. "Discuss the new guest and possible war?"

The word 'war' is punctuated by a new roar of fire and fresh logs being plopped onto it. The flames are situated beside the teepee behind Aiden, Eliza, and Dyson. It was doused with collected fat from our earlier hunt's carcass, and an immediate bellow of smoke quickly reaches the first row of branches swaying above our heads.

I scoff. "Don't pretend you didn't know there would be a war."

She crosses her arms behind her back, content on watching Eliza hug Dyson with tightly shut eyes. "I thought there may be, but my hope was to deliver their assassination swiftly. That plan is long gone."

"Indeed," Jaemes mumbles, shifting weight to his other foot. "And the mascot's charge? Has she returned?"

I narrow my eyes at Jaemes whose lips twitch in amusement. I flap my wings once to prove my worth, stirring the snow gathered around our ankles.

"No," Erline responds, a hushed whisper. She doesn't find it funny, and immediately, I rein in my smile. "But I suspect Dyson will collect her soon."

Silence and heavy emotion settle in the area, too great for me to further endure for more than a few more minutes. It adjusts, this emptiness where I hold Erma in my heart, reminding me that I can't escape my own troubles for long.

"Do we have a new plan?" I ask, grasping the subject to banish my hurt.

Erline nods, her head bobbing as she considers her next words. She tucks a stray white hair behind her small ear. "I believe Thrice Born has his own agenda, and it'll surely work in our favor. I also believe Kat has her own as well, though she has yet to voice it or draw from it."

She already took a go at her own plans of war. She ventured to the Death Realm in hopes of ending the fee, but I keep these thoughts to myself. I don't think she went there to start a war. I think she went to save the people in it because she was the only one who could. Except, it didn't end that way . . .

I quickly flick my gaze to Erline. Her expression is grim with worry, and I chew on the inside of my lip with a bout of anxiety. "She's in trouble, isn't she?"

"The darkness is powerful, Tember." She draws in a shaky breath, a rare moment of her seemingly indestructible demeanor shifting to great concern. "It's seductive, and Kat needs to find a way to pull herself from it or make peace with it."

I swivel back to Dyson, the snow crackling as it compacts further beneath my shoes. "If she doesn't . . ." I gulp, my mouth suddenly thick with saliva. "We've lost the war before it has truly begun."

An elf, one who refuses to look Aiden or Eliza in the eyes, hands two fur blankets to them. Aiden gratefully accepts the offer and murmurs his thanks to the creature. Erline twitches a smile, also caught off guard by a caring demon.

"He's a fine creature, isn't he," she says, but neither Jaemes nor I respond.

Gracefully, Aiden slides the thickest one over Eliza's shoulders before he covers his own. Eliza shivers once underneath it then sighs with audible relief. Aiden, however, shows no signs of enjoying the warmth it provides.

"Indeed," she says. "Indeed."

It's unnerving how Kat holds our future in her hands. Doubt lingers in my thoughts, and I breathe deep, hoping to demolish the idea that she may be our greatest weakness instead of our best chance. She's the largest weapon we have, the only dragon and magic wielder, and with a reputation that frightens the fee. But even with these strengths, the opposing fee outnumber ours. Those odds are useless to consider, for even with Katriane as an aide, we may still lose.

"Perhaps…" I begin. "Perhaps we aren't looking at the full picture here."

"Oh?" Jaemes quips, his voice thick with sarcasm. "Finally admitting to ignorance, are we?"

I ignore his jab, my mind consumed with my train of thoughts.

Tilting my head, I observe the three before us with a different set of eyes and voice my findings aloud. "Look at what we have here." I sweep out an arm. "We have a demon, pulled from the void, with unimaginable abilities. He can clearly love - his power must be great." I nod at my own assessment, agreeing with myself, and continue. "We have a mate to King Death, himself. Don't tell me you can't smell her power from here. It tastes as the split moment before a bolt of lightning strikes the land." I look back to the wolf pack, anxiously waiting for their packmate to return while stealing glances into the forest for Kat's reappearance. "We have them, the elf tribes, and we have Kat's mate."

Erline smiles with hope. "Dyson could be the key to her own plight."

"Would you look at that," Jaemes whistles. "We have ourselves an army."

"And the angels?" Erline asks, quirking a brow at me. "Will they fight for the greater good?"

I consider this, chewing on the inside of my lip and tasting a bead of my own blood when I bite too hard. "Some will, but it'll take some convincing. After the discovery of Erma and me, I'm not completely convinced of their allegiances. You felt it; there was a distinct rift when we were there." It's why we sought safety with the elves.

"It's a provoked hornet's nest," Jaemes mumbles. Uncomfortable, he fumbles with the strap of his bow nestled over his shoulder.

I look to him, my eyebrows furrowed. "You know what hornets are?"

He huffs. "Why do you continue to think so little of me?"

"It's a talent," I say quickly. I turn my attention back to Erline before he can respond. "Where's the sandman?"

She flicks her thumb over her shoulder. "With the children, telling tales of his realm. They've taken a quick liking to him."

"Excellent. Come," I say to Jaemes, taking charge. He bristles to the order, mumbles something about the rules of being a mascot, and I allow myself a small grin of a temporary victory.

I should expect retaliation for it, I think to myself.

CHAPTER ELEVEN

KATRIANE DUPONT

GUARDIAN REALM

The chill from the land has long since creeped into my bones and numbed my toes despite the elves' warm furs and cloths. I don't know how long I've been here, contemplating what Fate had proclaimed.

Fate's absence is felt as clearly as the bite of frigid air. I don't know what he meant when he said he'd always be with me. What am I to him? Another pawn in a grand scheme?

I do, however, hold his last words close.

Find your future in your heart. Seek Hope with your eyes. Discover the greatness of Choice. And whatever you do, don't cling to Despair.

I wish more than anything I could go back in time and change what was, to bring Myla back or undo the curse I set into motion. She would still be a spirit in Erline's grip if it weren't for me. But this can't be fixed. What's done is done, and there's no sense in pondering it further. Fixing what was will never be my fate. No. My fate rests in the future of all that is around me, in the beating hearts I seem to hold in my hands, and in the realms who have no other savior. Clinging to Myla, to all the deaths, is my disparity. My future is with the living and my choice to be their hope.

But how do I quench the darkness?

A twig snaps behind me, muffled by blankets of snow. I quickly look over my shoulder, around the bark of the tree I rest upon, and into Dyson's kind, glowing green eyes.

He holds up his hands, a gesture of peace, while pausing in his wade through thick snow drifts. "Kat," he calls, a tone so warm my numb fingers tingle.

His gentle gaze travels away from my eyes to my middle. I follow it, wondering what holds him captive there, and lift my hand out in front of me. The flames are at the ready, tugging at the tips of my nail beds.

I close my fist and squeeze my eyes shut with obvious embarrassment, willing the fire to retreat.

Carefully and cautiously, he closes the distance between us, stopping when he stands before me. His body's heat radiates as his frame blocks the wind, and his scent replaces the crisp dry air with wafts of a delicious aroma only belonging to Dyson.

When he doesn't say anything, I slowly open my eyes and study the side of his face. Instead of returning my gaze or even announcing why he sought for me, he stares at the frozen lake just as I have for the past several hours.

182

The way his eyes shift to each object makes me wonder if he is searching for inner peace, too.

In a visual caress, I sweep the expanse of his ivory skin, taking advantage of his momentary distraction. He causes me pause, and his touch had extinguished my inner turmoil on the Death Realm. I want to know why.

His jaw curves at just the right angle, and his lashes touch the bridge of his brow, casting shadows across his cheeks whenever he blinks. They're impossibly long and thick, and though black, they glint like slick ice.

Just under his chin is a birthmark, shaped like a tiny teardrop but with more jagged edges. His jaw is encased in the beginnings of thick stubble. Around his neck is chafed skin where a rope had strangled the life from him during his first death.

His thick coat rustles as he tucks his hands into his pockets. I watch his chest expand and his nostrils flare while he breathes in every scent, cataloging it in a way every animal does when they arrive at a new place. The glow in his eyes brightens when he does, just for a moment, before returning to a normal wolf shifter hue.

The glow of a shifter's eyes doesn't happen often. Usually when their wolf is agitated or angered, the animal will make itself known like this. But he's not in any danger here. Not with me.

Even as I think those words, I doubt myself, and my lips pinch at my own limitations.

Despite being in an unfamiliar realm, he's so sure of what he is and his place in this world. Every part of him looks like it's connected to nature in a way I can't understand. In a way I'll never have. And yet, gazing at him is more peaceful than the landscape I've been trying to soak in, as though all my answers are with him.

"Why are you here?" I ask, slightly breathless. I hadn't realized I had been holding my breath, distracted by his close proximity, seemingly memorizing every curve and finding beauty in the flaws.

Dyson's scent calls to me with a new gust of wind, a content hum where the cold fingers wrap my heart.

Unknowingly, I almost step forward. My center of gravity shifts, and his hand snaps from his coat, gripping my elbow to steady me. The touch is hot, searing, and my stomach clenches. I swallow and double blink to the sensation.

It's not unnerving - this sensation. It's like aloe to a festering burn. A relief to a deep pain.

Slightly tilting his head, he considers me from the corners of his eyes. "Because you are," he says, his voice gruff, the wolf speaking for him.

I frown. "What's that supposed to mean?" I don't need a rescuer.

Then why haven't you backed away? Why drag him down with you? my conscience mocks.

With a shudder, he turns his body fully toward me and searches my face just as I had done to him. His bottom lip twitches, finding the right words, and I'm drawn to it.

Have his lips always been this dark of a red?

184

Slowly, his gloveless hand lifts from my elbow, and he trails the fingers across my jawline. I suck in a sharp breath, my teeth chilling. The direct touch sends a shiver over my frozen body, a wave of luscious warmth. A ghostly smile tugs at his lips this time before it fades with the weight of his next words.

"I see you, Katriane DuPont," he mumbles.

His breath fans my face. Mint. Clove. Freshly shaved pine. And something sweet like peaches. I inhale greedily, like a newborn's first breath, and sag against his hand.

He leans in closer. "I see you."

In the space between us, his eyes glow a brighter green, and I meet them to greet his wolf with a different expression than when he first arrived. My face relaxes, my eyes water, and my soul rejoices.

"And what do you see?" I whisper back, asking the wolf and the man.

"Wariness. Blame. Heartache," he says. "A search for who you truly are."

"Oh?" I ask, attempting to square my jaw with defiance and failing miserably.

Dyson leans forward, guided by his wolf. "Do not hide from me, Dragon. I *see* you."

As if called from within, the dragon side of me returns the glow of eyes, green meshing with orange in the small space between us.

185

"I hide to survive," I answer, raspy with my confession.

Dyson's lips curve in a small smile with triumph. "There you are," he coos, ignoring my words, for he knows they're as false as they sound. I hide because I'm scared, and he knows it.

His fingers lower from my jaw and brush their way to the nape of my neck. The touch is featherlike, and despite my newly warmed body, I shiver. It's enough to snap me from his spell.

"Why do you care?" I ask, turning my head away from his touch and denying myself what he offers - a white knight sent to slay the dark villain.

"I chose to save you, and freely so," I press on, wanting him to understand that having me in his life would only mean disaster. Nobody needs my problems tethered to them. "You owe me nothing, and I don't need you to return the favor. I can deal with this on my own."

Seek Hope with your eyes.

Dyson's hand hangs in the air, giving me a moment to collect myself. Carefully, he pulls his other hand from his coat pocket, cups my cheeks with gentle fingers, and tilts my face back to his. "I will always care for you, Katriane DuPont. You are more to me than the stars, than the moon that calls me to the trees." He swallows, emotions thick in his next words. "You mean more to me than what's left of my pathetic soul. You're my gravity. Don't tell me you don't feel the same."

He leans in, his nose almost touching mine. "How could I not *see* you for what you are?"

186

Does he truly see me? For the darkness that I've become?

"What does this mean?" I ask while his nose inches dangerously close to mine.

"I think you know exactly what this means," he mumbles, and my eyelids flutter once more as I greedily steal the scent of his voice.

Feelings like this shouldn't be immediate, but even I can't deny what's happening. My heart swells, and my mind clears with only future metaphorical visions of him. I allow myself to dream of what a brush of lips would feel like, of what years of being in his arms would mean and how I'd soak in every moment of it, afraid to close my eyes in case it might be the last. Even my darkness can't banish what's clearly and undeniably here. It basks like a sore body in warm waters.

I exhale his scent, and clarity returns when the wind steals it from me. My eyes widen, and I pull from his grasp. "No," I state, firm.

Ducking under his arms, I scoot around him but not before I catch the look - the one that tells me I had just shattered his heart into a million pieces. I had painfully denied him.

His eyes follow mine, and his wolf retreats inside him, wounded by my refusal.

"No," I shake my head and close my eyes tightly, banishing his crumpled face from my vision.

I hear the swish of his coat as he stuffs his hands in his pockets once more. He's silent. Too silent, wordlessly waiting until I collect myself, until I can courageously return his gaze and name him a liar for what he claims I am.

Guarded, he considers me under his long lashes. His expression is simple like a parent waiting for a child's tantrum to subside. I bristle.

"Yes," he decides, challenging me to deny him. His voice is deep, firm and sure, full of an emotion I've never had directed at me.

Shaking my head in small denials, I stare square back in his eyes, and for a long while, we look at each other. Each soul probes for a glimpse of the other. Each soul begs the other. I huff my breaths, fighting against it.

The wind rustles his dark hair. The snow swirls around him. The branches creak. He looks like the white Knight I see him as, and he feels all too right in what he claims we are.

But still, I deny it. "I can't be your mate," I whisper, the breeze carrying it to him. "I'm not a wolf. I'm only a witch. A dragon. I'm nobody except a pawn in a game I don't know how to play."

"You are my mate," he says in the same tone. "You are not, and will never be, my pawn."

Hearing the words uttered from his mouth snaps me, an internal switch that's been grasping for reality for hours. I hold up a hand to silence the rest of his declarations. "I'm not."

And with that, I leave the conversation, and Dyson, behind, turning on my heel and pushing through the snow. With every step away from him, my darkness returns, and I work to shove him and his lingering touch from my mind before I reach the village.

AIDEN VANDER

GUARDIAN REALM

Down the way, past a few teepees, I watch as a woman with short black hair crosses the forest line. She stomps into the village and disappears inside a hut with a snap to the fur door. I recognize her from the Death Realm as the one who turned into a dragon. Fear wafts from her in waves, but it is not the village who she fears. It is herself.

My goal has been to seek out this woman, but something tells me she's as much of a slave as I am to Corbin. I'll have to approach her at a different time because I have no doubt she will gain the upper hand as soon as she sorts herself out. Then, and only then, can she be a true asset to my plans if I can convince her to be.

In front of me, a female elf clears her throat to gain my attention to the task at hand. I murmur my apology and take what she offers when she hands me a chunk of charred meat. Her shocked look at the fluent elvish accurately flicking from my tongue doesn't go unnoticed.

Just as the others, this elf doesn't want us here, and her sneer is hard to miss despite my obvious gratitude. None of them do. This much is clear by the stares like needles sliding through each vertebrae of my spine.

Eliza watches them with extreme curiosity akin to the study of a true scientist. Since Dyson dived into the trees and left us to our own devices, she and I have immersed ourselves in the village atmosphere in hopes of distracting ourselves from the future. We both know I'll be leaving soon, and it hangs in the air between us, clogging all the words we want to share with each other but allowing the interference not to.

We strode down each snow beaten path, hand in hand. Eliza had bent down to giggling children and tugged on the pointed ear of the littlest one. Their mothers weren't happy about it, but they allowed it nonetheless. We even watched warriors leave on their matuas, a mission clearly in mind. During all this, we never once discussed anything of importance.

Despite the lack of exchange, she hovered, afraid I'd disappear at any second without a single goodbye. And I let her because I, too, felt the same.

I clear my thoughts, wondering what I can say to ease her rigid form, but there are too many prying eyes and just as many listeners. As soon as I know she's safe and settled, I'll leave and make sure it stays that way. She is my only priority. My only reason for living and the only reason I've been semi-accepted here.

After Eliza is gifted her portion, we slowly head to the teepee Erma had dubbed ours, passing the sandman along the way. He's been chucking questions to the shifters since Dyson left, consuming their focus so they don't feel obligated to go after him. Packs seem to be funny that way, hovering just as Eliza and I are doing with each other.

It's a dark world, a dark time, we find ourselves in, and we fear that each exchange with the ones we love will be our last. We can't leave the other for fear we will never see them again, for worry that something will happen to them if we aren't there to stand in harm's way.

These are my worries as well, and it nearly brings me to my knees each time it rises in my thoughts.

I lift the teepee fur door, allowing Eliza to duck inside. Before I follow her through, I watch Dyson shuffle back into the village, his head hung with shame. Whatever happened in the woods with Kat, he isn't too proud of. He has his own demons to battle, and unfortunately, being refused is a mental war he'll have to win himself.

He lifts his eyes, feeling my gaze. The worry lines are prominent on his face, and he doesn't bother to hide them behind a false grin. I recognize the look - that feeling. I had felt it the first time I saw Eliza in her dreams. It's the knowledge he'll never truly have what he seeks, not while they're emotionally worlds apart. The dragon has to accept herself for who she is, as do I. I sympathize with her more than I do with Dyson.

He loves the dragon, but she doesn't love him.

I nod to him once, a reassurance which feels fake even to myself. But he returns it solemnly, and then his pack and the sandman swarm, beating him with questions like a mob of curious teenagers.

Ducking inside, I find Eliza already seated pretzel style and biting into her first chunk of meat. Hers appears less charred than mine, and I wonder if that's on purpose. Eliza's kind soul is palpable to even those who don't feed from emotion.

I stand like a fool for some time, my own meat heavy in my hands, before she swallows and lifts her eyes to mine. Instead of warm attention, it's filled with dread and a slightly trembling lip. She worries for me as much as I do for her.

"Are you going to sit?" she asks me tentatively. "Or are you finally going to ask the question that's been on the tip of your tongue since we came to this realm?"

My lips curve at the edges, adoring her forwardness. The woman is perceptive.

I sit next to her, kick out my feet, and lay on my side along the fur carpet. Running my tongue over my top teeth, I hand her my food.

She frowns. "Aren't you hungry?"

"This isn't what I eat," I mumble.

Dawning widens her eyes, and heat floods her cheeks, rosy in the center and dusty pale pink around the edges. Her attitude is tentative toward me like she's conversing with a stranger. I don't like it and wish for a moment we could go back to the way things used to be: Easy.

"So," she says, taking another bite. "What is it?"

I lift an eyebrow. "The meat?"

She scowls, and I find the chastising expression adorable. "No. What's on your mind?"

I raise the other eyebrow. "Why don't you tell me?"

Stopping mid-chew, she observes me with frigid muscles firming her cheeks.

"Really, Eliza." I shift my elbow underneath me for a more favorable position. "Are you going to tell me you can't read my emotions as easily as I can read yours?"

"No." She swallows, and I watch her throat constrict. "But I won't pry. I want you to tell me on your own."

She peers quickly at the carpet, my absent response dampening her normally forward attitude. I allow her to collect her thoughts, to give her a moment without me speaking.

"I still can't believe they're gone," she sobs, speaking of our mothers.

Dyson had told us as much, the burden as great as when he murdered me. It had been a bigger blow to Eliza, knowing without doubt she'll never see her mother again. The void is an ugly place, a place which strips you of everything you are. Their fate is there now, and there's nothing we can do about it.

"I should have saved them," she mumbles frostily. "I *could have* saved them."

I lean forward and grab her hand, hoping to give her the support she needs. I've never been good at consoling. "They gave their lives for the others, for us, knowing it was for the greater good."

"I know," she agrees, refusing to meet my eyes.

"Do you blame me? For taking you away instead of saving them?"

She shakes her head. "No, of course not."

I wait, and finally, a tear streams down her still rosy cheek, trailing all her grief in one drop. She meets my firm stare, and I study her, watching her try to battle her inner sorrows.

The question she's been waiting for me to ask fumbles from my lips as though I'm unable to hold my doubts in any longer. "Do you fear me?"

"No." Eliza's answer is absolute yet full of everything she isn't saying. How she feels about me. How she can't breathe when I'm not near. The secrets of her own. The self-doubt, thick in her voice. The fear of my well-being against her troubled lips.

Reaching automatically, I run the pad of my thumb along her plump bottom lip, soothing them. I would die for this woman. I *have* died for this woman, and yet, she's stronger than I give her credit for. She's lost me twice, and still, she refuses to give up on us.

"I don't deserve you," I admit.

I lean forward and brush my lips against hers. It's feather-light, different than it was before. She shakily sighs, the air tickling my tongue as I deepen the kiss.

"Are you still mine, Eliza?" I ask in desperate hope to hear what I desire most.

"I'll always be yours," she whispers, her lips playing against mine in perfect harmony.

A pang rocks inside my chest, one I wasn't expecting. I gasp at the pleasure of it. It's love, her love, something I thought I'd never feel again. Not to this magnitude.

Gathering myself to my knees, I reach and blindly grasp her food. Carefully, I try to set it aside, but it drops with a thud to the fur anyway. I lean into the kiss, towering over her. A sense of euphoria washes over me, sending my unease running for the hills.

Her eyelashes tickle my heated cheeks, and I open my eyes, my gaze meeting hers. Her magic swirls, uncontained, and I smell it with a deep inhale, mixing with her original scent I've so longed for. Blue electric bolts meet my molten ones, and she says words I've never heard her say.

"I love you."

And I believe her, pushing her back into the fur, nestling her spine against its soft strands.

I stare down at her, and her eyes plead with mine to return the words.

"You're everything a demon shouldn't have," I mumble, my attention drifting to her wet cheeks. Cradling her head with both hands, I brush my thumbs against the wetness and then bend to murmur in her ear. "You're everything I shouldn't have, and the one thing I cannot resist. You are my greatest love."

I work my lips down her jaw with slow pecks, feeling her breaths heavy from deep within her chest. I kiss my way to the tip of her chin, featherlike and tickling. I still, and she whimpers her displeasure.

"If you think love is one-sided in this relationship, you're sorely mistaken. My life is yours, Eliza."

Gripping her knees, I spread them wide and settle myself between them. My shirt rides up my abdomen, and the warmth which radiates from her is more delicious than any meal of terror.

I grind against her, once, twice, unable to control the sensation. She moans, and I capture the sound. Then, I capture her.

Some time later, we lay side by side, our naked bodies bright despite the lack of light. The fire in the middle has eaten its way through the one log available and now glows in a silhouette of what once was.

It's dark inside the teepee we've claimed as our own. I have no idea how long we've been here, staring at one another, our souls speaking instead of our voices. There are not enough words in any dictionary to describe what I feel anyway.

I lift my hand and brush her swollen, chapping lips.

"What is it?" I ask when her eyebrows dip slightly.

She shakes her head, pulling my finger from it. "Everything is different this time."

Affectionately, I seize her hand, bring it to my face, and kiss the soft flesh of her palm. I am different. We are different - heated, intertwined with a barely contained magic. We had been quiet, my mouth muffling her sounds of pleasure with each stroke, each passionate slow yet exhilarating thrust. She had writhed beneath, her sparking fingers gripping my shoulders. My shoulders tingle at the reminder.

"It was different," I whisper.

Eliza's thin red brows deepen. "But?"

"But," I nod, kissing her hand once more. "Despite our feelings, both physical and emotional, I must leave soon."

She closes her eyes, her emotional pain a great deal. "I know."

"Eliza," I call to her. "I won't rest until he's dead. The bond will be broken, and I will truly have you as my own."

She nods.

I open my mouth for more words of reassurance but stop short when the village outside quiets. Within seconds, the songs and the chatter disappear entirely, a hush falling over the village.

Eliza frowns, and a single scream echoes through the village, filtering into our tent as though it seeps through the skin walls. More quickly follow. She immediately pulls herself to a sitting position and her eyes glaze over, a brilliant hue of blue.

"Eliza?" I sit up and grip her shoulders, turning her top half to me. She doesn't respond, and I panic. Is Kheelan calling back his mate?

Her head bobs and her red locks rock freely when I shake her. "Eliza! What is it?"

More screams – women, men, children – come from the village, and goosebumps raise the hair on my arms. My demonic instincts feed from the obvious fear, my pores lapping the thick potent emotion.

"They're here," she says.

CHAPTER TWELVE

DYSON COLEMAN

GUARDIAN REALM

Flint's laugh quickly fades when silence washes over the village. His jokes about the sex going on in the other teepee had grown tiresome, and even Bre, who usually laughs at whatever pops from his mouth, quickly became annoyed.

The teepee we're in is large enough so that we can each stretch over the fur and peacefully sleep without touching the other. We hadn't been able to sleep though, too busy catching up on everything I've missed.

Shaking off the immediate, unnerving silence, I open my mouth to reminisce another memory when a wave of unease pricks at my wolf.

Danger, my wolf's growl warns.

A scream vibrates the teepee walls.

A boom shakes the ground.

Hoofbeats run past, hurried, a foreboding thunder which echoes the frantic patter of my pulse.

Evo quickly stands, his gaze moving to the teepee door, then slowly, he swivels back to me. My mouth dries when his eyes harden. As Alpha, he's seen many a battle, and his instincts when they arise are never wrong. He's preparing for a fight we have yet to understand.

Again, I open my mouth, prepared to say it's probably the elves and their weird traditional behaviors, when more hollers and blood-curdling screams thieve the sentence from my lips.

We jump to our feet, our bodies vibrating with the shift to wolf, and our eyes glow brighter than the small fire crackling in the middle. The walls brighten under the green and banish the remaining shadows. The snowflakes which fall from the opening at the top look like sparkles among the coloring shades, more illuminated than before.

The tent door pushes open, and Bre visibly jumps, emitting her own scream. Her hand flies to her mouth to hush the sound when she realizes it's only Eliza and Aiden.

Aiden yanks a shirt over his face, ruffling his already tousled hair, and covers an impressive set of abs while Eliza's bright blue eyes shift electric bolts inside them.

"What the hell is going on?" I bark.

"The village is under attack," Eliza yells over the ever-growing noise. I can barely hear myself think.

"Under attack?" Kenna asks in utter disbelief. "But this is the Guardian Realm! Who in their right mind would attack a realm full of warriors?"

Aiden's eyes change to an impossibility, lava dribbling down the orbs inside until it covers them entirely. Sulfur emits from him during the sudden change and stings my nose.

Kenna recoils with a "Sweet baby Jesus," whispering across her lips. "It's the devil in disguise."

"The angels are rebelling," Aiden answers, his voice deep and almost unintelligible while completely ignoring Kenna's prejudices.

She's right, though. It does look like a devil has a leash on Aiden's soul, and maybe it does. And maybe it's a good thing, at least in this moment. If the village is under attack, a little evil is needed.

"The fee have made their first move," I say, and Aiden nods tersely.

I slip off my clothes in a hurry, fumbling with my arms inside the holes. Eliza shifts her gaze from us to the wall, ever the modest lady.

"Where's Sandy?" I ask, breathy, while unzipping my pants.

Aiden tilts his head, an odd appearance with his molten eyes. "The sandman? Herding the children." As if he could see him, he swivels his head back to the door.

Sandmen don't sleep. When it was time for us to retire, he stayed by the fire deep in thought. The children must have found him at some point and dragged him back to their games. Bedtimes don't seem to be a thing here.

I breathe a shaky sigh of relief. Tugging down my underwear as quickly as I can, I almost tip over in my haste. "What's the plan?"

His lava eyes tighten when they meet mine. "There isn't one."

He manages to get the words out before my bones begin to crack and reshape. The sensation is like no other, a tingle where there should be pain, a stretch to stiff muscles.

"And Kat?" I manage to ask before my nose and lips point with a snout.

In answer, the unmistakable sound of a dragon roar rumbles the ground beneath our paws, and another boom quickly follows. Brenna's wolf yips as she bristles, and in return, Flint nips her flank.

Shit, I think to myself. Leave it to Katriane DuPont to take the entire matter into her own hands. When will she learn that she doesn't need to be the savior of every situation?

Aiden peers straight into my eyes, his expression hard as a rock. "Go," he demands.

The pack barrels through the door before I do, pushing past Aiden and Eliza and kicking snow back inside. I wrestle control with my wolf like a cowboy fiercely grabbing at the reins to anchor an unruly horse, to bring him to heel from doing something irrational. If I let him, he'd try to take on the entire fleet of enemy in a mad dash to save his mate who most likely doesn't need saving. He paces in place, stamping his paws and baring his teeth to me.

Once I have him seeing things my way, although in complete faithlessness, he snorts, his body rigid for command. I've seen shifters with a rogue wolf. Flint had suffered from such a thing, and it was difficult to watch. I won't let mine become one. Disaster can happen without a clear head, and more harm than good can come about.

"Dyson," Eliza yells to me. "Go!"

My wolf snaps his jaws, and against my better judgment, I allow him from the safety of this structure when I'd rather bench the beast instead. He skids in his tracks to a full stop, and hope drains from him quicker than it does me at the sight before our eyes.

TEMBER

GUARDIAN REALM

The wind and enemy give chase with each swoop through the village territory, having taken flight as soon as the first arrow caught light to my neighboring teepee. It pushes against my feathers, a steady resistance.

My black wings glitter reflections of electricity zipping past me, and I tuck and roll in the air, swaying left and right to avoid them while dodging each protruding tree limb that reaches higher than the others. The reflection of my frost-tipped wings is a beacon to the enemy like a lighthouse at the edge of a foggy sea. Compared to their white, I stand out with stark contrast.

I dip to the forest for a moment of cover, narrowly missing an arrow to my chest. Jaemes and his matua are leading a group of warriors on the ground below – mostly consisting of his brothers whom I was introduced to before I retired to my teepee for some peace.

Their animals' large, six-legged bodies are intimidating as they canter on. I eye them for a split second, the branches my cover, and watch the beasts jump over bodies, friend and foe, already broken and dead. Some are bright embers, having caught the flames of Kat's fire.

Fallen angels dive into the trees after me. I grit my teeth and angle my wings to soar up and perch myself on a sturdy branch.

Ire already within my steady grip, I aim, exhale, and release. It whistles as it cuts through the wind. Then, a boom shakes the forest when it finds its target. The fallen angel's wings flutter on descent before the body thuds to the ground directly in Jaemes' path. His matua rears and screeches, its smoky tail whipping in obvious displeasure.

As it rears, it shuffles its back legs, angles its body, and provides Jaemes with the perfect opportunity to glance my direction. His face transforms from curiosity to edgy, seemingly unaffected by his matua's aggression. We catch each other's gaze, but I'm forced to look away. I aim again, striking my next target.

There are too many of them. My fingers release as quickly as they can but to no avail. The breath hitches in my chest just before I'm overcome, but Jaemes' group comes to my aid. Their own arrows release in a wave, hitting their targets as one. The dead fall faster than the snow.

I grip the bark of the tree and flex my stiff fingers. The fog of my breath lingers in front of my face. I look down and nod my thanks to Jaemes then drop from the branch. Midway down, I flap my wings once to slow my fall. Snow lifts from the ground, disturbed by the gale of my feathers, and swirls around the elf warriors.

Jaemes growls as he bats at the flakes. "Tember!" he yells at me.

"What?" I mock, exhilarated. "Fallen angels you can handle, but tiny frozen water you cannot?"

The warriors turn their heads to each other, clearly confused by it. Mitus had put his youngest in charge of this group. They're uncomfortable with my presence and the way Jaemes and I speak to one another. Jaemes ignores their obvious discomfort, bares his teeth, and hisses at me like a feline. The expression is humorously despicable, the horns haloing his head and his long, pointed ears tipped along his scalp.

"Ah," I coo, and a sly smile spreads across my face. "The little kitten doesn't have fangs yet."

He hides his smile well, but I can see the twinkling laughter in his eyes. Does he find glee in my adrenaline rush? It is quite easy to banter when war pumps in my veins.

"How about a little wager then, ugly duckling?" he begins. "That is the story, is it not? The outcast among the flock?"

I narrow my eyes suspiciously and bristle against this new 'endearment'. "Yes," I say, drawing out the word.

"Excellent." He nods mischievously. "Whoever kills the most of Tember's flock, and this includes you," he says, pointedly beaming at me, "will have no hunting duties for a week."

"We're not keeping score, Jaemes," I protest and switch Ire to my other hand. "You can't bet on lives! We need to find Erma and protect her."

He opens his mouth to retaliate but snaps it shut. His matua whips around without obvious command, and its tail of snaking smoke disappears in a gust of snow.

"Get ready," Jaemes rumbles to the warriors and myself.

Angels, running on the ground, stampede our way. Their halos glisten from this distance, bouncing off the trees' dark trunks while illuminating the grooves of bark. They choose land instead of flight, *a wise move*. A dragon is in the sky, and this group knows she's impossible to tangle with. Plus, the cover of the trees makes it difficult for an air assault, which is why we pushed them from the village's sparser trees as soon as we could.

Smiling grimly, I lift Ire and wait for the first line of angels to reach shooting distance. They grow nearer, and the weight of their stomping vibrates my calves.

Recognition clicks when the face of one of Jax's friends is the first I spot. "Dena," I murmur.

It's unnerving, almost heartbreaking, knowing I'll soon end a life of someone I've once talked to. I swallow my guilt as a bolt of lightning brightens my bow, awaiting release despite my reveries. Jaemes beats me to it, taking advantage of my hesitation. The swift arrow pushes into Dena's chest, and her body slams into the angels behind her.

"One," Jaemes counts, shouting to the group. Laughter rings among the warriors. I don't share in this victory. My heart serenades my sorrow.

I shake my head, clearing my thoughts and emotions before they render me useless, and vow to grieve for the losses after this is over. All the losses that will come by my hand or another's.

"A pack of heathens," I mumble under my breath and sling my bolt at another.

It won't be long before we mesh with the foe, and there aren't enough warriors here to pick them off before they reach us. A hand to hand fight is inevitable. They run quicker than I imagined they would, smartly using their wings to gain speed.

I leap into the air, swinging Ire's long tip. The wood smacks against the side of the head of an angel. Stunned and bloodied, he staggers, his eyes unfocused like he's seeing everything and nothing at once. I grab his red hair at the roots and twist his neck. The spine cracks. It doesn't kill him. No, it won't kill him. The only thing that will kill the betrayers is. . .

Before he slumps to the ground, I twirl and aim. My bolt zings in harmony with the string's vibrations, striking the angel's wrist. This is the deadly blow. This is what will truly kill them, kill us, kill me. The heart of an angel is in the wrist.

Ironically, the beat at our sleeve is supposed to remind us we have an obligation. These angels have forgotten compassion. It burns my gut, their betrayal, their need for revenge. Their insistence on blood over a matter of a love they don't understand. My nostrils flare as I watch the life leave the angel's eyes, and sympathy sheds from my skin.

A wolf barrels past, a blur of fur, and the rest of the pack quickly after.

"Aim for the right wrist!" I shout.

Upon my instruction, the pack changes their approach of attack. They move as one, as though they're one body - one mind. Clamping the necks of angels, they use their weight to take them to the ground. Throats are shredded, blood sprays, and then their teeth clamp their wrists.

A stream of fire engulfs neighboring trees at the back end of the opposing group, followed by shrieks and bodies raining from the sky. Branches break as flaming angels hit each one on their way down.

I smile as Kat's dragon flies over the tree branches above me, her size impressive. The angels who are still in the sky attempt to take her down. Bolts sore after her. She spins her body, tucking her wings to miss them before she's completely out of my sight.

My heart thuds in fear. *She's fine,* I reassure myself, killing another angel with emotional disconnect. I break her wrist, the bone severing the heart and slicing through skin. Expanding my wings, I turn abruptly and sever another's head using my sharp feathers. Both angels drop at my feet at the same time.

She's fine, I think again, but this time it rings completely false to my own conscience. I grit my teeth and grip Ire tighter. My wings beat once, twice, and then I'm weaving between branches. The fresher air greets my skin once above the canopies, sending a sliver of freedom, of pure, undiluted delight through my chest. Until I get a look at what we're really dealing with.

Several angels pepper the sky, an impressive number still traveling this direction. They're originating from the Angel's ground off in the distance. I'm sure of it. My delight evaporates with a gust of breath passing my lips like I've been punched in the gut by shock alone.

The Angel's Ground has been overtaken by the fallen. Can I blame them? No. We all but abandoned it at the first hint of hostility, and something was bound to happen in our absence. Still, this is a well conducted attack, and something of this magnitude needs a leader. This leaves one question: who's the mastermind, the General, behind this? Who convinced this many angels to rival against us? I think I already know the answer to that.

Hovering, I harden my determination and then take immediate action. I pick off the angels in flight, one by one.

Kat is up ahead, dealing with her own hoard of white wings. Each one is eventually consumed by a stream of fire. A sure death wish, I imagine. They're not in their right minds, attacking a creature they can't win against. Even their arrows fail to penetrate her scales.

She roars, deafening, the sound waves crashing into my chest.

To catch up with her, I ride a stream of strong wind. As I travel, another arrow releases from my bow, then another, then another. I grab the wrist of an angel passing by who is swooping toward the village. There are children huddled in the safety of the teepees, and our purpose is to keep those who can't defend themselves safe. No enemy is meant to reach the village - a simple order by Erma and Mitus.

I whip the angel's body underneath mine, wrap my legs around her torso, and drive a bolt into her arm before she notices I'm her enemy.

ELIZA PLAATS

GUARDIAN REALM

Death and fire's smoke taint the air. With all the battling bodies blocking the wind, there's nothing to sweep away the stinging smell. I breathe through my mouth, desperate for fresh air. My huffing lungs cry for untainted oxygen, and the chill burns my teeth with quick inhales.

The enemy was driven out once, but it hasn't taken long for them to find a way back in. Teepees are on fire.

Children scream. Women rush to aid their young. Men drive arrows into chests.

Aiden's skin almost glimmers, a black substance rippling beneath his skin. It's as though he's fighting to hold on to his own body, to keep the demon in check.

He is *the demon*, I remind myself. A shiver trembles up my arms and settles in my tight chest.

This reminder is driven home when he punches his way into an angel's gut, his hand going all the way through the body cavity. I can hear the crunch of spine from where I stand and the slick slosh of organs. Dumbfounded, and unsure how to help without tipping Aiden over the edge, I gulp the bile burning the back of my tongue.

I've never been squeamish to injury, but I've also never witnessed an injury occur. Not in this manner and certainly not on this realm. I was only the one who stitched them back together again inside the four walls of a hospital's surgical room. The sharp light, which made the body seem less gory despite excessive blood loss, helped to dislodge my thoughts about a life's vitality under my trained hands. There, it was a job and easier to focus on patching them back together. Here, this is war, and death isn't prejudice. It comes for us all, no matter the side you fall on.

The angel looks to him, eyes wide. His once ferocious features are now fearful. Aiden feeds from it. I can see the hues and shimmers transferring to the predator.

Prominent crease lines above the angel's blond eyebrows stand out within his shadowed face, shrouding the finer details. The bright yellow halo beaming above his shaved head shines against the smooth skin and sluggishly pulses to a retreating heartbeat.

Without a second thought, Aiden grabs his wrist and breaks it in half. It crunches like a thick stick bent in two. A shuttered breath racks my joints. My hands clench in sympathetic-pain while I watch in horror.

The light leaves the angel's eyes, and the halo disappears in on itself.

I lift my head to the grey puffy clouds spitting snow and use their chill to force the vomit back into my stomach. The clouds' shrewd edges are lined with an orange hue. It's reflected by streams of fire the dragon makes as it flies by, attacking those in the sky. I observe flakes as they come into view and notice they mesh with sprinkles of bright red. Both substances pepper my cheeks, one cold and the other ash-like. At first, I think it's a trick of the mind, the orange tinged clouds the cause. Or perhaps, ashes of body and feather. With the guardian's different make, possibly an unknown chemical substance entirely, I can easily hypothesize why their ash is red instead of grey. Plus, the flames aren't traditional either, coming from a dragon and all.

Both float to the ground, and I watch as some gather inside a sticky substance – a black puddle - the blood of dead angels surrounding Aiden. They're bodies are skewed at nauseating angles, their wounds feeding the puddle. I lick my lips upon examination, my theory quickly probable.

I hold out my hand, allowing Aiden to keep the enemies from me for the moment. Not that I have a choice. I've been ordered to do nothing and let them protect me.

212

Having been told using my magic could call Kheelan to my whereabouts, I reluctantly obliged.

The tiny red specks capture in my palm while the snow quickly melts against the warmth of my skin. I lean forward, watching, and examine the substance with a medical eye.

Gathering a pinch with my other hand, I rub it together, and it smears like chalk. "Interesting," I whisper to myself.

I don't have time to draw a more definitive conclusion, however. The enemy angels surround the love of my life, and his roar brings me to the present.

Panic patterns my heart first, a moment of tense muscles. But an internal wave soothes them, a rush of power which calms my fear. It's automatic, uncontrollable.

Heat floods my chapped cheeks. My vision focuses. Blood rushes my ears. Every nerve pricks like my limbs are awaking from sleep. And then, a wave of intense adrenaline. Anger - white hot and utterly consuming - dries the saliva pocketed in my cheeks. The smell of electricity tickles my nose and zaps the lymph nodes inside.

An angel punches Aiden's jaw. Aiden's head whips to the side. He swings back, connects, and then another enemy jabs his thigh. Driven to one knee, Aiden grunts.

No, I scream in my head.

Hand still open, a bolt of bright blue tamed lightning slithers sporadically across the thin lines of my palm. I close my fingers around the bolt, lift my arm up and over my head, and throw it forward, a lashing whip that extends across the distance. It latches around the nearest angel and curls around her ankles. Once firmly gripped, I yank with all my strength and hurtle the angel over the flaming teepee tops. Her cries of surprise are cut off when a thud shakes the ground, her body hitting a tree trunk.

Again and again I do the same with the others, my bolting whip faster each time, until Aiden's surrounding enemies are manageable.

Heavy huffs of breath whistle through my nostrils and my chest heaves with the exertion. I look to my hands in amazement, twisting them this way and that, while leaving Aiden to his own devices. I swallow with an effort to quench my dry throat and stiffen as a prickling sensation raises the hairs at my nape. It's greasy, this feeling, like oil sloping down a paved driveway. I turn, slow, knowing who's standing there. And knowing why. I used his power, called it to me, in fact. Of course he would come. He'd been waiting for it.

My eyes meet the hems of black robes and travel up the length. I stare squarely into Kheelan's pinched eyes which mischievously glint fire's light. The gaze we share immediately sucks away my freewill, a compulsion of sorts, and renders me completely hostage. Blood roars in my ears, and time feels sluggish under it.

His lips move. Though I can't hear what he's saying, I can read my name slowly crossing his lips. The tip of his tongue touches his top teeth on the second syllable. A shiver trembles my body, waiting for his command.

The black orbs of his eyes glint again, and I'm sucked into their pits. My feet move of their own accord, each footfall measured, perfect in distance.

A wide, wicked smile extends his face, and when I'm mere feet from him, a grey ball of fur leaps in the air from my left. Before contact, Kheelan disappears in a wisp of smoke. It's almost as though he was never truly there in the first place, like a mirage.

My limbs break free from his invisible trance, and I plant both feet back in the snow. The wolf spins, snarling and searching for Kheelan.

"Dyson," I whisper, my voice harsh and parched.

The wolf whips his head to me, ears pinned. He approaches, crouched, a bloody paw smearing the white snow, and sniffs the air. A feral growl rumbles his massive chest when he scents Kheelan's power wafting from my charged hands.

For a moment, his ears flick forward, and his eyes look past my right hip. The growl deepens, and he stalks forward low to the ground.

"No," I gush, breathy, to the wolf. "Dyson, please!"

Fear spikes the rapid rate of my heart, pricking each chamber, and I scream when he lunges. I duck and cover my head. The grey wolf soars over me. A paw's claw catches my hair and rips a lock from my scalp. I grunt in pain and clutch my head. A thump vibrates the soles of my shoes, and I pivot in my bent position. Dyson's sharp teeth sink into the flesh of the enemy.

CHAPTER THIRTEEN

DYSON COLEMAN

GUARDIAN REALM

"Where is she?" I ask, my voice booming through the devastated village. A growl tinges each word.

I slip my shirt over my head and the collar smears a glob of black blood down my cheek. My stomping is muffled by packed snow while I approach Erma, Erline, Aiden, and Tember. They're huddled at the end of the village where the last attacking angel was killed moments before.

I had quickly shifted back and dressed when the fight ended, knowing mine is only just beginning. Fear coils in my gut. Fear for my mate who I have yet to see.

Tember lifts her head from their circle and watches on with a deep frown. She turns toward me, crosses her arms, and widens her stance, preparing to fend me off against her lover. I sneer at her protective display. The angel can't hide her affections from me. It's plain as day, and I'll call her out if I must to get what I want.

"Where is she?" I yell again, more frantic this time.

"Dyson," Evo commands, hot on my heels. His wider frame plods, crunching the snow, quite the opposite of mine. But his alpha command holds no weight over me anymore.

Tember's chest puffs as she takes an extensive breath. She unfurls a hand from her middle to rub the back of her neck. When I stand before her, she surveys the destruction, her face crumpling with stress-etched eyes, anything to keep from meeting my gaze.

"She headed into the woods," Tember divulges with weighted emotion. She finally shifts her eyes toward mine. "I saw her land in them."

I turn on my heel, an easy feat in the slick, blemished snow. When she grabs me by the arm, I snarl, a deep sound I've rarely made before today.

Mates can change a wolf, even mates who want nothing to do with the other. This thought alone twists my gut further, and my growl muffles with the pain it causes.

"Dyson, listen to me," she begins with urgency, and her call beckons attention from Aiden and Eliza down the well-beaten path. "She's not herself."

"She's my mate!"

Tember opens her mouth to say something else, but Evo shakes his head at her, trying and failing to be subtle. She licks her bottom lip and tries again. "I cannot protect her. Not anymore. She's far beyond my capabilities."

I swallow thickly, and my aching fingers and biting nails unfurl from my palms. I didn't even realize I had fisted them, not until her words extinguished my hatred. She didn't exactly say it, but I can read between the lines. Kat's mind is gone, and mine instantly finds someone to blame.

"Did you know?" I pin a glare to Erline behind Tember, watching on distractedly. When she realizes I'm speaking to her, she tilts her chin up defiantly and slips her ego back in place with a straighter spine.

"Did you know Kheelan was here?" I add.

A frown settles over her features as she thinks of how to respond, but her silence gives me the answer to my question. I make a disgusted sound at the back of my throat. Turning once more, I push off to the woods at a jog.

Someone has to retrieve Kat, and I know this lot won't lift a finger to do it. They're frightened of her.

"Come up with a fucking plan," I shout over my shoulder. Sandy passes me at this moment, children dragging him along by his large hands, and he lifts a chiding eyebrow to me, gesturing with his head to the children's sensitive ears. It's not like they understand me anyway.

"I'll go wrangle my beast," I add quieter to myself.

I slow to a walk once I hit the trees. I don't know how far in she is, but I also don't want to rush to her side. That could have the opposite effect of what I want.

218

The hike through the trees is quite a distance. As I pass dead bodies, I close the eyes of a few and grip the shoulders of the ones I knew. The village will be along for them shortly, I'm sure, but I can't pass them with a blind eye. They deserve compassion for their sacrifice.

My muscles cramp from overuse, and I limp despite my best efforts to soothe the knots. Shivers rack my body and chatter my teeth, my coat forgotten at the village. I eventually dismiss the discomfort, distracting myself with the hunt instead, with the pull to my mate. The acrid aroma of burning wood doesn't obscure her sweet scent. It left an invisible trail lingering in the brisk wind, and after a while, I spot her and stalk as stealthily as I can.

I'm as close as I dare though, one hand pressed firmly to a tree's rough trunk, steadying my wobbling legs.

She stands on all four scaled limbs, her head bowed, and her chest heaves excessively. She's still, statue-like, almost as though every ounce of humanity is gone, except the twitch at the tip of her tail. It curls and uncurls soothingly like a content cat.

Flexing my jaw, I gingerly push off the trunk and quiet my limping by moving at a slower pace.

"Kat?" I quietly call when I'm inches from her tail. I watch the sleek glint of her scales, each outlined with the underlying fire beneath the surface. The snow comes to a final rest along them and instantly melts and sizzles.

She doesn't respond, her dragon lost in deep thought. Or perhaps her mind is gone entirely. I don't know which, but I can't do nothing. I *won't* do nothing.

My nose twitches, hope making it itch, and against self-preservation judgments, I reach forward and touch the smaller scales along her tail. I can feel the heat, know it's flaming hot, but it doesn't burn my skin.

Before I can marvel and speculate to this anomaly, her body stiffens under my cool fingers, and she whips around to face me. Her tail hits another tree in doing so, and the whoosh of wind her large body's swift movement created ruffles my shirt. The intimidating orange orbs of her eyes portray murderous thoughts as she stares back into mine. They don't soften with recognition like I had expected them to. A shiver hardens my muscles.

A roar rumbles in her chest, fire inflating within, and smoke curls from her nostrils. The heat from within fans my cheeks and brings feeling back to my numb cracked lips. It burns the slitted, chapped wounds.

She's prepared to kill me, I realize. And if I don't act soon, she will.

"Kat," I whisper again, my hands loose and limp at my sides.

Something flickers in her eyes, a fleeting shadow in the dilation of her irises, and I slowly turn my palms out.

"I see you." My voice is hoarse as her heat steals the moisture from my mouth, and my vision blurs with unshed tears. She's in there; I know she is. She has to be.

I lift my arm cautiously, and the dragon's eyes narrow before characteristically chomping the air between us. The hairs rise along my skin, and my conscience screams to halt my actions.

"I see you," I repeat, putting as much emotion behind the words as I can. My heart pours out my feelings for her, begging her to see reason. New saliva pools in my mouth. I swallow with much difficulty.

The dragon observes the honesty, my emotions evidently spread across my unwavering posture, and her eyes sweep my face repeatedly. The fire expanding her chest sluggishly sinks inside her, and I allow a small, genuine smile for my victory.

I reach out further and take a step forward. "I see you, Katriane DuPont."

The glowing eyes watch my hand, and as I close the distance, she reluctantly pushes her muzzle into my palm. It feels like hardened leather, sleek armor, and just as hot as her tail though it still doesn't burn me.

A single tear spills from her right eye and trickles down the jagged slope of her face. The drop touches the tip of my finger and I gasp as the tear absorbs into my skin. A warmth seeps into the bone, wraps the stiff joint of my wrist, and travels up the length of my arm. Quickly, the warmth spreads to each muscle and relieves their knotted tension then quests to areas of my body I was unaware ached until they healed with the blissful sensation.

Kat's tears can heal, I marvel in numbing awe.

A wider grin tugs at the relaxed muscles of my face, pride vibrating in my veins, and I run my hand further up, settling at the top of her rounded jaw. Enjoying the sensation, her eyelids flutter closed with contentment. A deep sigh whooshes from her lungs, pushing away the chilling breeze and stinging flakes.

I lean, and inside me, my wolf sneaks closer to the surface, a pressure-like sensation in my brain. The green glow of my wolf's eyes sparkles against her wet scales, searching hers. When she makes no move to harm me, I close them and lean the rest of the distance, gently placing my newly-healed lips to her muzzle.

The scales shift and stack under my hands, rough against my kiss, and when I open my eyes, the soft pale skin of Katriane DuPont is under my lips. Her short hair is wet and tousled, and when the wind whistles in the space once blocked by a dragon, she shivers with no defense against the chill.

She's naked, I realize.

I remove my hand from her jaw, unbutton my shirt, and fold her inside my warmth.

Her cheek presses against my skin, and she's silent for several moments as we listen to the soft fall of snow.

"I see you, too," she whispers.

Tucking my chin, I look down at her. My wolf sighs contentedly and retreats with satisfaction that his mate is safe, taking his glow with him. Kat's dark eyes glint my reflection, and when a small grateful smile replaces her chattering teeth, I bend and touch my lips to hers, a proper kiss. A wordless promise.

A soft sigh presses her chest against mine, swelling my heart. My name is exhaled next, emotions behind the syllables, before she falls limp in my arms.

I freeze after I grab her, a spike of adrenaline burning my chest for fear she's dead. When a cloud of evaporation slithers between her nostrils, I breathe an audible gust of relief.

If she were dead, I would be, too. We are tied in more ways than mates, and my heart literally belongs to her.

I hoist her in my arms with little effort, marveling that such a tiny person can cause so much destruction. With effort, I tuck her inside my shirt as best I can, leaving her legs to dangle in the air.

Bending my head, I peck the bridge of her eyebrow. "I've got you," I whisper to her.

Turning, the village my destination, my attention is caught by a flicker of movement.

"Dyson Coleman," someone calls. The voice carries in the breeze, and my eyes pin to the movement, a rotating swirl of black and gold sparkles.

My wolf flashes his glowing warning and growls inside me, prepared to protect our mate.

What is it? Extraterrestrial? A new creature of the Guardian Realm? I've seen the prenumbras. They had fought alongside us in the village at the beginning and had stayed behind when the Cloven Pack ventured into the woods to beat back the threat. But this *thing* is something else entirely, hovering well above the ground with no mouth to speak words.

The male voice chuckles, hearing my thoughts. "Dyson Coleman, protector and mate to the savior of the realms . . ." He trails off, a gesture of arrogance.

I step back, and my spine jars against a tree. "Who are you?" I ask cautiously.

"Always the same questions. It matters not what or who I am." The swirls take shape to a human form with no facial features, resembling a thick stick figure. "It only matters what your next move is."

I narrow my eyes. "Why do I get the feeling you have the answers?" I know an extra angle when I see one. I've dealt with double-meaning phrases like this before.

"Because I do, Dyson, Born of Strategy." The glittering black and gold shoulders lift with a slow shrug.

Despite my desires to do so, we talk for quite some time. He speaks for longer than I like, spinning Fated tales and future dos and don'ts. I learn a great deal from him, secrets I'm meant to keep, and finally, when my patience wears thin, he lets us leave. Kat's toes are beginning to turn bright white, and the last thing I want is for her to have frostbite. She'd never believe my excuse for dead toes.

As I shuffle into the village, Kat's dangling feet jab my hips. Exhaustion slows my gait, and the cramping muscles are beginning to return. I survey the village and tuck Kat's head under my chin.

I find the group gathered in front of the teepee the pack has claimed, and once spotting me, they turn at my approach.

"Thank the Divine," Erma swears.

I meet Sandy's gaze squarely, his brows dipped in a question. Nodding my head to him, I let him know my mate is well. His tense shoulders drop with relief, and he blinks his thanks.

Erma places a hand on Kat's forehead and then checks her over for injury, lifting my shirt away to do so.

"Just fainted," I supply before she can pummel me with questions. She nods and backs away, arms tight across her chest.

The entire group tightens in a circle protectively. I understand the gesture. They care for Kat, and without her, many more would have fallen today. It's funny how a miniature war can change someone's opinion of another. Not so funny . . . more pathetic.

Scratching the stubble of my chin against Kat's hair, I look around while discretely inhaling her scent.

Smokey teepees and trees backdrop the group. Children no longer cry, and the prenumbras have been left to roam as an extra precaution. One of the brave creatures pads between Evo and Kenna and approaches me tentatively, his long ears drooped in submission. In a silent plea, he leans forward precariously, back legs outstretched as though to balance himself. I cluck to the sightless aura dog. With this verbal acceptance, the prenumbra licks the bottom of Kat's cold foot. The saliva leaves behind a trail of green aura which quickly slicks from her foot and splats to the snow.

Erline thunders forward and snatches the fur blanket draped on Kenna's shoulders, despite her shout of disapproval, and shoos the creature away before laying it over Kat's body. She mutters curses when her touch grazes Kat's cold skin. Her eyes meet mine, searches their depths, and then she backs away under the weight of my possessive gaze.

Watching Erline's retreat to the circle, Flint strides to my side and peers at Kat over my shoulder. "What happened out there?" Flint murmurs, concerned.

His closeness doesn't bother me, nor does it raise the need to protect my mate from another male. I know his own is waiting at home for him, back in the Earth Realm. She's taking care of Kat's shop. Irene is my mate's best friend, and I would do nothing to jeopardize the intertwined relationships, not when love and friends are what we need most right now. There's an enemy everywhere I turn these days.

"I -" I stop and frown. "I don't actually know."

"Huh?" he gently grunts. "As in you don't remember, or the English language is failing you?"

I eye him and half smile.

He shrugs. "Hey, it happens to me all the time, especially where my mate is concerned. There are no words in the English dictionary to describe how much she infuriates me *and* makes me love her all at once." He snorts and crosses his arms. His coat swishes with the action. "Women."

I chuckle my agreement. "Do you miss her?" I ask soberly.

The humor flees his eyes, taking his grin with it, and he ticks his jaw. "More than words," he admits, and I know exactly what he means.

226

When Tember approaches, Flint and I fall silent and warily watch as she smooths her fingers through Kat's disheveled hair.

"You're her mate then?" she inquires with a whisper.

"I am."

Her cheeks puff as she tucks the corners of her lips inside her mouth. "She is our means of survival, Dyson. I've never been able to truly care for her - not the way she deserves." She lifts her eyes to mine. "Promise me you'll protect her in a way I never could."

I search her face then flick my eyes to the elf, Jaemes, behind her. He nods to me once and returns a concerned expression to his friend's back.

"I will," I vow. And with that, she nods and slinks away. Jaemes trails after her, flicking me an exasperated but apologetic expression, and the prenumbra obediently follows on his heels. He hisses the creature away before I'm pulled from watching their retreating backs.

"Dyson," Evo rumbles, his hands on Kenna's furless shoulders. "Dyson, you should hand her over."

"Let this brute take her to rest," Kenna adds, flicking a thumb at Mitus' looming form.

I narrow my eyes at the mated pair while Mitus scowls. The look is funny on the tribe leader's face, and I have a difficult time holding my serious expression. Brenna looks away, tucking a smile between her teeth, and Erma pats Mitus' bulking forearm comfortingly.

Erline steps forward again when Mitus makes no move to do so. "I'll take her."

Flint growls at my back, but she meets my gaze the same way the prenumbra did, a gesture of submission with her hands clasped neatly in front of her, her chin tucked tightly.

I nod, and she approaches, holding out her arms. Reluctantly, I pass Kat's sleeping body over, but not before I inhale deeply and take my fill of her scent.

As Kat's weight is fully transferred, I hover my arms under her body, a moment of concern that Erline may not be able to hold her. She looks so slender. But Erline gracefully turns and escorts Kat to the nearest vacant and still-standing teepee. A gust of wind blows by, opening the fur door, and Erline dips inside with my mate.

"So," Brenna begins abruptly, rocking on the back of her heels. "This is a shitstorm. Would anyone mind sharing some sort of plan?" She studies the group and observes everyone's discomfort. None give her answers, and she pops her lips to fill the awkward void.

Luckily, I have some.

I survey the village, still in disarray, and watch as puffs of white smoke rise to mix with the somber clouds. I push a hand through my hair and tug on the ends. My arms feel abandoned without Kat in them, and my wolf urges me to leave the group and explanation in favor of my mate.

"Look," I begin with a shaky sigh.

A sense of deja vu resurfaces, whisking my words away. It's a memory of when I was assembling a rebellion with the shades. Then, the people who had gathered to hear what I had to say were reluctant to do so, but now, these people look to me for answers. My people. My friends.

I swallow and bob my head in small, quick successions. "None of us expected this. A year ago, I would have told you this was all impossible." I look to Flint over my shoulder, and his eyes avert from mine. My words bring back terrible memories for him, but it needs to be said.

In a comforting gesture, I touch his shoulder and squeeze the muscle there before pressing on. "I know I hold no authority here." My gaze flicks to those who do, but they intently listen, unwilling to interrupt my speech. "We won this round-"

"At a great cost," Mitus adds, cutting me off, his accent thick.

"Yes," I admit, and cross my arms. "At a great cost. But we can't say we weren't expecting a retaliation. We stirred a lot of trouble in the Death Realm."

"And trouble will continue to follow you." Mitus jabs a long finger at me. "Each of you come with your own set of complicated problems. I should have never allowed you in my village."

Flint scoffs and paces shortly behind me as if the action would hold his tongue.

"There was no warning," Erma declares in my defense. "None could predict the angels would swap loyalties and attack a tribe of warriors."

"Did you know the angels had planned to join the opposing team?" Mitus barks.

The sparkling man had told me about this. The majority of angels have sided with Corbin, fallen from grace for more favorable pastures. Those who haven't, fled back to the Earth Realm to hover over their charges. They know something terrible is brewing.

He also claimed there is no way to prevent it. This plan has been set in motion for a while, and Corbin's motives and manipulation have been in play since the day he bound with Myla in marriage, hundreds of years ago. The discovery of the relationship between Erma and Tember was the tipping point.

Obviously, Erma is aware of this and has been discussing it with people of importance while I was gone. None of the group seems shocked by the news, and we already know Sureen, Kheelan, and Corbin are bound and determined to watch evil snuff the light.

She doesn't give a definitive answer and directs the conversation to another matter consuming her thoughts. "I have to take back the Angel's Ground." Her declaration leaves no room for open discussion.

Despite Mitus' obvious bristle, I nod. "And you should."

Their home is their home. No one should be kept from their own home. It's not up to Mitus whether the good angels decide to take back what's theirs. If I could, I'd do the same. My gaze flicks to Kat's tent. I *am* doing the same.

I turn to the rest of the group and widen my stance. "Aiden." He lifts his head away from Eliza's ear. "You wish to go after Corbin?"

He had said as much when we were reunited, making sure I knew he wasn't going to stick around while discreetly asking me to watch over Eliza while he's gone.

Aiden blinks his confirmation. He's never one for many words. "Good. We need intel and you're the only one who can get it." I pause, choosing my next words carefully. "I'm going to ask once, and I'll respect your answer, whatever you choose. But choose wisely."

"Hmm?" he grunts, and shifts his arm around Eliza's waist. A slow blink of adoration fans her long red eyelashes when he tucks her tighter to his chest. I didn't fail to miss the gesture, nor the sour expression. He's not pleased that Eliza will be hearing his plans and intentions, but she can't be kept in the dark. I wouldn't want my mate to keep secrets from me, and I won't allow him to do so. The time for secrets is over.

"I'm going to ask you not to kill him," I say briskly.

Eliza pins a murderous glare to Aiden's chin, the adoration quickly fleeing.

I continue. "We don't know what we're up against, and we have no inside man. I want that man to be you."

He watches me, unblinking, while he mentally goes to war between our needs and his desires. Finally, he dips his chin in confirmation. I don't trust it. All I can do is hope that when he's face to face with Corbin, he heeds my request. I don't know if Aiden can even kill Corbin, but I don't want to chance it.

"No," Eliza says firmly.

I point at her, knowing what she'll demand next. "You cannot go. Did you notice Kheelan arrived when you used your magic?" She averts her gaze. "You're a supernatural GPS when it comes to the enemy. You must stay here. You mustn't use your magic. And you were a doctor before. They could use your help here."

Mitus grunts, cutting off my speech. "We're guardians, wolf. We heal quickly."

I blink twice at the leader of elves. "Still," I grit. "You could use another healer."

"And what about you?" Sandy inquires, his deep voice jarring my hearing.

"We - you, Kat, and I - will be going to the Dream Realm."

Fear twinkles in his white eyes, and he crosses his arms to hide his trembling. He doesn't want to go back, and for a moment, I sympathize with him. If someone told me I was to go on a mission in the Death Realm, I'd probably flat out refuse. There are just too many grievous memories held for me on that realm.

Returning to his own will be a great emotional risk for Sandy, but we can't navigate it without him. With my luck, I'd stumble into a pile of dream dust, like a raked stack of brittle autumn leaves, and slumber for the rest of eternity.

Erma props her hands on her hips. "You can't."

I hold up a hand and practically snatch the protest from her next words with the gesture of silence. "The choice isn't up to you. You have your job. The three of us have ours. Aiden and Eliza have theirs. Erline will stay with the Elves and make sure they're not harmed while ensuring Eliza remains away from Kheelan's grasp."

"Eliza cannot control her emotions, which seem to be tied to her mated magic. Whenever she's frightened, she uses it." Aiden adds and kisses the top of Eliza's red tangled hair to soothe the frown marring her features. He would know - he does consume fear. "Someone needs to make sure she doesn't draw attention to herself. Erline is a good choice."

Mitus mutters another language under his breath and stalks off, disappearing around the teepee Kat rests in. He reminds me of a bear lumbering on only two legs.

"You gave Sureen the ability to create life, did you not?" I ask Erma.

"How did -"

"How did I know?" I bite out.

It boils my blood that she would even consider such a thing, knowing this war is inevitable, and it frustrates me to the end of the realms that the fee sling around power like it's leprechaun gold and to be equally shared.

"Let's just say a little birdy told me," I add.

"There are no birds here," she starts, but I silence her with a simple look.

They don't need to know where the information came from, not until I've discussed things with Kat. She needs to know, but an inkling in my gut tells me she already does. Most of the time, she seems one step ahead of the rest. She was born to lead if not made to do so.

Everyone has kept her in the dark for fear they'll be her next target or to keep her ignorant enough to control her. I don't want to be the person she runs from. I want to be the person she runs *toward*. The only way to do that is to earn her trust, respectfully, and it begins with no secrets.

Bending, I pick up a white feather next to a black puddle soaked into snow and twirl the stem between my index finger and thumb. "Sureen is building creatures of war, creatures we know nothing about. We need to know what we're up against. Then, we can plan our next move before they begin theirs."

"Must have been some bird," Kenna mumbles.

Erma lifts a glowing hand, and the feather evaporates. I look up and scowl at her before fully standing once more.

"Then it's prudent we take action immediately," she supplies.

The sandman fidgets by rolling his shoulders, and it steals my attention from the tiny woman with red curls. "I have friends there," he says. "We can recruit sandmen and dwarves. We can bring them to this realm." He pauses as Tember and Jaemes shuffle back to the circle.

Tember's posture is more erect - shoulders pushed back and her brown curls returned to their original bounce. She's more composed than when she left. Jaemes, whose

234

hands are tucked behind the small of his back, puffs his chest, and his mischievous air slides back into place. Perhaps Jaemes spoke some sense into the stubborn Angel. They have an odd friendship, but I understand it completely. Flint and I share the same relationship. Sometimes friends don't pick each other.

"The dwarves are quite cunning," Sandy adds, pride heightening his tone. He's excited at the prospect of familiarity. Of someone he can talk to whom he trusts more than the group around us. It's the first true emotion I've seen from Sandy since the Death Realm. Witnessing death firsthand can be a traumatic experience, and I mentally note to talk with him at a later time just to check on his well-being. He needs someone to unload on. We all do.

Tember nods. "And Nally. Don't forget him."

He swivels his head to her, and his smooth forehead wrinkles. "You know Nally?"

"We met once."

I sigh impatiently and smack my lips together. This conversation can happen later. As Erma stated, time is of the essence.

"Any more questions?" I blurt.

"Shall the ugly duckling and I go with Erma and win back the castle of demented swans?" Jaemes asks, lifting his arm up and over his head and snatching an arrow from his quiver.

"I almost prefer mascot," Tember growls, her eyes a shade of murderous. For a split second, her halo blinds the group and disappears as quickly as it came.

He pokes his arrow against the tip of her feathers as if to prove his point. "It is I who won the bet, little duck. Perhaps you can ride my matua and wave our banners before the real warriors play a game of death and blood. Is that mascot enough?"

"You don't have any banners," Erma says.

He twists his lips. "It can be arranged."

Tember mutters under her breath. I cross my arms and watch as she kicks her foot to the side, landing a sharp blow to his shin. Jaemes' soft grunt is the only indication that it hurt.

I shut my eyes, willing the throb behind them to dull, and put my hands on the back of my hips. With a sharp tongue, I give instructions to the group, catching the attention of the two bantering creatures. Aside from grouping this tribe's elves and preparing them for battle, the angels who fled need to be found and convinced to return.

Kicking out a defiant leg, Erma cocks her hips and crosses her arms. "You know where the angels are?" she asks.

I nod and brush flakes from my eyelashes. She narrows her eyes, silently watching my face and expecting immediate answers. I don't give her any.

"I can do that myself," she adds slowly. "I can assemble them and -"

"No!" I pin my bottled-up emotions on her. They spill over the brim and unload the exhaustion of the entire day. "No fee will be running anything. This may be your war, but you can't fight it alone. You need us, and I'll be damned if I allow any of you to be in charge." I point at her. "You all created this mess in the first place, leaving us to clean it up."

"Sweet baby Jesus," Kenna mutters, uncharacteristically quiet until now. "Who is this new Dyson, and where has he been my whole life?"

The conversation diminishes after that, and most of us depart to help clear the destruction. Sandy is the only one who disappears from the village. He leaves with the elves to gather the dead – they seem to accept him more than they accept us.

This mind-numbing work helps us get lost in our thoughts and spend time with the ones we will shortly depart from. I'm grateful for it, especially losing myself in a task while my mind wanders to more pleasant memories.

Jaemes and Tember quarrel over a meticulous plan while refusing to agree over strategies. Their voices often carry, and nervous glances are flicked their direction by the villagers passing by with chunks of burnt materials. Erma has to step in several times when the disagreements sour past the point of civility.

Erline hasn't emerged from Kat's teepee the entire time, and despite my best efforts, I haven't been able to keep my eyes from the skinned walls. With this continuous distraction, I've bumped into several elves who were shuffling by carrying the dead from the forest.

I'd love to know what Kat and Erline are doing in there. I feel as though I should be a part of it, whatever *it* is, even if Kat is still unconscious. Maybe I should be sitting by her side. Do I bring her something? What if she doesn't want me in there?

With a sigh and a slouched back, I resign myself to the fact that I don't know exactly what Kat and I are now. It isn't my place to decide for us, so instead, I work meticulously on clearing the path of debris, setting it in a pile for the elves to take to the edge of the forest to be burned.

Finally, with most of my chores completed, I stand next to a fire pit, staring at the flames while I wait for the rest to return from their tasks. It's a short time and half a dozen repaired teepees later when we subconsciously draw back together like each of us knows that the time is now.

Aiden and Eliza are by the trees, huddling close together and saying their goodbyes. The touches are sweet, the kisses gentle. I hope they see each other again, but Aiden's mission is equal parts dangerous and vital. He may not survive Corbin's realm, even to return to tell us what he's learned, and this causes their display of love to sour my mood further.

"Is she awake?" I ask Erline, feeling her earthly presence behind me.

"Yes," she whispers. "And she's doing fine." She steps forward and stops beside me. "Dyson, may I ask you something?"

I shrug, and she takes it as an invitation. "You met him, didn't you?"

"Who?" I ask, knowing well the *him* she speaks of. I make a point not to fidget under my false truth.

238

"The Divine," she says patiently. "At least one of them. You had reeked of their realm when you returned, of my home realm."

Slowly, I inhale a deep breath and roll the tension from my neck. It's all the confirmation she needs.

"Did he give you information you needed to know?"

I nod curtly.

"I see," she sighs. "Please, whatever you do, do not share the information with the others."

Swiveling my head, I turn to face her. My eyes burn from the wind's chill as I stare, fixed, at the side of her porcelain face. "And why not?"

"Information given from the Divine is only meant to the deliverer." She licks her bottom lip, refusing to meet my gaze. "Sharing the news with others defeats the purpose, and the information could soon be tainted like any secret would. The Divine doesn't intervene unless there's a greater meaning for it."

Her words are filled with hurt. Does she know Fate is planning against her race? This war could very well end the entire fee species.

She stops speaking as soon as Aiden and Eliza stride, hand in hand, to the fire pit.

"I'm ready," Aiden mumbles, ignoring the sniffling Eliza who warms her hands over the fire.

We stare at each other for a moment, this feeling too real. He's an impossibility. Someone like him shouldn't exist. And what we're asking of him may come at a great

239

cost to the very thing he fights for. What will happen to Eliza if they kill him? What will happen to us if he dies? I feel guilty because this entire plan came from my mouth. She'll blame me, again, for his death.

Unexpectedly, I pull him into a hug. "Good luck, Aiden. Stay alive."

"Take care of her Dyson," he says. And just like that, his body wavers and shimmers under my hands, and then he's gone. It's so abrupt that it makes me wonder if he's as scared as I am for the future. A long goodbye would only prolong this fear.

I stare at the space where he once stood, frowning at the emptiness.

"Neat trick," Jaemes says sourly as he approaches with a prenumbra. The sandman follows him, his strides resembling a leisurely giraffe. Upon exhale, a pent-up sigh puffs his dark cheeks, and his arms swing freely at his sides.

"This war truly isn't a place for beating hearts," I mumble, watching Eliza's face visibly crumble. Many will die.

But love is worth fighting for.

CHAPTER FOURTEEN

AIDEN VANDER

DEMON REALM

When I shimmer into the Demon Realm, the stench of sulfur stings the inside of my nose. I should be used to this aroma. In fact, it's part of who I am and should calm me, but it's having the opposite effect. Every fiber of my being wants me to return to the realm from where I came, and anxiety curls in my chest as I resist.

Before my body fully materializes, my feet stride along the familiar path I know to take me to the Domus Timore, home of the demons. My gait is thunderous, and revenge is the only thing consuming my thoughts despite Dyson's request.

The realms are not my problem. Eliza is my only concern, and I have a one-track mind. I know I'm capable of ending this if I so choose. Taking Corbin out of the game, removing him from existence, could only benefit Eliza's safety and my future. I'd be in a fight for my life, but

I believe I could manage to hold my own once I figure out how to kill him, aside from the dragon. There has to be something here that can do the job. A weapon, perhaps. Or a poison. Or me...

Sending those angels was his idea. We all know it. He's searching for the upper hand and carelessly so. Or maybe it's meant to look that way.

Either way, it is my hope Dyson and the others find a way to make him pay if I fail.

I hear a disturbance in the black lava to my left side, bubbling goop, but I choose to ignore it instead of acknowledging the presence of another being. I already know who it is. Figures she'd come when I don't want nor need her.

"Aiden," Ferox hisses, swaying her arms against the flow, swimming to keep up with my purposeful, long gait. "Aiden, stop. If you go in there, you'll die. Do you hear me? You will die. I can promise you that."

Clenching my jaw, I stop, my breaths rushing through my nostrils, heavy with adrenaline and pure rage.

"Corbin is not alone," she quickly adds.

I turn to face her, my top lip lifted in a snarl to match my mood. My face is pinched with stress, and the skin around my eyes strains, pulling against bone.

"I know," I growl.

Her eyes widen, and for the first time, I feel and see fear secreting from the pyren's soft, green flesh. Large, almond-shaped jade eyes roam my expression, desperate to probe my mind for what knowledge I hold and the plans

242

that form around it. She swims back a few inches, eyes darting to my hands as they clench and unclench. "Kheelan, Sureen . . . they arrived shortly after you left. There are many formidable creatures here. You cannot charge in. You cannot take on three fee. Not by yourself."

Tilting my head back, I laugh a sullen chuckle. "Does a mighty pyren have a plan? Because I assure you, mine sounds pretty damn solid."

"You're a madman," she hisses. Her pointed ears flatten against the tentacles along her head, oddly catlike. Charging forward, she manages to make herself seem taller, more vicious. "It would be unwise to continue to insult me, Thrice Born. Brute force of one powerful creature will not destroy three more powerful than thee." Her voice drops a deadly octave, and behind her, more heads emerge from the black lava. Dozens of eyes are narrowed in challenge as they fix on me. I steel myself, prepared to take on the entire school if I must.

"There are more of us than there are of you," Ferox warns.

Though there is seemingly no gender, each pyren is female by looks, their hair the same identical black, their skin the same bluish-green. Their tentacles curl at the ends with irritation, and their arms sway in the lava, ready to charge. A few hiss a deep, inhuman passing of wind. I feel their fear, see it waft from the depths of their bodies, floating to me and fueling my demonic nature. But I also see courage.

They're determined to stop me even in the face of their own fear. It makes me question why. Is it me they fear? Or the changes occurring in their realm?

243

A smile tilts the corners of my lips, and my cheeks heat when I gather my wits. "Is that a challenge?"

Ferox's head juts, a quick snake-ish lashing, and she screeches. "We want to be free just as much as you. You've been a demon for days. We've been in servitude for thousands of years. If you die, there is no hope for us."

Behind Ferox, another pyren takes charge. Her voice is raspy compared to Ferox, and she lifts a hand from the lava and points it at me. "He's feeding from us," she mumbles to her sister.

Ferox tilts her head over her shoulder, glances at her sister, and returns her eyes to mine. "Corbin has starved him, throwing snacks his way here and there. He knows nothing of a true feeding." She inclines her head. "You need a true full feed, Thrice Born, or you will never be strong enough for what's to come. You can't deny yourself your nature. This isn't a place for warm, beating hearts full of love and revenge. This is a place of Terror, and you must heed to it."

I cross my arms and widen my stance. "And what's to come?" I already know the answer, but I'm curious to her conclusion.

"A war," she pledges.

"That ship has sailed, princess."

She shakes her head. "You cannot be the only army. Thinking you can kill them yourself is foolish. At least feed and gather your strength. You must be an asset, not a hindrance."

My nostrils flare, agitated, and I stand there for a long while, holding Ferox's eyes in a silent battle of stubbornness. Eventually, I do as she says without another word, and shimmer to the Earth Realm. She's right. Taking on the pyrens just to deny myself sustenance is foolish.

With a purse of my lips, I shimmer away. It didn't take long to find the perfect prey. In fact, it felt all too easy like a moth pulled to a light.

A middle-aged woman vacuums her couch cushions, humming a tune above the suction. Black hair streaked with white strands are tucked into a messy ponytail at her nape, and a few pieces curl around her damp forehead.

The house is small, dank, and shadowed by piles of newspapers. It's void of other signs of life at this time of night, aside from the mice scavenging for crumbs. The vacuum doesn't pick up the crumbs, and the hose whistles, clogged.

Dirt and old food chunks litter the paths between magazines, and as the woman moves to the next couch, I get the feeling she's not all right in the head, aside from the hoarding. Who would clean at this hour? If cleaning is even the right word for it.

I have chosen to remain unseen, invisible while I watch her. She lives alone in a house too small to hold a family, and if she had children or a husband, they're long gone. She turns again, displaying her face for my full view. Stress lines are prominent with age, and her eyes swirl with madness. A hooked nose takes up most of her face, and deep pores are greased over with a layer of filth. What has she gone through to get to the state she's in?

Her faded clothes are tattered with holes. She isn't of wealth, and what can be seen of her décor is aged beyond what's been popular since at least thirty years ago. She reminds me of myself when I was human – alone, poor, without love. I hit people for a living, which was probably the only thing that had kept me sane, but I also provided the mercy due. I wasn't a killer, and sadly, that's no longer true.

She has nothing, no one besides the papers reminding her of each day she spends alone. Whereas, I have Eliza, the only reason I've killed. And I'll do it again if I must.

I stand in the archway of her living room, the inner wall exposed, the outer crumbling. My stance is wide with my hands fisted in my pockets. I've never fed before, not like this, not actively hunting. I don't know how to begin.

The invisibility came as an instinct, to remain hidden until the right moment. But is there truly a right moment for what I'm about to do? For what mind frame I'll need to slip into just to do it?

The woman moves to the green and broken reclining chair, yanking on the vacuum hose. A gold framed decorative mirror hangs on the wall behind the seat, miraculously dust free and completely intact. My *need* drives a knife into my chest, and it takes all I have to not double over. I press each finger against an aching rib instead, easing them with a wordless promise. This pain, this hunger, is consuming - driving - my inevitable actions a slave to an internal master. It can't be helped, and it can't be stopped.

246

I inhale and dip my chin, feeling my eyes burn inside their sockets. I can see myself in the mirror though I know I remain invisible, and I watch my eyes molten. Manipulative emotions sting my pores as they exit the ache within, traveling to the oblivious, aging and lonely woman. I tilt my head, my shoulders bunching as I watch it seep into her back, through the tattered shirt. Slowly, her spine stiffens, and goosebumps visibly raise along her skin.

I know what she's feeling: she's no longer alone.

She raises from her crouched position, her muscles tense and rigid, and the worn handle of the vacuum trembles inside her shaky grasp. Leveling with the mirror, her eyes search the glassy expanse, too terrified to witness her on-looker for herself. She knows I'm here. She knows I wait for her, and by the fear, tangy in the musky air, she's aware of the immense danger she's in.

I push another round of manipulative emotions from me, and this time, it doesn't take its time to search out its victim, following the trail of her terror instead. She gasps as it crashes into her. She drops the handle, and her body shakes in terror. I watch her eyes round in the mirror, her mouth open with a scream that has yet to come. The next wave of fear exits her pores in intense puffs of invisible smoke.

"Who's there?" she yells to the wall she's facing. When I don't answer, she slowly turns, knocking a stack of papers over. I become solid, fisting my hands once to do so. Her eyes lock with mine, and her eyes water. She sucks in air, her lungs preparing to scream.

Scream, I silently beg her.

Leaving the crumbling wall behind, I shimmer inches from her, nose to nose. I smirk in her face. A growl rumbles in my chest, and my breath fans her face. Her mouth opens wider, her fear's smoke clouding my vision though I know she can't see it. It fogs the room, billows a feast which soaks into my body. It's a surge of adrenaline, lighting each nerve with brilliant tingles, and builds inside to a level I've never felt. I feel invincible, powerful, and my smile widens to the pressure-like sensation where the ache once was.

The lids of her eyes slam shut, and the scream finally sores from her throat. Hot spittle flies from her quaking tongue, and the high-pitched tone rings deliciously on my ears.

My head droops between my shoulders, and I suck in a deep breath, drinking the new wave. Uncurling my hands from my pockets, I lift them to my sides, shoulder blades prominent as I hunch further.

"Yes," I gush, basking in my victim.

The woman thumps to the ground, collapsed to a heap of unconsciousness. I remain where I am, my feast yet to be done even as her heart beats its last. I've taken too much from her, so much so that the most vital organ couldn't continue to pump in such duress.

The rumble travels up my chest, the feast fueling me like a waterfall into an awaiting bucket. I've never felt so alive, so complete, so powerful: a drug to a new addict. My head tilts back, my chest bows, and a roar erupts from my throat, rebounding off the walls and echoing back to me. More stacks of paper tip, and the mirror crashes to the floor, shards scattering in every direction. Chest puffing, heart pounding, the last of her fear-laced cloud quickly finds me with my next inhale.

My roars of victory come to a hoarse close, and I stand, taking in this new sensation I've been deprived of. Everything is sharper: the smell of mice urine, the jagged edges of crumbs, the strands of hair meshing with carpet fibers fallen from a scalp long ago.

The room is silent, the woman lifeless against the floor. I step back to observe my meal, and my shoes crunch the mirror's glass. Her face is frozen in a scream, eyes wide, dilated, and unseeing. Her finger twitches against the floor, the nerves dying, and the action seems like the body is trying to call back her soul. I watch it like it's some sort of magical testament for what I've done. It's an image I'll never be able to erase and a guilt I'll never be able to get rid of.

Along the ancient stand propping her TV, a cell phone vibrates. With much effort, I tear my gaze from the twitching woman and look at it, watching it ring for a moment. Slowly, I reach and grasp it with loose fingers.

I could ignore it, shimmer back to the Demon Realm and take my vengeance. I could leave her dead and think nothing of it. What I do next will define the demon I am to become.

Mercy, a male voice mutters in my head. *Mercy in the face of death, Thrice Born. Choose humanity.* I look around but know no one else is here. I frown, thinking I imagined the voice.

Fixing another stare at the woman, then to her phone, I read the screen which displays the name of Dr.

Cassandra Grant. It reminds me of Eliza, and guilt further cripples me. She'll never forgive me for what I've done.

Convenient, I think to myself, *that a doctor would call at the precise moment one is needed.* Fate, almost. I purse my lips and press the green, flat screen button and raise it to my ear. I don't speak. I don't greet. I wait.

Mercy, the voice echoes.

"Aunt Helen?" A woman asks chipperly.

I hesitate and grip the phone tighter in my grasp. She's an aunt. She's somebody's somebody.

"No," I answer, my whisper hushed and foreboding.

Dr. Grant doesn't respond at first, but I can hear beeps of medical equipment in the background. "Who is this?" she demands, her voice as quiet as the mice who had skittered from the room.

Licking my bottom lip, I lower my gaze to the shards of mirror and stare back at myself, a broken image. My molten lava eyes are bright, a brilliant orange, and full of the fear I've consumed.

What am I? Who am I? These are excellent questions I should be considering myself.

"I am responsible for her end, and this is my mercy," I finally answer. This is the truth. I cannot change what I've been made to be, and I cannot help that I'm a monster. I can only be *me.* How I choose to be *me* is up to myself.

I press the end button, lower my hand, and crush the phone in my palm. My eyes remain on myself, watching as I shimmer from the room, leaving the woman's fate to the cycle of life.

I'm either the predator, or the prey. And if I manage to be somewhere in between, mercy and vengeance will tango as one.

CHAPTER FIFTEEN

TEMBER

GUARDIAN REALM

I watch Dyson enter Kat's teepee, and quickly following, her expected shriek of anger shrills offensively against my ears even from where I stand. I suppress a shudder. The suggestion of leaving so soon doesn't appeal to my old charge like I knew it wouldn't. The last time she was in the Dream Realm, it didn't end well. She was roaring mad when she returned from the past. I chuckle at the memory, at the challenge she had forced the fee to endure because of it. It seems like a lifetime ago.

Turning and leaving Kat in the capable hands of her true mate, of her true protector, I approach Erma. She stands beautifully, her arms crossed while she watches the snow softly fall in the forest. It covers the black blood which taints it.

The snow never ends here, everything is white except the stark colors of life who roam it. There is no other place as beautiful as this, even if I do enjoy what the Earth Realm offers.

Her red curls whip in the wind which whistles between the trees, and the bottom of her dress tickles the edge of a pile of chopped logs.

"It's beautiful, isn't it?" she whispers, plucking the words from my thoughts as though we are one mind. "The way the snow falls and how it settles without a sound. But it does have a sound, doesn't it? Only if one is patient and quiet enough to listen to its silent song. If only we were quiet and patient enough to listen to every serenade that surrounds us." She pauses and blows a deep breath from within her chest. "Did you know I created the angels to mimic the snow?"

"No," I admit quietly.

"Angel's wings are soft. Majestic. A whip of wind." She plucks a stray hair stuck to her moist lips. "It's why we didn't hear them coming. Not even the prenumbras heard them, the wild or tame packs. The wind's song was too loud."

I tear my eyes from the peaceful sight and look at her. Her jaw grinds, but she doesn't meet my gaze. Is she drawing a parallel to her many failures?

The indifference hurts me, and it breaks me to see her second guess everything she's ever done. So much can be said with a single look into another's eyes. I muffle my shattered exhale by releasing it agonizingly slow.

If she'd return to me, if she'd give me all of her, I would protect it. I'd listen to her song and serenade her when she's silent. Surely, she knows this or has even considered it. I've proven my worth over the centuries. I've testified to what she means to me. But chances are, I'll never get the opportunity to protect anything aside from her well-being and her realm.

"We shouldn't dwell on the past," I soothe, banishing my emotional pain with difficulty. For a brief second, I wonder if I'm admitting this to myself as well. "But we *can* change the future with our carefully formed plan. We can't dwell on where we went wrong. It would mean our downfall, for we cannot fix what causes us grief. It serves only as a distraction."

Her colorless cheeks puff, and she sucks in her bottom lip, chomping her top teeth against the tender flesh. "When did you become the voice of reason?"

"I'm only one voice," I begin, touching her cheek and forcing her to look at me, "when it's needed most. Right now, we need to focus on how we will evict the fallen from the Angel's Ground. Has Jaemes started on a plan?"

She closes her eyes and pinches the bridge of her nose. "He's gathering his brothers now."

"Good." I wait for her to drop her hand from her face, but she doesn't. "Erma?"

"Hmm?" She focuses at me with tired eyes, and her hand falls to her side with a sway.

Steeling my nerves, I lean forward and brush my lips against hers. She tastes just as I remember and exactly what I ache for. "I love you, too."

A tentative, wobbly smile graces her stressed face. We stare at one another for some time, soaking in unspoken words of truth - words we can't say for fear we will lose the other in the coming days. She may be trying to protect me by keeping a firm distance, but I'll fight for her. On the grounds, for her affection, nothing will stand in my way.

Memories surface of tangled sheets, stolen heated kisses, and whispered promises. The heart in my wrist thuds with a wicked beat, forcing me to feel each emotion accompanied by every memory. I swallow with difficulty when her eyes well with tears.

A cough sounds at my back, and I bristle at the disturbance. I peer over my shoulder, my curls momentarily obscuring my pointed glare to the offender.

"Are we interrupting?" Jaemes asks, gripping the handle of his bow draped over his shoulder.

His brothers stand behind him, wary of the angel with black wings. Since the forest, I've been treated less as insignificant and more as formidable. The respect is there, but their full trust remains to be seen.

"Your very presence is interrupting, no matter the circumstance." I release Erma's jaw from my gentle touch and turn fully to him. "Do you have a plan?"

Jaemes straightens his spine, clears the quirked expression from his features, and nods his head. "Yes. At the risk of going against Dyson's wishes, I think it best Erma calls the angels. Those who still side with her will come."

His assessment is correct. I had originally planned to search for them, but they may not come with me. In times like this, they have no reason to trust another angel, especially one who's shunned. Though they remain loyal to their creator, many will still bristle just by my very presence due to the secrets Erma and I have kept. I can't expect them to be accepting of it even if it's what I desire.

"And those who don't?" I ask, pointing out his flaw by jabbing my finger in his direction.

He shrugs. "Most of the fallen who thought to attack my village are being burned as we speak. Those who don't should follow the same fate. Disloyalty will not be honored."

I purse my lips as I consider this truth and then tip my head to him, accepting his decree. Now isn't the time to allow such crimes to go unpunished.

"I agree," I begin. "Erma?"

"It is done," she says, and I turn to look at her. Her skin shimmers with her calling yellow glow, and then her eyes harden with the difficulties of what's to come.

Those who arrive will surely cause drama with the elves, and those who don't will die. Jaemes' brothers' murmurs attest to my own hypothesis of the coming struggles.

I flick my eyes back to Kat's teepee. The flaps of skin furiously whip with an internal wind. They're leaving by Erline's portal, and silently, I wish them well. Erline will return once they're in the Dream Realm. She'll be here to protect the village and all the innocent within in case we fall today.

"Good," I cajole while concern and dread envelope me.

ELIZA PLAATS

GUARDIAN REALM

Standing outside the teepee we had hastily constructed for the seriously wounded, I twist the ends of my frosty auburn hair, feeling electric currents flowing through them. I'm wound, the adrenaline pumping through my veins despite the fact that the battle has been long over by now. Time works differently here, I've noticed, just as it does in the Death Realm, so I don't have an inkling of how long ago it actually was.

The wounded will heal, I've been told, but they need a safe place away from the rebuild to do so. There's not much I can do for some of them, the occasional injury too great for a miracle. Those this seriously injured won't survive. They've held out longer than any human would be able to. Through their suffering, the village healer has been feeding them herbs to ease their discomforts while lulling them to a groggy state before their journey ends.

Angels arrive by Erma's yellow portal, stepping through and gathering with the assembled elves huddled at the far end of the village, their postures stiff. I've been told they don't get along, and after this last battle, I don't see why. Everyone is at war, even those who should be on the same side.

I look to the teepee Kat was in, knowing they've already left. Kat seems so broken, struggling to find herself. I know that feeling - to be scared of what you're becoming. The only thing I don't share with her is that I know what I'm capable of. My powers are what Kheelan has, and I know their strengths and limitations. I'm able to choose, easily, for good instead of evil. I don't think Kat has this luxury. It seems to happen against her will and sometimes when she has no other choice. I also understand that. Capabilities aside, I'm not entirely sure how to wield mine absent instinct.

My gaze swivels to the warriors gathering, and Tember and I swap blank glances at one another. Just as I, she's scared - not for herself but for the others - and she's trying not to show it.

I share this too. Something doesn't feel right, and I can't place the reason as to why.

Why would the enemy attack so swiftly, knowing they wouldn't survive? What plan do they have tucked in their cheek?

I dip my chin and break the eye contact with Tember and stare at the snow pressed with footprints. The red ash has yet to be covered completely, and in some places, it's smeared like chalk smudged on a chalkboard.

A gentle hand is placed on my shoulder, and I jump before I look up from the post I lean against. Mitus peers down at me, his square jaw softening. Is my emotional state that evident?

Saying goodbye to Aiden once again, wondering if I'll ever see him again, makes my chest ache and my breaths shallow. I hated watching him leave, and the feeling of impending doom doesn't help matters.

Being a spy in enemy territory won't turn out well for him. I don't know how I know. I just do, and the fear that accompanies this knowledge almost brings me to my knees every time I dwell on it.

I should have gone with him. I could be more use than a doctor in a realm with creatures I don't know how to treat. What if he loses his way and needs to be reminded of who he truly is? I won't be there to whisper those words in his ear.

"Yes?" I ask, my voice cracking.

"You are needed," he mumbles, inclining his head with respect.

I've been rubbing ointment on the fortunates' wounds and tending to the broken bones, resetting them with spine-chilling cracks. Moans come from the tent, pain thick in the air, and the healer, old and greying, hobbles as nimble as she can to each of the dying. The fallen angels did a number on them.

I nod my head and look back once more. An elf to my right is sewing together the skin of his teepee using some kind of vine and bark flayed from a tree trunk. His family watches, the mother comforting two boys with sullen postures.

Another elf scuffs the ground with his foot, frowns, and then bends. He runs his hand along the snow and red dust. Lifting his fingers, he brings the red to his nose, sniffing the substance. He turns, just slightly, to take in the rest of the path's floor, and a gashed wound on his upper arm gleams in fine glory. I'm just about to beckon him in and demand he be stitched up, but Mitus' voice stops me.

"Yami will come when he's ready."

Reluctantly, I nod and follow Mitus under the cover of the large teepee opening. He struts with authority to the table of a child I had already stitched. The memory of his cries still prick tears in my eyes. He cried for his people and not the injury, which somehow felt worse. Children are innocent and should never have to witness such a thing, no matter their traditional upbringing.

"I don't understand," Mitus mumbles and then clears his throat. He spits the phlegm to the ground, and we share a momentary frown.

"Neither do I," I start. Why am I being brought back to the same child I've already treated? "Is he not well?"

Mitus shakes his head, his black hair cascading over his shoulder. "He was treated, yes. But he is very hot to the touch."

"Like a fever?" I ask but receive no answer. Elves don't get sick, not with guardian's self-healing abilities. They wouldn't know what a fever is.

I lean forward and cup my hand over the sleeping child's forehead, feeling the heat emit from his sticky skin. My frown deepens.

"This shouldn't be possible," Mitus says quietly as though expecting I wouldn't hear.

"Indeed." I lift the dressing over the gash in his hip, examining the wound. This dressing is made from some sort of moss the village scavenges for. "It's not infected."

Mitus takes some time to collect himself, his posture stiff, and thinks over the situation before

260

answering. "We are guardians, healer. We shouldn't feel pain, and yet..." He sweeps his hand through the crowded space. "We now do. And we certainly aren't subject to illness."

As though it just dawned on me, my hand freezes, the dressing falling from my fingertips. They don't feel pain, yet they moan with it.

I whip my head back to him and untangle a lock of red from my eyelashes. "You don't get sick. You have no pain receptors. You can self-heal."

Mitus' jaw ticks my confirmation.

I curse in a mumble. "It's not the wound. This is most certainly not an infection due to his injuries. This is some sort of bug." I stand upright and stretch my spine while hiding my concern.

"A bug?" Mitus questions, trying the word on his own tongue. He picks up the extra moss from the table and squeezes it in his hand then sniffs it.

"Yes. I worry about a contagion."

"Contagion?" he echoes, placing the ruined moss back on the table.

I nod. Even with the impossibility and practically indestructible bodies, I'm sure of it. "This could spread. Has anyone else had symptoms?"

Perhaps they don't moan from their injuries. Perhaps they moan from the symptoms of their illness. They wouldn't know the difference and wouldn't be able to tell me.

Mitus crooks a finger and takes me from patient to patient, most who I've already stitched or bandaged and some who are at the brink of death. The healer ignores us as we travel throughout the teepee, often getting in her way.

"The time for healing has passed, and I worry they won't survive it," Mitus adds on our way back to the child.

"Oh?" My voice is tinged with malice. Their timeline for self-healing isn't stored in my medical brain. It would have been nice if they told me their little secrets before I started all my hard work. I shouldn't have expected them to, though. Patience is often difficult without information, no matter the species. And they have no reason to trust me with it.

"Let me get this straight," I begin and tap my chin. "Your magical non-pain abilities are faulty, along with your healing abilities, and some strange illness is conquering a land that's not susceptible to diseases."

"Yes." His answer is firm and business-like.

I press my middle finger to my right brow and rub the ache beginning there. "If we don't get this under control, the entire village will go down. We don't know if the bug has to run its course, but I suspect it's designed to kill its host."

Even with their self-healing, this isn't going to end well. The evidence is showing that this is a swift illness.

Mitus crosses his arms and his peck muscles ripple. "Tell me what to do."

I look to him, speculating if I can trust this man to follow my orders. Not long ago, he didn't want us here and couldn't return the trust we had placed in him to keep us safe. Chewing the inside of my lip, I come to a conclusion. I have no choice.

"This structure is now a quarantine. No one in it can leave, and no one out of it can enter. Not unless they become infected too. We need to be cautious, magical healing capabilities or not."

CHAPTER SIXTEEN

KATRIANE DUPONT

DREAM REALM

"This is your home?" I spin in a full circle, observing the absence of décor. There are no personal objects and no hint of the sandman's interests. It's bare and basically a Neanderthal cave, only with sparkles.

Satchels hang from every protruding edge of black, sparkling stone. The satchels remind me of my bag, the one I was gifted at my Right ceremony to hold the contents of potions and spells that I'll no longer need. It makes me miss home. It makes me miss the past when life was simpler.

The floor sparkles, too, and I can only assume it's sleep dust. I visibly recoil, lifting one of my feet in the air as though that'll keep me away from the substance. The last time this stuff touched me, I was dropped in a time period where witches were executed.

"No thanks," I whisper to the sleep dust.

Dyson is touching every bag he comes across, sweeping his fingers over them gently. And while he does so, Sandy's persistent gaze on my cheek lifts the hairs on my arms.

"What?" I spit to Sandy. I'm not happy about being here. Did I have a choice? No. Will I ever make my own choices again? That remains to be seen.

"Do you have your dragon under control?" Sandy rumbles in a mild temper. His tone echoes in the small space.

Dyson glances at me, and in doing so, accidentally bumps a satchel where it is dangling. It drops, and sparkles spill from the bag. Cursing, he squats to the floor. I suppress a smile. Though he's a Shifter, he's anything but graceful. Somehow, this makes him more attractive.

Hovering his hands, he tries to figure out how scoop it back in without touching it. His tongue darts out to the corner of his lips and sticks there in the midst of concentration.

With a flick of my finger, the dust swoops back in through the opening, and the satchel soars back to the cave wall, hooking on the rock. Dyson curses again, unnerved as he scrambles to his feet.

I tighten my arms further around my chest. "Yes," I say to the sandman, grinding the word between my teeth.

I'm moody and exhausted, but with Dyson this near, I feel the darkness kept more at bay. I can't explain what he does to me. He says I ground him, but he truly has no idea what that means. He's the light in my dark. He subdues it just by proximity. If he weren't here, I wouldn't be confident of my state of mind because without him, I wouldn't have come back from my dragon form in the woods. It had been like I was floating in a pit of blackness. I could hear voices that weren't my own. I could feel emotions that weren't my own. The voices were scared and all speaking at once. It was peaceful there; perhaps not for most, but for me it was. I was free, truly free, of the burdens I have to hold on my own.

But Dyson had pulled me back. I had felt him, heard him call my name like a muffled echo underwater. I swam then. I swam in the sea of black, his voice my map. And his lips. When they had found mine, his wolf's eyes glowing in the space between us, I felt it - the feeling of a true home. Home isn't a place . . . it isn't a possession, but rather inside those we love.

I fight with myself not to gaze at Dyson as my thoughts surround him and what he makes me feel. The word love frightens me more than death itself. With love, I have more to lose. And if I keep the word to myself long enough, it won't hurt as bad if Dyson falls in the coming days.

"Why do you ask?" I add.

Sandy sweeps the cave as though soaking in memories of a past life. He lifts a hand, points a finger, and sweeps the wall. "This is inferaze. The entire Dream Realm is made of it. It builds my species and makes the dream dust, but also fuels the entire realm. Its magical capabilities are vast. If it were to catch fire..."

"Are you saying that if Kat becomes a dragon and spits one flame, the entire realm will combust?" Dyson asks.

The sandman nods. Then, he flicks his gaze to my hands, watching for any evidence of fire. I drawl a stream of curses and look around the room with a new pair of eyes, now afraid to touch anything. Fire flows through my veins, and most of the time, I can't control it.

I whip a hand out from its tightly tucked position across my middle and smack Dyson in the chest.

"Ouch!" he grumbles. "What was that for?"

"For bringing a dragon inside a sleeping bomb!"

Placing his hands on his hips, he turns to me. It's adorable, his stance, while channeling an authority he can't beat. "We had no choice, Katriane. We each have our mission. This is ours. We couldn't come to an enemy territory without -" he stops short and looks away. His cheeks redden.

"Without a formidable weapon?" I accuse. I drop my hands to my sides, and my palms slap my hips.

I stare at him for a long time, my dominance rising above his. His guilt is tucked between the straining of his tight lips. Shifters are a dominant species, and male shifters tend to man-handle their mates. If that's what he's expecting here, he's going to be disappointed.

Pinching the bridge of my nose, I close my eyes and speak to the inside of my palm, knowing both creatures will be able to hear me. "What's the first move?"

Sandy glides to the wall and snatches the satchel I had just returned. "To blend in."

"To recruit," Dyson adds.

"And gain intel," I say, dropping my hand from my face. "And what's the plan when we run into trouble?"

Both men turn their gazes to me, blank expressions. It's the obvious choice then.

"Burn them to the ground?" I ask, innocently.

Of course.

We leave Sandy's room soon after. With the sandman in the lead, we follow behind him, shuffling along the cave's tunnel wall until he nods to carry on. A variety of sandmen and sandwomen pass, and I immediately marvel that each has a different feature than the last - a bigger nose, wider set eyes - but all the same beautifully dark skin color. I had originally thought they'd all be identical.

They barely give us a second glance. The dwarves, however, hold curiosity and fear as they scuttle by at a quicker rate than when they met us.

It startles me, the emotion that's in all of the creatures' postures and features. They're afraid, and before I can ask why we aren't trying to recruit all those we come across, we bend one more tunnel's path and enter the main area of Dream Realm.

I gasp. In the center, a dome pulses with light, almost identical to a hologram heart. Instead of a heart's red beat, the light is a blinding yellowish-white. This has to be where I woke back to my time, greeted by Sureen with all her majestic egotism.

Surrounding the dome is what looks to be trees. The leaves are like diamonds which reflect and blind the dome's light with each pulse. The weight of the leaves is too great for the branches, and they almost touch the ground, making it look like the trees are weeping.

Yellow, almost transparent fluorescent tendrils snake through the spikes of the cave's high ceiling, and every few seconds, more filter in. They gravitate to the dome, and the dome sucks them into its core.

"What are they?" I ask Sandy, awe in my voice.

"Dreams," he whispers.

A machine, butterfly in shape, swoops from above, and I duck, worried it'll crash straight into us. But at the last second, it spreads its mechanical wings with an audible grinding of gears, angles the body, and dives into the cave tunnel we had just exited from. I turn and get a better look at it as it travels at a daring speed. The back end is scooped, like a wheelbarrow bucket, and empty of any objects.

Dyson asks the question on the tip of my tongue. "It carries things?"

"It carries the inferaze which fuels the dome's mechanics," Sandy explains. "Built by the dwarves, of course. Their minds are brilliant. If Sureen wasn't afraid of modern technology, we'd be far more advanced than the Earth Realm."

I shiver. The last thing Sureen needs is modern technology.

"Sandy," I say. "What all can inferaze do?"

A small smile tilts his dark lips, revealing a rare show of pride for his realm. "It does a great deal of things, little dragon." And then his mood swiftly darkens. "Even I do not know all of its capabilities."

Dyson rocks his lanky frame on the back of his heels. "Let's keep going before we get caught."

I watch as the sandman's sparkle fades from his white eyes, and the rest of his pride visibly deflates. "This way."

"What about Sureen?" I question while jogging to keep up with his long legs.

"She is not here," he answers simply.

I scoff. "And how could you possibly know?"

He doesn't answer and quickens his pace instead. It seems almost rude, the way he's escaped as though my simple question offended him. Even his back is stiff, and each step is rigid and robotic.

Dyson trails back and stuffs his hands in his pocket. With a twitch of his nose, he indicates for me to do the same.

We let Sandy get a safe distance ahead. Scaling the descending rock with careful steps to the main level with weeping trees, Dyson focuses on me, a silent question tugging on his face.

"My next voodoo doll will be him," I mutter, peeved at being ignored.

Perhaps I'm blowing it out of proportion, but just the same, I never wanted to come here in the first place. With every step we take closer to the dome, I become more wary. It's too peaceful here. The enemy's land should never be peaceful.

Dyson quirks a brow. "You keep voodoo dolls?"

"In my mind," I say with a petulant nod. "I stab them. Frequently. With dark thoughts."

He chuckles under his breath, but it fades too quickly to be true humor. "Don't ask him about Sureen," he cautions. "They had a relationship."

I quirk a brow at him. "Like husband and wife? Mates?"

If they were mates, how could we trust him? Mates are loyal to each other first.

Dyson subtly shakes his head and lowers his voice. "It was an unwilling relationship."

"Oh." At first, it's all I can say. All of my emotions and blame are knocked out of me with this revelation.

I harden my eyes as images of these "unwilling" events filter into my mind. For a brief moment, an overwhelming urge to defend the sandman lowers my guard, and I stumble on a protruding rock.

It's ironic how quickly allegiances can form and protective instincts can blossom by simple facts of the past.

"Don't, Kat," Dyson warns. "He doesn't need you to defend his honor."

I look at him. His wolf is prominent in his eyes and ready to speak reason into me. He's right though, despite my protective instincts. The sandman has been through much since I met him, and every time, he's survived.

Dyson carefully places a hand at the small of my back, tentatively in case I deny his advances, and circles a pattern. The touch sends shivers across my body, and my back arches into the contact.

"Breathe," he cautions again. "It's of the past, and we can't change the past."

I nod solemnly.

We arrive at the first tree, and groans come from seemingly nowhere and everywhere. It sets my teeth on edge, not knowing where the moans originate from.

"What is that?" I ask.

I get my answer as the sandman holds open a nearby tree's crystals, and they clank together like tiny chimes.

"In," he beckons while his gaze sweeps the forest of dark trees and sparkling leaves.

Sharing a look with Dyson, a question becomes evident on my face. He only shrugs and dips to enter. I wait a heartbeat and then follow, dutifully curious. Once inside, I stop short.

A dwarf, hand mid-raised to hang satchels on the branches, stares with wide large eyes. Nervously, his tongue darts to the corner of his lips.

"Sandy," I caution.

Fear spikes in my chest and lights my nerves on fire. Mindful of Sandy's earlier warning, I fight to keep the flames inside by clenching my fists, and my nails dig into my palms. He's either a friend or an enemy, and if he tries to dart from this tree, he won't get very far. Not if my aim is good.

The sandman gingerly touches his hand to the back of my arm, steadying me, and his voice rumbles over my head.

"Nally," he greets.

I look up to the sandman's tall height and shiny bald head, then to the dwarf, and then back again.

"Friend?" I ask. I get no answer. Just several seconds of the dwarf's stare locked on Sandy.

Dyson steps forward, his hand extended in greeting. "Dyson," he introduces.

Nally flinches, and his short and stocky body quivers as though he's expecting swift punishment from the gesture.

I soften toward him, my tense shoulders relaxing, and Sandy drops his hand from my arm. "He's terrified," I murmur.

"This isn't possible," Nally mumbles. He lifts his gaze back to Sandy and retreats by one step. The action bumps his back into the crystals, and they clink once more.

Lightly bending my knees, I coo, "We won't hurt you," as though I'm talking to a frightened pup. His prominent Adam's apple bobs as he swallows my truth.

A moan, louder than those on the path, vibrates the trunk of the tree, and I look to where it's coming from. Inside the tree is a face through an opening just large enough to see the pained features of another sandman.

Anger spreads through me and tingles the tips of my fingers. I pin the dwarf with immediate blame. "What are you doing to him?"

"It is all right, little dragon," Sandy cautions. "Nally is simply tending to the infant's needs."

"Infant?" Dyson says with a scientific inquisitorial tone. "He looks full grown to me. Do they not go through the typical human infant growths?"

Bristling to Dyson's indifference, I head to the hole in the trunk and peer at the man inside. Upon exhale, my breath fans the sandman's face. His wrinkled eyelids soften like my presence soothes his agony, and the rigid muscles in his cheek smooth.

"But he's in pain," I whisper, reaching inside and touching the sandman's cheek.

"Yes," Nally answers simply, rushing over with a hobbling shuffle and batting my hand away. The slap stings, and I rub the tender skin. "He is growing. It is how it's done here."

Dyson snakes forward and gapes at the trunk. "This tree is made of inferaze."

Sandy's earlier words bring light to my tangled emotions. The inferaze creates sandmen, he had said. It's cruel, though, and less magical than I had pictured. No one should be born or created with pain.

274

Nally keeps his hand up, prepared to whack mine away again if I dare to think of touching the sandman once more.

"Yes," Nally snaps bitterly to Dyson. "What are you doing here, sandman? I've heard the rumors. You're dead."

"I was, my friend" Sandy admits, strolling slowly to Nally. He holds out his arms, and Nally peers at him with an underlying wariness.

"Do you not care for me as you once did?" Sandy asks.

"Of course I do," Nally spits. "But this isn't possible. It's a trick of the mind." He tugs on the ends of his long brown hair pinned back by a leather strip. As he paces under the crystal leaves, his tongue darts out again and coats his lips with another layer of gleaming saliva. "They said I was going mad. They told me so. I didn't believe them. They're right though. I am mad."

Sandy blocks his path and wraps his arms around the dwarf's bulky neck. "You're not mad."

Through all the seriousness of the situation, a delirious chuckle bubbles up my throat, and I cough to clear it. "I beg to differ," I mumble, and Dyson shoots me a warning scowl. I look away, smiling anyway.

"Why are you here?" Nally asks, sniffling into the sandman's borrowed fur from the Guardian Realm. Realizing what he sheds his tears on, he quickly lifts his head and clutches the fur with meaty, calloused fists. "You - This - You've walked with the Guardians."

Sandy inclines his head. "I have. It is why we are here."

"Oh?" Nally questions. He retreats from Sandy's embrace, needing the space for an immediate explanation.

With a deep exhale, Sandy explains everything, even details I knew nothing about. His time in the Death Realm, the battle, the fallen angels and how it came about. It is a tale I am familiar with, but to hear his side of it - the things he had witnessed and what he had to do to survive - it's almost like I wasn't a part of those memories at all.

Something he said hits me most though. I had no idea Tember had such deep love for Erma. My heart sinks, and I swallow my guilt for being so absorbed with myself. I should have known. The way she would talk about Erma, the wonder that had glistened in her eyes were telling enough when I reflect on them. The mere mention of the fee had a smile tugging at her lips every time.

However, I can see why their love would be conflicted. My own coven disowned me because of the simple request I had asked of Erline. My relationship with her is beyond complicated. Though I wish more than anything I could change history and never have met Erline, I know that if I did, we wouldn't be fighting for freedom today. And I would be motherless. And Dyson would be in the void. And Sandy would still be forced to tend to his Fee's needs. The devastation would go on and on.

My mother. It's better to know she's alive, knowing we'll never have a proper relationship, than to know I'll never see her again. My mother would have been in that battle on the Death Realm if I had not stepped in on the cold, wintry night, and she would have died again, spending eternity in the void.

Small blessings, I tell my inner sorrow.

Dyson feels my turmoil, notices my rigid posture, and snakes his hand into mine. His prodding forces me to uncross my arms. I give him a small smile, thanking him for his support, and squeeze his warm fingers in mine. My smile quickly fades though, and Dyson's hand is whipped from mine, stolen by the dwarf on bended knee.

I squeak when he kisses the flesh of the back of my hand, and horror shrouds my face.

"Dragon," Nally coos. "I have much to thank you for and much to beg of you. Your dreams filtering into our realm have gifted most with the ability to feel!"

I double blink. "Come again?" My what? Is that why Sandy can feel emotions? And the others we crossed paths with on our way here?

The sandman chuckles. "Does this mean you will help?"

Nally stands and pulls his smock away from sweaty skin. "Yes. But first . . . first you must see what we're dealing with."

With an exaggerated huff, I wipe the slobber from my hand onto my jeans and grumble under my breath at Dyson's low chuckle.

The two exit together, and just as I go to follow, Dyson grabs my arm and whirls me back. My chest bumps into his, and I look up, bewildered. His eyes twinkle the reflection of the crystals, and the hues of yellow shining

277

through them play across his face. He searches my eyes, and when my face softens, he bends and brushes his lips against mine.

CHAPTER SEVENTEEN

DYSON COLEMAN

DREAM REALM

Somehow, we had managed to sneak our way through the rest of the eerie tree wombs undetected. Nally knows every crook and cranny, every path that's always taken and the ones that barely show any travel. I trail at the end, contemplating what Fate had bestowed upon me like a king to his knight.

Fate is an alpha dog, a command you can't ignore but one I know I can trust in word. My wolf warmed to him instantly, seeming to know more about him than I did. Animals have a sixth sense, even the supernatural kind, but it can be irritating when he has more information than I do.

His voice keeps echoing in my head though, telling me what I must do, what I must discover for myself. If I close my eyes, I can still see the swirls of his sparkles. It sort of reminds me of Reaper's Breath, the way the specks had moved, and for a second, my thoughts touch on the creature of the Death Realm and what Fate has in store for it. I miss that cunning creature.

It'd be easier if Fate had just told me what I needed to know. Instead, I feel like I'm on a wild goose chase. This, the creatures Sureen is building for her own personal army, is one of them. The dome, another. He wanted me to see it for myself, perhaps to understand the severity of the situation.

The dome is the entire realm's life force. It's Sureen's beating heart of magic; where she draws her power from and where she fuels it. If it were destroyed, does that mean she would be destroyed as well?

But now is not the time to consider these possibilities. I just hope Fate will tell me when the time is right.

I lower my gaze from the dome back to Kat hiking in front of me. I'm aware of what she feels for me - reluctance yet trusting. And I can still feel the tingle on my lips where hers brushed mine. I can also understand her deeper feelings like the love she keeps carefully tucked away. She's scared of it, of what I offer.

I believe she only trusts me because her instincts demand it. She feels more herself when I'm around, when I'm touching her. Getting her to feel more for me is the true challenge, and because of this, I feel like I stole the kiss in the forest. I couldn't pass up the opportunity for a true one, so I snuck it while I could, under the tree womb.

Kat's not a Shifter. Not really. She wouldn't feel the bond like I do. Anything more than this first step in a relationship is lost to me. Wooing women is Flint's area, and even though he gave me advice in all aspects female, I don't think his advice will work on this complicated woman striding in front of me.

As if she's aware that I'm thinking of her, she peeks at me from over her shoulder. I smile and give a saluting wave.

She's deliciously stubborn and formidably strong. I have one shot to make her mine and one shot only. The last thing I want to do is make it seem like I manipulated her into loving me. She has enough of that going on in her life - a life which is no longer her own. The fate of the entire realms rests solely on her shoulders.

Fate warned me of this also, to make sure she stays on the right path. He told me by simply being near her, I'll be able to keep her intentions on the straight and narrow. I've witnessed how easy it is for her to lose herself when faced with choices concerning life and death. Kill or be killed.

That's the true reason I brought her with me, for fear her darkness would chase away what I offer - solace - while I'm away.

I halt as a festering tickle scratches at my throat. Bending, I cough and splutter, using my knee to support my upper half.

"You okay?" Kat asks, hovering over me. She pats my back and jars my spine with the strength of it.

Breathing in a large gulp of air, I stand upright. "Yeah," I croak and wipe sweat from my forehead. I gaze at the beads of precipitation incredulously, and a chill raises goosebumps over my skin.

"Come on," Kat whispers and tugs on my sleeve.

A few long strides, and we we're back in line behind our two escorts, my lungs oddly huffing and puffing with the effort. Maybe the air is different here, and it's just a matter of getting used to it. After all, these caves are mined. That should kick up dust enough for a bout of allergies.

Passing piles of satchels, a momentary thought nags my conscience about taking some of them. Sandy said this place is a warning label of flammable objects. If the dream dust is the same, it would make one hell of a weapon.

Instead of acting on this instinct to arm myself and my mate, I stride past them and pocket this information for a later time.

We reach the edge of the trees and start traveling around the curve of the dome. Kat shields her eyes from the bright light it pulses, and I squint, refusing to allow her from my sight. This area may be void of travelers right now, but I'd be a fool to believe we aren't being watched. Inside me, my wolf takes in each detail, each subtle movement of my friends, ready to defend his mate if the need arises.

It isn't long before we arrive at a brass, rusted door which couldn't possibly lead to anything but underground. I suppress the urge to tip the ever curious Katriane - who examines it with more interest than I do - over my shoulder and demand we return to the Guardian Realm where it isn't as foreboding as a door leading to the unknown. Underground is a death sentence with only one way in and one way out. Only a fool would go in there.

282

The handle looks to be the only thing which isn't deteriorating, and Nally opens it with a firm, muscular grasp and one heaving yank.

Stale and rotten air wafts my face, and I turn my head from the offending smell. I cough, cupping my fist over my mouth. The cough feels deeper, rooted in a spot I can't ease. When it subsides, I turn back to the group and eye the pitch-black entry suspiciously.

Kat hesitates at the opening and then squares her shoulders.

"Wait," I demand, grabbing her upper arm as she moves forward.

She whips her head to the side and squints at my hand. "What?"

"What if -" I begin and shoot Nally with a speculating expression. "What if it's a trap?"

"Well," she says with little patience, shrugging off my grip. "There's only one way to find out, isn't there?"

And with that, she ducks her head and dives into the darkness. Her feet patter against the stairs, and Sandy and Nally shoot impatient eyes at me.

"Nally can be trusted, Dyson. I give you my word."

I clear my throat. "Right," I grunt and follow Kat in.

At the back of an absurdly large room, the stairs step out into an opening that's hidden from plain sight by rows of machines. White stone, identical to the Death Realm, holds the walls up in haphazard and sporadic placement. It's as though it was assembled hastily. I suppose you can't have inferaze walls with the inferno burning in the center of this fortress. Its flames are as tall as I am, a blue so bright it's almost clear, and two dwarves feed it with small chunks of inferaze. The smell of the fire is like some kind of alluring spice, almost indistinguishable from a heavy scent of decay lingering in the air, though I can't pinpoint where it's coming from.

As we sneak to the first machine, Nally pushes us behind. The big, boxy machine grinds and turns gears. It looks like Frankenstein's lab in here, and an uneasy feeling settles over my sixth sense.

I cough again and wipe another odd layer of sweat from my brow. The sweat is pouring from my body in the heat of this place. I flare my nostrils and take in a proper breath, but it's useless, and I cough again under Kat's watchful concern.

Mindful of the hot metal, we inch as close as we can get to the machine. Sandy, Kat, and I peer our heads over the top of it after two chatting dwarves hobble by.

Instead of hiding with us, Nally continues forward, weaving between the dwarves working this misshapen factory and the gears poking through slits in the ground. With a destination in mind, unbeknownst to me, he composes himself by straightening his spine, acting as though he belongs. I suppose he does. This is his realm, and after listening to the conversation he and Sandy had on the way here, mostly one sided, it sounds like he's a dwarf in a high-ranking position if not someone respected. I had suspected he was boasting because not minutes before, he was rambling about how insane everyone thinks he is while slapping a dragon's hand from touching his infant sandman.

"Did Nally build these?" I ask, eyeing each machine.

Sandy brushes his hands against the rusted metal of the machine we duck behind and hisses when his skin sizzles. "Yes, this is his work, his design," he says, shaking the burned flesh at his side.

"Then how can we trust him?" Kat mutters, and I roll my eyes. Now she asks? Now? When I had voiced my concern not moments before?

Women.

"Because like I, the dwarves are forced to serve."

There's no choice but to trust him, I suppose. Either he tattles, and we're dead, or he doesn't, and we're caught and then very dead. Hysteria threatens to bubble in my chest. Our chances of getting out of here undetected by a loyal creature of Sureen are slim to none. Come to think of it, I'm surprised we haven't tripped some sort of alert already.

"We need the dwarves, but I have a terrible feeling about this," Kat mumbles.

She's right. We do need them. If they can create these machines, there's no telling how their brilliant minds could aid us in the coming days.

"What do these machines do?" I ask.

Kat grimaces after taking a whiff. "It smells of corpses."

"Because it is," Sandy mumbles, keeping his eyes on his friend's whereabouts. "Nally said that not all of the shade humans competed in the arena. Some were taken here and stripped of their skin. Their skin is fed into these machines and sown together for a new creature."

Katriane flashes wide eyes at the side of Sandy's face. Guilt lingers there before malice replaces it. This truly is some sort of Frankenstein bullshit. Many of those people were my friends.

I turn forward, my jaw ticking, and I wince as the muscles ache. My legs strain when a wave of exhaustion overcomes me, my limbs jelly.

"Are you guys hot?" I ask, but neither answer.

Suppressing a cough, I squint at tall and wide podiums which reach from ground to ceiling. Each one has a large, hinged door at the base, and I jump when several open in unison. Steam exits the openings, and giant feet step through. Their movements are robotic like a march of nutcrackers, only these aren't nutcrackers.

Kat gasps beside me, and I hoarsely curse under my breath, wobbling limbs forgotten. The ground shakes with each stride as several orcs emerge and file in a line. Marching, they head in a direction we can't see from our position.

"An army," Sandy mumbles, his attention divided between the orcs and the safety of Nally who still converses with his friends.

"You've been busy, Sureen," I mumble. "It would seem the Colosseum was not only to feed a twisted mind but to line the humans up for slaughter in more ways than one."

"And to test the new creature," Kat growls.

Oh, it was for more than that, I think to myself, remembering my promise with Fate not to share what he's told me.

"You are correct," Sandy agrees.

"What's he doing?" I ask, worried Nally's spilling the secrets of our whereabouts. Normally, I'd be able to hear what's being said with my sharp shifter hearing, but a ringing sound is vibrating my eardrums, threatening a massive headache.

"Gathering our army," Sandy mumbles.

"I don't think a few dwarves are going to compete with that," Kat grumbles, flicking her thumbs at the exiting orcs.

Sandy's anxious face spirals to grim. "They're knowledgeable, young dragon. Brain will always beat muscle even if we only have a few on our side."

I cough into my hand, barking, and something wet splats against my palm. Pulling it away, I observe the liquid, fingers trembling.

Blood.

"That's not good," I whisper. In a pocket of my mind, I acknowledge that allergies wouldn't do this.

Kat's attention is hesitantly released from the scene of filing orcs and chatting dwarves, and she gawps at the red staining my fingers. Her eyes widen and lift to mine, slow and filled with such fear. Then, they flicker with her dragon's immediate presence.

Sandy's voice calls from far away, an echo down a long hall even though he's directly beside me. "Your eyes are bleeding, Dyson."

CHAPTER EIGHTEEN

AIDEN VANDER

DEMON REALM

I shimmer to the same spot I left Ferox and her sisters. They remain exactly as I left them, as though they didn't move a muscle while they waited for my return. Time works differently on each realm, this I'm aware of; I didn't know how different until this very moment.

Ferox watches me, wary but expectant. "Is it done?"

"Can't you smell it, sister?" Another answers, her voice shrill and displeasing to the ear. Her slitted nostrils flare, and she pulls in my scent. "It's unlike any other feed I've encountered."

Stuffing my hands in my pockets, I tuck my feelings to hide my guilt.

"Did you kill your victim?" Ferox asks.

My jaw ticks, and I narrow my eyes, my head still tucked. She takes my unvoiced answer as confirmation and tilts her head while her eyes roam my body. "Interesting. You feel sympathy."

A sister pyren swims forward, level with Ferox. "Perhaps he's more formidable than we realized." This one's voice is pleasing but childlike. I peek under my lashes to place the face with the voice. "A demon who feels, a demon who's most powerful . . . you were right to choose this one, Ferox."

"Choose me?" I question, confused. No one chooses me. I'm not a possession.

Ferox smiles. "Yes, Thrice Born. I chose you because as it stands, you're the only one who can free us. The rest blindly follow Corbin and do his bidding without a second thought. You . . . you feel. A heart beats in your chest." She points. "How do you feel?"

"Different," I admit with reluctance. And I do. I've never felt so alive.

"As you should. Now. . ." she whispers, inching closer to the path I prowl on. "I've helped you twice, given you advice when I could have remained silent. What will you do with what you've consumed? How will I benefit from our arrangement, Thrice Born?"

My eyebrows raise into my forehead, and I curl my hands inside my pockets. "You mentioned a war?" She nods. "I cannot free you on my own. There are others -"

"We know of the others," Ferox's shrill sister spits.

I narrow my eyes at her for the interruption. "When the war truly begins, the others will get involved. However, you cannot be an innocent bystander. If you are to be free, you have to be willing to fight for it."

Ferox considers this. "And what do you propose to be our next move?"

My voice drops an octave. "You wait to be called on."

The collective group bristles at the order, and their hair tentacles curl quickly and unpleasantly as though the tips were burned on the black lava's hot surface.

I refuse to be a servant to another being. If they want my help, they'll have to be patient as well as willing to get their hands dirty.

"And how will I know when I'm called on," Ferox growls, irritated.

"Listen for your name."

Shimmering from the path, I leave the pyrens behind, my purpose due elsewhere. But mid-shimmer, I'm yanked like someone swiped my feet out from under me. Unconsciousness descends immediately.

When I wake, slow and disoriented, a roar of blood whooshes in my ears. The wooden chair I sit on creaks when I adjust my weight against the uncomfortable strain. My hands and legs look to be untied but they're stuck, bound by invisible restraints. I yank against them, testing the strength and earning myself a few burns along my wrists.

Murder in my gaze, I swivel my head to get a better look at my hands and feet. Nothing is wrapped around my wrists, but I feel it there, tight and painfully pinching. I look to my feet and try to move them, but the heels refuse to leave the ground as though they're cemented to it.

Vexed, I growl and sway my rump against the chair. It does no good. The chair doesn't rock.

The room is dark and dimly lit by a reddish glow at my back, casting eerie shadows across the clear glass floor underneath my feet. My hearing tells me it's a lavafall, most likely inside a fireplace chimney built with the heads of screaming skulls identical to the ones in the main area of the Domus Timore. That's where I am. The castle of demons, but in this part, this room, Oleum rain doesn't fall to feed my skin like it does everywhere else.

Under the glass floor is black lava, a slow flowing river, and red fire veins snake through the hot goop. Occasionally, they burst and fog the glass with sulfuric smoke.

Small, yet subtly hexagram-shaped, the room wafts a damp dungeon smell. Underneath the musk, the aroma of a freshly struck match burns my eyes.

I fight against the restraints once more and call on more of my strength with renewed determination. Whatever they have planned for me won't end with negotiations over tea.

"Be no point in fighting it," a familiar voice mumbles. I freeze and lift my head from my strained struggles.

The demon whose skin is flayed over most of his body, the one who escorted me from my black pit rebirth, hobbles and limps into my line of sight. "Corbin be knowing when you enter his realm." His one eye roams my body, my chair, then the walls.

"Tormentis Cubiculum," he hums, naming the room while watching the red reflections flicker like water at the base of a pool.

I grunt my displeasure and curl my fingers into my palm. "Torture Chamber?"

His eyes snap back to mine, and his loose skin slaps against bones to the sudden jerk. "Oh yes."

"You plan to torture me?" I chuckle low in my chest. "For what?"

He frowns while crossing his arms. Where his eyeball is missing, the skin invades the space of his cheekbone. "Why you wait so long to return to the Demon Realm, Thrice Born?"

I lick my lips and prepare myself for what's to come. "Errands."

TEMBER

GUARDIAN REALM

"They're everywhere," Jaemes confesses beside me in a displeased sort of way.

We crouch at the edge of the forest behind bushes that have miraculously withstood the torrential winter weathers and the earlier battle. Everything in this region of the Guardian Realm endures the cold, wind, and snow. A war is constant here, both physical and elemental.

The slender branch I hold out of our way nicks my skin along my wrist, and beads of blood drop to the snow by my shoes. The bush has hundreds of inch-long needles which drink the blood of any species in order to thrive. I use my free hand to cover it up with a handful of flakes, absentmindedly appeasing my level of stress.

As if the realm itself had divided lines of territory on its own, not fifty feet past the Elf's forest clearing, the snow stops, and green grass immediately replaces the frosty white. It makes the blades look greener than they are.

Earth's climate is much different than ours. I remember being in awe, watching the seasons change while protecting my first charge so many moons ago. Times were different back then, and beauty or horror could be found even in such tragic, quieter moments.

"Observant," I mutter back to him, gazing at the Angel's Ground floating high. The roofs dip into the clouds, and beyond that, the stars twinkle as the ceiling's backdrop. I miss it. I miss my home, and I'll do what's necessary to take it back.

Many of my white feathered brothers and sisters soar the sky, protecting those who hold it hostage while others are stationed on the ground below. They wait, still and silent, as they absorb every sound and sight, including detailed stretches of the forest line.

They knew we'd come. How could we not?

294

I growl and slam my fist against the bark of the tree beside me. It groans from the blow.

"Do you think we have enough?" Jaemes asks, his eyes flicking to each visible fallen angel, and his fingers clench, mentally tallying their totals.

"No."

Deeper in the forest, the angels who did not side with the rebellion wait with the elves of all four tribes. Not many of the other tribes came, and I didn't ask why. Why would they fight those they despise if the enemy is destroying itself from the inside out? I can only guess that those who've come are here on a volunteer basis, and our numbers suffer because of it.

Erma was forced to stay with them and keep the peace between her creations while Jaemes and I venture out to scout the enemy. But what we're seeing is something we didn't expect. Their numbers are on a grander scale than we had anticipated.

"Come," I demand.

I turn on my knees and flatten to the ground. Using my arms, I drag my body through the snow in hopes of maintaining some cover. It helps that our clothes and exposed skin were painted white by the tribes before we left, a camouflage to nature, but quick movements would surely give us away.

Many of the elves are dressed in armor but more as a scare tactic than a shield for vital organs. Shoulder pads with spikes from bushes like the one I cut myself on, belts made of dry creature intestines to hold their various weapons, and breastplates made of white feathers from past kills match the white paint. The weapons they wield are based on their tribe's trade.

My black wings, however, had refused to hold the white paint and even from the corner of my peripheral vision, I can see them glinting.

"Have you forgotten your role here, Wingless Wonder?" Jaemes asks, disturbing my fleeting thoughts. He's easily keeping up with me by crawling on all fours instead of flat to the ground.

I turn my head in his direction, and my white painted curls fall over my shoulder. The stiff tips drag in the snow and snag against the exposed brush. "Have you forgotten that I am no longer wingless? Should I be worried about your eyesight?"

"You will always be wingless in my eyes, little duck."

"You're a fool," I grumble.

Deeming this a safe distance from the edge of the forest, I stand and wipe the thawed snow on my hands against my jeans, smearing the paint. My wings rustle, tickling the back of my thighs while shaking flakes from the feathers.

"A fool? Should I be worried about delusions?" Jaemes asks. I hear the hint of a smile in his voice but refuse to acknowledge it.

Our feet crunch the stiff crystallized snow when we make our way back to the group. The closer we get, the more we can make out the shouts and bickering between sides. Jaemes and I share a look of annoyance as he holds a branch out of my way. The war is past the forest line, but we won't be able to begin it unless the one under the trees is resolved.

The two groups are divided - angels on one side and the elves on the other - and Erma is in the middle with her hands in the air, threatening her creations with an expression that'd smite a rainbow for daring to cross the sky.

"These are our fools," Jaemes corrects.

I run a wet hand through my hair and my fingers snag in the tangles. With the paint, it feels more like straw than the silk strands I'm used to. "It'll take a sudden miracle to convince them to work together." I look over at him. "Luckily, we have you."

Jaemes adjusts his bow over his chest, grumbles to himself, and marches forward. I raise my brows in surprise. I had expected some sort of verbal retaliation or egotistical retort. I received neither.

He whistles loud, gathering everyone's attention, and a small pack of prenumbras obediently pad to his side. I cringe and glance over my shoulder, paranoid the enemies will hear his call for silence.

"If you kill each other here, there will be no one left to save our realm," Jaemes yells. The muscles along his back ripple with each agitated twitch.

A green tattooed elf belonging to another tribe lifts his hand and points to the group of angels. His lips move, but I'm pulled from what he has to say by a disturbance of wind to my back.

The hairs on the back of my arms stand on end when a breath whispers in my ear. "His plan will not work," a male voice says.

I frown and glance over my shoulder. Nothing stands behind me, and only the snow sways with movement. I mask my expression, hardening it to look the part of being unnerved, and then mumble back to the invisible person. "Who are you?"

"*What*, not who," he chides. "What I am does not matter. The tribe leader's son is who we are discussing. His plan will not work."

I grind my teeth. "I do not trust what I cannot see."

The voice waits before responding. "And that is your largest fault, Tember."

I look over my shoulder again, expecting to see the person or creature who whispers sweet insults in my ear. My head and heart cry an internal war, one knowing the voice speaks truth and the other begging me to ignore it. I sigh through flared nostrils and glance back to the group. Jaemes is gesturing with his hands in another attempt to make them see reason.

"His plan – we have no choice," I announce. It's the only solid plan we have, and everyone had agreed to it before we left to scout.

"There is always a choice. Fate is only but a ripple of Choice."

I jut my chin. "Fate . . . You're –"

The voice hisses a laugh in my ear. "You are smarter than the elf gives you credit for. Now, the question

298

is, are you willing to follow my orders, or are you willing to perish?"

"Is that a threat?" I growl, fisting my hands and preparing myself to fight something I can't see.

"Fate does not threaten, young one." His voice is quiet and patient but hushed with contempt. "Fate is certain. But alas, it will not be by my command in which you fall, but by the choices you make."

"Many will fall," I correct, and my eyes immediately flick to Erma whose back is to me. If I ask, would he tell me her fate?

"Indeed," he agrees, the whisky voice carried by a gusty breeze.

No, I shouldn't ask. Erma is a fee who's been around since the beginning of time. This isn't the first war she's endured, and it won't be the last. Yet, my heart pumps in fear anyway.

"Then why are you here, whispering in my ear?"

"Because of your destiny. It's time to be brave."

I shuffle uncomfortably, catching the attention of a few before they dismiss me altogether. "Destiny?"

"Yes, Guardian. Your destiny. Do you wish to hear more?"

My eyes sweep those gathered, their attention solely on Jaemes. His shoulders are pulled back, and his arms ripple with power at each hand gesture. He was born to lead; this much is clear. And just like I, he is overlooked by his father. It is my hope that this war will prove his worth.

"Yes."

CHAPTER NINETEEN

ELIZA PLAATS

GUARDIAN REALM

Sweat beads at my brow. I swipe it away and return to my task, tending to the female elf on the table before me. The quarantine teepee is filling quickly, and there's only so much their healer and I can do. I've taught some helpers how to care for the infected, but even some of them have fallen ill.

At the far end, Dyson's shifter friends sleep under a heavily medicated state, the illness affecting them too. They stumbled in a handful of minutes ago as though the illness swept them as one. Dread curls my toes. If I lose them, Dyson will never forgive me.

"There's another," Mitus shouts weakly from the entrance. He coughs into his hand, and I raise my attention to him with wide eyes.

Sweat covers his head, the illness taking its hold. I swallow thickly, and the dread turns to defeat. It's a wonder he's even standing. Everyone else can barely hold their own weight when they stumble into the structure of death. That's what this place feels like to me. A tent to cap the many deaths.

But if we lose him...

Two elves, one holding the arms of another and one holding his legs, shuffle in directly after Mitus' proclamation. I blink rapidly, and my open mouth, which was ready to order Mitus to sit, shuts quickly.

"Yami," I utter, recognizing the elf who was investigating the red specks earlier.

I rush to the table they place him on, and my knee painfully bumps into the ledge along the way. The red ash is still smeared across his fingers, splayed open for immediate notice. The red...

"No," I whisper. Lifting his hand with a gentle grasp of his wide wrist, I inspect the leftovers staining his black striped skin.

Slow in stride, Mitus lumbers over to me. "What is it?" he demands, his voice raspy and weak. He grips the edge of the table for support.

"The red specks - they fell from the sky," I say, lifting my head and revisiting the memory as though it floats across the skin of the teepee.

"Yes," Mitus nods, peering over my shoulder to inspect the hand I hold up. "I remember. It clouded my eyes. The others say it never hit the forest. Only the clearing."

I turn to him, and the elf's hand falls to the table with a thud. I wince and send a silent apology to the unconscious patient already dripping sweat from the deadly grips of the infection. "It's the illness."

He tilts his head, not following my train of thought.

I ball my fists, frustrated at their lack of medical knowledge. I shouldn't be because they've never needed it, but right now he's my blame-goat. "The red specks are an infection. It was sprinkled over everyone here. Even you." I eye him as his body precariously sways.

"You need to lay down," I add slowly.

Waving off my remaining elf assistants who quickly rush to his side, he pins me with an unconvincing glare. "Why aren't you infected then?"

I frown, open my mouth, and snap it shut when Erline walks in. "Because she's the wife of a fee. She's immune. Kat will also be immune as well as Aiden because of their fee blood. All those who were in the forest are safe. All the children who sought shelter with the sandman are safe. Only those who inhaled the dust will be infected." She looks to me. "This is not spread in the traditional way, doctor."

I hear her words, but my brain only echoes one. Aiden. How could he possibly be immune? Kat has fee blood, and a lot of it from what I understand. But Aiden? He was right there with me when the dust settled. Could the fee blood come from his third birth?

Mitus drops to one knee, smacking against the packed snow. I bark out orders to get him to a table, and the demand is quickly delivered by waiting elves who have volunteered to help. Erline follows me, and together we hover over Mitus like fretting mothers. When he tries to sit up, Erline holds out a palm and uses her magic to lay him back down.

"What is this?" I frantically ask, taking a cold cloth from a waiting elf. "What are we dealing with?"

In the ER, I had a stellar reputation for remaining calm, but there, I knew what I was dealing with, no matter the injury. I knew what to expect and when to expect it. My hands would fly over a body with practiced ease even with the impossible cases. That isn't the case here. I'm helpless and utterly alone.

She takes the cloth from me and lays it over Mitus' head. "The Red Death," she conveys.

"You've seen this?" If it has a name, and she knows it, she's definitely seen it.

She nods grimly and fusses over the wrinkles in the cloth. "It was what Kat made a deal with me for - to cure her coven of The Red Death in exchange for Myla's soul in her body."

I have no idea what she is talking about, and my patience is wearing thin. I suppress a growl, demanding answers. All the fee tend to talk in riddles, and I'm about done with it. We're running out of time. "Well then," I spit. "How do we cure it? What's the antidote?"

She slowly lifts her eyes to mine. "The tear of a first born witch."

I slam my hands on my hips at the same time the healer drops the bowl to the ground, shocked. "Point me to the witch, and I'll make her cry."

Erline closes her eyes and breathes deep as though she's about to spill a secret she doesn't wish to share with me. "Katriane DuPont."

"But -" I splutter, my hands falling to my side. "She's... she's in the Dream Realm."

"Correct," she whispers with more grace than due when talking about a deadly illness. Lifting her head, she ganders out the wide-open door she came in. "The battle is about to begin."

How can she be so utterly at ease?

I growl and lean toward her, threatening, "I don't give a rat's ass about that battle. We have one here. How do we reach Kat? How do we get her back here?"

She fans out the towel, taking her time to place it back on Mitus' head. "We don't." She lifts her eyes to mine. "I do."

DYSON COLEMAN

DREAM REALM

"Over here," Nally urges in an underground hallway. It's unoccupied and echoes with the thud of each foot.

The joints in my knees quickly give way, and a wave of heat turns my muscles to jelly. I feel and look like a puppet, pulled by the strings of a quick sweeping illness. I try to command my legs while allowing two dwarves to support my weight, their hands on my arms. But I can't. I can't move them. Whatever is happening is swift, and for the first time in a while, I truly fear how long I have left to breathe.

"What is this?" The sandman asks hurriedly, grasping my upper arms from behind me before I can hit the ground. A couple dwarves rush to aid him, and they help support me by wrapping strong arms around my waist. My lanky body must feel like a fish under their grips.

They lay me gently on the floor, and Kat's frightened expression looms over me, stealing my view of the hallway ceiling. The beautiful curve of her eyebrows is distorted in raised positions, and she runs a shaky hand through the hair above her ears, pulling on the short black hair. The light of the blue fire, reflecting through the hall from the Frankenstein lab we just fled, shimmers against the strands.

I cough again and blood sprays, soaking her jeans around the calves. With much effort, I scratch the hollow of my ear, and shakily pull my hand back. The tips of my fingers are coated with more blood. Not only is it shedding from my eyes and mouth but every exit in my face.

More faces, new and recognizable, arrive and hover over mine. Nally's, the sandman's, and a few other dwarves. Nally licks his lips nervously, his tongue darting to each corner. *He was successful after all*, my mind thinks, the thought irrational in such a dire moment.

The heat seeping from my veins dissipates, and a cold draft shudders through my bones. I grunt, squeeze my eyes shut, and clutch my stomach when my insides feel like a knife cut through my diaphragm.

"I'm dying," I croak with an exuberant amount of energy. More energy than I feel like I have. It drains quickly as though it travels with the blood pouring from seemingly everywhere. Despite the pain, it feels peaceful, right even. That thought alone should scare me, but it doesn't.

"It's The Red Death," Kat mourns, her hot fingers lifting my eyelids further than I can. I yank away from her to cough once more. The cough roars in my ears, replacing external sounds with the rush of blood. Their voices become mumbled, wavering in and out of audibility.

"How did he get this?" I catch Sandy asking. His long fingers touch my forehead, but I barely feel it. Each blink is difficult to make, my eyes a heavy weight. If I just shut them, if I rest for a moment, I know peace will be delivered.

Peace. I wonder what that truly feels like. Is it as promising as its allure, like a bright warm light at the end of a cold tunnel? Inside me, my wolf sighs with relief at the prospect.

The sandman picks up my hand and cradles it in his. I marvel at the size difference. His is much larger than mine, too large. Alien-like, almost, and the skin is smooth with fresh soft callouses under the knuckles.

Another chilling wave sweeps from my head to my toes, but this time, it doesn't frighten me. I internally reach for it like a toddler grasping for his favorite blanket. More coughs jar my spine against the ground, and they don't cease. Blood chokes me, fills my lungs and splutters from my mouth. My eyes widen. I can't breathe.

A bright light comes from behind those gathered above me, and for a moment, I believe it to be the light I seek. But Kat whips her head around when it illuminates the tunnel and banishes the blue hued reflections of the fire down the way.

"Erline!" she yells.

I choke once more, but it's half-hearted, an attempt by my body to try for life once more. But my brain has accepted my fate. It knows this is my end, and Erline's bright light welcomes me. The voices become a blur, my consciousness fading quickly. I mentally grasp the light as it wraps itself around me, thinking it's my ticket to the void, and snuggle in for a peaceful, eternal sleep.

CHAPTER TWENTY

KATRIANE DUPONT

GUARDIAN REALM

"He'll be okay?" I ask Erline while watching Eliza bark orders within the teepee of the infected. It's quite a remarkable structure, and it battles the chilling breeze and holds strong against the elements.

Pulling at my fingers hovering about my middle, I'm unable to stop the nervous gesture. When my anxiety becomes too much to bear, I pull harder, and the knuckles pop, a jarring audible crack of a twig snapping in two.

I can feel Dyson's beating heart in a back pocket of my mind, just as the sandman's. Sandy's vitals are strong while he hovers at the entrance, and Dyson's are gaining in strength. The fear I felt on the Dream Realm when he was slipping away was unlike any other. The way his eyes had looked, unseeing, still haunts me. It was close. Too close. But what frightens me most is how he seemed to welcome it.

With a tube tucked at the rim of my eye, the glass ice cold as the wind whistles inside the small ledge, Erline continues to gather my freely falling tears. The salty wetness trickles from my eyes and leaves a chilling trail along my frosty cheeks, freely flowing by my heartbreak for Dyson.

I've come to care for him despite my best efforts to deny everything. It's how the fingers around my heart loosen with every minute he's near. How I can breathe when he looks at me. How he chases away my darkest thoughts with three little words.

I see you, the memory taunts, his voice just as crisp as the last time he said it, pulling me from the pocket of my mind my conscience hid in.

But my sorrow isn't the only thing I shed tears for, unable to stop them as they flow at a fast rate. With every step the elves carry Dyson away from me, I can feel the darkness creep back forward, squeezing my heart as a reminder of its presence. I want revenge for Dyson's state, for almost killing him.

"Yes," Erline answers. "And so will the others once they receive your tears."

She sloshes the liquid to accentuate her authorial statement, and the tube brings forth memories of the last time she captured my tears. That day, inside an Earth Realm's frigid forest, I was the deliverer of a cure, and I wonder idly why she's taking charge of this moment instead of myself. I am the one, after all, who swiped my tears with quick fingers and dipped them into Dyson's mouth on the Dream Realm. And not a moment too soon, either.

Behind us, three dwarves, those we were able to gather, Nally among them, quietly rave to one another. Their tones sway in awe, and I'm drawn to it. When I tip my chin to get a better glance at them, to see how they're fairing, Erline grasps my jaw and forces my face forward again. I sniff my agitation, and the fog from my hot breath obscures the immediate space between us.

I don't imagine the dwarves have ever been to the Guardian Realm, and the way Nally has spoken about it tells me they hold it in high regard. Perhaps they'll feel safer here, freer. No doubt they'll be discussing plans and inventions soon. Without Sureen here to tell them no, they'll be able to construct anything they want. But right now, they're in shock over the legendary elves.

With my face frozen in Erline's firm grip, I angle my eyes and sweep what I can of the village. It looks more put together than when we left mere hours ago, or so it feels. But here, it seems to have been a good day or two.

The skin of the teepees, which once smoked with an extinguished fire, are brand new and seemingly more elaborate and larger than before. Instead of the cracked and dry surfaces from battling the drier elements, they're smooth and flawless and easily bow to accommodate the wind without tipping the structures over. The blood and red specks are covered by fresh prints marking a new layer of snow, and the objects that were skewed in a hasty exit for safety are now back to their original places and pieced back together with what this realm's nature has to offer.

My eyes sweep past Erline's shoulder. "How many are infected?" I ask and blink a few more tears when I watch a family weep over their now dead child. Their cries and pleas in their native tongue pierce the agonized moans of the others.

"Almost all who defended the village."

I frown, flicking my attention to Erline's concentrated expression. Her eyebrows are furrowed, and her black orbed eyes reflect my concern. My face is smudged with dusty dirt and the already dried blood belonging to Dyson.

"How is that possible?" I whisper. "Isn't this contagious?"

"The red dust only fell inside the village, daughter." She lifts an inquisitorial white brow to me. "Did each of your coven fall ill when it swept through the Demi-Lune home?"

"Well, no." I shift uneasily. I hadn't fallen ill at all, and there had been a few witches who tended to those who were. They had remained unaffected by The Red Death, too. I had never asked how they contracted it. I was gone when the first fell to the illness, tending to my shop.

She returns her attention to the tube, satisfied with my pondering. "An anomaly. This illness was made by magic, and magic isn't perfect. It is my hope those in battle remain unaffected and fall by the sword and not The Red Death."

"Excuse me?" I ask, snapping from the memories of what I once called home. "What battle?"

Standing fully erect, Erline passes my tears to an elf when he hastily approaches. He's scrawny as though he has yet to come into manhood, but his tall height is foretelling that he soon will. The elf bows and backs away as quickly as he came. He straightens when the cover of the structure casts shadows across his tattooed skin, and he disappears inside, weaving between the grieving, the healers, and the ill.

"The one at the Angel's Ground." She tips her head to the side, and a lock of white hair catches in the breeze, whipping like a sleek ribbon under her chin. "Have you forgotten already?"

I stretch my neck and relieve the tension settled at the base of my skull. I had forgotten about that and briefly recall such an update inside my teepee after the first battle. With everything we had witnessed over this short period of time, it had slipped my mind that while some fight for their lives, others are fighting for their homes.

Looking past the triangular structures, I peer into the eerie forest, trying to get a grasp of where I am. The trees were witness to many deaths, and I briefly wonder what else they've seen over their long lives. "I can't see the Angel's Ground from here. Are they at least winning?"

She averts her gaze, tipping her chin and following the path of an elf's print. I didn't miss the glossy film slipping over her black eyes - the telltale sign she's peering into another part of this realm. My mother would get the same look with her visions.

"I don't know," Erline begins, her voice hushed with secrets she's unwilling to share.

For a second, I wish I had the power to tap into unseen occurrences like this. I'd be able to tell a great many things. But I dismiss the desire quickly. Those who can peer into the future or can see through another's eyes have a great burden to bear. I don't need another burden. I have a collection of them to keep me warm.

"Tember is out there," I declare unnecessarily. A primal instinct to protect her hushes my words as the rush of needing to do so swiftly takes over my thoughts. But the thoughts are swiftly stolen, and a flicker inside the teepee averts my gaze from things I can't see from here.

With much effort, Evo, Kenna, Bre, and Flint filter out of the structure, concerned looks on their gaunt and bloody faces. I had forgotten how quickly my tears can heal, and memories of my mother's own miraculous recovery surface. I was almost too late for her, too, just as I had been for Dyson. My tears can't heal the dead. The soul is always swift to cross realms, and when it does, only a powerful hand can bring it back. Only the cruel would taunt a soul this way, and Kheelan and Corbin's faces flicker in my mind.

Evo folds Kenna in a loving embrace, the kind only true love blossoms, and she tucks her face into the crook of his arm.

Their clothes are stained with their own blood, and the iron scent fills the air. In this moment, I see them differently than I once did. I think, on some level, I felt superior compared to them, but that feeling is quickly whisked away. They're survivors, having seen and endured their fair share of disasters. The earlier battle wasn't the first we've fought together. It won't be the last, either. Fighting alongside each other makes them family.

Sweat still clings to their bodies and spreads the red droplets of blood in odd patterns along the cloth of their shirts. Bre releases Flint's hand when she sees me, rushes forward with open arms, and wraps them tightly around me. My body sways precariously with the abrupt affection, and I note how her body is still warm to the touch from the fever.

With a deep shuddering sigh, I return the hug, more for greedy comfort than for fear she may crumble under her weakened body.

"Thank you," she confesses. "For saving Dyson. For saving us."

I pat her on the back awkwardly, the comfort quickly fleeing, and I busy myself by glaring at Erline whose knowing smile dares to grace her face.

"How are you feeling?" I ask instead of the traditional *thank you.*

I've never been one for such affection. At least, not lately. When my coven banished me from my home, I had to learn to console myself. Gratitude has been rare, even when I had saved the witches. The thanks I had received was to live a lonely life as they kicked me from the only place I called home.

She pulls away, taking her feverish warmth with her. "Better. The antidote worked fast. Even now I can feel my strength returning. It feels like a recharging of batteries."

I double blink and quickly mask my surprise by smacking my lips once. Were they not told what the antidote was? I look to Erline and she dips her head, answering my unasked question.

She's preserving the knowledge of my healing abilities to only those who need to know. Trusted people, perhaps? I wonder who the all-mighty Mother Nature classifies as trustworthy. I suppose wolf shifters are a pack species and gossip notoriously as second nature. It is a wise choice to keep it from them, at least for now.

And I suppose it's for the best. If their gossip would reach the wrong ears and word got out I could cure the incurable, every last tear would be drained from my body. The thought of how they'd acquire those tears makes me shudder and instantly douses any kind notion of curing cancer. There isn't enough *me* to go around.

I pull my coat tight around me and eye Bre's bare arms with a scowl of concern. Erline follows my gaze, and with a flick of her wrist, each shifter's coats are returned to them, magically zipped. The fabrics crackle with the next immediate breeze.

Jumping in shock, Kenna fists her coat before pinning a glare at Erline's blonde hair. I don't believe she likes Mother Nature, and the thought of such a prickly wolf disliking the very thing she's meant to love tugs at the corners of my lips in a rare show of a smile. She drives home her point with a few choice curses.

I've always enjoyed Kenna's constant sour mood even if the little Queen Alpha frightens me, and this time is no different. Evo and I chuckle together despite our best efforts to squash it.

Bre runs a hand through her blonde hair, seemingly oblivious or immune to her best friend's attitude. "How can we help? What can we do?"

I raise my eyebrows at her, look to Erline once more, and then to the pack as a whole. I banish the grin, harden my face, and square my shoulders as the wolves wait for my answer. "Prepare for battle." My sudden mood switch throws them off, and Bre backs up as though my words lashed at her grateful mood.

Turning on my heel, I start to march toward the forest. Tember has been there for me, pulling strings in the background - which often led to trouble - just to keep me safe. The least I can do is show up to have her back even if Erline won't. I won't leave them to the odds. I won't let another die on my watch.

Erline's voice slices through the silence. "Katriane, you cannot."

I laugh though it's anything but humorous. It's darkness. A darkness I can control. "Oh, but I can. And I will."

"We need you here," she barks.

I whip around to face her, sneering, and the prenumbra flanks me. A fierce growl rumbles from the creature's chest, and quickly after, the pack of green aura creatures fall in line.

"I've sat back long enough," I snarl. "I won't stand by while others fight for their freedom, for their home. It's up to me to fix the wrongs you and all of the fee have done. You've sealed our fates by ripping our choices from us, and I won't sit idle and watch you do it again. I'm not your puppet, Erline. Not anymore. Nor will I allow it to continue for the rest of the realms and all those supposedly under the fees' care."

317

Turning and passing a few elves, I mentally pause, startled by the sight before me. Starting with the elf nearest me, they bow one at a time, a wave of bent bodies down the village's main path. At first, I believe them to be doubling over in pain.

Dwarves abruptly drop gathered logs propped in their beefy arms and beam brilliant smiles at my scouring face. I slow as the wave of bows continues. I stop my determined strides as a hush of a breeze punctuates the gestures of respect, of one displaying such unworthiness to another.

The village quiets to blissful silence, even the children, except the tinkling of each snowflake colliding with another, a beat to their proclamation. A creak of branches vibrates the shifting air. A chirp of a creature sounds in the distance. A fire crackles nearby, and a wave of adrenaline surges through me, the cold fingers squeezing my heart as every vein and nerve lights with flaming power. It waits to be called on … waits for me to give the remaining elves orders to do my bidding, to share in a victory of blood and enemy lives lost. It's what they wait for, too. They honor me. They see me as a savior, a worthy opponent to the fee.

Gulping, I allow my gaze to sweep the expanse of bowing creatures. And then I vibrate with the possibilities. Not once has Erma or Erline been bowed to. A shiver creeps up my spine, slithers over my shoulders, and settles cold on my collar bones.

An odd sensation coats my palm. I glance down and meet the tall green wavering form of a prenumbra, its tongue licking my skin and its saliva tingling the nerves. And then it, too, bows. As the elves, they wait for orders.

They wait for the same honor and glory. They wait for battle and bloodshed. For compassion over those they've lost, they desire for me to lead them to vengeance.

Grinning maliciously, I stalk off, and as footfalls sound against crunching snow behind me, I know I'm not alone. I'll never be alone if I don't wish it.

A single tear slips from my eye. It drips to the snow from the edge of my jaw as we reach the first layer of trees.

CHAPTER TWENTY-ONE

TEMBER

GUARDIAN REALM

My mind swirls with the information I've acquired from Fate. He talked mostly in riddles about my future and destiny, but his battle plan appeared flawless on the surface. It was more so than anything Jaemes or I could have mapped out. Indeed, I wouldn't have thought of such a plan. Could it be he knows the future? Of course, he does. Fate would know any outcome. Perhaps I do not give Fate enough credit. His only wish is to side with the lesser evil - to ensure his creations' wrongs are righted.

Despite credibility, I am not sure I like the idea of a battle strategy built on a future which has already been seen. It feels manipulative, and it's difficult to grasp the dynamics of it.

Jaemes stands beside me, his bow in one hand. His stance is solid as the rest of the elves, and he braided his white painted hair to keep it at bay. Each muscle ripples in anticipation of what's to come. His instinct as a warrior is clawing to reach the surface and begin the bloodshed.

A gust of chilly wind sweeps through the trees, whispering between the branches, and whips our hair. When it reaches the angel's wings to my right, it creates a whistling sound, playing the features like a stroke of a violin. Their wings are poised and ready for flight, arms bent and angled at a running position.

Jaemes has yet to summon his matua, I note. The elf warriors, including his brothers, are already mounted on theirs. The large black beasts' hooves paw at the snow, and their necks arch. They can feel the stiff atmosphere, the adrenaline. Puffs of heated mist gush past flared nostrils while their riders look on, surveying the green grass which will be tainted with the rift in creatures in mere moments.

"Are they ready?" I ask Jaemes.

Without looking at me, he nods his head once. I swivel my gaze back to the front, a full view of the scene. I picture the outcome - feathers, arrows, and blood meshed with the blades of grass.

"Do it," I mumble, widening my stance and tucking my arms behind my back.

Jaemes tips his head to the elf mounted beside him - his brother Kai, I've learned. He had introduced himself after Jaemes barked threats to them if they didn't learn to get along. He looks almost identical to his brother but has a lighter wit to him.

Kai turns his matua without any obvious command, and the creature takes off at full speed, kicking up snow in his wake. He travels along the edge of the forest to the appointed destination. Seconds tick by, the snowflakes tickling my cheeks and melting at a brisker rate due to the heat settling under my skin.

"You have been avoiding my question," Jaemes says in a serious tone.

"Have I?" I ask distractedly. My gaze sweeps the trees where Kai had disappeared.

"What gave you this idea?" His voice is deep and concerned, his accent thicker than usual.

I don't answer and, instead, run my tongue along the inside of my cheek to keep my mouth busy and my secrets prisoner.

"There," Jaemes points.

A thunder rumbles the ground below our feet despite the distance, and the thrill of it travels up my legs and centers in my gut, sparking my nerves with exhilaration close to nausea. I suck in a deep breath, and as planned, a herd of oxtra stampede through the tree line, flattening the wild bushes within it.

Their size never ceases to amaze me, and my breath exhales with a whoosh. The surrounding blanket of snow quakes with the tremors. They bellow in fear, having been chased from the woods by the wild prenumbras on their heels, and it carries in the gale. A herd of angry, frightened oxtra can be dangerous and deadly. This I know firsthand.

The fallen angels protecting our stolen territory take notice, and Jaemes scoffs his dislike to their wavered loyalty. A few on the ground conjure their Ires, drawing the strings and releasing blue, crackling electric arrows.

From here, nestled in the protection of the trees, I can hear the sparks sizzle as the arrows soar. With a resounding boom, they strike the herd. The few oxtra who are hit stumble along the ground only to regain their footing and continue the same path. The angels try again and again, and in time, they change their targets to those who give chase. The prenumbras can't be taken down so easily. The arrows soar directly through them, their forms built on auras rather than solidity. It takes much more than lightning arrows to bring down an oxtra, too, especially from that distance.

A small smile lifts my cheeks, and Erma's bright form glows beside me as she arrives through a portal. She's come from where the prenumbras chased the oxtra. It was she who called those who gathered and asked they lay down their life for their creator.

"It's working," she says with a smile, her body breathless and huffing with effort.

I nod my head to her, giving her the signal to commence the next portion of Fate's plan. As she lifts her arms, I look to the sky.

The angels who are soaring above swoop, their attention focused on the angry creatures heading their way. So far, they suspect nothing besides a hungry pack hunting for their next meal.

If we would have gone in without Fate and the creatures' help, too many would have lost their lives. Our plan is working.

White light forms around Erma's fingers, expanding in the shape of perfectly rounded orbs. The hairs on my arms stand on end as I observe her power gaining in intensity.

This next portion of our plan will take much out of her and make her an easy target. However, I trust her to protect herself, even weakened. After all, she's the creator of guardians – of warriors. Surely, she's a formidable one herself.

Squinting her eyes, she focuses her power and directs it to the Angel's Ground. The floating island shakes and rumbles. The clouds quiver. Wind gathers speed, slapping my hair into my eyes, and a deep unearthly groan reaches my ears.

"It's working," Jaemes proclaims with excitement. He side-steps closer to me.

"Indeed," I pledge, watching my home lower.

My nostrils flare as the fallen angels feel the change in the air and notice the island's descend, dividing their attention from the hunt to the Ground.

"Save themselves or save their falsely claimed territory," I mumble grudgingly, hanging on my own words. *Pick one.*

"We fight for our home," I say to the group, shouting above the wind. "For equality and justice." My gaze sweeps all the warriors, and my voice raises with each following word. "Dying is not an option. Disloyalty is not an option. A rift has begun, and yet, here we stand as brothers and sisters. As Guardians."

My words visibly charge the group, and many smile wickedly. When the Angels' halos wink and hover above their heads, I add, "As one!" while pumping my fist in the air. As I do, Ire appears in my grip. Pride swells the heart in my wrist.

"Now!" I yell to the angels.

They spread their wings to full expanse and grip their own Ires tight. It only takes moments for them to shoot from the snow like rockets, leaving a trail of cold flakes behind, and hurl themselves to the sky.

Once above the tips of the trees, they release electric arrows, lighting the somber clouds in brilliant hues of blue. Unaware, many enemies fall, plucked from the sky with precise aim.

My balance precariously teeters as the descending Angel's Ground slams into the soil. Chunks of dirt hurtle from the destruction. The matua's shriek. Oxtras roar. Prenumbras bark. Booms of electric bolts rock the atmosphere.

"Ready?" I scream to Jaemes.

"I was born ready," he growls the familiar phrase. He conjures his matua, the creature appearing in puffs of smoke, and easily glides on the back of the two-headed horse with a single graceful swing.

Staring, his shredded body completely still, my demon escort considers me with a blank expression. He waits for me to cave and answer the question he's been repeating over and over again.

"Be I ask one more time," he says, his voice shaking. "Shall I inquire again, I be not able to stop what next."

I ponder his words and consider his threat mumbled in a merciful air.

Corbin fears me, or I wouldn't be sitting here, confined and subjected to the beginnings of an interrogation. That's what the demon is telling me - what happens next won't be pleasant. I already knew it wouldn't when I woke stuck to this chair.

"Doesn't Corbin have his Oleum?" I ask. "Why doesn't he pull the information from my mind like he does with everyone else?"

Unless he can't. Unless I'm too powerful for even him. The thought thrills me, and goosebumps raise over my skin. If I remain silent and get through this interrogation, I can kill the man who can't kill me himself.

The demon bends his knees, lowering himself with difficulty just to peer into my eyes. The skin dangles from his thighs and slaps against the glass floor. "Remember? I told you to trust no one?" he asks, a parent speaking to a toddler. I nod once and grind my jaw. "He could pull your thoughts, but this be more entertaining."

Lie, I growl inside my head. The odd turn of the question to the conversation is his way of telling me I'm correct in my wordless assumption.

He straightens back to full height and continues. "This be a lesson more than a search for information, Thrice Born. Trust no one, I said. There be no humanity or mercy here. You did not listen."

Wincing once, he grips the exposed bone in his thigh and yanks, popping his hip back into place. "Two options. Speak, or endure?"

"Endure," I say, tilting my head with a wicked grin and peering at him from under my lashes.

The demon sighs, and his one eye lowers to the glass. "So be it," he states, his voice foreboding as if sealing my fate.

I frown when he doesn't do anything else but instead watches the lava, transfixed and mesmerized. I nearly jump when he finally does.

"Filii Noctis," he calls.

Laughing without humor, I recognize the Latin words filtering into my mind. "You plan for children to interrogate me?"

"Oh, they not be children, Thrice Born," he murmurs with wonder. "They be Children of the Night."

In three short points of the hexagram, three beings shimmer and fully materialize: the child demon I remember

327

from the room of mirrors, a shadow in the shape of a tall man, and a large demon whose face is half monster, gnarled and contorted with knobby warts which ooze. His features are oddly gargoyle-like.

The demon points to the child. "Do you remember Terror?" he asks and then chuckles as though he's sharing a private joke among friends. "Timore Venandi be his true name."

I eye the child in question and hide a smile threatening my scowl by tucking my top lip between my teeth.

"Umbra Malum," the demon continues, moving his hand to point at the shadow lurking a few inches from the ground. The shadow isn't still but, instead, shifts like mist in a breeze.

"And Chao Mortis," he adds, pointing to the oozing wart demon. Chao growls his greeting, exposing pointed teeth, and the vibrations of it search the pores along my skin for points of weakness and fear. It finds none.

"Should I be afraid?" I ask, shrugging and quirking a brow.

The scrappy demon narrows his one eye. "Any being, be demon or otherwise, should be afraid. The Filii Noctis are Children of the Night, Thrice Born. Each represent their own specialty of terror." He dips his voice to a haunting tone. "Things which make the sane-minded sour to mad."

He limps his way past my chair, and as he passes, he bends to my ear and whispers. "Tell me, Thrice Born. What be you fear most?"

328

The demon doesn't give me a chance to answer. Not that I would. He shuffles his way and leaves my sight. The child, Timore Venandi, steps forward.

I glare to the tiny demon, and he giggles musically. His face darkens, the humor whipped away as fast as it came, and he stares, soullessly, back into my eyes.

"What was your errand?" he asks with pure innocence.

I smirk and bend closer to him, as much as my invisible restraints allow. "I took a trip to Wonderland, little buddy. If you're a good boy, I'll take you with me next time."

Slowly, Timore shakes his head, his thick brown hair waving, and he clicks his tongue like a child chiding his parent. Cocking his slim hips, he crosses his arms over his chest. "I've heard about you."

"Have you now? Do I give you bad dreams, peanut?"

He giggles, the sound of insanity. "Quite the opposite."

I pucker my lips in mock disappointment. "Shame."

We dwell in silence before he mumbles, "Last chance, Thrice Born."

I pop my puckered lips. "I was sucked down the rabbit hole."

With barely any time to finish my sarcasm, my back arches and a gasp rushes up my throat. An intense wave of pressure pushes along my spine and settles at the base of my skull, bulging my eyes. My body slumps against my will, and I'm cast into complete darkness, awakening to a different scene.

Now standing, I frown at the room he took me to, and the scent of freshly washed laundry tickles my senses with familiar pleasure. Everything is blurred and wispy - the deep purple curtains, the white carpet, the black leather couches which make the living room's decor. Nothing hangs on the white walls.

I bring my hands to my cheeks and touch my fingers to my skin, trying to grasp if this is reality or not.

"I am the mind of the three," a child's voice says behind me.

Failing to mask my surprise, my muscles bunch in my shoulders, and I slowly swivel my head. Timore takes a step and stands beside me, his head reaching the height of my elbow.

Without looking at me, he adds, "It'll be interesting to see if you can withstand me. Will it not?"

He nods to the curtains draped in front of what can only be a window. I follow his gaze and choke back a gasp. Eliza stands in front of them, robotic and eyes unseeing with limp hands dangling at her sides. Just as the objects in the room, she doesn't look completely solid but, instead, more Dream-like.

"Is this a dream?" I ask hesitantly, my voice deep.

The child demon doesn't answer me, and my attention flickers to the kitchen knife as it poofs into her hand, gleaming in her slender clutch.

"Eliza?" I call to her. She gives no notation of hearing my voice, not even a twitch in her eyelids. "What's going on?"

"I know what you fear most, Thrice Born," Timore goads. "Fear is what drives us to the edge. It can do a great many heroic things, or a great many disastrous."

He pauses, letting the words sink in. "When someone is frightened, it is then we can uncover the weak. Fight or flight mixed with nature verses nurture. There is one exception, and this is if the fear is forced upon us. There's no way to control or stop it, no way to swipe it aside, and when there is no escape, fear blossoms insanity. Insanity is the most delicious emotion to feed from." He jerks his torso to me, the gesture quick and unnatural. "Shall we begin, or do you wish to save yourself and explain your whereabouts?"

"I do not fear you, Fear Hunter." But my words belie my actions, my thumbs counting the tips of my fingers.

"An ego serves only ignorance," he growls in his tiny voice, displeased at hearing his true name in English. Sighing, he turns back to Eliza's still frame. "Do it," he barks to her.

I begin to doubt if she'll listen because she didn't acknowledge me. But I'm painfully wrong.

My eyebrows pinch, and I watch as Eliza raises the knife. With a calculated, robotic movement, she settles the blade at one side of her neck, sharp edge against soft skin.

"No," I demand. I attempt to take a step forward, to stop Eliza from a certain death, but I can't move an inch. My feet are cemented to this very spot. Desperate, I reach for her by outstretching my arm, my eyes pleading. "Eliza, don't."

Her eyes finally flick to mine, and I breathe an exhale of relief. She sees me.

With a swift pull, she swipes the blade across her neck, leaving an open wound in its place. It's deep and exposes the white spine nestled in severed muscles.

"No!" I scream in the room and yank at my legs. "No!"

Blood pours from her neck and her mouth gapes, gasping for air which can no longer pass a severed cord. Crimson foam gathers at her lips. Tears shed from her eyes. Her shirt soaks with black cherry red, staining as it flows rivers down her torso. The carpet is marred with a spray of blood to each beat of her heart. The laundry scent is replaced by a thick aroma of iron and musk.

The knife drops from her hand, and she falls to her knees, fingers clutching her neck.

CHAPTER TWENTY-TWO

TEMBER

GUARDIAN REALM

The dusty dirt snakes around shuffling feet fighting for the upper hand. Enemy angels continue to pour from the Angel's Ground entrances and absent roof. Off in the trees, a blizzard has picked up, and beyond that, a vicious storm is visible, wreaking havoc over the Kaju tribe territory. But here, where the angel's call home, moans, grunts, and yells echo in the clearing as each creation of Erma's fights to kill the other.

We're overrun. We're outnumbered. I've greatly underestimated this outcome.

Stationed next to the Grounds, my small team is behind Jaemes and me, including Erma who Jaemes' brothers circle to protect. They wait for my command to slip inside while hidden behind a white pillar on the outside of the structure. We watch the scene unfold, waiting for the perfect opportunity. Our dwindling warriors battle with cries of victory and wails of frustration.

With much effort, we have fought our way to the Grounds. It is prudent to have as many of the enemies out of our home for Fate's plan to succeed. We need to get in and even the odds, but the fight to get here has been difficult. Black blood layers along my skin, smearing the paint, and my hair sticks to my forehead and cheeks.

To take back our floating castle, we must seal the gates from any who try to reenter. But nothing is going according to plan. From where I stand, we're losing. Our warriors are falling quickly, crumpling to the grass and dropping from the sky like comets. We can't enter if we lose. We can't leave everyone to die if my team can make a difference out here.

The zaps and jolts of bolts charge the air, and the bellows of the oxtra herd vibrate my bones while they continue their rampage in utter chaos. The oxtra cannot fly, however, and their numbers are being picked off due to that single flaw in their makeup as a team of enemy angels kill them from above. Oxtra may be strong and tough-skinned, but they cannot handle several rounds of electricity at once. And because of that, their numbers are dwindling at an alarming rate.

"This was not a good plan!" Jaemes yells above the noise. "My people are dying!"

I ignore him, my huffs of breath matching the tune of beating wings and pounding hooves. The clash of weapons better suits my frantic heart throbbing against pulsing veins in my wrist.

"We should retreat while we can," he continues, slamming his fist against the pillar to grab my attention. A chunk breaks away and tumbles to my feet.

I curl my fingers, and my face darkens. "No," I say, firm. I choose to place my trust in Fate. "We've come this far. We can't turn back, not when we are almost inside."

Beginning with Kai, Jaemes' brothers eye each other and begin speaking rapidly in their own tongue. His expression is grave yet murderous as though I've become his next target, friendship be damned.

"If you do not pull our people back," Jaemes warns with clenched teeth. "If we do not retreat to safety, all will be lost. With no guardian left to fight for it, this realm will be destroyed."

I open my mouth to retort, but snap my jaw shut when a shadow overcasts the lands. I lift my head to the sky, and a deafening roar rebounds inside the clouds, followed by the sherbet smear of orange brightening them. I cover my ears as it echoes in the clearing, and the matua's screech their cry.

"Kat," I stammer, my voice tinged with a grateful whoosh of air. Jaemes follows my line of sight, and his braided hair swings from one shoulder to the other.

The black sky and numerous twinkling stars are visible when she cuts through the clouds, leaving an opening in her wake which quickly swirls closed. The fire follows her entrance, hurtling closely behind her as though her talons grab the flames. Her black dragon comes into view, her wings tucked while she dives, and the scales gleam their impenetrable armor.

Another roar quakes the land, and as she passes over our heads, her belly is alight with an inferno within. Heat wafts from her, but she continues on her flight without pause or recognition, swooping past the Angel's Ground.

A stream of flames leaves her muzzle, engulfing angels midflight in scorching heat so bright it snuffs the hues of electric arrows arching into the air. Her chest puffs again, and she exhales, aiming and slaughtering the enemies in the sky with a moving torrent of fire.

Immediately following, a howl erupts inside the forest, then a chorus of them, until the sound almost replaces the war happening before me.

"Wolves," Jaemes calls over the chaos, alerting our small group to new potential danger.

A smirk lifts my cheeks, and the paint plastered there cracks. *Kat brought a few friends.* "Not wolves. Shifters." I tip my head back and laugh, pure delight taking over my actions. "The odds are now even, my friend!" I slap Jaemes on the shoulder.

The large wolves drum through the trees, kicking snow into the air with massive, sharp paws. Their bodies are low to the ground as they gather speed, and the two in the back yip and nip at one another.

The lead wolf takes down the first enemy angel it leaps on, the two skidding across the grass with the wolf's paws firmly planted on the angel's chest. The animal is swift and deadly, the others following their Alpha's lead. The angel's wings bend at an odd angle under the wolf's weight, and with a quick chomp of his jaw, he bites the wrist of his prey. From the chest of his victim, he leaps to the next.

Jaemes brothers whoop and shake their bows into the air with victory.

"Let's go," Erma shouts to us from behind Kai.

ELIZA PLAATS

GUARDIAN REALM

From here, I can hear the roar of a dragon in the distance and the boom of bolts of lightning as they strike. The vibrations shake the quarantine teepee walls and quake the ground below my feet. I get the feeling it's not a thunderstorm brewing, but the beginning of a raging war. It's the result of the rift which had settled over the realms and blackened the hearts of all those in them.

The thought is fleeting, however, as my own battle is beginning with my incapable, and well-trained, hands.

"Why isn't it working?" I yell to the crowd gathered around Mitus' table. He's fading fast, and no matter how much of these tears I dribble into his mouth, it's not working. His skin is pale even under the striped tattoos, and blood seeps from every opening in his body.

The turnaround with the others was nothing short of a medical miracle, swiftly curing this illness faster than anything I've ever seen. It was instant, and Mitus had refused the treatment until his people were cured first. That wait may be the very thing that kills him.

I understand magic and everything around me are against the laws and science of my realm, but if it worked so well with the others, why isn't it for him?

It's too late, a voice says, deep and gentle. Though it's a male voice chiming in my head and not my own, I ignore it with a quick dismissal of my warped conscience trying to seep through my panic.

Erline wades through a crowd who eventually parts automatically for her. "He's too far gone," she murmurs when she reaches the table. With a slow sweep of eyes, she observes his slick and sweaty, bloodied body.

A light beams around her hand, and she touches it to Mitus' heart at the wrist. I know what she'll find - she'll find it barely beating just as I heard moments ago. A splutter gurgles in his chest, and his lips turn a shade of greyish-blue. He convulses, rattling the table.

"Move!" I shove her aside. But nobody listens, and instead, they watch on in horror. "Move!"

I grab Mitus' jaw, open his mouth wide, and pour more clear liquid in with a shaky hand. Nothing happens, and when I release his face to see if it has any effect, his jaw slacks. A last hush of breath whistles between his teeth.

"No." I try again. Nothing. "No!" I shout, slamming a fist to the table. Sparks surge from my hand and crack against the surface next to his shoulder.

"Eliza, do not use your magic," Erline cautions in a sea of whimpers.

I look around, watching the elves comfort each other and visibly crumple in defeat. They've admitted failure. I'm not ready for that yet.

I meet her gaze. Fear and determination shake my voice. "He can't die. Not like this."

Her face, though with a firm set of black eyes, softens, and she holds out her hands in a gesture of peace. "He is dead, Eliza. It is not up to you if he lives. He's gone."

"I refuse to let him go to the Death Realm!" I shout at her.

Turning, I pour more into his mouth, and when I let go, the dragon tears drip at the corners of his lips. They trail a dreaded, sluggish path down the dried blood along his skin to the curve of his neck and find a final rest at the scoop of his collar bone.

Tears stream down my cheeks, hot and salty. "No," I whimper.

My back curves, and I dip my head, sobs wracking my frame. I know he's gone. There's a numbness when someone's spirit is no longer in their body. The atmosphere is eerie, silent, as though the body is only a shell which contains one's soul. When a dead corpse lays in front of me, I don't feel the comfort of another. The air feels just as empty as though they're nothing else but a material object.

Erline places a gentle hand on my shoulder, squeezing comfortingly.

His sacrifice was his choice, the voice whispers again.

AIDEN VANDER

DEMON REALM

"Your fear is exquisite," Timore murmurs with his eyelids fluttering in ecstasy.

Slumped in my chair, sweat beads across my forehead and dribbles down the slopes of my back. I fight for air, for one pain free moment. Not because there's a lack of oxygen, but instead my mind fights to control the situation I'm finding myself in: reality or non-reality.

Again and again, Timore had forced me to watch as he ordered Eliza to kill herself, each way a different suicide. He's a demon who specializes in manipulation of the mind, but this wasn't what I had expected. I don't think I can endure it one more time.

It's not real, I chant, and squeeze my eyes shut, forcing myself to believe.

The child demon bends in front of me and demands my gaze. I pin him with a glare which promises an agonizing revenge.

"I must admit, Thrice Born, you held out longer than anyone I've had the pleasure of tormenting."

I grind my teeth but blank my face, refusing to show him how much he's shaken me. My muscles quiver anyway, exhausted with fighting my sanity and restraints.

"Perhaps we should move on," he sighs. "Umbra Malum?"

With much effort, I lift my head and gaze at the misty shadow. He leaves his corner of the hexagon, floating to a few feet before me. Muffled moans come from within his core, blacker than his edges.

Timore backs up and crosses his arms once more. "As I was the mind, Umbra is the soul," he says. "Fear is the kiss of death, demon. Save yourself this torture. Tell me what I wish to know."

Between clenched teeth, I hiss. "Never."

He smiles a grin that was meant only to adorn an innocent child's mouth. "Excellent. Then let's continue."

Umbra's murky shape swells and spreads his ferly shadow, taking most of my immediate and peripheral view. The edges curl and wave, a content tail of an impish house cat.

Clearing my throat uneasily, I push my spine against the back of the chair, and the wood creaks. I squint to his darkening middle, and featureless faces emerge, pressing into the dense black gloom as though it is a thin plastic sack. The many faces' mouths open in silent screams, jaws ostensibly unhinged.

"Umbra consumes the souls of his victims," Timore supplies optimistically. "It's a fascinating thing to watch."

The expanded shadow creeps forward, and I jut my chin to the side with a grimace. The tail-like curls reach, writhing and twitching fingers, my sternum their aim. My breaths come faster, harsh bursts, and I prepare myself for what's to come by curling my restrained hands into tight fists.

Uncontrollably, fear wafts from my skin and coats the room with a thick, powerful aroma, feeding the Children of the Night. If they get to my soul, it'll no longer belong to the woman I love.

"Yes!" the child demon cries, holding out his arms to his sides while he drinks what my pores offer. His pinched features morph to pure glee.

I grunt as one of the shadow's fingers dip into my skin, through my ribs, and directly into the flesh of my chest. They search within like a prying, blind hand, coiling around organs, vessels, and bones. My nails bite into my palms, and I suck in a sharp inhale when they touch my lungs, cold against my internal warmth. The fingers grasp and clutch something inside tucked securely in my middle, and an internal pop vibrates my ribs and aches my collarbones.

My soul.

My pinched eyes widen as I stare at the silent screaming souls within the shadow, their open mouths just before my face, and I roar as the fingers yank.

Seconds? Minutes? Hours. Hours which I fight to keep the soul within my body, all the while picturing Eliza's face in my mind's eye. Her smile, her waving red hair, her fear in the face of her true husband's presence. I have to protect her, and so I had fought with every internal will-power I had to keep my soul in my chest.

My soul is hers!

When the shadow retreats to the corner it came from, unsuccessful, its murky fingers twitch with displeasure. The faces sink back within, returning to his core with a chorus of moans.

"You are powerful," Timore professes in rage. "I've underestimated you again."

"It happens to the best of us." I shift in my chair, righting my posture, and gasp. My body aches like a festering torn ligament, soul in agony, and a sharp stab throbs where I mentally tugged to keep it my own.

"You've survived two of the three Children of the Night, Thrice Born. A feat not many can boast. Not even the mighty Kheelan and Sureen could manage when we were sent to frighten them into compliance. They caved quickly. It almost wasn't any fun."

Kheelan and Sureen. His slip of admission doesn't go over my head. Is this how Corbin man-handled them to join his side?

With effort, I lift my heavy eyes to his, tucking that nugget of information into a deep pocket of my mind. "Do you give up?"

"Never," he growls, a contorting snarl.

"A shame." I attempt to click my tongue, but instead, the action sounds more like a sloshing of spit. Even my mouth is too exhausted for mockery.

"Chao Mortis," he calls to the half-faced monster, anxiety creeping into his beckoning and cracking his voice.

I worry him. *Good.*

One more. I can endure one more. Perhaps then they will believe my lie.

Chao strides forward, graceful compared to his legendary creation. His name means *of chaos*, but I have no idea what he's truly capable of. If Timore is the mind, and the shadow the soul, that would deem Chao the body - the muscle of the three.

He wastes no time. Even before he strides in front of me, he begins his torture.

A burning sensation blossoms along my neck, a fresh slice from an invisible knife, and I hiss against the pain, whipping my head to the side. Another slice along my chest, deep and festering, and then another, each healing themselves before the next wound is opened.

I clamp my jaw and curl my fingers into tighter fists, straining against the pain. The slices are random and a few seconds apart from each other. A cut is made against my inner thigh. I moan. The severed soft flesh trembles my thighs against my will.

Eliza, forgive me, I weep to myself.

A long slice reaches from my chin to my groin, slow, deep, and my chest bows as I wail.

CHAPTER TWENTY-THREE

TEMBER

GUARDIAN REALM

What do normal people do when their homes are overrun? What do good, kind-natured souls demand from it? Do they fight for their territory? Or do they flee and save what little they have left?

These are the questions which absorb my thoughts after we enter the Grounds, bombarded with immediate attacks. There's no way further in, and the only option left is to run or fight our way through.

My questions are simple, but any answer I choose can decide my fate forever, and that of the realm I've been taught to protect with my very last breath.

"Tember!" Erma shouts past the masses of taunting hollers directed at us and the shattering of weapon against weapon outside. We're shoulder to shoulder.

Every voice, every evidence of death, seeps into my heart, and my wrist dangerously thumps, regret driving the beats.

This feels like a trap.

With little choice, we have to duck behind pillars as soon as we slip inside, and I currently press my spine against one. A ripped portion of my shirt exposes the skin along my back to the smooth marble, grounding me and my wavering choices.

I breathe slowly, deeply, attempting to calm my nerves. This has never happened to me - this fear in battle. But this time I have more to lose.

"Tember!" she yells again, vibrating my ears.

I turn my head to her and tensely lick my bottom lip. My dry tongue feels like sandpaper against the tender flesh. She is what I could lose.

"Are you ready?" she mimes while watching my mouth.

An arrow flies past her head, ruffling her perfect red locks. The electric bolt pops as it whizzes by and booms when it strikes the pillar Jaemes ducks behind. The marble cracks, a spider web from top to bottom, but the structure holds steady. Fallen angels fire upon us again, desperate to keep the Angel's Ground as their own.

Jaemes focuses on me, his face hard, steel. The muscles tick in his cheek, displaying his pure determination and his unwavering faith in me. He nods his head, a silent demand to pull myself together. But how can one pull herself together when we are outnumbered ten to one?

How can I pull myself together when the one I love fights alongside me?

Turning his head, Jaemes nods to his brothers using their own pillars as shields while waiting until our next plan can be devised.

Ire in hand, I dangerously tighten my grip around the smooth wood and pull the string to my cheek with my other hand. I gulp. Not long ago, I was chastising gossiping angels next to this pillar. Today, I contemplate which will die by my hand.

The muscles in my biceps quiver. Erma watches Ire shake unsteadily within my grip, and her lips part. She lifts her eyes to mine.

With a tender expression, she raises her arm and strokes my forearm with soft brushes of fingers. This rare touch of reassurance and affection soaks into my core, and my nervous energy dwindles under her watchful gaze. Her eyes say it all – the love, the memories, what we feel for each other despite our differences.

In a slow blink of long red lashes, she wordlessly promises to stay alive.

She gathers herself on the tips of her toes and leans forward, brushing forgiving lips against mine. It's an affectionate kiss, and I melt into it, into her. My heart thumps a different beat, steadying the grip of my weapon, and her hair brushes my cheeks with a feather-like tickle when she reluctantly pulls away. Her sweet scent retreats with her, and the smell of dust, blood, and electricity replace it, sharper than before.

She searches my face and lowers her voice. "Are you ready?"

I swallow hard, memorizing every feature, curve, and color of Erma. I may be here to massacre those I once called brother and sister, but I'll do anything to keep her alive, to take back what's mine.

Nodding, I inhale a deep breath and turn from behind the pillar, releasing a materialized arrow from Ire. The string snaps beautifully, and then the arrow strikes the closest angel. It sinks into her chest, and the force causes her to sail backward, straight into a sturdy wall. With the deadly blow, she crumbles, limp, to the floor. A pool of feathers rain down over her still form.

This momentary feat causes immediate pause to the taunters, a temporary gain of the upper hand.

I take a step, aim again, and release another. And then another. Jaemes and his brothers tread behind, each step equally measured with mine while allowing me to take the lead. We pluck away at the angels as they swivel past their pillars and hallway curves, poised to aim. They never get the chance to strike and fall lifeless by our hand.

Yellow blinding lights shoot from Erma's palms, striking her own creations with a look of pure determination and justice. I observe a ball of light quickly gliding through the common area, growing in size before colliding with an angel. It consumes the fallen guardian, wrapping around him like a blanket, and bursts the creature into tiny particles. The entire process is completely soundless, and the particles float upward, disappearing one by one as the air absorbs it.

An arrow clips my arm and I yell from the surprising sheer of pain. I stumble from the force and agony. I've never felt pain, nor have I ever been hit by my own species. The wound quickly heals and seals the pain in a pocket of electricity under the freshly closed flesh. Jaemes calls my name and steadies me by the shoulder with a firm grip that digs fingers into my muscles. We share a quick look - his dipped in concern and mine a steady stream of rapid blinks - and then he shoves me upward again, throwing me back into the fight.

"Stand your ground," he yells to us.

A wave of bolts arch in our direction, intent on one deadly raid. Erma claps her hands together and spreads them wide, conjuring a small, blue shield, a barrier wall in front of us. Like a rubber band, the shield snaps into place, and the arrows pop against it.

The elves and I gaze wondrously at the transparent blue wall. This is our fighting chance.

Jaemes lifts his bow and aims, and the arrow slows as it cuts through the shield but gathers speed once on the other side. The weapon plucks an angel from her feet, and she soars into the descending mass of enemy, intent on breaking down Erma's protection.

But the shield doesn't last. Minutes that feel like seconds, we are given to dwindle the numbers, but some still remain. Erma's shield wavers with her exhaustion, and an arrow hits my leg, sizzling the flesh.

A fallen angel prepares to attack me from my side with raised fists, to bring the fight to a hand-to-hand combat. He runs at full speed, flapping his wings to accelerate his pace and punch.

I turn last minute, striking him with my black wings. It knocks him off guard, and I continue the turn, kicking up my leg and connecting my heel to his jaw. The angel falls, and I quickly aim Ire, striking him in the eye.

Another angel charges, and I jump into the air, flapping my wings to propel me higher. Pulling back my free fist, I punch her in the cheek. Her head snaps back, but she grabs my ankle and rips me from the air. My shoulder hits the ground first, and she raises her Ire before I have a chance to recuperate.

My muscles tense as I prepare for the final blow that'll end my life, but her chest bows forward, eyes wide. She turns to the side, intent on discovering who struck her between the wings with an arrow. Before she can make a full turn, she falls to the ground beside me, her white feathers blanketing her dead frame. I look up and see Jaemes poised with his bow still hovering.

I prop myself up on an elbow. We lock eyes, and he puckers his lips before flicking his gaze back up to the fight. He grabs another arrow from his quiver, aims, and releases in a swift motion. The arrow flies overtop my head and thuds into a new chest, sickly-wet sounding. Another fallen angel replaces that one.

Growling, I lay flat to my back, kick my legs, and propel myself to my feet.

An angel swings at me with a closed fist. I bring my arm up last minute, blocking the blow.

For a split second, all the time I'm allowed, I frown as I take in the face of the fallen angel who had pursued me. Black blood tears spill from her eyes and the corners of her lips. Her cheeks are sunken, and dried blood is smeared across her neck as though she had been bleeding before we had arrived.

She swings her other arm, and again, I block it. Her movements are sluggish, and huffy breath splutters past her sickly pale lips.

Lifting my thigh, I kick forward, my foot connecting to her stomach. Blood sprays from her mouth as the wind is knocked from her lungs. She falls to her back, landing on tangled wings. Distracted and concerned, I stab her heart with an electric arrow while sweeping her body with my eyes. Her blood seeps from every opening, and my scowl deepens.

I look around, curious as to what's happening and why. Each fallen angel has the same symptoms – blood oozing from their eyes and mouths and a sickly pale body. I recognize it for what it is, having seen this in the witches when Kat was my charge.

"They're infected," I mumble. "They're infected!"

KATRIANE DUPONT

GUARDIAN REALM

Two ally angel's flank me, their aim swift and accurate from a lifetime of skill. We have something the enemy does not. *I* have something they do not. I have the blood of fee. I have the power of the first born and a dark conscience that walks hand in hand with my light. I have those I love whom I fight for.

With these convictions determining every swift move I make, and my immediate imposing threat, I've become the primary target.

What do they fight for? What fuels their desire to win that's more so than mine?

Nothing, the darkness growls inside.

We raise ourselves to the clouds, gathering more warriors as we dip. Our formation reminds me of geese, my dragon at the front of a triangular tip.

The dive grants us speed, and the gathering winds tickle my scales. I tuck my wings against its forceful caress and angle for the pack of wolves being overtaken.

It's easy to tell who is the enemy and who isn't. The enemy delivered The Red Death to this realm and, in doing so, infected themselves. The effects of the illness are already showing, and it's weakening them more than our efforts to destroy them.

My roar is deafening as we grow nearer, stunning a few enemies long enough for the wolves to steal the advantage. Electric arrows fly past my head, and a wicked gleam brightens my eyes, the battle exhilarating, the fall from the sky just the same.

Fire puffs black smoke from every corner of the scorched clearing. At the last moment, I open my mouth and snatch two enemy angels off the ground. I glide a few feet, and chomp my jaw around their middles, severing them in two. Blood gushes, slithers between my gums, and sprays the blades of grass I sail over.

I swoop around, and as I do, the angels who were flanking my sides drop to the blackened grass and engage in battle next to their elf alliances.

The wolves form a line, and before they close ranks, I land on all fours between their Alpha Female and Alpha Male. Their fur is soaked in their own blood and the enemies, but each is still alive.

In my expanded peripheral vision, blue hues descend from above, spiking fear in my heart. At the last second, I inflate my wings, almost a moment too late. The stream of electric bolts pummel from the sky. My wings take the hit, blocking the blows from their wolf targets.

CHAPTER TWENTY-FOUR

AIDEN VANDER

DEMON REALM

Inhuman sounds gurgle up my throat, gasping agonized rumbles. Chao tilts his head to the side but leaves his expression blank. Yet, there's a certain curious twinkle catching in his eyes. I can almost see his thoughts churning. I managed to hold out, and he wants to know how and why.

How do I survive? How do I not give in and heed to their desires?

That answer is simple: love.

Chao, Umbra, Timore – they'd know nothing of it. They don't know the strength love has against fear. They could pull the fear from me until the end of time, but the love I have for Eliza, the pure strength and torment I'm willing to go through to keep her safe… it'll be their undoing. Not mine.

I want to be everything Eliza hasn't dreamed of yet, everything she thinks is impossible. I want to be her *home* in whichever realm we seek refuge. I won't give up on her, nor would she for me. She's trusting me to keep her safe.

"Tell me what I want to know!" the child screams, infuriated.

"Go. To. Hell." I pant each word. Perhaps he doesn't know we're already there.

I shift in my chair and bite back a groan. Each muscle is on fire, and though the wounds had instantly healed, every inch of skin is hypersensitive. I can feel every nerve within my body as though they're exposed to the open air.

The child demon's hands fist into tiny balls at his side, and he sneers. "You will die, Demon. I will kill you if you do not answer, orders be damned. Is that what you want?"

I raise a shaky eyebrow, and a trail of sweat dribbles over, stinging when it spills into my eye. "If that's what it takes."

Chao's head tilts back, and he roars with rage. It echoes and vibrates against the walls, and I wince.

Inch by inch, quick excelling wounds open upon every pressure point and every soft expanse of skin. I scream, the action uncontrollable. The pain is too great, the wounds too deep.

Eliza, my thoughts scream as the wave continues.

An internal click switches inside me. Anger floods every vein, every pore, my very soul. It drives through each

355

nerve, each bone and lymph node held within the shell of a human body.

But I'm not human.

I'm the Thrice Born. I'm the impossible, born for the third time in the depths of black lava. I was yanked from a void, a place of utter black and nothingness, a home of cries to those undeserving.

Closing my eyes, I hang my head and shake it, chuckling to myself as my wrath unleashes like the floodgates of a broken dam, hot and heavy. The invisible bands of restraint are willed away with a simple thought. Everything I am, everything Corbin made me to be, comes forward. He has no idea what he created, no sense of the doom that'll be brought upon him.

I'm ready to own what I am.

Snapping my head up, I smile so wickedly it could melt the wax of a candle. I bring my arms forward, held out at my sides. The child's eyes widen as each muscle ripples and contorts under the skin of my pale white flesh. Hot tears of lava travel down my cheeks, spilling from the depths of my eyes.

Like the melting of butter in a hot pan, my skin disintegrates, replaced by a pitch-black, rock-solid shell which sparkles, a milky way on a clear night.

"You're wrong, you know," I begin. My voice is an overlapping of many tones as though several dwell inside me. And they do. I can feel them just like I could in the void. With this transformation, this empowering sense of what I truly am, I've taken pieces of them for strength, their fear and sorrow my food, willingly given by the souls lost

356

there. "Fear isn't the kiss of death. Fear is a gift by the grace of love. Those who don't fear have nothing to lose."

I stand with grace, the hems of my clothes ripping at the seams as my torn muscles rebuild into solid rock. Hot red tears fall from my chin and splat against the floor, sizzling with steam.

"Let me ask you something, Timore," I add. "What do you believe to happen next?"

With one step in my new, morphed body, I reach and grasp the child by the neck, lifting him from his rooted spot. Fear wafts from him, a delicious taste coating my larger, more sensitive tongue.

He thought the three would destroy me. He believed to be victorious by day's end. Oh, how wrong he was.

I bring him to my face and chuckle once more, the laugh reflecting a wrath he'll soon experience. My jaw opens wide, and I roar in his face, unleashing the fury he built inside me, the conviction due. It sounds like a thousand wails of agonized victims, high-pitched and eerie.

The black, shiny hair atop the child's head waves in the breeze of my breath, and the pupils of his black irises grow. I lower my jaw more like a snake before he consumes his meal. Inhaling, I drink the cloud of fear and then take more, demanding his body to give me everything it has. He struggles, pulling at my massive black, sparkling hand circling his neck, and his feet kick the air.

I give no mercy. I continue to consume him. I drink him in as though he's mine with which to do so.

The hollows of his cheeks swallow what was once plump skin, and his flesh wraps his bones tightly while I suck every fear this demon contains. It belongs to me, willingly killing its host to give me what I desire. His body quivers in my grip, each bone exposed under a thin layer of grey-ish skin.

He kicks. He pries. His lips twist. And then, his shifting eyes still. Slowly, the lids come to a final close.

Hinging my jaw, I grunt, staring at the dead demon within my grip. He's mummified, a hollowed husk, dead from existence. Uncurling my fingers, one by one, I drop the tiny demon with a thud to the glass floor. As soon as the carcass hits, it breaks into pieces, scattering like shards of ice. The floor sucks it in, pulling it into the solid glass, and the lava takes it away as soon as it's through.

The shadow demon speeds forward faster than any shadow should be able to travel. I smile and hold out my massive arms to my sides, conjuring the only thing I know to kill a shadow: a light.

Bright white, blinding light gleams from the white sparkles along my black skin, illuminating the room. The shadow screeches like a tortured pig, forced to halt its advance. The glow around my body brightens, and his shadowing wisps twitch, my light consuming every inch.

Without warning, Chao punches me in the jaw with the back of his elbow. I stagger. The light continues to glow as I turn, slow, deliberate. Ready.

This demon causes me pain. He is the finale to this entourage, thinking to drive me insane by a thousand painful slices across human flesh. He doesn't know pain, but he's about to.

The last screech of the shadow disappears, and I know I've killed the host. I drop the light and scream the thousand voices once more.

Chao holds his ground, delivering a slice against my abdomen with thought alone. The new wound is meant to be deep and deadly . . . if I were human.

I glance at my stomach, lava dripping from the gaping flesh before it heals. The goop knits the rock back together.

Smiling, I close my fists at my side, my body obeying my command and lighting with a blazing fire. The sparkles along my black skin heat and detach, floating forward and circling around Chao. He bats at them, swatting the tiny, flaming specks to no avail.

As each individual ember touches his skin, it lights that area on fire, consuming the demon until the sparkles have all attached. Chao opens his mouth to scream, but no sound comes out. He falls to his knees as the blaze continues, consuming from the outside, in.

When he thumps to the floor, a heap of death, the floor consumes him, too. I slowly extinguish my flames. The specks return to my body and reattach to my black skin.

TEMBER

GUARDIAN REALM

Placing his foot on the chest of a dead angel, Jaemes yanks his arrow free. Throughout the large room, each of us examine the dead. Every angel has the infection: the trails of black blood seeping from their unseeing eyes, slack mouths, and sickly emaciated bodies. I bend to my knees and finger the withered feathers attached to an angel's wings.

"What is this?" Jaemes asks Erma who stands behind me.

"The Red Death," I answer.

"The Red Death?" Kai says.

"It circulated through Erline's witches about a year ago," Erma claims. "It's what Katriane made a deal for. She asked for a cure."

Standing, I rub my hands together, desperate to dust the disease off. "It's only contagious by red dust if I remember correctly."

Erma nods, nostrils flared.

I bend and pick Ire from the black marble flooring as Jaemes continues peppering questions. "And what's the cure?"

"The tears of a dragon," she claims.

"Of course, it is," Jaemes disapproves a little too loudly.

With careful balance, he steps over a few bodies, a limp in his gait. He slightly slips on a bundle of feathers on his way to stand beside me. His brothers hover next to each entrance of the room, poised and ready in case there's another attack.

He continues, a snarl on his lips. "It's too much to ask for everything to be simple with you crazy people." He looks to me, expectantly. "How did the disease originate?"

I frown. "Do you think I have all the answers?"

His eyebrows flick and a small shrug rocks his shoulders. "You march around with a superiority whipplemonk on your shoulder, chirping opinions and demands. I only assumed."

I turn to face him, angry. "Says the elf whose own people refuse to leave the Guardian Realm to protect those who can't."

Tilting his head back, he laughs without humor. "Says the angel who sleeps with her creator for favors."

My face heats, and my hands curl into fists. He knows that isn't true.

I open my mouth to retaliate, but Erma cuts me off before a word can be uttered. "Enough," she spits. "These are unfortunate circumstances and pointing fingers at one another will be our downfall. There's no sense in it. We need to continue through the Grounds."

Jaemes peels his hard stare from my face and bows, sweeping his arm out. "Mascots first."

I growl as I shove past him. Perhaps the heat of the moment is getting to my head and causing me to pick a fight with the elf who has saved me on numerous occasions, but I just murdered dozens of my own species. He could cut me a little slack.

As we get near the hallway entrances, we remain silent except for my stomping feet echoing my anger.

Refusing to look at Jaemes, I nod to Kai, and he silently motions with his hands for us to split up. Jaemes remains with Erma and me, and we watch as his brothers divide into teams and head through the other archways before we go our own direction.

"How are you holding up?" I ask Erma, spotting the lines of exhaustion around her worried eyes as we stealthily roam down a hallway moments later.

"Tired," she admits. "The losses today have taken their toll."

I frown. "What do you mean?"

She brushes hair from her face. "My lives are tied to those I create, Tember. By killing them, I'm weakening myself."

"Excuse me?" Jaemes says as we halt.

I rapidly blink as I stare at her.

CHAPTER TWENTY-FIVE

ELIZA PLAATS

GUARDIAN REALM

Sitting on a log in front of the quarantined teepee, I dig a stick into the snow while watching as a group of elves chant a haunting tune. They wrap Mitus in fine furs, a customary tribute to their fallen leader.

"What happens to him?" I ask Erline who nobly sits next to me, hands neatly clasped and rested on her thighs. It's as though she sees this every day of her life. I suppose she has.

"There will be a ceremony for the dead and another for Mitus," she begins. "In the past, Erma has assured me it's quite a beautiful tribute."

"Hmm," is all I manage. A tear swells in my left eye, and I swipe it away before it can fall and betray the sorrow I'm keeping carefully hidden. "And a new leader will be elected?"

Erline puckers her lips. "No. A new leader is already elected. As royals on my realm, it is by blood."

My incessant poking halts, and my finger's hard grip breaks away a few chunks of wood on the splintered end of my stick. "His oldest son then?"

"No," she quietly drones. "His youngest."

I whip my head to her. "Jaemes? Why the youngest?" I ask.

From what I've witnessed, the elf in question is a great warrior and stalks around the village like a panther hunting his next meal. He'd make a fine general, but a leader of this tribe? I don't know Jaemes well, but even I don't believe he'd give up battle for such a position.

She slowly tips her head, and her black eyes gaze into mine. "The youngest brings youth to old traditions as well as ferocious strength that can age over time. Mitus had made these arrangements when it was evident a war had begun."

A great leader will sacrifice himself for the many. It's exactly what Katriane is doing, and Tember and Jaemes, whereas Aiden is fighting for my freedom just as Dyson is fighting for Kat's affections. I wonder what would transpire if we all fought for the same thing. To me, my own personal battle against a chemical warfare feels lost. All this power inside me, and I couldn't even save the one who counts the most to these creatures.

Erline scoffs with a whip of her head. "Do not pity yourself. You have a purpose. Find it."

A deep sigh lowers my shoulders, and my back hunches. She's wrong. There's no purpose in a war when the enemy is my husband. Many choices are no longer mine to make.

"Does Jaemes know?" I mumble, desperate to stick to the subject. If anything, to wipe Erline's attitude from her scowling face.

A subtle shake of her head supplies my answer, and a ruckus pulls our attention from the conversation.

"I should have anticipated this," Erline grumbles and excuses herself to help the sandman keep an angry Dyson from going after his mate in battle. He's just recovering, and already he desires to dive, paw first, into battle. That would do more harm than good. He almost died. Running into another fight for his life wouldn't end well.

I swivel my attention back to the teepee of death and let the elves' song serenade my sorrows. This won't be the only death today. I can feel it in my bones. Something terrible is happening. Something I have no power or knowledge to stop.

You are more than what you feel you are, a voice jabbers in my head. It's the same voice who told me Mitus was gone before I could recognize it for myself.

A great loss is about to come, sweet Eliza. But this shall not be your only concern. The voice pauses, and I can feel thoughts and memories being plucked from my mind. *Your love will return to you, but prepare yourself. He will not be the same, nor will this war have a favorable outcome.*

"What do you know of Aiden," I mumble aloud. I drop the stick and sit up straighter.

I know he's endured great pain in the face of your well-being. In doing so, he's accepted his nature, and his appearance is now that of true form, forever altered in his sacrifice for your safety.

I gulp. "Sacrifice?"

Oh yes, he hisses. *But he will be yours just the same.*

"When?" I ask.

When the time comes, do not lose faith in me, he cautions without answering me.

I scowl. How can I lose faith in someone, something, I don't even know? "Who are you?"

He waits, and I count the seconds, almost believing him to have left my mind. *I am Fate, and I come to you with a confession, Eliza, the Born to Love.*

"Oh?" I ask while scowling to the added name.

Your fate, your lover's fate, and Dyson's, Katriane's, and Tember's are all tied together because of the choices the fee have made for you in the past. You are each set on a prudent path, one I needed to implant to right the wrongs of my children.

"And who are your children?" My eyes flick to Erline, directed by Fate as though he pulled them there himself. I growl and mimic Erline's earlier snarl. "You're using us to do your dirty work just like them." I had heard

Kat's shouts before she took over half the village and charged into battle.

He continues. *If you do not fight as one, you will lose Hope, and Despair will fill the Realms. All will be lost.*

Fate speaks of them as people - living beings. I shift in my seat, working frantically to categorize his revelations.

"Why are you telling me this? I have no authority here."

You, Eliza, have a heart of gold. You find the ability to love with a pure heart even in the most impossible circumstances. Each of you are the chosen five, the five appointed saviors, born of love, compassion, strategy, mercy, and vengeance. The rise of a greater destiny for the Realms is in your hands.

My eyes swivel to the barren tree branches as if to find him there, staring at me. "And if I refuse to participate?"

Then all will be lost, he whispers. *You are the voice of love. A war needs it. Hope follows it. And Fate becomes of it.*

The pressure of his presence lessens, easing the ache in my skull.

"Fate?" I call to him, but he's no longer there.

What will become of us?

AIDEN VANDER

DEMON REALM

It's quiet. Too quiet. The only thing left to hear is the gentle slosh of the lava under the clear floor.

Breathing heavily, I lift my arm, turning it this way and that, and examine my new skin. I've never seen anything like it, and the sparkles distract me, my eyes flicking to each speck. The muscles quiver, begging to find my next feed, but I push the urge down with a deep inhale through my nose.

I had expected to feel different once my true form emerged. But instead, I feel the same as I did before entering this realm, aside from the void's voices who speak too fast for me to distinguish.

Turning, I look at one of the walls, and just as predicted, a black lavafall tumbles inside a chimney constructed of skulls. Instead of traveling through the portal, I form a different plan. I half shimmer to invisibility like a shade, thunder forward, and travel straight through. Once on the other side, I reform and slowly swivel in a circle, frowning.

This is Corbin's room. The bed's canopy sways, and the familiar scents tickle my senses. The last time I was here, it was under better circumstances. I was a willing slave then.

"May the Divine help us," a female voice utters to my left.

I turn my head to gaze upon my audience. I knew he was watching. I just didn't think he'd be so close.

Corbin, Sureen, and Kheelan have themselves seated on the Victorian-styled red couch. The puddle of oleum is at their feet, risen to their knees in the shape of me.

Sureen is situated between the men, dark eyes wide, and a trembling hand hovers over her shrewd mouth. Kheelan grips his black robe around his collar, his face sickly pale with sweat beaded at his temples, and Corbin props his hands at the nape of his neck, leaning into the back of the cushion with ease.

Hot feelings return to the pit of my stomach at the sight of the two men. It churns and swirls, urging me to retaliate while I have the chance - while their guard is lowered. But instead of lunging at them, I take a page from Fate's book and practice mercy like he cautioned. They have much to pay for, but my desire to see how this plays out is greater.

"What have you created, Corbin?" Sureen hisses, slapping her hand against her thigh.

A smile spreads across Corbin's face – his telling smug grin which shows a moment of his dark intentions. His black eyes, his focus, remains on me.

"You've been hiding more than errands from me, Thrice Born," he gently chides, his subtle way of telling me he watched the entire interrogation.

Kheelan angles his head to look past Sureen's and straight to Corbin. "How did you do it?" His voice is as weak as he looks.

"Do what, dear brother?" Corbin inquires, innocence dripping from every word.

Sureen chuffs. "Come now, Corbin. We all saw it." She points to the Oleum. "He holds each element from the five realms. A beating heart, inferaze skin, transparency, the pure soul of a guardian, and he feeds on fear."

I soak in this knowledge as it throws me off guard, but before I can ponder too long, I'm distracted.

Corbin leans forward, placing his elbows on his knees, and sweeps my demonic frame from head to toe. "So, it would seem."

"Is this because of the void?" Kheelan splutters, spittle coating his chin. "Or because he's your child?"

My head juts to the side, eyes blinking rapidly. Did I hear that correctly? I flex my fists, refusing to speak, and search each fee, wondering how I'll defeat all three at once. And then wondering if I should. Knowledge is power.

I, indeed, have magic from the void and have been gifted many powers associated with each realm. The shocking knowledge that Corbin is my father further confirms Kheelan's speculations and my own. It would explain how it's possible.

"My child?" Corbin questions with a smirk.

Sureen growls. "Don't play us a fool, Corbin. We know you impregnated that human. This is your child. All the evidence points to it. Why else would you have pulled this one from the void? Why else is he so different from the others?"

The others? At first, I believe her to be talking about the demons, but somehow, by the way she said it, I know my assumptions are incorrect.

"It wasn't to torment me," Kheelan mumbles, a dawn of understanding. "Your Children of the Night did a fine job of that, and now they're dead! You pulled him because of blood. Your blood." He turns to me, sweeping his gaze from my head to my toes. "Now, you've created something impossible! We can't even delve into his mind!"

"Quiet, Kheelan," Corbin murmurs. "You need to gather your strength. Killing the ties to your life must be replenished by rest."

A drop of lava slips from my cheek and splats on the floor. "Son?" I ask, unable to move past the thought. My voice's tone draws the attention of the three but only for a moment.

Sureen turns back to Corbin. "What is the plan? The other side now has formidable creations. We've been bested twice, and Kheelan is in no condition to fight or lead, not even with his new mate as an anchor. They have the advantage. How will we gain the upper hand?"

Is Eliza the only reason he's still alive? Because her heart still beats? I knew Kheelan was tied to his shades, and by killing them, he has weakened himself. It brings back the first conversation Corbin and I had, right there on the couches. No doubt this is Corbin's insistence. He likes his allies as weak as his enemies. It's a smart plan, I'll give him that.

Kheelan shifts in his seat. "The fallen angel's first attack was fruitless. We can only hope they'll hold the Angel's Ground."

"No," Corbin mumbles, his attention still on me. I hold his gaze, unafraid of my supposed father. "It wasn't. When those angels arrived, they sprinkled The Red Death across the village. Every being it encountered will suffer from the deadly disease."

I stiffen. A disease is sweeping the elf's village?

The urge to flee and check on Eliza ripples across my skin, and Corbin's face brightens at the show of muscular strength. The sneaky attack wasn't to dwindle our numbers traditionally. It had a double purpose: sweep the village with deadly force then a deadly disease.

"The Red Death was your creation?" Sureen asks Corbin, noticing my stiff, wild posture.

"It was," Corbin says curtly. "The most excruciating death. No doubt Eliza is suffering the consequences."

Kheelan grumbles like a child, but his words ease my troubled mind. "I doubt a fee wife will be affected."

"But it still won't be enough," Sureen demands, her fists balling against her thighs. "Not with a dragon reborn. And you can't trust that thing," she spits in my direction, "to be any use for us. He killed his own kind without a single drop of remorse."

"Correct," Corbin begins, standing and taking slow, deliberate steps in my direction. "That is why my plan has yet to unfold. Thrice Born, child of my blood, will not be the only one I pull from the void." He reaches forward and touches the lava flowing from my eyes. I yank my head away from his hand. "And if Thrice Born wishes for his beloved to live, he will do as he's told."

"Like hell I will," I growl. There's no point in playing spy when they already know what I'm capable of. I have no doubt they know why I'm here as well, but even I know I can kill all three at once.

Tucking his chin, he whispers to me. "If I can't contain you, how do I control you?"

He thinks on this for a moment, his posture frozen, and considers his next move.

In a swift spin, he turns back to the fee seated comfortably on the couch. "Come. The fallen angels should have returned by now. It's time to prepare for the coming battles."

It doesn't take long for the three fee to exit his chambers and lead us out of the Domus Timore. And as we do, many demons follow obediently as though drawn to the powerful.

We hike along the path which leads to and from the demon's lava castle. I continuously question myself why we don't travel in more conventional means, but the rows and rows of demons who follow may not be able to shimmer.

I could destroy so many with a simple thought, too. However, my mission for revenge has turned into a mission of information even if they know why I'm here.

Dyson was right. I wouldn't make it out of here alive if I tried to unleash my wrath. The demons marching behind are loyal to their creator, and they'd surely follow me back to Eliza. All would be lost if that happened.

As we stride, our marching makes an impending song of doom. One by one, pyrens surface from the black depths of lava, curiously watching. I lock eyes with Ferox to find her expression wide with shock, sweeping the length of my new body.

I clench my jaw and return my attention to the path, wondering not for the first time where we are going. The lavafall portals are to my right, yet we head to the place of my birth. We don't plan on leaving the realm then, and this thought alone works in my favor. They aren't planning to attack yet.

Corbin shimmers to my side, matching my pace. "Do you think you can hide from me, Thrice Born? Did you think I wouldn't know you were aiding the enemy in favor of keeping Eliza alive?" I don't answer him nor acknowledge that I've heard a word of the crap sprouting from his feeble mouth.

He chuckles at my resolve. "She will die, you know. I'll do it myself, and I'll force you to watch. Or... I'll take her for myself. Perhaps then you will fall in line."

I allow a small smile, a grin of wickedness. He could sure try. The note of wavering confidence in his voice didn't go unnoticed. It almost sounds like he's trying to convince himself more than he's trying to sway me.

I wonder if Kheelan knows he plans to kill his wife. In doing so, Corbin would kill Kheelan.

"Is that how you normally talk to your offspring?" I ask.

He clicks his tongue once. "Only the ones who question their allegiances."

The rocks and boulders lining our path become smaller the farther we go, our footfalls echoing off the solid forms. It gives me a better view of what's ahead, and I grind my teeth. We, indeed, are not leaving this realm.

"What have you done?" I growl.

The surrounding lava of the place of my third birth, the once flowing expanse, has become solid ground. Orcs, many more than I thought possible, are saddled on top of their necrocorns. They wait, poised with a self-control which should be impossible for such a large towering beast.

Filed in perfect rows of battle formation, their steeds paw and scrape against the ground, impatient for orders to spill blood. Hundreds of vampires linger beside them, some hissing while others participate in a brawl like wild animals.

Above, winged people - angels - fly through the thick red sulfur lingering there, their feathers expanded as they cut through the specks. I note how the specks look oddly like the ones that fell in the Guardian Realm, delivering what they called The Red Death.

"How did you get the others to sacrifice themselves?" I ask, watching the angels.

"Haven't you heard?" Corbin asks gleefully. "I thought your pyren friend discussed this with you." I stiffen. Did she tell him, or does he have eyes everywhere? "A war is on the horizon, Thrice Born. A side must be chosen."

I tilt my head, glancing at him. "How —" I begin.

"How did I know you spoke with Ferox? I have many ears. I may not be able to dwell in your thoughts, but I have many watching you." His voice dips dangerously, shedding his handsome, charming act. "You forget who I am."

An angel with bright orange hair swoops down and lands gracefully beside Corbin. "It's done," he speaks quickly, eyes darting. "But many were destroyed on the Angel's Ground."

Corbin quirks an eyebrow. "Destroyed?"

The angel nods his head in rapid succession, and an ache forms in my skull just by watching the action. "Erma came with elves and the angel with black wings. Those that didn't fall by their hands fell by the disease they carried there."

Sighing, Corbin mumbles, "I should have foreseen that. Erma may be pint-sized, but she's the only one of us who created formidable warriors in a selfless act." He scoffs, the sound unattractive. "No doubt she knew I'd try to overtake her realm when I all but implied she travel to the Death Realm and retrieve her lover's charge. Instead, the fool sent only two guardians and left herself to cower behind her walls."

The angel sneers, disgusted.

"This is why the angels attacked their own realm?" I ask. "To weaken Erma?"

"I pushed my move too soon," he continues, a mumble to himself though we both heard him clearly.

Demons file by, marching obediently to the gathered army and finding a place among the gnarled creatures. Some hobble, and some are large enough to shake the ground beneath my feet.

He turns his attention back to the angel. "And what of Erma?"

"That plan has yet to unfold," the angel claims in a clear voice, bowing at the waist. His white wings arch over his back at the gesture, a tinted red hue due to the surroundings.

"Very well," Corbin mutters and carelessly flicks his hand in the air. "You are dismissed."

The angel nods, straightens, and spreads his wings. He soars back into the sky, graceful, as though he didn't just help murder his own kind. A humid breeze follows in his wake, tickling my solid skin with a rush of damp heat.

The sulfur aroma of this realm must be uncomfortable for the guardians, but like all troubled souls, they'll make do. This thought doesn't mean I don't wish the thick air would smother them. They'll get what's coming to them, and by the jittery demeanor of the orange-haired angel, he knows it too.

"What do you plan to do?" I ask, eyeing Corbin suspiciously.

He huffs, crosses his arms, and puffs his chest. "It's not a secret. If you used that thick skull of yours, you'd have figured it out by now."

The mention of another plan yet to unfold has several scenarios of death flipping through my thoughts. Will the Guardian Realm be able to keep Eliza safe? How am I supposed to rely on information if everyone on that realm has a battle of their own going on? Who knows who's going to survive it?

Corbin strides forward, stops in front of the puddle of black from which I was born and peers down into it. "If you'll excuse me, Thrice Born, the dragon is loose and providing much power I cannot pass up. I have shades to resurrect."

My heart sinks in my chest. *He wouldn't...*

CHAPTER TWENTY-SIX

TEMBER

GUARDIAN REALM

"How many are in there?" I mutter to Erma, turning my head over my shoulder to do so. I'm still upset with her about the information she divulged a little too late, and my voice comes out harsh.

If I would have known this battle would weaken her, I would have never allowed her to come. It makes me question why Fate himself didn't suggest it.

Our sides are pressed to a hallway wall as we listen for signs of life in a nearby room. Like every room in the Grounds, each given to an angel for their own space, a large, sturdy door tucked in an archway blocks the view from passersby.

I swivel my head further, the muscles down my neck straining, and tuck my wings tighter along my back to get a better look at the woman who hasn't yet answered my question. Sweat beads down her porcelain forehead, and her black eyes seem oddly unfocused. Her energy is spent.

She takes a deep breath and closes her eyes. "Three fallen, and many hostages."

Flanking Erma to protect her back, Jaemes pokes his head around her small body. "We can't leave them in there, Tember," he whispers.

I tick my jaw and hardened my words with harsh syllables. "Did you think I would?"

He shrugs. "You've been distracted. It's my job to make sure you stay on a true path."

"The true path is very clear, I assure you," I say and look to Erma. "Can you create one more distraction?" I hate myself for even asking, and the unease curls in my stomach and radiates to my toes.

I watch as her throat constricts with her next swallow. She squares her shoulders and nods one curt nod.

"Ready?" I ask, placing my hand on the knob.

Jaemes curls his hand tighter around the wooden arch of his bow, arrow resting on his finger, and he slowly relaxes his shoulders. With my next breath, I turn the knob and slam the door open with my heel. The door crashes into the next wall, and a few shouts come from within.

Shoving herself from the wall, Erma quickly darts through the doorway. Her skin glows, and with a swipe of both arms, she sends the power blast into the room. It's not a lethal blow, but it does serve as the needed distraction, temporarily blinding all those within.

Erma sags, her knees momentarily giving way. Jaemes and I rush through the doorway, releasing arrows. Erma stumbles inside after us, gripping the door frame to steady herself before resting against it.

It is immediately obvious who the enemies are. Within seconds, they're disabled, lifeless against the black marble floor, two with arrows poking from their bodies, and the others with smoking torsos where my electric bolts hit. Jaemes quickly reaches them, stabbing each in the wrist.

The hostages slump against the far wall, beaten to a bloody mess. To keep angels in this sort of physical state, it must be repeated frequently.

In a corner, the discarded wings of the hostages have been carelessly thrown, ripped from their backs during whatever torture they endured. I grate my teeth against each other and run a hand over my paint plastered hair.

I turn back to Erma after toeing the dead, and her hand fumbles against the wall as she makes her way along it. Lowering Ire, I go to her and immediately reach, touching her cheek void of color. My blood-stained hand coats in slick sweat, and her normally chilled skin is hot to the touch. Lips parting in an "o," I sweep my gaze along her body, but no obvious injuries can be seen. She's depleted of power and struggling to stay conscious.

Perhaps I asked too much of her. This war may kill her, and it is I who may have signed her death warrant. This is my fault, and just the thought fills me with dread.

"Erma?" I call to her softly.

She lifts her eyes to mine, a struggle.

I bend my knees slightly and bring myself level with her height. "Can you free them? Jaemes and I can continue without you."

It wouldn't take power to free them, only two hands to untie the knots twisted around their roped wrists.

"Yes," she responds, her voice weak.

"Erma?" I lick my bottom lip, second guessing if I should leave her side.

With effort, she narrows her eyes. "I'm fine, Tember. Go."

Slowly, and searching her eyes for acceptance, I lean forward and place a gentle kiss against her soft, feverish lips. "We'll be back. Stay here."

She nods, her hair momentarily tangling with mine and getting stuck in the chips of paint.

Leaving quickly, we weave through each hallway and room, light- and sure-footed, and each one is vacant but destroyed. Papers are strewn, furniture slashed, and the dining hall's intricately carved tables resemble splinters. I stare at the debris of wood, remembering when my young hands had first skimmed the freshly carved surface many years ago. They were built from the black trees the Kaju elf tribe uses to construct their tree homes, and their inner rings are a deep purple. The color was striking against the black marble, but this is now a catastrophic scene to behold.

"This is the final room?" Jaemes murmurs, pointing his arrow to the last door of this hall.

"Yes," I whisper back, banishing the reminder of my destroyed home. Why would the angels do such a thing to something they once held dear? Perhaps the same question could be asked about their choice to fall from grace.

Our steps are quiet like a predator stalking its prey, and this last room isn't far from where we left Erma and the hostages. I'm eager to return to her side and find it difficult to be stealthy.

"What do you think?" he asks, checking over his shoulder once.

I shrug subtly. "I think it's far too quiet." I look to him. "Ready?"

Bows raised, arrows aimed, we enter the room quickly.

"It's empty," Jaemes says quizzically after searching every hiding spot.

I understand his concern. This is too easy. I had expected to find many more holed up in their rooms or favorite places, poised to strike the unsuspecting.

"So observant." I lower Ire, the electric arrow popping from position, and loosen my grip on it. "This doesn't feel right."

"Perhaps we are frightening to them, Mascot." Jaemes exits the room back into the hall, and I follow him with stomping strides.

"Will you stop calling me that?" I growl, Ire disappearing in my grip.

"Come now, Angel. No need for a sour mood. We won. Take pleasure in it."

The sensation which victory usually brings has yet to surface, and his words ring false to my own ears.

We patrol in silence, each lost in thought while returning to Erma's side. I've never seen the Angel's Ground so devoid of life. Perhaps this is why my instincts are roaring a warning of danger. These halls are always roamed, and without the rustling feathers and flung gossip, it's eerie.

We approach the room, and I open my mouth to further voice my concern, but my jaw quickly snaps shut as I take in the situation unfolding inside.

"Jax," I say breathlessly. He swivels his blonde head to mine.

At arrow-point, Erma is backed into a wall next to the doorway entrance, struggling to hold herself upright while Jax threatens her life with the very weapon Erma granted the angels.

Erma turns her head, her black eyes reflecting my face.

"Leave," Erma demands, but her command slithers over my skin, slick, while my attention is solely focused on the situation at hand.

Blood drips from Jax's hard and crazed eyes, the same infection the others had.

"The lover has finally arrived," he taunts.

Clenching my fists, I move into the room. "What are you doing?"

Jaemes follows me in, his bow raised, his arrow ready.

Jax coughs, spraying blood from his mouth, but keeps his aim. "Are you blind, betrayer?"

"Betrayer?" I say, astounded. "From where I stand, there is only one who has betrayed us today."

Erma flinches as she adjusts her position. "He's been sent for an assassination."

"A trap," I whisper to the room, repeating my earlier thoughts.

"By who?" Jaemes asks, a deep venomous growl. "Who sent you?"

"Corbin," I supply and then swallow thickly as I take a small step deeper into the room.

Jax fleetingly eyes my movement and then looks back to Erma. "Did you really think I wouldn't fall, Erma? That we all wouldn't if we found proof of this betrayal?"

"I never created the guardians for jealous rages," Erma spits with much effort.

Jax purses his lips, blackness dribbling from the corners as though the action is squeezing it from the pocket of his cheeks. "Perhaps you shouldn't have granted us choice then, or so you say. I've never seen much choice under your ruling. Mainly just orders backed with little love.

Except for Tember, of course. She gets all the love, doesn't she?" He raises his arm higher, his muscles shaking as the illness takes further effect. "It matters not. Not anymore."

Despite the fact that he sounds like a desperate man, though his words do sting, if we can get him to keep a flowing conversation, we may be able to get him to see reason before he strikes Erma. All he seems to want is compassion. But as the thought crosses my mind, as I take a step forward to get him to see reason, his blood-smeared fingers uncurl from the string.

Several things happen at once in seemingly slow motion and perfect detail for how quickly everything truly occurs. A cautioned "be brave," vibrates my skull in tune with the whip of a bowstring, the voice of Fate. My body coils and springs, lunging in front of Erma to take the bolt for myself.

But I never make it there.

Jaemes grabs my wrist and yanks me back, my body slamming into the floor, and my wings bend at an odd angle underneath.

Using only his hand, Jaemes hurls an arrow at Jax like a titan with a spear. It hits Jax square in the eye, slamming his head backward while Jax's arrow hits Erma in the chest. In a normal, intentional incident, this would do her no harm. But with every death today and her energy completely depleted...

Jax and Erma fall to the floor at the same moment, a synchronized thud, and the Grounds fall quiet.

Be brave, the voice whispers again.

I breathe once, twice. I blink, observing past the hair fallen over my face like a curtain trying to save me from the view before me.

"No!" I scream.

Scrambling on my feet, running and skidding across the floor, I collapse at Erma's side. Her face is relaxed, and her black eyes are aimed, unseeing, to the clouds above as though they're beyond them and seeking the stars.

"Erma," I beg, placing my hands on her shoulders and shaking her small frame. I gather her into my lap and cover the smoke emitting from her chest with a flat palm. "Erma!"

Jaemes bends, hovering over us, and the hostage angels shuffle to their feet for a closer look.

I pat her cheek, searching for any sign of life. Tears well in my eyes, warm.

"She's gone, Tember," he pleads.

"Erma!" I shake her again.

"Tember!" Jaemes shouts above me. "She's gone!"

"No," I grit. "No, that's impossible."

I look up to Jaemes. His drapes of black hair shroud his crumpled face. His grave expression is pinned on his friend, his creator, and he ticks his jaw to banish his own unshed tears. If she's gone, we'll quickly follow. Our lives are tied to hers.

"It's fate," a familiar voice echoes in the room.

Jaemes lifts his bow and takes aim, swiveling his posture throughout the room, searching for the body to the voice. He will find none. Fate doesn't have a body.

A halo forms around my head, and I grip Erma tighter to me as his *be brave* echoes as a memory. "You knew this would happen," I say to Fate, my voice cracking with rage.

"Who?" Jaemes asks.

"I did," Fate confirms with genuine sorrow.

I slam my fist into the marble floor beside Erma's hip and half curl my body around her to shield her from the enclosing hostages' sight. "You knew she'd die."

"I did," the voice repeats.

Jaemes peeps at me through the thin string of his bow, confused. "What's going on, Tember?" His question is harsh, thick with grief.

"This is Fate," I growl the introduction. A hot tear trails down my cheeks, and many more follow, fueled by sorrow and fury.

"*The* Fate?" Jaemes cocks his head to the side and lowers his weapon. He nods to Erma, hopeful. "Can you heal her?"

"I am the Fate, but I cannot bring back my dead children. It is against our ways."

I gently lower Erma from my lap and stand, searching the room though I know I won't see Fate himself.

"What was the point of all this," I demand, throwing out my arms. "You manipulated me. Why?"

"You are destined for greater things, Angel."

I huff, the breath full of emotion. "By your decree, yes?"

Fate doesn't answer for several moments. "Let it begin," he says.

I open my mouth, prepared to deliver the lashing he deserves, when my heart in my wrist thuds an incorrect beat. I lift it, examining my wrist, and a blossoming pain begins there.

Pain. So much pain.

A roar, beginning as a weak whimper, grows in intensity and volume, ripping from my throat. Agony snakes up my arm to my shoulder and ripples down my spine. I drop to my knees, gasping for air when it clutches my lungs.

Jaemes takes a step back, his eyes wide as my body glows bright, a star. "Stop!" he yells to the room.

My back bows, a yank to my sternum, and a frigid chill sparks every new and old nerve, working its way from my face to my fingertips, to my very soul.

"To replace a Fee, only the finest are chosen," Fate whispers in my ear, and I'm lifted into the air, wings draped until only the tips touch the marble.

CHAPTER TWENTY-SEVEN

AIDEN VANDER

DEMON REALM

The last soul pulled from the void emerges, hands on the ledge as it hoists itself out of the puddle with maximum effort. Thousands roam the expanse with the rest of the army from the three realms, but they have no personality. Like each one has been purged of any choice.

However, as each one is created, the voices in my head from the void grow louder and multiply like their souls are being split. Their true humanity lying with mine while the scraps are inserted into the demons.

A four-fingered claw, coated with the black, hot goop I remember so well, rises through the flowing surface, followed by a hairless head adorning two thick horns and pointed ears. The creature resembles a feline with a catlike nose and eyes. Its mouth, with fangs as long as a snake's, opens wide, the liquid spilling inside as the newly formed demon gasps for breath. Its cheeks are protruding, boney, unlike the rest of its naked body.

Though the creature is short, it is also stocky. Its neck muscles are thick, growing straight into its shoulders, and each limb is roped with impossible muscle.

As the goop slides down fresh skin, the claw slaps against the solid ground, desperate for purchase. They're monsters, all of them, very much unlike how I emerged. This is because Corbin is my father, his blood aiding me to remain more powerful. My earlier hypothesis is now confirmed.

"What are you calling these creatures, Corbin?" Sureen asks, watching the new demon emerge and perch his feet on the ground. Its tail is rat-like, but the end is tipped in the shape of an arrowhead, sleek and deadly.

"Gula," Corbin mumbles, his eyes transfixed, watching his new creations lumber to group with the others.

"Gluttony?" Kheelan asks, translating the Latin.

Corbin inclines his head. "They're flesh eaters, brother. Look at them." He crosses his arms over his chest and smirks.

Though he isn't talking to me, I turn my attention to the new demons, the gula, watching as a few feast on another, tearing flesh from fresh demons, exposing bones while they fight over the meat. They don't make a sound, even the one being eaten. They're faces remain unpinched, without agony, and their silence is more eerie than their appearance.

"They don't feel," I whisper.

"No," Corbin responds, voice flat. "I've learned from my first creation." I flex my jaw, irritated at the dig. He turns toward me, face emotionally dark and dangerous. "They will not feel, they will not disobey. I do not make the same mistake twice."

I swallow. "Have you tried this before me?"

"I have," he says. "When my wife was still alive, I drew her power when she fought a hoard of vampires in our home village. Though I did love her, it was a sacrifice I had to make."

"For power?" I growl.

"For war," he corrects.

"It was a careful plan before but too impulsive to properly achieve." Sureen says. She steps closer and rests her hand on Corbin's forearm. The gesture is sickly seductive, and her fingers create small circles on his shirt. "Are we ready?"

He flexes his jaw, nods, and together, all three move to the black pit once more. I frown, watching as, in unison, they bring their index finger and thumb to their chest, pinching the sternum. Their expressions remain blank as they slowly pull their hand away, a wisp of white fog wrenching from their torsos. My eyes widen when I recognize the fog – on the Death Realm, they called this creature, Kheelan's creature, Reaper's Breath.

"What are you doing?" I ask, demanding to have answers.

Distractedly, Corbin watches as his fog floats over the pool, hovering, awaiting orders as the other two join his. "A seed from three will resurrect a firstborn of her kind."

"Of blood," Kheelan mumbles.

"Of enemy," Sureen whispers.

"Of love," Corbin adds.

There is only one connected to all three. Only one who I know of that is the first of her kind. *Myla.*

At Corbin's last word, the three fogs begin to spiral around one another like an hourglass of life. It lowers and emerges inside the pit. The black goop swirls like a vortex, once touched, and lifts into the air just as oleum does when it conjures a person for Corbin to gaze upon. It forms a cone, a tornado, electric bolts crackling inside, doom booming my ears and shaking the ground.

Whatever emerges will be enormous and unstoppable, based on the height it's growing. It won't be Myla – only her soul. Everything she once was will be gone just as the rest of the gula. Except...her conscience inside me, mixed with all the others.

My muscles tense, the sparkles along my black skin lighting, prepared, as a deafening roar ricochets from within the black tornado. Streams of fire shoot from the top, and Corbin claps his hands together, laughing hysterically.

The vortex lowers in one splash, revealing the creature within: A dragon, one like nothing I've ever seen. It matches that of the gula, gargoyle in make. Short, sharp spikes stick out over every inch of the dark grey dragon.

Each feature it has is sharp and jagged, including the muscles. Wings like a tattered bat's expand, casting deep shadows over the army.

The dragon sucks in a breath, deep and impossible, and the ribcage enlarges, billows of flames leaking out between the bones. In another roar, the breath is released along with a stream of fire to the sky which narrowly misses the angels soaring above.

"Here's to the next phase in our plan!" Corbin yells over the noise, toasting his glee.

I look to Kheelan who shouts weakly in victory, pure pleasure on his sickly face. Why would Corbin weaken this ally after a display of trust and companionship like this? And then it hits me. He needed Kheelan and Sureen to help pull Myla from the void. But later, he'll kill them. He won't need them anymore. If he kills Kheelan, he'll kill Eliza.

My breath freezes in my chest.

Eliza, my conscience screams.

I shimmer away before I become the enemy's first target. First, I travel to the Earth Realm, going to several places and never staying more than a few seconds in hopes of them losing my trail if they happen to be following or tracking me. And then, I seek the woman of my heart. My duty is no longer on the Demon Realm. They know I'm there to spy anyway. My time will be better spent protecting the woman I love, surrounded by guardians to help us through this perilous situation we now have.

Thank you for reading Rift (Rise of the Realms: Book Three). Please take a moment and leave a review. I'd love to read your thoughts. Book Four will be available soon (2019), so please follow me on Amazon, or travel to my website at dfischerauthor.com to receive updates. I won't leave you hanging long on what happens next.

ALSO BY D. FISCHER

| THE CLOVEN PACK SERIES |

| RISE OF THE REALMS SERIES |

| NIGHT OF TERROR SERIES |

| GRIM FAIRYTALES |

| OTHER |

Christmas Stranger

Author Planner

ABOUT THE AUTHOR

D. Fischer is a mother of two busy boys, a wife to a wonderful and supportive husband, and an owner of two hyper, sock-loving dogs. Together, they live in a quiet little corner of a state that's located in the middle of the great USA.

Follow D. Fischer on Twitter, Facebook, Goodreads, Pinterest, and Instagram.

DFISCHERAUTHOR.COM